ROYAL RAIDERS

The Tories of the American Revolution

Royal Raiders

The Tories of the American Revolution

NORTH CALLAHAN

THE **BOBBS-MERRILL** COMPANY, INC.
A SUBSIDIARY OF HOWARD W. SAMS & CO., INC.
Publishers • INDIANAPOLIS • NEW YORK

Library of Congress catalog card number 63-19000
Copyright © 1963 by North Callahan
All rights reserved
First printing, 1963
Printed in the United States of America

To
Thomas L. Norton
Who Enlivened the Idea

Foreword

If, as is believed, the American Revolution, within the course of not quite two centuries, has become worldwide, and the shot fired in April of 1775 has been heard around the world and waked up the whole human race, then this Revolution should be better known. Or at least our knowledge of it should be better balanced. To us, for virtually a century, that engaging war has taken on the partisan aspects of an American crusade; now it is beginning to be better realized that the conflict was not only colonists against the British, but also Americans against their neighbors.

The one-sided conception existed so long because we, through our historians, assumed that the American Revolution was "right." We have been so justly proud of the results, of which we are a part, that, beguiled by the well-meaning but chauvinistic writings of such men as George Bancroft, our people have swallowed with fondness the mistaken idea that the colonists rose as one united and super-heated body to drive out the hated and heinous redcoats. Yet even John Adams estimated that only a third of the Americans were wholehearted patriotic Whigs, a third were indifferent, and the remainder loyal Tories. This was a rough but significant estimate. Adams also told a friend that he feared no good history of the American Revolution would ever be written, not only because the participants were dying off, but because he felt the best materials had been carried off to England and Canada by such Tories as Thomas Hutchinson, Jonathan Sewell and Peter Oliver. It surely is true that when the Revolution drove out some 100,000 Tories, our young nation not only lost some of its best historians, but also paved a smooth way for ardent nationalists who willingly took their place. But no one more opposed the Tories than John Adams. He said, "I would have hanged my own brother if he took part with our enemy in this contest."

In order to understand the American attitude of the eighteenth century, it is necessary to realize that these English colonies inherited a tradition of individual and legislative rights from their motherland that was unknown or ignored by other nations and their colonies then. An even better way to view the situation would be, as Charles M. Andrews observed, for the historian or his reader to stand, as it were, on the shores of England and look across the ocean at the American colonies, and at the same time be able to place his feet in the Western Hemisphere and look back at the British Isles. Such a contradiction being only fanciful, one may at least try to see both sides instead of the one which has so often been presented.

It is the purpose of this book not to adopt the Tory viewpoint, but to present it and the exciting actions resulting therefrom. Much of the

contents of the volume is based upon Tory materials and this should be
kept in mind, although care has been taken to identify and describe the
sources so that their nature and worth may be unmistakenly known.
Also, in especially significant portions, sufficient information from patriot
origins has been included to afford a proper balance.

Writing a century after the Revolution, the Tory-minded historian
Egerton Ryerson stated that our Declaration of Independence was not
only that, but "the commencement of persecutions, proscriptions and
confiscations of property against those who refused to renounce the oaths
which they had taken, as well as the principles and traditions which
had, until then, been professed by their persecutors, as well as by themselves. The Declaration of Independence had been made in the name
and for the professed purposes of liberty; but the very first acts under it
were to deprive a large portion of the colonists not only of liberty of action, but liberty of thought and opinion." Ryerson added that the American Congress conducted its meetings secretly, while the British Parliament
was open to the public. And he comments that "the war carried on between American Tories and Whigs was more merciless than any other,
and more cruel and wanton than that of the Indians." Though this last
statement may be exaggerated, it contains much truth.

Whigs and Tories in the country differed even over definitions of
words, but understandably so when the words were so vital. "Treason,"
for example, was a disputed designation, for the Tories held that the
kind of "treason" they were charged with committing took place prior to
the time when a government to which such "treason" could apply was
even created. Therefore, the argument went on, this was not treason,
but obedience of the only laws that were then in force. So they regarded
the upstart Americans as dangerous rebels, and successful rebels at that,
who stupidly broke away from benevolent British rule and hence deserved no sympathy.

It is true, as Clinton Rossiter reminds us, that the American colonies
moved fast and far between 1765 and 1775. While King George III
fumed, while his ministry blundered, colonial assemblies protested; mobs
rioted and Samuel Adams plotted. Even so, it was too much to expect
that two and one-half million loyal subjects should break through all
former attachments and unanimously adopt new ones. As late as July,
1775, the Continental Congress was still declaring its loyalty to Great
Britain, avowing that the colonies were attached to his "Majesty's person, family and government, with all devotion that principle and affection
can inspire . . . and deploring every event that tends in any degree to
weaken the ties between them" and desiring that "a concord may be
established between them upon so firm a basis as to perpetuate its
blessings, uninterrupted by any future dissensions, to succeeding generations in both countries."

The decision to break away from England was a difficult one, made
only after a long period of deliberation and after the colonies had been
in armed revolt against the mother country for more than a year. About

three-fourths of the colonists were of British descent, and nearly all were accustomed to thinking of themselves as Englishmen. For most, independence came as a last resort; so it is no wonder that many chose to remain within the maternal fold, or at least were not convinced of the urgency of leaving it.

The Tories saw more clearly than did their opponents the inherent values of their colonial past; they clung to the security of union with the Empire and feared the uncertainty of a new government founded by inexperienced leaders. The loyal colonists, and most who were not so, wore English clothes, read English books, followed English politics, and looked across to England as the source of their cultural life. Over and over, Leonard Labaree has observed, the records show that even colonists who had never been to Britain wrote and spoke of it as "home." Being, in their broader aspects, of a more conservative turn of mind than the Whigs, the Tories shrank from change and chose not to leave the royal circle. Wallace Brown points out that fear was the great underlying factor of their attitude. Officials had their jobs to lose, lawyers their fees, merchants their trade, landowners their proprietorships, Anglicans their dream of a bishop, king-worshipers their idol, Anglophiles their membership in the Empire, and others their hope of royal help. Descendants of these Tories who live in Canada today, the United Empire Loyalists, are proud of their dissident American ancestors.

In England, the historical school of Sir Lewis B. Namier, and in this country the followers of scholarly Lawrence Henry Gipson, have gone far in revising historical concepts of the American Tories. Inevitably, the colonial moderates who were not with the patriots were said to be against them, and many siding with the neutral ones were forced to take sides. A considerable number of those who were loyal felt that corrective measures should be applied to the blunders of the British government, and admitted that a little rioting was all right as long as it was meant to bring the English government to proper terms. But when destruction of property began to be relished for its own sake by those who had no property, and the cry of liberty came loudest from those without political privilege, it was time, the Tories believed, to call a halt.

With this conviction, they were unavoidably drawn into the war, 8,000 being in the British forces in 1780 at a time when the army of Washington numbered only about 9,000. An estimated 50,000 Tories served the crown during the American Revolution, in one combat capacity or another. And although they were out-generaled, weakened and finally dispersed until the once-powerful Tory faction was virtually effaced from the pages of American history, the following account will show, it is hoped, that they gave a vigorous and exciting account of themselves.

The materials for this book have been obtained from sources both distant and diverse, although a veritable mine of original information was found reposing elegantly in the Manuscript Room of the great New York Public Library. Here the American Loyalist Transcripts, 60 formidable volumes in all, were, it is understood, researched completely for the first time in the preparation of a single work. Out of the great welter of seemingly endless testimony by Tory claimants of Great Britain who sought restitution for personal losses in America, emerged the pattern of this book. Needless to state, the selection from and organization of this huge amount of raw material, plus that obtained from other original sources, has been a task of much magnitude.

The aim is to present a coherent account of what the Tories did in the American Revolution, and why they did it. The pattern ranges from significant portions of background, through the war, and up to the peace treaty in 1783, as represented by exemplary act and attitude. A subsequent volume is planned to cover the activities of the Tories after they fled from the United States to Canada, Great Britain and the West Indies. New material on this later phase of the eventful life of the Tories is increasingly coming to light.

As the bibliography in the back of this volume indicates, various manuscript collections in Great Britain and Ireland, which afford new information on the American Tories, are being organized and made more available. Modern historical methods of putting such valuable data into convenient form for use by authors have greatly enhanced the possibility of telling a reasonably complete chronological-geographical-topical story of this neglected side of the American Revolution. The greatest amount of original information on the Tories is in the English Public Records Office in London, but through such media as the Transcripts from them, in New York, these records are more and more in readiness for use.

Other important sources of documentary information utilized are in the New York Historical Society, the New Jersey Historical Society, the New Jersey State Archives, the Library of Congress, Chicago Historical Society, Clements Library of the University of Michigan, the State Historical Society of Wisconsin, New York State Library, Boston Public Library, Massachusetts State Archives, Massachusetts Historical Society, American Antiquarian Society, Fordham University Library, Historical Society of Delaware, Maryland Historical Society, Virginia State Library, Virginia Historical Society, North Carolina State Library, Southern Historical Collection of the University of North Carolina, Duke University Library, Georgia Department of Archives and History, the Filson Club of Louisville, Kentucky, and the Florida Historical Society.

Additional manuscript repositories researched are found listed in the bibliography and footnotes at the back of this book. The acknowledgments of help given to the author are but small expression of the appreciation due to all who had a part in the making of this volume.

North Callahan
New York University
New York 3, New York

April 30, 1963

Contents

ROYAL RAIDERS

The Tories of the American Revolution

1. *The Bridge That Wasn't There*

Inward from the lower coastline of North Carolina, the long and slender inlet beside Cape Fear points like a menacing finger at a small plot of ground set apart by the national government in memory of a battle. Here kilted Scots who fought the English at Culloden Moor, but who were known in America as Tories, fiercely attacked a patriot stronghold at Moore's Creek Bridge on February 27, 1776. The startling results were enough to influence North Carolina's delegates to vote for independence from England a few weeks later at the Continental Congress. North Carolina was the first colony to take such extreme action.

Beneath the blackish-brown waters of Moore's Creek, a branch of the Cape Fear River, lay a bottom miry with the accumulation of many years of swamp wastes. The bridge itself, some twenty miles above Wilmington, was located on a sandbar, the highest point in the low-lying tidewater area where the creek crawls through the swamp in a series of twisting loops. Although it was not as highly publicized at the time, this early southern battle of the American Revolution was in some respects as significant as the clashes ten months before at Lexington and Concord.

Earlier in the year, Royal Governor Josiah Martin of North Carolina had been confident he could raise a Tory army and beat the rebellious local Whigs. The nucleus of his force, he felt, could come from the back-country "Regulators" who five years before had been defeated in a fight at Alamance with the better-armed tidewater provincial troops. The "Regulators" resented the favored treatment of the coastal settlers by the King's government in the colony, which had imposed its own "taxation without representation" on the back-country people. Since these same victors at Alamance were now leading the Revolutionary forces, their former opponents might well wish to wreak vengeance on them.

The high-spirited Scotsmen who had settled in the Cape Fear region seemed especially likely recruits for the royal standard. Although they had revolted thirty years before against the king of England, when, led by "Bonnie Prince Charlie," they were defeated at the battle of Culloden, they had subsequently taken an oath of allegiance to George III. Having given their solemn word, these Highlanders typically kept it. Also, they feared reprisals both in the colonies and in England, particularly the confiscation of their lands, if they did not support the crown. Adding weight to the collective allegiance were a number of retired British officers on half-pay among the local Scots.[1]

To help organize and lead these men, General Thomas Gage sent from Boston Donald MacDonald—hero of Culloden and Bunker Hill—and Donald MacCleod, who were made brigadier general and colonel, respectively, in the North Carolina militia. En route from Massachusetts, these two officers were stopped by a patriot committee and questioned; but being in civilian clothes, "they pretended they were officers who were wounded at Bunker Hill and had left the army with a desire to settle among their friends." [2] Allan MacDonald of the local Highlanders was made a major, but his famous wife, Flora MacDonald, was better known and more conspicuous than he. She had been credited with saving the life of Prince Charlie after the Culloden battle, for which she had been imprisoned by the English in the Tower of London for a time. After her release, she had come to America and was a commanding figure among the Scots in North Carolina, riding a white horse and exhorting them to do their duty. Her husband was a major, her son a captain and her son-in-law a colonel. After the Revolution, Flora returned to Scotland, while her husband remained imprisoned in America.[3]

In order to gather the Scottish residents for action, a call went out for them and other Tories to assemble at Cross Creek, now Fayetteville, North Carolina. The response was only partial. Some answered the call; others apparently preferred to remain out of the war, as did many men throughout the colonies. Some who had been driven from their homes by the rebels were hiding in the forests. Others started for Cross Creek, but were driven back by the Whigs, as the rebels now called themselves. Some were slapped into jail. Still others were too frightened to stir from their firesides. And a number of the Tories who did arrive at the rendezvous took a look at the motley army already there, decided they wanted to be no part of it, and returned home.

This activity was not lost on the Whigs. In an even more unmilitary manner, they too moved on Cross Creek—ill-trained men in untidy clothes, marching along to the rat-tat-tat of a beaten-up drum and the sound of a whining old fiddle. But meanwhile patriot units of a more martial nature, under Colonel James Moore, also headed for the meeting place. In general, "each side was attempting to intimidate the other, many were afraid to join the Tories, and were equally afraid not to." [4] There were signs of dissension among the Tories also, since some older provincial military officers were jealous of the Scottish newcomers. None of these was very young, most of the Highlanders by this time having reached the age of fifty or more. It was rumored that when they should arrive at Cross Creek, the Tories were to be met by Governor Martin and a thousand regular troops. When they found neither Martin nor troops there, many, especially the ex-Regulators, lost confidence in him and returned home.[5] But the governor was having his own troubles trying to get the warship *Cruizer* to sail up the Cape Fear River in order to divert patriot attention from his Cross Creek force. The ship started out, but rebel rifles spoke sharply from the bushes lining the banks and kept the sailors from maneuvering the ship upstream.

At Cross Creek, the Tories had finally gathered and General Mac-Donald was striving vigorously to form some kind of army out of his very raw material. Taking stock, he found that he had 700 Highlanders, 700 civilian Tories and 130 "Regulators," but only 520 out of the 1,430 had arms. All the muskets and rifles which could be spared by the people of the neighborhood were collected and distributed. The outfit did not even have a British flag, so a tailor was put to work to fashion one out of some red, white, and blue cloth.

It was February 18, 1776, and Scottish bagpipes skirled a martial pibroch as General MacDonald gave the command to march. The Highlanders had come from the wide plantations on the river bottoms and from the crude cabins in the depths of the pine forests, dressed in tartan garments and feathered bonnets, with their two-edged claymores flashing at their sides. There were the Clans MacDonald, MacLeod, MacKenzie, MacRae, MacLean, MacLachlan and others—a spirited moving picture out of old Scotland.

The colorful kilted procession did not go far. Seven miles from their starting point at a place called Rockfish Creek, the Tory army slowed to a halt. Confronting them just across the creek were Colonel James Moore and two thousand patriot soldiers. The Tory troops paused, then an odd exchange of communications took place. MacDonald sent a flag with a copy of Governor Martin's proclamation—which called on the rebels to "join the royal standard"—to Moore. But actually the flag-bearer was sent as a spy. Moore replied with a copy of the patriots' Test Oath, which, if signed by MacDonald and his men, would entitle them to join the Continental Army. Neither accepted the other's invitation.[6]

MacDonald realized that he must act quickly before Moore's men were reinforced so strongly that he could not face them. Already two companies of the Tory forces—part of Colonel James Cotton's corps—had, upon hearing of the forthcoming battle, quietly taken their weapons and faded into the forest. Disgusted with such cowardice, the elderly Mac-Donald drew up his men in formation and addressed them in a loud voice. Those who were not ready to die for the cause, he said, should say so then and there. To his chagrin, twenty more men admitted that their "courage was not warproof," sheepishly stepped out of ranks and, laying down their arms amidst the jeers of their comrades, fled into the woods. The remaining Tory troops cheered General MacDonald.[7]

One of the Scots, Farquhard Campbell, seemed to have a penchant for changing sides. He visited the camps of both the Tories and patriots, giving each information about the other. Campbell informed MacDonald that Moore expected reinforcements shortly, and since the royal forces would then be outnumbered, he advised MacDonald to avoid a battle. At least to some extent, this influenced MacDonald to lead his soldiers along the southwest side of the Cape Fear River toward the coast. There he hoped to unite with the forces of Sir Henry Clinton, who was to come down from Boston, and with the seven regiments under Lord Charles Cornwallis then en route from the British Isles. Campbell promptly re-layed what he knew of this revised Tory situation to the patriot forces.[8]

Slipping his men quietly up the river, MacDonald had them cross it in boats, which he then destroyed to forestall any pursuit by use of the same craft. Not until next morning did Moore, even with the intelligence he had received, discover that the wily MacDonald had given him the slip. Then Moore moved fast. He sent soldiers to occupy the post of Cross Creek in order that the Tories could not return to it. Hearing that patriot troops under Colonel Richard Caswell were marching from New Bern, Moore ordered them to change course and, in an effort to cut off MacDonald, to take a position at Corbett's Ferry on the Black River. Moore then led his own troops toward the sea to block off roads which the Tories might take in that direction.

Slowly MacDonald's army pushed its way through the wilderness and approached Corbett's Ferry. His wagons creaked over the rough ground; bridges had to be repaired to hold them, while patrols kept sharp watch for a possible ambush. On February 23, MacDonald reached the ferry. One of the alert scouts had spotted a five-man patrol of the patriot forces. It was quickly captured, and from it MacDonald learned that Colonel Caswell and his men were waiting eagerly for him on the opposite bank of the stream.

Again the craftiness of the veteran Tory commander showed itself. He left a small body of men at the ferry, while his main force moved stealthily upstream. The men left behind proceeded to outdo themselves. They cunningly kept out of sight of their opponents and made every kilt count for many times its number by making all the noise and commotion possible. They tramped back and forth through the woods, loudly break-ing branches and rustling leaves. Those a bit distant from the rest purposely shouted to their comrades. Some of the Scots beat drums;

others answered them on shrilling bagpipes. While all this melee was going on, selected members of the detachment posted themselves along the river bank and added realism to the exaggerated uproar by the sharp crackle of their rifles, which sent bullets whining into the patriot camp. So effective was the cacophony of the demonstration combined with the firing that Caswell thought MacDonald was readying for an assault with all his troops. He ordered his men to dig in. All this time, the crafty MacDonald was scurrying upstream with his main force, picking a good place to cross and building a bridge there. By eight o'clock on the crisp morning of February 28, his Highlanders and other soldiers had made the crossing and were once again marching toward the coast, on the opposite side of the stream—with no time to spare.

Colonel Caswell learned to his vexation that a few soldiers with drums, bagpipes and rifles had outwitted him. He blared out orders to his men to hit the trail after the enemy. They complied with such alacrity that by taking a different route they arrived at Moore's Creek Bridge ahead of the Tories. Here Caswell found that another patriot leader, Colonel Alexander Lillington, was already on the ground and had begun to throw up breastworks beside the stream. Caswell crossed to the opposite side and had his men begin to dig in there.

MacDonald, driving his men hard, found when he was within six miles of the bridge that even with all his maneuvering he had lost the race to Caswell. Undaunted, he sent a messenger into the patriot camp to demand surrender. MacDonald did not expect Caswell to comply, but felt he could in this way obtain some intelligence of the enemy's positions. He did. The spy returned and said that Caswell was alongside the creek with about 800 men, while Lillington had about 150 in his camp nearby. To the south and too close for comfort was Colonel Moore with an additional thousand of the pesky rebels.

Night had come and the strain of intensive activity began to take its toll of the venerable MacDonald. Particularly had the punishing pace of the forty-mile march through the wilderness and the responsibility for the movements of his men exhausted him. He was forced to take to his cot, though he remained alert. Then, regretfully, the seasoned Scotsman called his officers to his bedside and told them he was ill and unable to continue commanding in the field. The younger men were sympathetically respectful but still anxious to have a go at the rebels. General MacDonald agreed that by all means this was the thing to do, *if* a reconnaissance showed that the rebels were vulnerable. Lieutenant Colonel Donald MacLeod was appointed by the ailing leader to take over the command.

The younger and more impetuous MacLeod called a council of the officers. Some of the experienced ones pointed out that their latest information showed the patriot force was strongly entrenched behind heavy fortifications. To attack such a position without artillery would be foolhardy, they argued. MacLeod and the younger officers scoffed. This was just a greater challenge, they indicated. Finally, when the older ones insisted on caution, the junior officers accused them of being cowards— and in turn, the wiser, older men scoffed.[9]

It was eventually decided to move in the night. Rifles, muskets and ammunition were checked. A number of the Tories were found to have no firearms at all, but this did not deter those who were Scotsmen. They felt that they could do very nicely with what they did have—keen-edged claymores, the trusted and traditional broadswords of the Highlanders, which their fathers had carried when they swept across England and terrified the inhabitants some thirty years before.[10]

The advance began at 1 A.M., led by seventy-five of the broadswords-men. This might have been a formidable array at Culloden; but it was not at Moore's Creek Bridge. The night was overcast with murky clouds and the resulting darkness both helped and hindered the Tories as they struggled to make their difficult way through the sticky mud in the swamps. Some lost their way; others slogged on through the night. Finally, just as the first rays of dawn were beginning to glimmer on the watery reaches of Cape Fear River, the floundering Scots saw the gleam-ing fires of Caswell's encampment shining through the trees. They felt relieved and thought that their long trek was now to be crowned with bright success.

Forming themselves into three columns, the Tories crept stealthily forward through the brush to surround Caswell and his men beside the campfires. But, coming close, they found their prey was gone. During the night, Caswell had slipped across the creek and joined the troops of Lil-lington, leaving his campfires burning as a ruse, in the same manner that Washington was to do at Trenton. This time, the Whigs had turned the tables and outwitted the Tories.

Disconcerted, but only for a moment, MacLeod drew his men together and prepared to push his attack across the stream. Just before the dawn broke fully, his men were to form near the creek, get set, then upon the order charge across and storm the earthworks before the defenders were awake enough to act.

In place, the Tories waited. The sun peeped through and reflected upon the shining claymores and the metal-topped sporrans of the Scots in front. This was the moment. MacLeod raised his huge sword and three cheers rang out along the kilted line. Drums rolled in the morning air and the Highlanders dashed forward, blades upraised as the bagpipes screeched.

"King George and broadswords!" the battle cry resounded.[11]

The onrushing men reached the murky creek, ready to cross it in a breathless hurdle. Then a chilling sight met their eyes and made them pause. The bridge which they expected to use had been stripped of its planks, and only two round pine logs, or sleepers, remained. Unknown to the attacking Tories, these logs had been greased with soft home-made soap and tallow. Beneath them in plain view the sluggish water ran dark and deep. But the brave, reckless MacLeod hesitated only an instant. Charging forward to the edge of the skeleton bridge, he thrust his sword into one of the slippery logs to balance himself, and shouted for his men to follow him. They did.

Up on the rise beyond the creek, the patriot troops behind the earthworks watched all this precipitous movement with great relish. Already they had the Tories in their musket sights. Now as the first wave of attackers swarmed furiously upon the bridge, a sheet of fire flashed from the earthworks. The distance was only thirty paces; it was a point-blank job. Scotsmen sprawled from the decimated bridge and slid into the deep water as the bullets showered upon them.

MacLeod was slammed to the ground by the fusillade just after he had made it across the bridge, his body riddled. But he arose, flourished his sword, yelled bravely to his men to come on, and lunged forward again, almost making the edge of the fortifications. Another volley of bullets ripped him, and this time he went down to stay, nine leaden slugs and twenty-four swan shots in his kilted figure.[12]

Now the cannon from the breastworks boomed and hurled death across the bridge, the shells and musket fire sweeping the oncoming Tories off the slippery logs and into the stream as fast as they came. Many were drowned in the creek. The few who reached the opposite shore had to take cover behind trees near the fortifications, from which they tried vainly to return the fire coming from within. Again their officers shouted the rallying cry,

"King George and broadswords!"

But it was too late for words or weapons. The Tory officers and men turned away from the bridge of death and fled in headlong rout.

"The insurgents retreated with the greatest precipitation," a New York newspaper reported, "leaving behind some of their wagons etc. They cut their horses out of the wagons, and mounted three upon a horse. . . . Lieutenant Colonel Cotton ran at the first fire. The battle lasted three minutes. Twenty-eight of the Tories, besides the two captains [MacLeod and John Campbell] are killed or mortally wounded, and between twenty and thirty taken prisoners, among whom is his Excellency, General Donald MacDonald. This, we think, will effectually put a stop to Toryism in North Carolina." [13]

Actually, this estimate of casualties was low, as more died later of their wounds. MacDonald, ill and still asleep, was passed by his fleeing men. The unfortunate general was unaware of what had happened until he was awakened and humiliated by being taken prisoner. For this worn-out Highlander, it was a miserable end to his valiant efforts.

Out among the fleeing Tories, the officers finally gained enough composure to pause in their headlong flight and hold a council. They quickly decided that further resistance to the patriot fighters at this time would be useless. They passed word to their scattered men to divide any ammunition they might have left and make their way back home as best

they could under such chaotic circumstances. This was a far cry from
the martial preparations and colorful fanfare with which the day had begun.

As for the patriots, they were not willing to halt the engagement so
quickly. Colonel Moore arrived with his force soon after the rout of the
Tories and assumed command, ordering his men to pursue the enemy at
once. Scouting parties filtered rapidly out through the woods and in the
general direction of the fleeing enemy. After capturing MacDonald and
sending him on to New Bern and to the confines of the local jail, they
grew bolder and dashed after the retreating men with abandon.

The Tories had traveled only a pitiably small distance, when upon
looking around, they saw the surrounding woods suddenly filled with
rebels, most of them mounted menacingly on horseback. There was no
argument in this second encounter. The Tories simply surrendered en
masse, 850 of them. The enlisted men were allowed to return to their
homes, but not before they promised never to fight again. Officers were
given more special treatment, being taking to the nearby Halifax jail.

As for the patriot interpretation of the results of the brief battle,
Colonel Caswell reported that his men captured "fifteen hundred rifle-
guns, all of them excellent pieces; two medicine chests, one of them
valued at three hundred pounds sterling; one box containing half Johan-
neses and English guineas; thirteen wagons with complete sets of horses;
850 common soldiers taken prisoners, disarmed and discharged." The patriots lost but one man killed and one wounded.[14]

Governor Martin, still safely aboard the *Cruizer*, could hardly believe
his ears when he heard of the rout. He was already none too happy; no
sailor, he had complained that he was "a wretched man not of Neptune's
element, in the tenth month of confinement on board ship." Despite his
burdens, he assured his superiors that the defeat at Moore's Creek Bridge
was nothing to be concerned about; that North Carolina would remain
a British colony. In explanation of the defeat, he pointed out that "the
Tories had not turned out to half the number expected." As for the other
side, the North Carolina Provincial Congress issued a proclamation in
which it jubilantly apologized for having to send the leaders of the Highlanders to other colonies for safekeeping. "Justice demanded it at our
hands," the document added, "and in the anguish of our hearts, we la-
ment the sad necessity which the frailties of our fellow beings have al-
lotted to our share; still, we wish the reformation of those who, in this
unhappy contest, are severed from us. . . . They may rest assured that
no wanton acts of cruelty, no severity, shall be exercised to the prisoners;
no restraints shall be imposed upon them but what shall be necessary to
prevent their using their liberty to the injury of the friends of America." [15]

After the debacle, both sides seem to have been moderate. The victors
at Moore's Creek Bridge issued a message of mercy; General MacDonald
had previously prepared one in behalf of his troops, to be issued if they
had won. This generous attitude of the patriots further aided in winning

over many of the Highlanders to the Revolutionary cause. In addition, those defeated had taken a parole which most of them kept inviolate. But though the large proportion of Tories stayed quietly at home in North Carolina for four years, other Highlanders served in the forces of both sides during the whole of the war for independence.[16]

Such a situation was not unusual. All over the colonies, men searched their souls to see what, if anything, they should do in this uprising against their English sovereign. Those who found an answer satisfying and lasting to themselves were fortunate; for many conscientiously did not see the necessity of the American Revolution and said so, often at their peril. Some were influenced by neighbors; others dared to differ independently.

After the battle of Moore's Creek Bridge, there was a lull in the activity of the Carolina Tories, which misled their adversaries into thinking that resistance to the Revolution had ceased. By underestimating the Tories, the patriots felt safer than ever. Even so the revolutionaries, despite their assurances of mercy, began to persecute their foes more and more as time went on. In the months following the battle, groups of Whigs raided, pillaged and burned Tory farms, thus causing much unnecessary suffering and hardship, until many of those who still favored the crown had to seek shelter in the woods and swamps. There in the sylvan recesses they found the few who had escaped capture after the battle.

The Whigs had obtained General MacDonald's muster rolls and so knew who had enlisted among the local people. Tory stragglers were afraid to show their faces near their homes for fear of being picked up. One of them, Duncan MacNabb, hid in the woods for weeks in the hope that the British would appear and rescue him. When they did not, he set out and walked all the way to Philadelphia. From there he marched to New York with the British, then sailed to Georgia and took part in the siege of Savannah. Meanwhile his wife in North Carolina was robbed of everything she had, even her clothes, and was forced to leave her child at the mercy of the enemy. Later she returned from Charleston, 300 miles away, and retrieved the child.

Tory Norman MacLeod was imprisoned in Pennsylvania for almost five years, his home and plantation in Anson County, North Carolina, being repeatedly robbed and plundered by the Whigs while he was gone. His wife fled to Charleston and, like Mrs. McNabb, later made her way back to rescue her children. She was captured and imprisoned for seven weeks, and her husband was forced to pay the expenses of her stay in jail. Captain Alexander Martin was incarcerated by the Whigs for a year. After his release, he claimed that his cell was filthy and that he had to endure many insults before he was set free. Later he joined the army of Cornwallis. During her husband's imprisonment Mrs. Martin and her children were robbed and then turned into the woods, where they probably would have died of exposure had not a kind-hearted patriot officer found them and escorted them to the British lines.[17]

These few instances coming in the aftermath of a battle between American neighbors serve to illustrate the kind of fate which lay in store for those who lost the war, or those in sympathy with the losers. In this conflict, much of the violence was not on the battlefield but rather in or near the homes of the settlers and involved the family and fireside as well as the rank and file. These early examples were only harbingers of more to come; and the causes behind the conflict, both in England and America, were not less weighty than the consequences.

2. *Backstage*

In the turmoil going on in England at the time, the battle of Moore's Creek Bridge proved disappointing, but its impact did not appear fateful to those in charge of the government. Britain would muddle through. She always had, and this was a small setback compared with those received two decades before at the outset of the French and Indian War. Then for a moment the royal standard had dipped; but it was soon raised by Amherst and Wolfe and others, and magnificently glorious victory was the result. There had been no lowering of the British flag since, nor were impudent American colonies likely to threaten its majestic luster, the King and his ministers reasoned. A few stern imperial measures, and victory would again be theirs.

The general situation in America at this moment, however, did not justify British optimism. In answer to war preparations in New England, Lord North, the English prime minister, had offered a conciliation plan by which Parliament would not lay any but regulatory taxes upon any American colony which would tax itself for defense and support of the government. But an act passed soon afterward by Parliament sought to restrain the colonies from trading with any nation but Britain, and this tended to offset the peaceful effects of the proffered olive branch. Patrick Henry thundered "Liberty or Death" in Virginia, while John Hancock and Joseph Warren fumed against the mother country in Massachusetts. The strokes at Lexington and Concord followed; George Washington was placed in command of the new Continental Army, and the battle of Bunker Hill was fought two days after Washington's appointment, before the new commander could even get to Boston. When he did get there, he sent an expedition against Quebec, led by Benedict Arnold and Daniel Morgan, which almost succeeded in making Canada the fourteenth colony. There was certainly enough lively opposition activity going on in America to make the leaders of the British government realize, had they been sufficiently alert, that here was a serious situation, both in respect to the homeland and to their subjects in America who chose to remain loyal.

It is so evident now that the British government was not alert to the true situation, that there are still those who seem to have the impression the American Revolution was caused by such leaders as Samuel Adams, John Hancock, Arthur Lee, Richard Henry Lee or Patrick Henry on the one hand, and George III, Lord North, George Grenville, Governor Thomas Hutchinson or Lord Dunmore on the other. "But to accept this interpretation would be to ignore the mass of available evidence of the growth of nationalism and a sense of self-sufficiency in the colonies after 1763," Professor Lawrence Gipson aptly observes.[1] Such an interpretation also ignores the active role the American Tories played, not only in the war, but in the events leading up to it.

Some of the Tory leaders who had already fled to England were being honored there at the time when anti-British sentiment reached a climax in America. On July 4, 1776, the very day of the Declaration of Independence by the colonies, an interesting ceremony was taking place at venerable Oxford University, where Lord North, the Prime Minister, was also chancellor. Honorary degrees were being conferred on exiled American Tories Thomas Hutchinson and Peter Oliver, formerly governor and deputy governor respectively of Massachusetts. This was early evidence of what England thought of her sons who remained true to her, even if they had to flee to prove it.

Lord North was to be held largely responsible for the inept British policy during the American Revolution. Later research has revealed, however, that he was chiefly the tool of the obdurate monarch George III, and was the only individual in the British government who for a time held the respect of both Parliament and public. It is appropriate to examine to some extent the personal activity of Lord North, who was to American Tories their friend and political master in England.

The principal efforts of the Prime Minister were directed toward maintaining the authority of Parliament and recognizing any legitimate complaints the colonies might have at the time. These were almost impossible tasks. Lord North had been head of the ministry only a month when on March 5, 1770—ironically, the day of the "Boston Massacre"—he moved to repeal all the Townshend taxes except that on tea. "It is interesting to speculate," Charles B. Ritcheson comments, "on the probable course of the Anglo-American conflict had there existed then the means of communication available today. . . . Had intelligence of North's motion on March 5 been known in Boston on the same day, would the clash between British troops and townspeople have occurred?" [2]

Not only was this lack of quick communication unfortunate, but the British Prime Minister was blamed personally by many for the Boston Port Act which closed the harbor to ships after the celebrated Tea Party there. At nearby Salem, to which the shipping was diverted, "the act was called, *Lord North's Act*," according to one of his supporters, Peter Oliver. "It was diverting to a traveller to hear the quaint curses which the simple drivers of the carriages would throw out at this great and good statesman. If a wheel ran into a rut, it always descended with a *this is Lord North's Road;* if it jolted hard over a stone, the rumble was accompanied with a *Damn Lord North!* Even the pious clergy propagated the sound; and when they left their cart-driving and ascended the desk, they had something to say in their prayers about *Lord North*, either explicitly or by implication; and one of them thinking it was best to be fair and above board with his Maker, uttered the following expression: *O Thou Lord of the East and of the West and of the South! Defend us against Lord North!*" [3]

That such castigation was hardly deserved is borne out by the fact that both Lord North and his stepbrother, the Earl of Dartmouth, Secretary of State for the Colonies, wished to confine the punitive action of their government to Boston, and hoped that the other American settlements would condemn the Massachusetts city for its incendiary acts. But they clearly were not aware of the desperate feelings of the patriots or of the lack of forcefulness on the part of the American Tories at this stage.

How remote the Prime Minister's prestige was from the conditions in America may be indicated by the high esteem in which he was held in England in the spring of 1772. Soon British complacency was to be shattered by the burning of the British schooner *Gaspee* in Narrangansett Bay, Rhode Island, by irate colonists who resented the interference of the ship in their profitable smuggling activities. The dramatic incident so alarmed American Tory leaders that they warned Lord North a revolution might follow.

But the Prime Minister nonetheless had cause to be jubilant. A government bond issue which he proposed was fully subscribed to by noon of the day of its being announced. Such a crowd of buyers surrounded the Bank of England, eager to buy the bonds, that the clerks had to be put in at the windows by a ladder. Brownlow North, brother of the Prime Minister, commented on how popular the latter was at the time and said that even his opposers admitted Lord North had "been very ill used." A more recent and objective observer stated, "North was an ideal leader of the House." [4]

As for reverses in the House, North took these more seriously than did the King—in fact, too seriously. Once the Secretary of the Treasury had to beg him not to take to heart a defeat in a division of the members over the matter of university almanacs! On February 4, 1774, Lord North suffered a defeat over a trivial issue in the House of Commons and ex-

perienced one of those attacks of melancholia which were to become
increasingly frequent during his ministry. So downcast did he become
that it was with great difficulty that the Earl of Suffolk, acting at the
behest of the King, persuaded North not to resign.[5]

In these as in later instances, the Prime Minister recovered, however,
and carried on actively if often futilely. Both his viewpoint and that of
the most distinguished American Tories have been echoed by Professor
Gipson, who asks, "When may coercion be applied by a state to restrain
subordinate units or groups within it? Was President Lincoln justified
in calling upon Congress to permit him to save the Federal Union by
use of force against the Southern secessionists who insisted that the Union
was only a conditional pact between fully sovereign states? Were the
King and Lord North justified under existing circumstances in asking
Parliament to take drastic action to curb the insubordination of the
radical elements in Massachusetts Bay in order to save the old British
empire from disintegration? In each instance, subordinate units set
themselves up as ultimate judges of the constitutionality of particular
measures, and in each case their stand challenged the concept of national
unity and defied the central government. In the face of this challenge,
George III and Lord North, whether wisely or not, did not hesitate to
act—any more than did Lincoln." [6]

For their part, the colonists had counted on the 1774 elections in
England to overthrow the North ministry in Parliament, and thus bring
about a more conciliatory policy toward America. But after the election,
the composition of the new Parliament represented a distinct victory for
King George and Lord North, with the House now having a comfortable
majority for the ministry. The elation of this victory probably lulled
North somewhat into believing that, despite the meeting of the Continental Congress and reports that the colonies were preparing for war,
the attitude of Massachusetts was substantially different from that of the
more peaceable colonies. Even so, North and Dartmouth sent a plan to
the king, which provided for the dispatching of a royal commission to
America to examine the troubles there at first hand. But George III did
not agree and the plan was dropped. It took the news of the battle of
Bunker Hill to remove any doubt from English minds about American
war intentions.

So, although Lord North was loyal, good-natured, hard-working and
a past master of parliamentary tactics, the oppressive and shortsighted
policy toward the colonies continued. It was this policy, set by the
monarch above him, rather than his own considerable bungling, which
chiefly brought on the conflict and its subsequent disaster for the American Tories. This was a war that was predominantly a territorial and
nationalistic revolution, animated throughout by patriotic American
hatred for the British attitude—especially as this attitude was represented
by those Americans who remained loyal to the Crown. Solidifying this
situation was the fact that in the political relationship of the colonies

and their mother country was the strong tradition of individual and legislative rights, inherited from the Glorious Revolution in England, and little known or regarded by other nations and their colonies at the time.[7]

In contrast to this tradition of individual rights was the idea that the colonies were subject to the legislative authority of Parliament, an idea subscribed to sincerely not only by Lord North and Mansfield in the House of Commons, but by the liberals, Burke and Chatham, as well. Even Charles James Fox believed that America was wrong in resisting the authority of Great Britain's legislature. So, too, Richard Jackson, even while opposing the Stamp Act, asserted the sincere belief of the American Tories when he said, "Parliament is undoubtedly the universal, unlimited legislature of the British Dominions."[8]

But if the colonies were subject to the empire, Lord North was virtually a vassal to the King. George III had found that he and North could work together, and that the genial Prime Minister was also one whom he could trust. Consequently the King had a deep personal attachment to him. Accordingly, the campaign of George to regain what he thought to be his rightful place in British politics as chief executive of the state, free of factions and parties trying to hinder him with laws, was brought to a victorious conclusion by the engineering of North. Thus, the Prime Minister found himself driven into the leadership of a war that was naturally repugnant to him, the outcome of which he was skeptical about from the first. In his fidelity to the King, Lord North endured distress and humiliation under conditions which no other ministry ever suffered and survived.[9]

An example of the personal attention which the Prime Minister gave his sovereign occurred on September 9, 1776, when, according to Lady North, her husband was very much fatigued. "He got up earlier than usual yesterday, expecting the King about 10 o'clock, but he did not come until One, when the Queen came with him, and they stayed until half after four. The King insisted on Lord North sitting in his great chair; indeed it would have been quite impossible for him to have stood all the time."[10]

Horace Walpole showed little sympathy for the Prime Minister when he wrote the Countess of Upper Ossory on December 11, 1777, that "Lord North yesterday declared he should during the recess prepare to lay before Parliament proposals of peace to be offered to the Americans. 'I trust we have force enough to bring forward an accommodation.' They were his very words. Was ever proud, insolent nation sunk so low!"[11] These proposals were the result of the urging of William Eden and helped to rouse North from the despair into which he had fallen. The Prime Minister immediately began a series of anxious conferences which lasted through the Christmas recess. Since he could not trust his cabinet colleagues, North consulted Eden, Jenkinson, Wentworth, Thurlow, and Wedderburn, all subministers. Under the strain of formulating in great haste a pacific plan which would be acceptable to Parliament and perhaps to the colonies, North drove himself without pity. By late January, though near mental and physical collapse, he had at least a plan. It was to repeal the tea duty and the act regulating the charter of Massachusetts and to create a commission to negotiate with the colonies on every point in dispute. The result was the Carlisle Peace Commission, which unfortunately came too late.[12]

Commenting on this plan, Walpole told Sir Horace Mann that "peace is not made, it is only implored—and I fear, only on this side of the Atlantic . . . it solicits peace with the States of America; it haggles on no terms; it acknowledges the Congress or anybody else it pleases to treat; it confesses error, misinformation, ill-success and impossibility of conquest; it disclaims taxation, desires commerce, hopes for assistance, allows the independence of America, not verbally, yet virtually, and suspends hostilities." [13]

What more, one might ask, could the colonists have sought at that time? Justified or not, the patriots, over Tory protests, did demand more. And so did the King demand more, of Lord North. Regarding some men who were urging cabinet changes, George III commented that "Intriguers should never approach a man of Lord North's cast, who with many good qualities too much tends to the difficulties of the moment and to procrastination, and he too often from wanting to get out of the evil of the day but too often falls into what may prove ruin in futurity." [14]

For his part, North told the King, "I am in fever with my situation. I have been kept in it by force. If the house falls about my ears, I cannot help it. All I can do is not to quit a falling house and to use every means in my power to sustain it as much as possible." [15]

On June 21, 1779, Lord North was unjustly attacked in the House of Commons for alleged corruption and treachery in the counsels of the King. Two days earlier, the Prime Minister had lost his fourth son, a child of two, whom he loved dearly. So that day he was understandably more sensitive to attacks in the debate, saying that he had been in a most laborious and expensive office without asking for a single emolument for either himself or his family, adding with feeling that he had a pretty numerous family. Whereupon, he struck his breast and burst into tears, doubtless remembering that one of them lay dead.

It was not long after this emotional occurrence that he received a letter from a Whig identified only by the name Nathan. Judging from the writer's sentiments, he could have been an American colonist. "My only motive in writing this letter," it began, "is because I am an enemy of your Lordship, because I consider your Lordship to be the greatest enemy to my country. Be advised—retire before the populace snatch the instruments of lingering justice into their own hands—fly to shelter before the pelting of the pitiless storm." At almost the same time, North received another attack, this from Lord Shelburne, who described the House of Commons as venal, declared the Prime Minister to be a guilty man, and challenged the government to send him to the Tower of London.[16]

In spite of these attacks, at the close of the thirteenth Parliament under George III, Lord North appeared to be firmly established in office, and his abilities generally admired. He was cool in debate and talented as a speaker. Many felt that he had good sense and unusual penetration, and if at times he seemed to nap in the House, he always aroused himself when any important point came up on the floor, and made quick, effective comment on it. Not overly vigorous, he depended on perseverance. He was fairly well versed in history and had an impressive knowledge of tax matters. Though a man of integrity, his heart, like that of Alexander Hamilton, seemed to be better than his head, his ambitions greater than his abilities. "Lord North, the noble commoner in the blue ribbon, stands forward as perhaps the most unfortunate minister that this country has produced," concluded a contemporary pamphleteer. "Misfortune overtook him in the assertion of the highest monarchial principles. In spite of misfortune, he adhered inflexibly to that assertion." [17]

Contrary to some accounts, Lord North did not resign on hearing the news of the American victory at Yorktown on October 19, 1781. Not until three months later did he send in his final and effective letter of resignation, and only then when he heard that a coalition of country gentlemen belonging to no party were going to announce their intention of withdrawing their support from the ministry. In fact, North commanded more than a hundred votes in the House in the winter of 1782.[18] Matthew Ridley wrote in his diary on September 29, 1782, "Lord North is in as much full power as ever in England—he went out of office entirely against the King's consent." Nor did he wring his hands in horror, as has been widely stated, upon receiving the news of Yorktown. Brownlow North wrote his father on November 11, 1781, that the Prime Minister "was out of spirits, but not so bad as he is sometimes." With the termination of the war with America, the principal ground of dispute between North and his colleagues was eliminated.[19]

This being the case, had Britain won the American Revolution, the reputation of Lord North would now be a vastly different one. Even so, a contemporary French writer described him as an "able financier, adroit orator, subtle courier, indefatigable worker and full of resourcefulness." Not so complimentary were some of the colleagues of the Prime Minister in the House of Commons. Charles James Fox cried on one occasion, in criticizing North, that "whenever the black and bitter day of reckoning comes, I shall convict him of such a chain of blunders and neglects as would bring vengeance on his head." But that day did not come; the time did come, however, after the Revolution was over, that Fox joined North in a Parliamentary coalition—an action which belied the former's bitter words. Equal acidity filled the words of Edmund Burke, who, in a moving peroration one day in the House, looked directly at Lord North, who appeared to be drowsing, and said, "Brother Lazarus is not dead, but sleepeth!" [20]

It is true that when North was a colleague of Fox in a later cabinet, the former admitted that earlier he had operated under a bad system, but "had not the vigor and resolution to put an end to it." But years and modern scholarship have brought new information about Lord North, and with it a more favorable appraisal. Personally, he was described as looking remarkably like George III himself; the Prime Minister's "tongue was too large for his mouth, his speech thick but indistinct. He was clumsy and had weak eyesight. His good nature and homely humor were his best assets." According to a daughter of North, his "character in private life was, I believe, as faultless as any human being can be; and those actions of his public life which appear to have been the most questionable, proceeded, I am entirely convinced, from what one must own was a weakness, though not an unamiable one, and which followed him through life, the want of power to resist those he loved." Horace Walpole is quoted as saying that "Lord North was the most popular man in England, even after his downfall." And Edward Gibbon, who dedicated his *Decline and Fall of the Roman Empire* to Lord North, stated, "The house in London which I frequented with most pleasure and assiduity was that of Lord North. After the loss of power and sight, he was still happy in himself and his friends; and my public tribute of gratitude and esteem could no longer be suspected of any interested motive." Reginald Lucas avers that "North had a refined and cultivated intellect, knew the classics, liked books, especially Shakespeare, was a linguist and spoke French and German well. He was a companion and intimate friend of his elder sons and daughters, and the merry, entertaining playfellow of his little girl." [21]

Lord North was able to endow Toryism with an intellectual meaning and to make his constituents believe that George III stood for the nation as well as for himself. Toryism became a philosophy at a time when farmers, Puritans, and democratic smugglers on the other side of the ocean were challenging the King as the national ruler. After 1770, it seemed to the majority of the British nation that colonial independence meant national disgrace. So Toryism and the King's friends were no longer thought of as the nation's enemies.

North knew better than Walpole and others how to "smile without art and win without a bribe," and the independent members often followed the genial premier where they might have deserted the cold Grenville or the haughty Pitt. The most serious weakness of Lord North seemed to be lack of firmness, due perhaps to a constitutional indolence. His refusal to answer letters and his apparent inability to control subordinates were responsible for both misunderstanding and disaster. He was certainly not deficient in common sense, but he appeared to lack the necessary driving power to inspire his ministers or his parliamentary following with zeal and enthusiasm, nor did he or the King effectually support the American Tories in their opposition to the colonial radicals.[22]

At times the explanations of Lord North to the House of Commons about the colonial situation seemed half-hearted, and he purposely de-ceived that body in regard to the danger from France in the winter of 1777. He glossed over the state of the navy in both peace and war, and when he talked of conciliation with America, he often breathed despair at the same time. But it is now plain that North had to kowtow to the King or he would not have remained as Prime Minister. In his place any of his colleagues would have had to do much the same thing. In this crucial period most Britons believed, along with the King and Prime Minister, that England must stand firm or lose her colonies. Both lenient and forceful measures had failed of the desired results in settling the colonial question, so now the administration felt it should not be blamed for the seriousness of the situation which developed.

In commenting on this situation, Philip Guedalla said, "King George III is out of place in Cockspur Place. That neat military figure, when America pays her historical debts, will ride down Broadway. For he helped more than most men for whom the claim is made, to found the United States. A similar piety should impel every town in the Union to erect a statue of Lord North. . . . A modest pedestal might proclaim that, though not strictly a Son of Liberty, he was yet a father of the Revolu-tion." [23]

The King and his first minister are described as "an odd pair, the two young men with their smooth faces and protruding eyes. Friendship and official duty united their fathers; but the sons, with a rarer unanimity, seemed to share a single profile. Both brows, both chins receded with a common design; and below the powdered regularity of dressed hair, each pair of eyes stared hard in the comic fierceness of weak sight. The King was thirty-two and knew his mind, the minister was thirty-eight and knew his place. For, inclined to compliance by his natural good manners, North held a doctrine which rendered his sovereign almost irresistible. Sharing Lord Chatham's queer *marotte* that party was less than country, he added a yet stranger notion of his own, that the country was personi-fied in its king." [24]

Even so, it was not always the principles which North supported that drew upon him parliamentary and public ire. Samuel Johnson in typical acidity observed that he would not say that what Lord North did was always wrong, but it was always done at the wrong time. In contradiction to this, Lord North as late as March 25, 1778, advised the King that England was totally unequal to a war with Spain, France and America at the same time. "Great Britain will suffer more in the war than her en-emies," he astutely predicted, "not by defeats but by an enormous ex-pense which will ruin her, and will not in any degree be repaid by the most brilliant victories." This critical situation was "enough to employ the greatest man of business and the most consummate statesman." [25]

That North himself realized that he was not such a man is pointed out by a twentieth-century historian, H. Butterfield, who has described the Prime Minister as being one "who was in the habit of behaving like a prisoner seeking release . . . who cursed the futility of what he privately called 'that damned American war.' " And yet "It is necessary to insist on Lord North's skill as a parliamentary leader . . . in his long tenure of office which lasted until 1782." Another modern authority, W. B. Pemberton, has passed the judgment that "He dominated the House of Commons for twelve years as not one of his contemporaries could have done." [26]

A Knight of the Garter and with the exception of Sir Robert Walpole the only member of Commons to wear the Blue Ribbon since the reign of Queen Elizabeth, Lord North was witty. When he dismissed Charles James Fox from his cabinet, he did it in these words: "Sir, His Majesty has thought proper to order a new Commission of the Treasury to be made out, in which I do not see your name." [27] In regard to Generals Howe, Gage and Burgoyne, Lord North stated, "I do not know whether our generals will frighten the enemy, but I know they frighten me." [28]

In home affairs, North believed that good, economical housekeeping was all that was required, but obviously that was not sufficient for the exigencies of the time. Edmund Burke, however, grew more generous in his appraisal of North, calling him "a man of admirable parts . . . with a mind most perfectly disinterested." [29]

Significantly, in the twentieth century Great Britain has repudiated its earlier stand that sovereignty was indivisible within the Empire, by letting its self-governing commonwealths have complete freedom.[30] The United States, on the other hand, has just as fully repudiated the Revolutionary War concept that each state is a sovereign entity within the Union, holding that sovereignty rests within the whole American nation. In this same concept, the Tories in this country were perspicacious if unsuccessful.

3. Into Three Parts

Who were those people in America who dared to uphold the standard of Parliament and the King, and in the attempt, to engage in an internecine warfare more bitter and brutal on both sides than that of the regular soldiers in the field?

They were contemptuously called "Tories" by their enemies, after their English counterparts personified by Lord North and his associates; but they called themselves "Loyalists" because of their adherence to Great Britain. In this account, which is principally concerned with their part in the Revolution, they are designated by the name of Tories.

All too often in history, the losing side of a conflict suffers not only defeat but oblivion. So it has been with the American Tories. Not only did they lose the war, for reasons which will be shown, but they lost their homes and property and often their lives. They have also virtually lost their place in history. This seems unfortunate when it is realized that an estimated hundred thousand of them were banished from this country, and that the impact of their exile has been compared in importance to the banishment of the Moors from Spain and the Huguenots from France. Certain it is that this exodus of the Tories deprived the new American nation of some of its best political, diplomatic and financial talent.

Why were the Tories not more successful? Although this question needs an answer, there is no simple one. Strenuous study seems to evolve three principal reasons: lack of unity, lack of leadership, and failure to recognize early enough in the conflict the need for arms and their effective use. The Tories never sufficiently developed that enthusiasm and cohesion so vital to victory. They were not usually sure of themselves, much less of their opposition. The Tories displayed snobbery toward the patriots and a remarkable lack of proper timing in their activity against them. Mainly, the loyal leaders failed in their efforts to rally the King's adherents against the growing rebellion. Too late did the British recognize that Americans could best fight against Americans; and as a result, the military utilization of the Tories mostly miscarried.

One cause for such ineffectiveness was the conservatism which held such a strong and respected place in the American Revolutionary era, many of the prominent Tories being naturally conservative. Instead of seeking aggressively to establish and vitalize a way of life in a new setting, they merely defended a 150-year-old system which had been eminently successful in building the British Empire. New elements of American society, however, were coming into political prominence and power, namely, the town laborer and the frontier farmer. These were challenging the leadership of the royal and aristocratic figures then in high positions. Moreover, the new and more democratic elements were developing a tendency to substitute public clamor and mob violence for the regular procedures of government. There was a strong trend toward social levelling. The period was one in which society seemed to be shaken to its foundations.

Even so, no revolution was generally intended at first. The colonists wanted merely a redress of grievances as British subjects and had no plans either for independence or for the formation of a republican government. There were thirteen separate colonies or states involved and each considered the move for independence in a somewhat different way. This was evident after the Revolution as well as before it. Their resistance to the colonial regulations had not been motivated by a desire for independence, but by a desire to maintain the rights of their people as Englishmen. Independence was a last resort, a means to secure these rights as Americans. But in a very real real sense, they had to decide after Lexington and Concord what kind of traitor they wished to be, a Tory or a Rebel.

As opposed to those more radical, the Tories consisted of officeholders, Anglican clergymen, Quakers and other pacifists, large landholders, merchants, and many artisans and small farmers. Whatever their category, their collective energy fell far below that of the patriots or Whigs, who organized their committees, held their Continental Congress, and passed test laws to coerce the indifference to their cause, while the Tories were arguing in their coffee houses and making clever, haughty remarks in their dwindling press. "Relying confidently on the armed power of their sovereign, they drifted in the wake of the British Army, gathering first in Boston when Gage arrived in 1774, then in New York after Howe occupied it in 1776, again in Philadelphia when Howe made his sortie there in 1777, and to Cornwallis' banner in the South in 1780 and 1781." [1]

At the start of this eventful progression, there were few partisans of American independence in evidence, although for a long time there had been those who thought in an academic way that such independence would some day come about. In the British system then in effect under the King and Prime Minister, the chief means of political action was the distribution of offices, many of which were sinecures with high pay. Holders of these offices in America had as part of their appointment sworn to execute the laws. Logically they were Tories and accordingly they felt, even in America, duty bound to obey the instructions of the ministers in England. Some Tories had taken military oaths of allegiance and did not wish to break them. One Tory, Hopestill Capen, wrote to the Court of Enquiry, from the jail in Boston where he was confined "in a Felon's room," that "as to the base, unkind, diabolical interpretations of some, that I only wait to see which will be the strongest side, and then join that, the simplicity of the Scriptures which my conscience is bound to attend to, forbids my acting in any such crafty, deceitful way. For I do not think if I was to take up arms against the King, whom I twice solemnly swore to be faithful to, when I took my commission in the militia, and thereby perjure myself, and after that be taken by the King's army, that I should have more to fear, if so much, as I now have to fear, in dissenting from some of my countrymen." [2]

As Moses Coit Tyler has pointed out, during the eight to ten years prior to 1774, it might fairly have been assumed that the Anglo-American dispute was but one of a long series of political disagreements that had broken out at various times in John Bull's large and vivacious family, and that this particular dispute would probably run its natural course and come to an end. This historian believed that New York had the most Tories, especially in New York City, and that large numbers of them lived in New Jersey, Delaware, and Maryland, with an extremely numerous contingent in Pennsylvania. Timothy Pickering called the Quaker State "enemy country" because of its number of loyal persons. In New England, Connecticut had the most Tories, Vermont next. There were fewer loyal people than Whigs in Virginia; the two factions were about evenly divided in North Carolina; there were more Tories than patriots in South Carolina; while in Georgia the loyal individuals were so numerous that they were preparing to withdraw the state from the rebellion in 1781 and probably would have had it not been for the battle of Yorktown. Those who were neutral have been called "the hesitating class who were wondering on which side their bread was buttered." They shifted from one side to the other, at times, depending upon the way the wind of victory was blowing.[3]

Although some colonial merchants were Tories, most of them eventually ended as Whigs because of the sharp restrictions on their trade applied so clumsily and with such bad timing by Parliament and the King. Threatened with bankruptcy by this legislation, the merchants were the instigators of the first discontent in the colonies, and they brought about the first nonimportation agreements. Oddly enough, several of them who were later to be distinguished as Tories were elected to the Stamp Act

Congress. It required time for these conservative men to see that they had started something they could not stop and finally could not even control. The rich merchants of Boston or New York might not mind greatly if the common people blew off some steam. But such demonstrations soon went too far. As Carl Becker said, "These men might not cease their shouting when purely British restrictions were removed." [4]

More conservative were the rich American farmers, who for the most part were Tories. On the other hand, the debtor class naturally chose the side of the Revolution. Inhabitants of Norfolk, Virginia, even "refused paying merchants' debts, esteeming it a patriotic measure and arguing that to pay money to an enemy was giving him a dagger to pierce their own bosoms." [5] Immigrants from England and Scotland, regardless of their differences with the government of the mother country, were as a rule Tories, as were the businessmen who were antagonized by the loss of trade caused by enforced participation in the nonimportation agreements or because of persecution they endured for refusing to participate. The higher ranking judges and most of the eminent lawyers and physicians sided with those loyal to the King.

The Tories felt that congressmen and committeemen were rascals who sought not so much to serve their country as to feather their own nests. The patriot leaders had selfish motives, their opponents charged. James Otis started the agitation because his father missed a judgeship; Joseph Warren was a broken man who sought to recoup his fortunes by upsetting those of others; John Hancock suffered from wounded vanity; Richard Henry Lee failed to get a position as collector of stamps under the very act he later denounced; John Adams turned rebel when he was refused a commission as justice of the peace; and Washington himself never forgave the British War Office for not rewarding him properly as a colonial military officer. So ran the Tory version. [6]

In Boston, the Tories formed a superstructure of wealth and social importance made up of persons who gravitated to the loyal side under the weight of inherited reverence for English institutions. Outside the town, an opposing sentiment crystallized among the farmers, who were more influenced by Whig propaganda than Tory elegance. A Massachusetts Tory as early as 1770 noted that "the spirit of discord and confusion which has prevailed with so much violence in Boston has spread itself into the country." This same individual told of some rebels who stole a horse, put an "image" on its back with a sign on it which read, "Wishing the Tories in hell," and let it loose to trot about Boston. At about the same time, a mob equipped with drums, horns, and whistles assembled in front of a Tory's house. Friends of the Tory appeared, seized the leader of the mob and threatened him "with a school boy's correction." The leader immediately drew a penknife and threatened to stab his captors. A cry of "murder" followed and the mob dispersed. According to the account, this incident was played up in the newspapers like the exaggerated story of the Boston massacre. [7]

The reputation of the British tax collectors also spread. John Adams has related how on a cold winter night he stopped at a tavern in Shrewsbury, some forty miles from Boston, and while sitting before "a good fire in the bar-room" overheard half-a-dozen substantial yeomen of the neighborhood talking in a lively manner about the Whigs and Tories.

Said one, "The people of Boston are distracted."

Another answered, "No wonder the people of Boston are distracted. Oppression will make wise men mad."

A third cut in, "What would you say if a fellow should come to your house and tell you he was come to make a list of your cattle, that Parliament might tax you for them at so much a head?"

Replied the first, "I would knock him in the head." [8]

As portentous as this remark was, not all of the colonists were so extreme either way. No examination of the men who failed to join the American cause in the Revolution is adequate if it does not take into account those moderates who preferred to remain neutral and who in many cases were driven into Toryism by the hostility of their uncomprehending and impatient fellow-colonists. After all, it was natural for many to remain loyal simply because of a deep attachment to Great Britain. Americans of means and culture reproduced, as best they could, English manners, dress, and conversation. They spoke of the mother land as "home" whether they had been there or not.[9]

Tories, as described by a sympathetic historian, were not always easy to recognize: "They were a numerous and intelligent portion of the community; were as interested in the welfare of the country as their assailants, yet were designated by every epithet and opprobrium and denied the freedom of opinion and privileges of citizenship." This same analyst points out in behalf of the Tories that the American Congress had declared to England that "the colonists were a unit" in advocating liberty, but that its own enactments and proceedings against the Tories refuted this statement.[10]

Whether this statement was accurate or not, those from the American patriots in regard to taxation certainly were meaningful. It will be remembered that until 1764, Great Britain did not exert a right of imposing internal taxes on the colonies. And up until the year 1768, the colonies could and did claim exemption from port duties laid on by Parliament. British authorities doubtless felt that Maryland, for example, showed impudence in resisting taxes, when the charter of Maryland reserved to the King and his heirs forever the right to levy imposts, duties, and customs. In fact, England and her American colonies were so close at one time that it was proposed America become like Scotland; but this mirage faded with the rise of patriotic opposition.[11]

Such opposition reached a boiling point with the Stamp Act, and its repeal in 1766 marked the beginning of real decline in British influence in her American possessions. From that time on, the spirit of democracy gained ground in America. And it is fairly clear that the English government was aware of its implications. A review of the debates in the House of Commons of this period reveals that one of the considerations influencing the ministry was the military factor. It became clear that when the relatively small number of British regular troops deployed over a vast area of North America was compared to the potential strength of the colonies, which possessed thousands of men trained in the use of arms, the military position of Great Britain in the thirteen colonies seemed a weak one. Any attempt to enforce the Stamp Act might have led America successfully to seek help from France and Spain. So it was not repentance and generosity alone that led England to repeal the unpopular law.[12]

Nor were the colonists fooled by the motives behind the repeal. A British writer on the scene at the time stated that "the concessions supposed to have been made by Great Britain on that occasion were considered by the colonists as more the result of apprehension and diffidence than a generous intention of atoning for an act of injustice or correcting a conduct politically wrong. . . . This unfortunate, ill-judged repeal almost instantly produced the effect which every sensible, moderate man in America dreaded: the laws were disregarded, the governors little respected, and the mother country considered as little more than a sister state in alliance with the colonies." [13]

From the Tory standpoint, not enough Americans retained such a moderate viewpoint, however. As Carl Becker said, the American Revolution was the result of two general movements in the colonies, the one concerned with home rule, the other with the question of who should rule at home. In each colony there were class distinctions, and in some cases the internal friction between the different economic groups and social classes was as fierce as the struggle between the colonies and Great Britain itself. Some of the lower economic groups used the external quarrel to diminish the power and prestige of the local ruling aristocracies. On the other hand, "Many of those wanting home rule cared little for the rights of the common man, for the democratisation of colonial policies and society." [14]

Such sentiment appeared to be among the motives of the "Indians" who in 1773 dumped 15,000 pounds' worth of tea into Boston Harbor, and also by the citizens of Maryland, who, the following year, publicly burned the tea ship *Peggy Stewart*, owned by Annapolis merchants. With such overt acts occurring, people were soon forced to take sides, even those who did not wish to do so. Bullet and bayonet were to take the place of reason, and the Tories were told by the patriots, "Those who are not for us are against us." [15]

This situation might appear to be somewhat anomalous, considering the statement of Crane Brinton that, leaving out the avowed loyalists and those who were indifferent, the group which actually engineered and fought the American Revolution was probably not more than ten per cent of the population. "The great majority were cowed conservatives or moderates, men and women not anxious for martyrdom, quite inca-

pable of the mental and moral as well as physical strain of being a devoted
extremist in the crisis of the revolution." The Tories, despite such intimi-
dation, showed much sporadic persistence. At times they provided the
British with information about the plans and forces of the new United
States. They intercepted postriders and seized dispatches. They counter-
feited money and operated as irregular forces in conjunction with the
British. They spread demoralizing rumors which hurt the patriots, and
they tried hard to circumvent the work of the Continental Congresses.[16]

Most of the colonial conservatives stressed the virtues of the British
constitution, the balance of power it exemplified, and the value to the
colonists of their connection with Great Britain. In emphasizing these
points, the Tories found it necessary actively to denounce certain tendencies of the radicals; but the loyal position was basically defensive—the
position of men urging the preservation of a political system in which
they positively believed and which they saw no reason to overthrow. For
many Tories, this was quite consistent, since they had a vested interest
in maintaining the existing political leadership and in the prestige and
material rewards which went with the political offices they held. As time
went on, however, direction and control of the colonies passed from the
original political spokesmen to men of little or no experience in government.[17]

At the outbreak of the hostilities, there were men who thought that
the overthrow of a government, however evil it might be, must lead to
worse consequences than submission to it. They had come to America
seeking legal and constitutional rights, but to go where Thomas Paine
now beckoned them seemed to be an abandonment of both law and
constitution and would mean "to risk their all in the untried and unrigged
ship of natural rights. Rather than board such a vessel, they would give
up the contest and accept whatever King and Parliament chose to give
them." [18]

This sentiment of the colonial conservatives was expressed by Cadwal-
lader Colden when he said it was most prudent for them to keep as near
as possible to that plan which the mother country had for so long experienced as best and which had been preserved at such vast expense
of blood and treasure. This was the mission of the Tories: to make the
British constitution work in the American wilderness. But despite their
protesting, most of the Tory leaders did not go so far as to take up arms
against the rebels. Nevertheless, these conservatives are believed to have
been largely responsible for perpetuating in a raw, new country much of
the best heritage of the old.[19]

It required more than latent sentiment to dampen the rebellious spirits
of Massachusetts. Doughty Nathanael Greene, the Quaker in arms, held
a Tory captive at Boston, explaining to Washington that he blamed the
prisoner for helping the British "when the veins of our heroic countrymen were inhumanly opened at Lexington." [20] The Continental Association of Worcester County agreed to boycott British products, the result-

ing document being signed by forty-one blacksmiths who also refused to do work for any person not strictly conforming to patriot principles, especially Timothy Ruggles of Harwick. He had warned General Gage that the patriots would fight if pressed, and now with the help of Gage, Ruggles was actively promoting a Tory organization for the purpose of defeating the Continental Association.[21]

Had such an organization been duplicated throughout the colonies by the Tories, and early enough, the war might have ended in a stalemate before it reached major proportions. In the Ruggles group, the Tories pledged themselves to defend with lives and fortunes, their "life, liberty and property" and their right of "eating, drinking, selling, communing and acting . . . consistent with the laws of God and the King." When the persons or property of Tories were threatened by the patriot "Committees, mobs or unlawful assemblies, the others of us will, upon notice received, forthwith repair, properly armed, to . . . defend such person, and if need be, will oppose and repel force with force." This strong pledge was published in newspapers, but the weakness of the resolution was its lack of fulfillment. Ruggles did not convince his own family; his wife, brother and children differed with him on the question, and five of his nephews served in the American Army.[22]

General Thomas Gage was encouraged, however. As John Trumbull put it :

> The annals of his first great year
> While wearying out the Tories' patience
> He spent his breath in proclamations;
> While all his mighty noise and vapor
> Was used in wrangling upon paper.[23]

Perhaps it was "wrangling," but the efforts of Gage had some effect. Hundreds of Tories came into Boston from neighboring communities to work in gardens and hospitals, cut firewood and procure forage for the cooped-up British. One of these Tories, Samuel Gilbert of Taunton, was struck on the head by rebels and lost the sight of one eye, as well as his hearing. Edward Stow of Boston was mobbed, his "house bedaubed with excrement and feathers and his head broken with a cord wood stick" for his efforts in behalf of the King.[24]

Acts of such violence were to come mainly, however, in the later periods of the conflict. In the earlier phases, it was often hard to distinguish American Whigs from Tories, so small were the differences in their attitudes. The burdens imposed by the British government were light indeed, the historian Charles H. McIlwain believed. The stamp tax had been withdrawn almost as soon as it was enacted. The taxes which did succeed were comparatively insignificant and of the least irritating kind. "The Americans knew they should pay their share of the Seven Years' War and they knew that they had not done so. It is difficult to characterize this as intolerable oppression." In addition, the colonists themselves knew well the laws of Parliament concerning America, especially regarding trade with other countries and its relation to English-American commerce as well as colonial domestic activities. They early evolved the idea that such legislation, in order to be binding, should be accompanied by representation of their own in the English Parliament. Yet, as Charles M. Andrews observed, "It is to be noted that in the years before 1684, Massachusetts taxed non-freemen of the colony without giving them representation in the assembly that taxed them; that Virginia and Maryland taxed the Quakers; and that the English inhabitants of St. Christopher taxed the French in the island without giving them the right to vote." [25]

Perhaps there was inconsistency in regard to vested rights, but the main difference in the viewpoints of the American Whigs and Tories was that while the former urged rebellion and accompanying violence if necessary, the latter considered themselves Americans but still subjects of the British Empire. The Tories felt that the best interests of the colonies would be served by remaining *a part of* what was, at the time, the greatest empire in the world; for even if some of them considered their lot to be a burdensome one, they believed that England's sense of justice would soon lead to the removal of the hardships.[26]

"My ancestors were among the first Englishmen who settled in America," exclaimed the loyal leader Samuel Seabury. "I have no interest but in America. I have not a relation out of it that I know of. Yet, let me die, but I had rather be reduced to the last shilling, than that the imperial dignity of Great Britain should sink, or be controlled, by any people or power on earth." [27]

The cultural attitudes of a considerable number of Americans were European. This was especially true in and around the seaboard towns where several generations of successful commercial contacts with Europe had produced a class of merchants and professional men with genteel aspirations and a cosmopolitan outlook. They found much to admire in fabulous eighteenth-century Britain, with its great wealth and wonderful ease of living among the upper classes.[28] It has been estimated that in New England itself, in 1775, more than half of the most educated, wealthy and hitherto respected people were Tories. Around eleven hundred of these were to leave with General Howe, and the thousand who followed took away probably a majority of the old aristocracy of Massachusetts, most of them never to return. The historian Trevelyan states that one out of every five of these was a Harvard man.[29]

Not long after these Tories arrived in Nova Scotia, a composer among them expressed an anti-patriot sentiment in song which was to prove more poetical than realistic. Nonetheless, appearing in the *Halifax Journal,* it was popular among these newcomers to Acadia:

> The Lion once roused will strike such a terror
> Shall show you, poor fools, your presumption and error.
> And the time will soon come when your whole rebel race

Will be drove from the lands, nor dare show your face:
Here's a health to great George, may he fully determine
To root from the earth all such insolent vermin.

Before these unfortunate people fled, they felt the cruel hand of persecution. For example, an elderly dock-worker in Boston named Malcolm
was picked up as an aftermath of the celebrated Tea Party, and stripped
"stark naked" on one of the coldest nights of the winter. Accused of being
a Tory, he was covered all over with tar, then with feathers, having one
arm dislocated in the tearing off of his clothes. He was hauled through
the icy streets in a cart, with thousands of jeering spectators looking on,
some of them beating him with clubs and knocking him out of the cart,
then into it again, according to a contemporary diarist. This treatment by
those who apparently were having a party of their own, by comparison
with which the preceding Tea Party was mild, went on for five hours.
Torturing him further, the mob demanded that he curse the King, the
British Government, etc., but all they could make him do was to cry
out,

"Curse all traitors!"

So they brought him to a gallows and put a rope around his neck,
saying they would hang him. He replied that he wished they would, but
that they could not, for God was above the Devil. Some doctors who observed the spectacle said that it was impossible for the poor creature to
live, since his flesh was literally torn off his back. Malcolm was apparently
singled out for punishment after it was discovered that he had been one
of the military force of Governor William Tryon of North Carolina in his
fight against the Regulators at the Battle of Alamance. The Governor
had praised Malcolm for his service there, "by his undaunted spirit en-
countering the greatest dangers." As a token of appreciation, Governor
Tryon had sent the victim a gift of ten guineas just before the tarring and
feathering. Malcolm had a wife and family and an aged father and
mother who saw the ghastly spectacle, "which no indifferent person
could mention without horror." [30]

This same diarist also tells of a lady at Roxbury, Massachusetts, a Mrs.
Ed Brinley, who "while laying in, had a guard of Rebels always in her
room, who treated her with great rudeness and indecency, exposing her
to the view of the [surrounding] banditti." They called attention to her by
saying, "as a sight, see a Tory woman, and stripped her and her children
of all their linen and clothes." [31]

Such instances of violent treatment of the Tories were often not known
to the British authorities in time for them to furnish protection, even
when they could. Also, it was a question whether the royal forces would
exert themselves in individual cases to the extent necessary to be effective. A London newspaper editorialized that protection and allegiance
were reciprocal duties between the state and the subject, adding that the

subject was not bound to endanger his life and property before the state was in readiness to assist and support him. It was, the paper stated, regretted that British citizens were subject to the *de facto* laws of the colonists who had usurped the sovereign power of their rulers, then declared it high treason "against that usurpation to aid, assist or even to correspond with the subjects of Great Britain." The publication assailed the colonial assemblies and committees who were persecuting "the most faithful subjects, without distinction of age or sex, for the sole crime, often for the sole suspicion, of having adhered in principle to the Government under which they were born, and to which by every tie, human and divine, they owe allegiance. . . . The protection and justice due to them from the State, and the duty they owed in return, were always before them. Impressed with a perfect confidence in the first, they resolved not to be deficient in the last." [32]

There was a deficiency in protection for Councilor John Murray of Rutland, Massachusetts, however. A "well behaved mob" of about 3,000 men assembled on Worcester Common on August 22, 1774, assaulted a "bigg Tory" there, then broke up into companies representing each town and marched to nearby Rutland to find Councilor Murray, who had definite Tory leanings. Additional recruits joined them on the way. Arriving at Rutland, the marchers searched Mr. Murray's house, but found that he had gone to Boston. Before dispersing, however, the mob took out their spite on the furniture, the wine cellar, and on a Copley portrait of their intended victim, running a bayonet through the picture in lieu of Murray himself. [33]

From this same locale arose the determined campaign of the patriots to force the Tories out of the colonial militia. It has been estimated that more than one-half of the officers of the Massachusetts regiments were firm supporters of the Crown, and that these held most of the higher ranks. Since there was difficulty in getting many of the men to serve under these Tory officers, a plan was put forth in which all officers were asked to resign their commissions, and then, in forming the new regiments, each company was to choose its own officers. This procedure eliminated the Tory officer corps. One who remained loyal took a parting shot at the patriots, saying: "Such is the army with which you are to oppose the most powerful nation upon the globe." [34]

More than the military opposed those loyal to the King. Tory sentiment in a man was sometimes taken by his overzealous neighbors as an excuse to appropriate or destroy his land and goods. In the confused days following Lexington and Concord, anyone on the roads in Massachusetts suspected of Toryism had "their eatables demanded of them." Tories were hated more than the British and were treated worse when captured as fugitives. In 1775 a group of them were paraded down a village street with their hats off, a mark of villainy, and then sent to the "dunjen," while at the same time captured British regulars enjoyed the comparative ease of the prison. Washington himself feared and disliked the Massachusetts Tories especially, although at one time he considered pardoning all such people in order to win them over with forgiveness.[35]

Yet not many people who believed the rumor wanted to forgive those accused in the "smallpox winter" of 1775-76 of spreading the disease. In something of a throwback to General Jeffrey Amherst who in the French and Indian War had advocated spreading smallpox among the Indians, a Dr. McCarthy of Fitchburg, Massachusetts, was accused by many of having introduced the disease into the town in order to obtain more business. He was suspected of being a Tory also, and this double suspicion added to the already prevalent belief that the British and Tories were spreading smallpox.[37]

Such hostile feelings spurred a small mob in the following months, when at Amherst a Tory failed to heed the call of a local committee to appear before it. Men were sent to bring him out, and when they found his door barred, they broke it down, dragged him out and with "sticks, clubs and fists, did bruise and wound him." When such suspected persons were summoned before a committee to answer complaints of being enemies of liberty, they were subjected to a grilling reminiscent of the earlier Puritan inquisitions of Roger Williams and Anne Hutchinson. These Tories were given a chance to defend themselves, but the committees were organized to convict, and they usually did so. If the accused happened to be found innocent, the committee had to pay the costs of the hearing; if convicted, the Tory paid, and if he could not, he was confined to jail. By devious maneuverings, the committees often found persons in contempt of the group, and fined them for their "insults." [37]

Those suspected of loyalty to the King were frequently forced to sign humiliating and abject recantations. These documents were usually required to be read in public by their authors, and then published in the newspapers for several issues. Commenting upon these unfortunate individuals, a Whig writer said, "These hearty wretches trembled; some confessed and like vermin crawling among the roots of vegetables, endeavoring to secrete themselves . . . or in sheep's clothing, secretly watching for prey to satisfy their voracious appetite." [38] There seems little doubt that many of the recanting Tories did not change their attitudes but simply took the easy way out of their dilemma. It was not hard to say, "I now renounce the Pope, the Turk, the King, the Devil and all his work; and if you will set me at ease, turn Whig or Christian— what you please." [39]

More dignified was the attitude of the Massachusetts General Court. While this body recognized that in every government there must exist somewhere a supreme, sovereign, absolute and uncontrollable power, it was held that such power resides always in the body of the people, and never can be delegated to one man or a few. "It is the will of Providence," the Court proclaimed, "that for wise, righteous and gracious ends, this Colony should have been singled out by the enemies of America, as the first object, both of their envy and their revenge, and, after having been made the subject of several merciless and vindictive statutes, one of which was to subvert our constitution by charter, is made the seat of war." [40]

The custom of parading effigies of Catholic Popes through the streets was prevalent in Massachusetts and elsewhere. The Reverend Ezra Stiles reported that in Newport on November 5, 1774, "This afternoon, three popes etc. paraded through the streets, and in the evening they were consumed in a bonfire as usual—among others were Lord North, Governor Hutchinson and General Gage." [41]

Those in such parades were not always readily identifiable as Tories or patriots. Dr. Benjamin Church was an example. Although his story has been told numerous times, and it is a question whether he was more Tory than turncoat, no account of opposing sides in the Revolution would be complete without him. A graduate in medicine from Harvard and the London Medical College, a writer, poet and speaker, Dr. Church resided in a fine mansion near Boston. He was a political confidant of Joseph Warren and Samuel Adams, active in the provincial congress and director of Boston hospitals under none other than General George Washington. Yet on October 3, 1775, Ebenezer Huntington of the patriot army wrote his brother that Church had been corresponding with General Gage and giving him secrets about plans of the Americans, that the plot had been divulged by the mistress of Church (he having "dismissed his wife"), and that the information had fallen into the hands of Washington. A few days later, great excitement was occasioned by the discovery of a secret correspondence which Dr. Benjamin Church had been carrying on with the enemy. He had had the highest respect of all, as a member of the patriot vigilance committee, and was especially recommended to General Washington on his arrival in camp as a trustworthy and valuable man and one deputied to meet the commander-in-chief and escort him from Springfield to Cambridge. Apparently, he was a Tory all the time!

Patriot leaders were amazed. Church was dismissed and confined to a jail in Connecticut, "without the use of pen, ink or paper, and no person to be allowed to converse with him, except in the presence and hearing of a magistrate of the town or the sheriff of the county where he is confined, and in the English language." In the spring of 1776, he was allowed to return to Boston where he was also confined. Church eventually obtained permission to go to the West Indies, but the ship in which he sailed disappeared without a trace, and the first traitor to the American cause vanished.

Although Church had done comparatively little harm to the patriot cause, his involvement as a spy added excitement to the situation of those in rebellion. As a recent English historian has stated, the American Revolution was an ideal situation in which young men who wanted liberty, who abhorred spies, who sought practical expression of their idealism, found an opportunity for glory and self-sacrifice. He points out that so active were the people of the Massachusetts metropolis at the outset of the struggle, that Americans were often called "the Bostonians." Their audacity "electrified souls, aroused universal admiration, especially among young people enamored of novelty and longing for glory." [42]

Even so, the measures resorted to when idealistic ones did not seem sufficient were unmistakably elemental. Regarding the common method, a young rebel asked early in the conflict, "O you poor Tories, when shall I get some tar?" [43]

This meant that while harsh steps were taken against some Tories, there were others less molested, at least for a while. General John Sullivan wrote Washington from Portsmouth, New Hampshire, that the "infernal crew of Tories who have laughed at the Congress, despised the friends of liberty, walk the streets here with a sneer, telling the people in the streets that all our liberty poles will soon be converted into gallows." [44]

Such confidence was, however, the exception rather than the Tory rule. At Hatfield, Massachusetts, where storekeeper Israel Williams and his son consistently refused to sign the local Covenant of those opposing the King, armed men appeared from a hill on the east, took the two into custody and confined them in a cabin overnight. One of the captors partially stopped the chimney of the hut in an attempt "to smoke old Williams to a Whig." When dawn came, the victim signed on the dotted line. But the Tories did not always take their incarcerations seriously. One group of them, held in a new jail which they themselves had only lately helped to build, found a boy to run errands for them outside, sent him to get some liquor and made a merry night of it.[45]

Events were more serious for the few Tories in storied Concord, Massachusetts. These were horrified at the aftermath of the skirmish there, when a youth who was chopping wood saw a British soldier crawling away after being hit by a bullet, and killed him with his axe. One of the local Tories, Daniel Bliss, a lawyer, entertained British Captain Brown and Ensign de Berniere when they went to Concord some weeks before the famous clash there, to report to General Gage on the condition of the roads. Bliss was forced by his neighbors to leave town with the soldiers. He never returned and his estate was confiscated. This was done under the provisions of the local laws which stated, "The estates, real and personal, belonging to the loyalists of Massachusetts Bay, are declared to be escheat to the commonwealth, as the property of traitors, and to annure to the use of the public." Such provisions were set forth also in the resolutions of the provincial congress of Massachusetts and signed by Joseph Warren, the celebrated patriot leader who later was to die in the battle of Bunker Hill.[46]

As for leadership of the Tories, General Gage would have been glad to furnish this, but their forces never came up to his expectations. In and around Boston, the Tories never seemed to do much except protest. This some of them did strongly. At a town meeting an able Tory, Daniel

Leonard, paid his respects to the Committee of Correspondence set up by Samuel Adams—who was also present—in the following words: "This is the foulest, subtlest and most venomous serpent that ever issued from the eggs of sedition. It is the source of the rebellion. I saw the small seed when it was planted; it was a grain of mustard. I have watched the plant until it has become a great tree; the vilest reptiles that crawl upon the earth are concealed at the root; the foulest birds of the air rest upon its branches." [47]

Nor was the Tory opinion of Sam Adams himself any higher. A Massachusetts historian, James H. Stark, in contrast to many orthodox accounts, near the turn of the twentieth century described Adams as being in his forties during the formative days of the Revolution, "but already gray and bent with a physical infirmity which kept his head and hands shaking like those of a paralytic. He was a man of broken fortunes, a ne'er-do-well in his private business, a failure as a tax collector, the only public office he had thus far undertaken to discharge. He had an hereditary antipathy to the British government, for his father was one of the principal men connected with the Land Bank delusion, and was ruined by the subsequent restrictions which Parliament imposed on the circulation of paper money. Apparently, Governor Thomas Hutchinson was a leader in dissolving the bank, and from that time on, Samuel Adams was an enemy of Hutchinson and the existing government." [48]

What Adams thought about the royal government at the time has been made clear in thousands of pages, both his and those of others. But Governor Hutchinson felt just as strongly about Adams. Describing the sale of the elder Adams' estate which had been put up to satisfy the unpaid debts left by the closing of the bank, under the authority of the General Assembly, the son, Samuel, "first made himself conspicuous on this occasion," wrote Hutchinson. "He attended the sale, threatened the sheriff to bring action against him and threatened all who should attempt to enter upon the estate under pretence of a purchase, and by intimidating both the sheriff and those persons who intended to purchase, he prevented the sale, kept the estate in his possession, and the debts to the land bank remained unsatisfied." [49]

Hutchinson himself is in the forefront of any study of the Tories. His ancestry had been active in the colony of Massachusetts since its founding. Born in Boston in 1711, the son of a wealthy merchant, Thomas Hutchinson was graduated from Harvard in 1727. He served in the local government, becoming speaker of the General Court or legislature of the province from 1747 to 1749. Later he became chief judge of the superior court of Massachusetts, a position James Otis, Sr., wanted, and which James, Jr., always resented Hutchinson's getting. The latter was lieutenant governor and governor in the crucial years from 1771 to 1774, being the last royal chief executive of the important colony. He left only when General Gage took over as military governor in the emergency. Hutchinson was on the whole a moderate, wise and dedicated public official. His father told him, "Depend on it, if you serve your country faithfully, you will be reproached and reviled for doing it." His great-great-grandmother, Anne Hutchinson, had certainly set such an example.[50]

When the Revolution broke out, Hutchinson was a successful merchant, a financial wizard and probably the wealthiest man in New England. Violence he already knew, for in 1765, following the Stamp Act—which Hutchinson had opposed but felt bound by duty to uphold—his elegant Boston mansion had been ransacked by mobs which broke open his door, destroyed his furniture, opened his bedding to get the feathers, tore an ornate balcony off the front of the house, and pulled down all the shade trees in the yard. Not content with this senseless destruction, they stole the family silver and pictures, destroyed many of his valuable documents which he had been collecting for thirty years, and drank or spilled thirty-four pipes of wine. Fortunately, a friend, Dr. Andrew Eliot, rescued most of the papers, including the material for the second volume of history which Hutchinson wrote from original papers to which no one else had access.

This royal governor detested the radicals and thought they were too common for consideration. He urged that the leaders of the band of Americans who burned the British schooner *Gaspee* be taken to England and hanged. Those who did this in 1772 were never convicted. Once, in an observation regarding the American Declaration of Independence, Hutchinson said that he doubted that men were created equal. But he showed bad judgment in getting the East India Tea Company consignments for a relative. And the outspoken John Adams lumped Hutchinson and Peter Oliver together in asserting that by taking the view that an abridgement of liberties would be good for the colonies, "they deceived themselves and became the Bubbles of their own Avarice and Ambition. The rest of the world are not thus deceived." [51] Yet upon another occasion, Adams expressed a different opinion, calling Hutchinson "the greatest and best man in the world . . . a sort of apotheosis like that of Alexander and that of Caesar." Hutchinson opposed the Stamp Act but was equally opposed to violence in resisting the King. He was misled by the lull from 1772 to 1774, as he told Lord Dartmouth.[52]

When Hutchinson felt compelled to leave for England on January 29, 1774, he did not, as some accounts state, slip out in the middle of the night. A courageous man, he walked calmly along the road in daylight, saying good-bye to his friends, then sadly departed. Two hundred prominent Massachusetts citizens signed a paper regretting his departure. In England where he became an adviser to the King and the government, Hutchinson was able to convince George III that the Boston Port Act was too severe in its closing down all such activity of the town, and he was also able to persuade Lord North that the Massachusetts General Court should not be required to recognize the sovereignty of Parliament formally, and that in the future the colonies should be warned before such measures as the Tea Act were passed. Thomas Hutchinson refused a baronetcy from the King, as well as a rich governorship, wanting only to help Massachusetts and be buried there. Today the weight of scholarly opinion is that Hutchinson is more deserving of respect than of apology.[53]

He certainly felt he deserved more than he received. After being in England a year, he happened to read in a Boston newspaper that all his property in America, including the country estate to which he had fortunately been able to flee after his house was sacked, was for sale. In his diary on August 16, 1779, he noted, "I hope the ingratitude as well as the extravagant cruelty of this act, will hereafter appear for the benefit of my posterity." In the confiscation sale his estates brought almost 100,-000 pounds in the then-depreciated currency, which was far below their real value. Even the family tomb was not respected by the purchaser. The bones of Hutchinson's ancestors, who for generations had been prominent in the history of the colony, were scattered and the name of the new owner unceremoniously carved upon the tomb.[54]

Judge Peter Oliver, also a distinguished member of the ruling aristocracy in Massachusetts for thirty years, was himself forced to flee to England. After his departure, his daughter-in-law Phoebe, in a petition to the General Court, said that she was a widow and that after the death of her husband, Andrew Oliver, she and her children had been supported by the estate of her father-in-law. Then the selectmen of Middleborough had taken possession of the property and were depriving her of the use of a cow, the grist mill, bacon, bread, etc. She asked that she be given relief, especially pleading that she and her family not be evicted from the Oliver house in which she had lived for seven years. The records of the Court indicate she was helped some in this respect.[55]

The appraisal of Thomas Hutchinson by Judge Oliver, while naturally in favor of his subject, reveals significant details: "Mr. Hutchinson was a gentleman on whom nature had conferred what she is sparing of, an acumen of genius united with a solidity of judgment and great regularity of manners . . . the people of the Province repaired to him with as much avidity as the people of Greece repaired to the Oracle at Delphi in their emergencies; but Mr. Hutchinson was so void of duplicity of soul, that he, unlike the priestess of Apollo, never returned an ambiguous answer. . . . In private life, Mr. Hutchinson was the scholar without pedantry, the polite gentleman without affectation, the social companion without reservedness, affable without the least tincture of pride, in commerce undisguised and open, in morals, regular without severity, in expression of his sentiments, candid and void of guile, liberal in his charity, without ostentation or partiality, amiable in domestic life, distinguished by conjugal fidelity and attention, parental affection and a humane, tender and condescending behavior to his dependent domestics. His religion sat graceful on his conduct; it was manly and free, undebased by hypocrisy, enthusiasm or superstition; it embraced all mankind." [56]

The editors of his recently published diary point out, however, that nowhere in it does Oliver speak of Hutchinson's love for office, "that peculiar lust that made him accept office upon office without ever considering the political repercussions." But even allowing for the bias of Oliver toward his contemporary, the verdict of history acquits Thomas Hutchinson well. He was a lover of his country, while he was here and when he was abroad, and was termed the best American historian of his time and the ablest financier in Massachusetts. The fact that, unlike most British officials here, Hutchinson was born in America and was not a member of the Church of England added to his popularity.[57]

It seems to have been the firm conviction of Hutchinson that the American colonies were not yet ripe for independence, that they would not be for another fifty years, and that it was foolish to try to overthrow British rule and impossible to revolt against it. He never felt himself to be an Englishman, but was always primarily an American who believed that the policy of moderation which he urged was the one most beneficial to Crown and colony. This also was the policy of most of the Tory leaders, who felt themselves no less American because they admitted a slender degree of British control. In 1773 the bitterest feeling was aroused against Governor Hutchinson by the publication of some letters expressing his political views, which he had written to the ministry officials in London. This correspondence fell into the hands of Benjamin Franklin, who sent them to Boston with the admonition that they were not to be published. Such precaution apparently caused the immediate publication of the letters, and although they contained little not already known concerning Hutchinson's views, the circumstances surrounding them brought patriot rancor down upon his head. Henceforth, he suffered under the stigma of having attempted to betray his country's liberties. By a strange paradox, Lord North and Governor Hutchinson, although each concealed his real thoughts from the other at the time, were in virtual agreement as to the utter folly of the royal policy which it had been their duty to enforce.[58]

This policy Hutchinson made clear in a speech to the Massachusetts Assembly, when he said, "I know of no line that can be drawn between the supreme authority of Parliament and the total independence of the colonies; it is impossible that there should be two independent legislatures in one and the same state; for although there may be one head, the King, yet the two legislative bodies will make two governments as distinct as the Kingdoms of England and Scotland before the Union." [59]

Trying to enforce the supremacy of the Crown, Hutchinson had run into interminable squabbles with the Whigs over taxation. Such arguments as those of Samuel Adams and his associates that heavy taxes and "horrid slavery" would follow if the governor continued to hold sway made lively reading in the patriot papers, which accordingly undermined the duller Tory news sheets. Hutchinson complained that seven-eighths of the people read nothing but the *Boston Gazette,* and so were "never undeceived." He believed correctly that if the colonists, as with people at all times, would take proper advantage of their privileges, they would have little worry about their rights. But such a reasonable attitude was not to prevail, even though it was from a seasoned mind in which the intellectual faculties matched the practical. As radical tides swept over New England, political power shifted into the hands of the popular leaders, and theories shifted as well.[60]

This trend could be seen in the Whig appeal that the corrupt rich were oppressing the downtrodden poor, which was much more appealing generally than the Tory appeal that "silly clowns and illiterate mechanics" were promoting social rebellion and deluding the people. The Reverend John Bullman of South Carolina said in a sermon that "every idle projector who perhaps cannot govern his own household, or pay the debts of his own creating, presumes he is qualified to dictate how the state should be governed, and to point out means of paying the debts of a nation." The same sentiment was expressed in a poem with the lines,

> Down at night a bricklayer or carpenter lies
> With next sun, a Lycurgus or Solon doth rise.[61]

This type of democratic sentiment was spreading to the other colonies, but, as John Adams pointed out, the case of Massachusetts was most urgent and "it could not be long before every other colony must follow her example." Even so, he still hoped that they would be wise "and preserve the English constitution in its spirit and substance, as far as the circumstances of this country required or would admit." The enterprising Adams was closer to the viewpoint of Hutchinson than he cared to admit. In fact, Adams stated in the summer of 1775 that "Nothing could be more false and injurious to me, than the imputation of any sanguinary zeal against the Tories, for I can truly declare that through the whole Revolution . . . I never committed one Act of Severity against the Tories." [62]

It is difficult to reconcile the clamorous charges of Samuel Adams that Hutchinson was from boyhood imbued with the principle that man should be governed by the discerning few, and that Hutchinson wanted to be the hero of the few, unless we consider the reasoning impelled by the British government to which Hutchinson was ever loyal. Nor does the echoing comment of Vernon Parrington that Hutchinson was a reactionary without a spark of idealism coincide with all the facts and circumstances. As Harvey Wish indicates, Hutchinson's interpretation of the American Revolution has more adherents today than it did a century ago. The argument of this Tory governor that the struggle was caused by colonial fear of events to come rather than current British abuses has been upheld by recent historians. Hutchinson tried to show that the fear of a disproportionate and unfair tax by Great Britain was groundless. He dwelt upon the growing prosperity of Massachusetts, emphasized the security offered by remaining in the Empire, and stressed the military futility and costliness of resisting England.

Hutchinson had rightfully pictured the "Boston Massacre" as an affair in which a mob abused and then attacked the British soldiers, although his contention that they fired in self-defense is open to question. There was logic enough on the side of the soldiers to enable John Adams and Josiah Quincy, the defense attorneys, to win virtual acquittal for them. However, there was a phase of the trial that disturbed Adams. He was paid only nineteen guineas for his strenuous services in "a whole year of distressing anxiety, and for thirteen or fourteen days of the hardest labor in the trials that I ever went through. Add to all this, the taunts and scoffs and bitter reproaches of the Whigs; and the giggling and tittering of the Tories, which was more provoking than all the rest." [63]

As to the belief of Hutchinson that the colonial newspapers played a major role in fomenting the revolution, Arthur M. Schlesinger, Sr., has plainly substantiated this in his recent book on the subject. Tory propagandists, like the Whigs, developed the newspaper as a channel for their ideas to a remarkable extent, but from the time of the Stamp Act—which applied irritatingly to printers—the preponderance of the press was on the patriot side. However, there were several newspapers open to the Tories, including the *Boston News-Letter*, in 1704 the first paper established in the colonies. The most important of the Tory papers was James Rivington's *New York Gazetteer*, published with one period interruption from 1773 to 1783. Most significant of the contents of papers on either side was the political essay, in which the two causes were variously praised and condemned. From this crucible of conflict, modern American journalism has grown, springing mainly of course from the patriot press, but also tinged with the poignant overtones of some sturdy efforts made in vain by their outnumbered antagonists.[64]

Mrs. Mercy Warren, sister of James Otis, wrote two plays which pilloried Hutchinson and his intimates and which were distributed to the public through the press. But despite all the efforts to condemn him to infamy then and through the later pages of chauvinistic history, Thomas Hutchinson has been proven to be more perspicacious in political wisdom than his contemporaries could know. As historian Esther Forbes has stated, no man ever loved Massachusetts more than did Thomas Hutchinson. He had written her history, fought for her boundaries, reestablished her currency, and seen to it that her courts and judicial system were kept to a high standard. Hutchinson lost everything by backing the wrong system at the wrong time.

The conservatism of Hutchinson was shared by prominent associates, among them Judge Samuel Curwen of the Admiralty Court in Boston. His grandfather was Judge Jonathan Curwen of Salem, Massachusetts, in whose house the unfortunate women accused of witchcraft in 1692 were examined by Justices Sewall and Hawthorne before being sentenced. Samuel was graduated from Harvard in 1735 and, after engaging in business, became an admiralty judge and was serving in this position at the outbreak of the Revolution. Curwen supported the policies of Governor Hutchinson, which of course offended the patriots, who tried to make him recant his beliefs through the newspapers. This he refused to do, saying that the prescribed recantation contained more than in conscience he could own, and that to live under the character of reproach, which the fury of the mob might throw upon him, was too painful a reflection to suffer for a moment. He decided to leave the country.[65]

On April 23, 1775, Curwen left Boston for Philadelphia, where he embarked for England the next month. There among his fellow Tories he kept a journal which has been published and which affords much information on the plight of those exiles. Prior to his departure, he began his journal at Philadelphia, and in it he made a revealing comment: "Having in vain endeavored to persuade my wife to accompany me, her apprehensions of danger from an incensed soldiery, a people licentious and enthusiastically mad, and broke loose from all the restraints of law or religion, being less terrible to her than a short passage on the ocean, and being moreover encouraged by her, I left my peaceful home (in my sixtieth year) in search of personal security, and those rights which by the leave of God, I ought to have enjoyed undisturbed there." [66]

His wife put the matter more succinctly: she said her husband was simply a runaway. As a result, the two were never reconciled, and apparently neither ever forgave the other. Curwen even left instructions that they were to be buried apart, for the reason that he would feel not a little deranged to find her by his side on the day of judgment.[67]

But Curwen, like many of his fellows, did not find the happiness in England for which he sought. He was one of those New Englanders in London whose sympathy for America grew as the war worsened. Because of neglect and penury, he even reached a stage in which he thought a dress of tar and feathers would be preferable to the distress of mind he was daily suffering. He became superstitious and wrote his friend Jonathan Sewall, another exiled Tory, then at Bristol, England, that he had heard strange news from America: that on May 19, 1780, a clear, bright day at first, "all at once a sudden darkness overspread the face of the heavens, and so palpably thick was it, that candles were lighted in the houses during its continuance until three o'clock in the afternoon . . . a short interval of light or twilight ensued, but was succeeded by a tenfold darker night than was ever known." What Curwen had heard was essentially correct, for the day was uncommonly dark in much of New England, and some thought it was the day of judgment. It did not portend any special significance in the events of the Revolution, however, since the nearest occurrences of importance were the capture of Charleston by Sir Henry Clinton a week before and a mutiny of hungry Connecticut troops under Washington at Morristown, New Jersey—unless one considers these "dark days" for the Americans to have been ominous.

At last Curwen determined to return to America. His final days in the mother country were pathetic ones. He paid a parting call on John Singleton Copley, the renowned painter and another displaced Bostonian who sympathized with the King, and who had fled to England at the outbreak of hostilities, also to find little happiness. Curwen visited once

more the Tower of London, and from its grim ramparts saw for the first
time a strange sight, a flag, the Stars and Stripes, flying from an American vessel in the Thames. He arrived back in Boston not long after the
peace treaty was signed, and his wife, upon learning of his landing, had
a "hysterick fit." For his part, Samuel Curwen bemoaned his absence of
almost ten years, "occasioned by a lamented Civil War excited by ambitious, selfish men, here and in England." [68]

As always in such conflicts, at times friendship recognized no martial
barrier. One such instance was that of Jonathan Sewall, able Massachusetts attorney and strong supporter of Governor Hutchinson, who was
also a close friend of John Adams. Sewall and Adams had studied law
together and later, while attending court, lived together, often sleeping
in the same bed. In fact, as they were walking on a hill one day, Sewall
tried to persuade Adams not to attend the First Continental Congress.
In reply, Adams spoke the memorable words, "The die is cast, I have
passed the Rubicon; sink or swim, live or die, survive or perish with my
country, is my unalterable determination." [69]

They parted to meet no more for fourteen years. Adams went his well-
known way and Sewall went to England, where he later denounced the
patriots as criminals and "the worst set of men who ever lived." But he
evidently had one exception to this denunciation, at least. In 1788 when
Adams was Minister to the Court of St. James's, Sewall was living in
London. Adams decided to visit his old friend. It was a heartrending encounter, for Adams was still fond of his former companion and considered Sewall "a gentleman and a scholar." At the simple Sewall apartment, John and his vivacious wife, Abigail, called. "I ordered the servant
to announce John Adams, I was instantly admitted, and both of us forget-
ting that we had ever been enemies, embraced each other as cordially as
ever. I had two hours' conversation with him in a most delightful freedom, upon a multitude of subjects," Adams recalled.[70]

This was not the only instance in which the astute and forthright John
Adams was involved in a personal friendship with a Tory. Late in 1774
when Adams was verbally jousting under the pseudonym of "Novanglus"
with the equally disguised "Massachusettensis" through the press, much
to the interest and entertainment of the citizenry, Adams thought at the
time that his hidden opponent was Jonathan Sewall. Not until forty years
later did Adams learn—or admit—that "Massachusettensis" was actually
34-year-old Daniel Leonard, another Harvard graduate.[71]

The purpose of the Leonard letters was to show that the course of the
English government was founded on law and reason; that the American
colonies had no substantial grievance; and that they were a part of the
British Empire and properly subject to its authority. Leonard was a scion
of an old New England family noted for its wealth and the public honors
attained by its men. Having married a Boston heiress, he soon adopted a
colorful style of dress and display, wearing a broad gold lace around
the rim of his hat, his coat glittering with still broader laces. He used an

ornate chariot and horses to travel to work and back, something it was said no Boston lawyer had done up to that time. Elected to the legislature, Leonard at first made the most ardent speeches in opposition to Great Britain that had yet been made in the House of Representatives. But, becoming alarmed at the mob outrages, he gradually changed until he became a full-fledged Tory.

In June of 1774 Daniel Leonard showed that he was a supporter of Governor Hutchinson, and when this was generally recognized, a mob of some 2,000 men gathered on the green near his home, uttering oaths, angry shouts and threats. They grew more violent until they were assured by his father that Leonard was not at home. Upon learning this, they went away. But next evening they returned, and seeing a light in the south room, which they thought was Leonard's, they fired a shot through the window. Actually, it was the room of Mrs. Leonard, who was in bed expecting a baby soon. The bullet went through the upper window sash and shutter with a loud crash, lodging in the partition of the next room. When the child was born, the Leonards' only son, he was an idiot, a misfortune which was attributed to the shock of the inhuman attack.[72]

If Daniel Leonard had any doubts about the vital question of the day, this outrage decided him. His attacks on the patriots grew more intense. "Are not the bands of society cut asunder and the sanctions that hold man to man trampled upon?" he asked. "The local people professing themselves to be true patriots frequently erect themselves into a tribunal where the same persons are at once the legislators, accusers, witnesses, judges and jurors and the mob the executioners," he complained bitterly. "Your war," he told the patriots, "can be but little more than tumultuary rage." Then, realizing that wide curiosity existed as to who he was, Leonard stated in his third issue of "Massachusettensis," "Perhaps by this time, some of you may inquire who it is that suffers his pen to run so freely. I will tell you: it is a native of this province, who knew it before many that are now basking in the rays of political sunshine had a being. He was favored not by Whigs or Tories but by the people. . . . Perhaps the whole story of empire does not furnish another instance of a forcible opposition to government, with so much specious and so little of real cause." He compared the treatment of the Tories with the persecution of witches by the colonies many years before. Leonard ardently believed that the Whigs had great advantages in the unequal combat, that their scheme flattered the people with the idea of independence; the Tories' plan supposed a degree of subordination, a somewhat humiliating idea. He also felt that the patriots followed the human tendencey to believe themselves injured and oppressed when told that they were. As to the charge that the Tories did not exert themselves sufficiently, Leonard replied that "they shuddered at the gathering storm, but dared not attempt to dispel it, lest it burst on their own heads." [73]

4. *Where Tories Held Sway*

Early in February of 1775, some gentlemen were dining together at a house in New York City, and in the course of the conversation one of the company frequently used the word "Tory." Finally, he was asked by the host,

"Pray tell me, what is a Tory?"

"A Tory," the other replied, "is a thing whose head is in England and its body in America, and its neck ought to be stretched." [1]

It is ironic that this stringent statement should have been made in New York, for here was the haven of the American Tories, the center of their activity as well as their sentiment. A man in Wethersfield, Connecticut, wrote to a friend at the time, saying, "The eyes of America are on New York." [2] Then, as in our national life today, the state was a pivotal province, winning its title, "the Empire State," from its huge area, its variety of peoples and its imperial resources.

New York had not even approved, or at least its influential Tory element had not, the more drastic measures of the first Continental Congress in 1774, and the next year its assembly refused to choose delegates to the second Continental Congress. Only after the blow against the British at Lexington and Concord did the patriot party wrest control of the New York provincial government and gain a favorable vote for independence. Typical of the sentiment there, a letter from London, jubilantly printed in the New York press, stated that Lord North, in the face of the uprisings, behaved with the greatest firmness and composure, and was resolutely determined to carry his point with the colonies, "smiling with contempt upon any tales of congresses and combinations in America." [3]

What the local Tories thought of the Whigs in both England and America, and of the Continental Congress, was summed up in a New York newspaper. The instigators of the Revolution were regarded as "an unprincipled and a disappointed faction in the mother country and an infernal, dark-designing group of men in America, audaciously styling themselves a Congress . . . obscure, pettifogging attorneys, bankrupt shopkeepers, outlawed smugglers, wretched banditti, the refuse and dregs of mankind." In poetry, the sentiment of the Tories was expressed thus:

> These hardy knaves and stupid fools,
> Some apish and pragmatic mules,
> Some servile, acquiescing tools—
> These, these compose the Congress! [4]

Although there are no exact figures on the subject, it is probable that most of the property owners in New York belonged to the Tory party. It was strong not only among the monied, but also among the middle classes of the towns and among the country folks. On the big manorial estates along the Hudson River, the tenant farmers, if they took sides at all, sided with their landlords. During the period of the British occupation, the city of New York was strongly Tory, and in Westchester County to the north of it, the feeling was even more general in favor of the King. The same loyalty existed on Staten Island and on Long Island. Furthermore, many persons were not eager to fight for either side.[5]

At no time before the end of 1775 was total independence generally desired in New York. The idea of such independence was publicly and privately resented by individuals of all classes and parties, on most all occasions. Complete separation did not become the issue of the contest until early in 1776, and as far as New Yorkers were concerned, it certainly was not the primary object of the war. Whigs and Tories stood together in demanding their constitutional rights, but differed more and more widely as to the means of securing them. Then when at last the patriot party brought out the new proposal of independence, the Tories labeled it as a revolution, as anarchy and political suicide, declaring that such radical ideas represented not only a violation of all earlier proposals but the worst possible way to obtain improved relations with Great Britain. So the Tories entered into a bitter fight with pen, sword and the Bible. In New York then, as elsewhere, the Tories represented every class and interest. Men tied to British political authority or commercial interests were logically inclined to maintain their allegiance to the King with greater consistency than those who had no such ties. Loyalism was in large part simply a residue of the people's long-standing attachment to Great Britain, and those who adhered to it were on the whole good men of respectable principles.[6]

How reluctant these people were to take sides may be judged by an incident which occurred on June 25, 1775, after the battle of Bunker Hill had taken place and even before George Washington had taken charge of the Continental Army. He was, in fact, then on his way from Mount Vernon to Cambridge, Massachusetts, to take command of the motley collection of soldiers gathered there, when the news reached New York that he planned to visit the city en route. The Royal Governor William Tryon had just arrived in the harbor from England. The New York Provincial Congress was considerably embarrassed as to how to act, since it was uncertain which of the two, the Patriot Washington or the Tory Tryon, was to appear in the city first. The Congress had thrown off the governor's authority, but still professed loyalty to him personally. Being in doubt, they ordered a colonel to dispose the militia so as to receive "either the general or governor, whoever should first arrive and wait on both as well as circumstances would allow." Auspiciously for the patriot cause, Washington came first and received a hearty welcome. Later, Tryon received one just as enthusiastic.[7]

Such was the indecision in this important colony. The theory that Great Britain waited until it was too late to make overtures to the colonies does not seem in this instance to be logical, judging by a letter from London as early as August 7, 1775. The correspondent told a friend in America that he had been informed by a member of the British government that "nothing could be more agreeable to them than any overtures which they could accept with any appearance of honor or coexistence or such as would get a negotiation on foot." This would appear to be inconsistent with the firm anticolonial statement made by Lord North and reported in the press some seven months before. The chief stumbling block in England seemed to be any recognition of the unauthorized government which the colonies had set up, for the correspondent continued, "but if any overtures should be made by the Congress, they [the ministry] will be difficulted how they can with any propriety treat with an assembly, which they have upon all occasions, stigmatized as an illegal, seditious Combination." Even so, the writer evidently felt that this obstacle could be overcome, for he added, "If the Americans do but act with union and persist in the most spirited, resolute measures, they will be able to obtain a reconciliation on their own terms."[8]

The measures taken by the American patriots were aided, it appears, not only from their own ranks and resources but from the mother country as well. In less than a month from the time the foregoing letter was written, the Lord Advocate of England was admonishing his customs officials that he had been informed of many embarcations of his Majesty's subjects from that country to America, some of them with money, arms and ammunition apparently for the purpose of "aid and support for his Majesty's rebellious subjects in the several Colonies in America." The Lord Advocate stated that he was determined to prevent such activity, and accordingly directed that no vessel be cleared from any of the ports in Scotland—this evidently being the most suspected region—with more persons on board than their proper complement of men. Realizing that the ocean was a two-way thoroughfare, the British government further directed that the brigantine *Industry*, with a Captain McFaslin in command, which was expected to arrive soon from New England, be searched. It had been reported that this vessel had "letters and papers on board from persons now in rebellion in America." For this purpose, the *Industry* was to be "rummaged in the strictest manner." Tories in America had evidently tipped off government officials in England.[9]

Those subjects loyal to the Crown did not tend to hide their feelings when the climax came. That of course was the Declaration of Independence, and New York was the last state to agree to it. One reason for this was the fact that the Empire State bordered on Canada and was influenced by the loyalty there. Also, as has been indicated, New York's commercial interests were such as to make the powerful protection of England desirable. In 1775 and early 1776 before the Declaration of Independence was proclaimed, at least ninety-five per cent of the state's people professed loyalty to the King, Empire and British constitution. The remaining five per cent were those ardent republicans who advocated outright independence. The Declaration of Independence, coming with dramatic impact, made loyalty to the King or to the Continental Congress the issue on which party lines were finally formed. The eloquent document divided those who tried to solve the problem by evolution from those who preferred to solve it by revolution. It placed the Tories on the defensive and forced them to choose sides.[10]

How this noble document is patriotically regarded is a matter of common knowledge. But how it was looked upon by those who did not approve of it has been of course less graphically presented. It is not to be expected that Thomas Hutchinson would have liked the great Declaration. But his use of the words "false and frivolous" to describe it is at least thought-provoking. John Adams did not like certain parts of the document, although he was one of the committee appointed to draw it up. Especially did he disapprove of the reference in it to "the last king of America," George III, as a tyrant. "I never believed George to be a tyrant in disposition and in nature," Adams later remarked. Professor Goldwin Smith called attention to the Declaration's "sweeping aphorisms about the natural rights of man . . . which might seem strange when framed for slave-holding communities by a publicist [Jefferson], who himself held slaves." [11]

Not content to criticize the document from a technical standpoint, the Tory-minded historian, Ryerson, has pointed out that two weeks before adopting the Declaration, Congress passed a resolution "That no man in these colonies charged with being a Tory, or unfriendly to the cause of American liberty, be injured in his person or property, unless the proceeding against him be founded on an order of Congress or Committees." This same writer adds that the resolution "amounted to practically nothing," contending that the Declaration of Independence was a result not of a great spontaneous movement but of agitation by radical leaders who tried to appease the Tories by such misleading resolutions as the foregoing. Writing about a century after the Declaration went into effect, the historian concludes, "After many years of anxious study and reflection, I have a strong conviction that the Declaration of Independence in 1776 was a great mistake in itself, a great calamity to America as well as to England, a great injustice to many thousands on both sides of the Atlantic, a great loss of human life, a great blow to the real liberties of mankind, and a great impediment to the highest Christian and Anglo-Saxon civilization among the nations of the world."[12]

These ideas were felt particularly in New York. Washington himself declared that most of the people on Long Island were Tories, and it was estimated that there were only forty-five Whigs on Staten Island. On Long Island, loyalty and rebellion blended, the balance of power before the arrival of troops being in favor of the former. The rich aristocrats and the Dutch were averse to disturbing the comfortable *status quo,* especially in Kings and Queens counties, which were largely Tory. British authorities believed, even after the Declaration, that a majority of the "honest-hearted people in New York" were still on the side of the King. But such sentiment did not mean that there was tranquillity in the state. Liberty poles had been set up early in 1775, and two of the still-loyal subjects, William Cunningham and John Hill, were coming from the Hudson River one March afternoon when they stopped in the town to watch a boxing match near one of the poles. Soon they were set upon by several of the young patriots, were called "Tories" and eventually "used in a most cruel manner by a mob of more than 200 men." Hill was soundly beaten up and Cunningham was brought to the liberty pole, told to go down on his knees and "damn his Popish King George." Instead, he called out, "God Bless the King!" Whereupon, the mob dragged him across the green, tore off his clothes and robbed him of his watch. Had it not been for some peace officers who intervened, the two Tories might have been murdered. Yet compared to other colonies, New York was still mainly loyal. At about the same time as the foregoing incident, James Madison wrote from his home, "How different is the spirit of Virginia from that of New York. A fellow was lately tarred and feathered for treating one of our county committees with disrespect; in New York, they insult the whole Colony and Continent with impunity."[13]

A wedding was held in March at White Plains, just north of the city, the main participants being Gabriel Purdy and Miss Clarity Purdy, evidently relatives. Both were residents of "that loyal town. What particularly is remarkable about the affair," said a New York newspaper, "is that the guests consisted of forty-seven persons, thirty-seven of whom were Purdys, and not a single Whig among them." This occurrence was typical of White Plains at that time, the majority of whose residents three weeks later signed a declaration pledging undying loyalty to the King and British Constitution.[14]

Before the arrival of the British army in New York, the persecution of the Tories grew rapidly. They were arrested for arming to support the

British or aiding the enemy in any way; for harboring or associating with each other; recruiting soldiers; refusing to muster; corresponding with each other or with the British; refusing to sign the Continental Association against the cause of the Crown; denouncing or refusing to obey congresses and committees; writing or speaking against the American cause; rejecting Continental money; refusing to give up arms; drinking the King's health; inciting or taking part in Tory plots and riots; and even for endeavoring to remain neutral. Isaac Youngs and Henry Dawkins were charged with counterfeiting Continental currency, not so much to help the Tories by cheapening this plentiful medium but to pay off their own personal debts in an easy way. A youth in New York who had stolen some public ammunition was confined to his father's farm for one year, and allowed to go out only for worship on Sundays and to funerals. A politician who drank to the King's success was taken to the guardhouse, where the soldiers knocked the end out of a hogshead and forced him to dance Yankee Doodle in it until the next day. Mere suspicion was sufficient for arrest, and by the end of 1775 the jails of the city were overflowing.

Instrumental in the continuing rejection of the Tories by the Whigs was the general Association passed by Congress which forbade purchase of British goods. It served as a political thermometer in New York. The Tories objected to this idea of "boycotting the whole world" in order to get rid of taxes and declared that "the remedy was ten thousand times worse than the disease." It was like "cutting off your arm to remove a sore on your little finger." Americans would have to live like dogs and savages until the English government relented. It stamped the individual as a Whig or Tory in the eyes of his neighbors, when some of those involved were members of neither faction. Hesitation brought suspicion, and refusal meant guilt and punishment. It was in the struggle against these regulations that the Tory party reached its summit as a political organization in early 1776. From then on, it declined, although it remained active in New York and in certain regions elsewhere until 1783.[15]

Especially active in opposing such measures of Congress was James Jauncey, New York Assemblyman, who was soon forced to leave his house when a mob broke in for the purpose of riding him on a rail. He retired to Throg's Neck, some twenty-two miles from New York, to the house of "a great Whig," but he and his sons were seized and imprisoned in Connecticut. Jauncey estimated his estate, which he lost to the patriots, to have a value of 100,000 pounds. Samuel Tilley of Westchester County furnished the British forces with "intelligence, beef, pork, butter, cheese and vegetables, without compensation." After he had returned home from this activity, he was "secretly betrayed" and jailed. His house was then plundered and his wife taken prisoner. She had to leave three small children at home to be cared for by neighbors, but Tilley escaped and joined the British troops. Isaac Low, president of the Chamber of Commerce in New York City, was an active Tory, although he had served in the first Continental Congress. Another Tory, Justus Sherwood of New

York, was taken by armed men from his home; the mob then wantonly destroyed his household furniture, clothing and food. Before he was brought to trial, however, for refusing to take the oath of independence, Sherwood escaped and led forty other Tories some 200 miles through the northern wilderness to join the army of General Sir Guy Carleton in Canada. These were said to be the "first body of Loyalists in America that joined his Majesty's Army." Sherwood was able to give Carleton and Burgoyne valuable intelligence of the American forces.[16]

Giving aid to Carleton also was Sir Guy Johnson of upstate New York, who was forced in the winter of 1775 to surrender arms belonging to himself and tenants of his extensive estate. The following spring, he and 170 of the members of his community escaped through the wilderness to Canada. Lady Johnson and their two infant children were detained as hostages for nine months, when she escaped to the British in lower New York. Johnson was given command of 500 troops by Carleton and reentered the state to fight the Americans. He later claimed losses of more than 183,000 pounds. John Munro was caught recruiting men for the British and sent as a prisoner to Albany. "It would almost make a volume to enumerate the many various hardships your Memorialist and family have undergone," he later wrote, "both in mind and body, being with his fellow prisoners loaded with irons, together with the cries and laments of their wives and children, on seeing their husbands and relations dragged from their cells to the place of Execution and executed in the presence of their fellow prisoners. . . . Nothing supported your Memorialist during eighteen months confinement but being conscious of the goodness of the Cause for which he is suffering." Later, he too escaped from the Americans and joined the army of Burgoyne.[17]

To much of the Tory activity, the *New York Gazetteer* of James Rivington sounded an echoing note. Its editor at various times seemed to be the friend of both Whig and Tory—or neither. He was the son of a well-to-do London bookseller and publisher, had married well and lived luxuriously. Rivington's paper joined typographical excellence with a naturally conservative viewpoint. He was a friend and correspondent of Henry Knox, Boston bookseller and future Revolutionary general and Secretary of War, as true a patriot as ever lived in America. Knox later started a newspaper for the American forces in New Jersey in answer to the Tory press there. This patriot paper eventually became the *Elizabeth Daily Journal*.[18]

As time and the rebellion progressed, Rivington and his paper became plainly Tory in viewpoint. An ex-shipmaster and privateer, Isaac Sears, took it upon himself to stop Rivington's ravings, as he called them. Sears set out from southern Connecticut with a hundred men, bound for New York and Rivington. He was no stranger in the city, in fact was known there as a mob leader. It was Sears who later seized guns when the news of the battle of Lexington and Concord reached New York, and for days terrified the Tories. Now it was his purpose not only to silence Rivington, but to disarm the principal Tory leaders in and around New York. At Mamaroneck the mob burned a small British sloop used to supply warships. Then Sears and his men crossed into Eastchester, where they entered the home of Judge Jonathan Fowles, placed him under arrest and confiscated his sword, guns and pistols. They then proceeded to Westchester, where they seized the Reverend Samuel Seabury and Nathaniel Underhill. The able and influential Tory Seabury complained afterward that they had rifled his desk, thrust a bayonet through his daughter's cap and cut to pieces the quilt upon which she was working.[19]

After sending their prisoners to Connecticut under strong guard, the raiders mounted their horses and went on to New York City, which they entered at noon November 23, 1775. With bayonets fixed, they clattered over the stone pavements and drew up in a rather grotesque close-order formation before the printing office of James Rivington at the foot of Wall Street. Part of the eagerness of Sears to "get" Rivington may be explained by the fact that the *Gazette* had previously termed Sears "a tool of the lowest order," a "political cracker" and probably most arousing of all, "the laughing-stock of the whole town." [20]

Placing a guard at the door, the mob crowded into the printing shop, destroyed the press and carried away the type. They left in mock payment "an order on Lord Dunmore." Outside on their horses, they wheeled to the left and in precise order rode out of town singing the newly popular "Yankee Doodle," to the loud cheers of the spectators, who joined in singing what was soon to become the nearest thing to a national war song of the Revolution.[21]

Flushed with success, Sears and his raiders on their way back took the opportunity to disarm all Tories with whom they came in contact. They arrived in New Haven on November 28. Along the way, they had been joined by a large group of curiosity-seekers and all of them entered the town with "the whole making a grand procession." They were received by the townspeople enthusiastically, and were saluted with the booming of two cannon. That day the raiders spent in "festivity and innocent mirth." Sears wrote to Roger Sherman, Eliphalet Dyer and Silas Deane that he had deprived "that traitor to his country, James Rivington, of the means of circulating poison in print, the latter of which we happily effected by taking away his types, and which may be a great means of putting an end to the Tory faction there, for his press has been as it were the very life and soul of it." But even Alexander Hamilton thought little of this predatory raid of Sears. He wrote to John Jay, "Though I am fully sensitive how dangerous and pernicious Rivington's press has been, and how detestable the character of the man is in every respect, yet I cannot help disapproving and condemning this step." [22]

The Provincial Congress of New York, however, resented this raid by Connecticut men on their territory, people and press, even if it did involve Rivington. The state leaders protested so that Governor Jonathan Trumbull of Connecticut released Seabury, Fowler and Underhill. But

66

 Royal Raiders

Rivington never got back his valued type, and so his *Gazetteer* made a temporary demise. This suited the patriots quite well, since many of them had called it "the lying *Gazette*." Even so, it was probably the most important Tory newspaper in the country. As for Rivington himself, he is later quoted as saying, "I have no desire either to be roasted in Florida or frozen to death in Canada or Nova Scotia, and if I go to England, it is not impossible that I might be accommodated with a lodging in Newgate." [23]

There were many who would have gladly consigned Rivington to the dreaded Newgate prison in London, among them a former British army officer, General Charles Lee, who rendered questionable service himself to the American cause. Said he of Rivington: "a ridiculous, pragmatical, slipshod coxcomb; they said he had not decency enough for the porter of a bawdy-house, learning enough for a barrack washer-woman, nor imagination sufficient for a Christmas bellman . . . they said that when he first set up his press, he used always to write musketeers, musk-cat-ears, dragoons, dragons, battalions, battle-lions." Had Rivington examined, in reverse, the professional career of General Lee, he doubtless could have returned the "compliments." There is documentary evidence suggesting that Rivington had secret contacts with George Washington, for the purpose of furnishing the patriots information about British activities, and that the editor was paid for this information at the same time he was acting his role as a Tory. It is interesting to note that Rivington was allowed to remain in New York after the peace was signed. [24]

Despite the loss of their main newspaper, the avowed Tories showed their feelings whenever possible by supporting the British. According to Claude H. Van Tyne, New York alone furnished 15,000 troops for the royal army and navy, this number being more than George Washington's entire army most of the time. As will be seen, however, the British did not accept or assimilate the provincial militia to any effective extent. Spies representing both sides were busily at work. Patriot leaders felt it necessary to identify strangers and travelers, who had to carry a certificate of Americanism from Congress or some local committee. Innkeepers and stage drivers were fined if they neglected to ask their patrons to show their credentials. Many Tories, not being able to obtain such certificates, were forced to stay at home, and this greatly hampered their organizing and effectiveness. Of course there were those who violated these strict rules—but they often paid for it with a coat of tar and feathers or worse. [25]

As an example, Thomas Sprague of Dutchess County, New York, refused to sign an Association paper and was taken into custody, but, as seemed to be almost a custom in such cases, he escaped. He nonetheless had to say good-bye to "a pleasant part of the country highly improved by his own labor, and to leave a large family to the mercy of the merciless, and after passing through much peril and hardship in the year, 1776, reached New York with twenty-eight men that engaged in Dutchess

County to serve as soldiers under him." He was part of the successful assault force on Fort Montgomery and received a ball which remained in his arm. His son was sent nearly fifty times by British officers into the country for intelligence.[25]

Trying also to remain loyal, A. D. Spalding of Norwalk, Connecticut, reported that the Whigs intercepted his mail and found that a gentleman in England was corresponding with him. "They had sworn to execute their vengeance on me . . . to take me . . . not to spare my life but to cut me up into pound pieces." Spalding heard that a mob was to descend on him, and feeling that it would be "neither true courage nor prudence for me to think of braving it out alone against a raving Mad Rabble, which, from what I knew, consisted of a hundred rough, infatuated, distracted desperadoes . . . I took my flight into the country, was pursued by 18 armed men for 20 miles, with guns, bayonets, powder and ball." He got as far as Old Pound Ridge, when he received word from his wife that it would not be safe for him to return home unless he signed the Association and joined in the rebellion. "But I do from my soul abhor the thought of rebelling against my Prince," he declared. "But what to do, I know not, to be absent from my family and business is cruel, 'tis hard. . . . This part of the world is filled with falsehood, and a lying spirit has gone forth in our land." [26]

Similar sentiment existed in Newtown, Connecticut, where an expedition of several hundred men, led by Colonel Ichabod Lewis, formed in order to disarm the local Tories. They took in tow the rector, the selectmen and some important citizens of Newtown, who were compelled to sign the Continental Association, swear not to take up arms against the colony and promise not to speak disrespectfully of the Congress. As an incongruous climax to the situation, Isaac Sears reported that he had "arrived at Newtown and tendered the oath to four of the great Tories, which they swallowed as hard as if it was a four-pound shot they were trying to get down." [27]

A Connecticut soldier of the American forces, Barnet Davenport, killed a Tory named Malley, his wife and two children, in Litchfield County, then plundered their home. Afterward, in order to conceal his crime, he burned the house and the corpses. But later he was discovered wearing the clothes of the murdered man, was arrested, tried, condemned and executed for the crime at Litchfield.

Acting even more energetically, the frisky riflemen of Daniel Morgan, head of Washington's rangers, while on their way from Virginia to Massachusetts to join the main army, grimly amused themselves as they went along by chasing Tories. Fascinated by the new-fashioned discipline of tar and feathers, these sturdy frontiersmen in fringed buckskin apprehended some of the loyal people who were accused of serious crimes and sent them tarred and feathered to the British lines. At New Milford, Connecticut, they found "a most incorrigible Tory who called them 'damned rebels' etc." Their answer was to make him walk before them to

Litchfield, some twenty miles, and carry one of his geese all the way in
his hand. Upon arrival there, the rangers tarred the Tory, made him
pluck his goose, then stuck the feathers on him. They made him kneel
down and "thank them for their lenity," then drummed him out of their
company.[28]

So the poor Tories—or so it seems at this date when viewing their hardships in retrospect—hardly knew which way to turn. Some wit, sensing
their excruciating indecision, paraphrased the soliloquy:

> To sign or not to sign, that is the question
> Whether 'twere better for an honest man
> To sign, and so be safe; or to resolve,
> Betide what will, against associations,
> And by retreating shun them. To fly—I reck
> Not where: and by that flight, t'escape
> Feathers and tar and thousand other ills
> That loyalty is heir to: 'Tis a consummation
> Devoutly to be wished.[29]

As the tension and violence grew, so did the rumors. A London newspaper reported in 1776: "Mr. Washington, we hear, is married to a very
amiable lady, but it is said that Mrs. Washington, being a warm Loyalist,
has separated from her husband since the commencement of the present
troubles, and lives, very much respected, in the city of New York." By
spring, Englishmen were reading in their press that Washington was
dead and that the American rebellion clearly would not long survive him.

At about the same time, American newspapers extended the correct—or
what it felt to be correct—definitions of the terms "Whig" and "Tory."
The former was said to have been a reproachful name meaning "sour
milk," first given to the Presbyterians in Scotland when they were persecuted by the high church. Because they were forced to flee from their
homes, hungry and thirsty, they often drank buttermilk whig or whey
which was given to them. The "Tories" or high churchmen stood on the
side of the King as being above the law. Their adversaries therefore gave
them their name, referring to Irish robbers or highwaymen who lived
upon plunder and were eager for any daring or villainous enterprise.
"Whig and Tory then," concluded the newspaper account, "are used only
with allusion to their originals, from whence they are borrowed—*sour
milk* and *highway robber*. Such as trust to our common dictionaries for
an explanation, will only deceive themselves." Another newspaper put it
differently: "Every fool is not a Tory but every Tory is a fool. The man
who maintains the divine right of kings to govern wrong is a fool and also
a genuine Tory." [30]

Regardless of the derivation of their name, the Tories in New York
were given comparatively moderate treatment by the revolutionary government, much to the disgust of patriots elsewhere. John Hancock urged

New York officials to attaint all Tories as well as counterfeiters—apparently not including smugglers, with whom he was all too well acquainted. George Washington complained to the Continental Congress in regard to this leniency and accepted Charles Lee's extreme recommendations of dealing with the "dangerous banditti of Tories." John Adams assured Washington that Tories were identical in status with the British troops and therefore the American commander had jurisdiction over them. But the New York Provincial Congress opposed the drastic control of the military men and this was supported by the Continental Congress.[31]

This encouragement was welcomed by the Tories who as a rule either received no encouragement or, if they did, it was not sufficiently backed up by the British government. As a recent writer has stated, a basic weakness of the Tories was not their attachment to Britain, but the fact that they held social or political opinions which could prevail in America only with British assistance. In order to counteract Tory propaganda to the effect that the tenants would get the estates of their Whig landlords, Dutchess and Ulster County patriots passed word around that when independence was established, the manors would be parceled out to such tenants as were in favor with the newly established government. And despite the opposition of the tenant farmers in southern Dutchess County to breaking with England, they were faced with the cruel choice of joining the patriot militia or running away.[32]

The choice had to be made by the middle of June, 1776, for by this time New York had temporarily changed its sympathies. General Washington had dashed down from Boston ahead of General Howe and had established his military headquarters in New York City. Taking heart, a group of patriots headed by some Presbyterians gathered and determined now to hunt out the Tories in the city. They searched, found and dragged "several from their lurking holes where they had taken refuge to avoid the undeserved vengeance of an ungovernable rabble." These Tories were placed on sharp rails with one leg on each side, the rail being carried on the shoulders of two tall men, another man being on each side to keep the poor wretch straight and fixed in his seat. Thus many Tories were paraded in extreme pain through the main streets, and at every corner a crier proclaimed their names and said they were notorious Tories, while the mob gave three cheers and the ludicrous procession passed on, even in front of the City Hall, where the Provincial Congress was sitting, ironically making regulations for the peace and good order of the city. Then the mob moved past the door of the headquarters of the American commander, and "so far did General Washington give his sanction and approbation to this inhuman, barbarous proceeding," said a contemporary Tory historian, Thomas Jones, "that he gave a very severe reprimand to General Putnam, who accidentally meeting one of the processions on the street, and shocked with its barbarity, attempted to put a stop to it, Washington declaring that to discourage such proceedings was to injure the cause of liberty in which they were engaged, and that nobody would attempt it but an enemy to his country." Putnam appealed to the Provincial Congress to stop such cruelty, but that body also declined.[33]

One spectator, Peter Elting, reported that "we had some grand Tory rides in the city this week. . . . Several of them were handled very roughly, being carried through the streets on rails, their clothes tore off their backs and their bodies pretty well mingled with the dust. . . . There is hardly a Tory face to be seen this morning." Some of the faces that could be seen had a sheepish look, those of American soldiers who had been frequenting bawdy houses to the extent that Generals Washington and Greene declared the saloons in the city off limits, "except the house at the Two Ferries." Special attention was given the soldiers who had been going swimming in Long Island Sound in open view of some of the Tory women, and coming out of the water naked and running toward the houses, "with a design to insult and wound the modesty of female decency." [34]

As if these problems were not enough, the persons who were supplying Washington's troops with beer reported that their barrels were not being properly returned. Whereupon he ordered "that the colonels of the several regiments strictly charge their quartermasters to take care of the beer barrels to prevent their being cut for tubs." Further complaints were to the effect that his troops were misbehaving at the food and vegetable markets, destroying the property of patriot as well as Tory farmers. Disciplinary steps were taken to stop this practice.[35]

The Tories were beginning to practice what they preached, Lord Stirling, ardent New Jersey patriot, reported to John Hancock, who was then president of the Continental Congress. Stirling understood that the Tories were assuming fresh courage, were talking daringly, had some 4,000 members in their Association, and were in possession of a supply of arms and ammunition which had been stored on the man-of-war *Asia*, off New York Harbor. Hancock was not much impressed, however, by the information, nor that contained in a new pamphlet issued by one Thomas Paine, entitled *Common Sense*, meant not only to encourage the patriots but to discourage the Tories. With typical naïveté, Hancock sent Thomas Cushing a copy of the pamphlet, saying it was for "your and your friends' amusement." [36]

Another blow was aimed at the Tories by the formation of a Committee of Safety by the New York Provincial Congress, with John Jay as chairman, and Philip Livingston, Gouverneur Morris and others as members. The group was to see that any person believed to endanger the colonies was to be arrested and sent away. Sessions of the committee were held in the New York city hall and at least once in the more mellow atmosphere of Scots Tavern in Wall Street. Manuscript records still extant show that the committee was in existence even after the British took over the city. Meeting at Fishkill, New York, on September 13, 1776, the committee considered reports from informants regarding "sundry speeches and declarations" by residents of Ulster County. It was decided that those accused had become dangerous and that they should be "apprehended, examined and secured." Five months later, John Jay interrogated Beverly Robinson, well-to-do owner of an estate, who had not yet made up his mind on which side he would be in the Revolution. Asked how he felt about the matter, Robinson replied, "I believe that committees through their severity have made a great many Tories, for it is natural when a man is hurt, to kick."

"Sir, we have passed the Rubicon," said Jay, echoing John Adams and others before him, "and it is now necessary for every man to take his part."

Robinson remarked that he was not yet sure which side to take, and wondered whether if he joined the "enemy," he would be allowed to take some of his effects with him. John Jay, who himself had had some difficulty in becoming convinced of the positive right of the patriot cause, or especially of the way it was being conducted, assured Robinson that he would be allowed to take his effects. The latter was given several weeks to make up his mind, and eventually, he decided—in favor of becoming a Tory. The historian Thomas Jones, a warm Tory himself, in describing the action against Robinson and others, commented that "the vindictive Legislature of New York, in order to get possession of these estates, took a step that no civilized nation ever before took, they attainted the women . . . for 'adhering to the enemies of the State,' that is to say, in eating, drinking, living and sleeping with their husbands, an injunction commanded by the decrees of the Almighty." [37]

Later, Robinson became a colonel of Tory troops, and he had an associate, Colonel Frederick Philips, who owned Philipsburgh Manor, the mansion of which still stands in Westchester County. The estate extended along the Hudson River for twenty-four miles and consisted of 3,000 acres, "not an acre, except the domain, not tenanted," and worth at least 100,000 pounds, in the estimation of Robinson. Philips was caught by the Americans and spent six months in Connecticut in a prison. But as seemed habitual in such cases, he escaped and took his wife and nine children into the British lines. Five of his sons joined the redcoat forces, Colonel Philips having "to borrow money to purchase their commissions." [38]

The picturesque and fertile region of Westchester County was a storied stronghold of Toryism in New York. Probably the most prominent loyal family was that of the De Lanceys, the county sheriff and later leader of the Refugee Corps of the Tories being James De Lancey. His grandfather, Judge James De Lancey, had presided at the famous trial of John Peter Zenger, in which freedom of the press was legally established in America. His uncle, Oliver De Lancey, was the senior Tory brigadier general in the British forces. Having been taken into custody by the patriots, then paroled, the younger James De Lancey decided he did not like such a neutral position, so he organized a troop of sixty light horse soldiers, all genuine Tories from the neighborhood. Getting what was for them a propitious start, they proceeded to steal the horses they were to use, as well as some cattle. Actually, bands from both sides raided the rich countryside, those from the rebel ranks being called "skinners," from their fondness for clothing which they badly needed, and which they often "skinned" right off the victims. The British and Tory raiders were known as "cowboys," because their main objective was the local cattle needed for beef by the British army.[39]

De Lancey's Refugee Corps, as it was called, soon embarked upon rounds of pillage and destruction. It was described by Governor William Tryon as being made up of the elite of the colony, three of its captains having the well-known last names of Knapp, Kipp and Totten. The corps was increased to a strength of 450 men, with De Lancey holding the rank of lieutenant colonel. These were not regular troops but a band of volunteers whose hatred and desire for revenge against their former neighbors was so intense that they preferred volunteer service without pay in the Refugee Corps to that in the regular British militia. Knowing their country so well, these raiders approached houses by the most stealthy routes and ransacked them from roof to cellar. If they could not carry off all the booty, often it was purposely damaged or destroyed. Houses were frequently burned over the heads of the occupants, leaving them suffering and destitute. In at least one instance a victim was tied to a chair from which the seat had been removed and beneath which a fire had been lighted in an effort to learn from the writhing occupant the location of valuable objects. Graves were opened and looted and the bodies were left grotesquely exposed to view. De Lancey claimed that a third of the supplies of the British in New York City was supplied by his men.

An army chaplain passing between the lines of both armies observed that "These Americans so soft, pacific and benevolent by nature, are here transformed into monsters, implacable, bloody and ravenous; party rage has kindled the spirit of hatred between them, they attack and rob each other by turns, destroy dwelling houses, or establish themselves therein by driving out those who had before dispossessed others." But such extremes did not seem to deter the Tories or their foes. They spied on each other avidly; the headquarters of De Lancey at Morrisania regularly received intelligence of the movements of the Continental forces and the patriot irregulars, often from alert Tory residents of the area. In retaliation, the patriot troops frequently raided the De Lancey headquarters trying to capture De Lancey himself, but he always managed to elude them. He never stayed in his headquarters at night and took pains not to expose himself during the day, for he doubtless knew that if he were captured, his fate would be a fantastically cruel one at the hands of avenging enemies. Around his headquarters was a cluster of Tory houses, the inhabitants of which subsisted upon the spoils of raids undertaken by the Refugee Corps. As time went on, the Corps was housed in some seventy log houses near the headquarters, this being the southernmost unit of the New York British defense line above the city. Its main purpose was to cover troop crossing in the nearby Harlem River area. This fort site is today the uptown campus of New York University.[40]

If Tory officers were sought by the patriots, the idea of capturing opposing officers was of course not unknown to the other side. General George Washington was to wage a losing battle for New York City, never being able to recapture it, but if one plot had materialized, he would probably not have succeeded even in keeping his life. David Matthews, the Tory mayor of New York City, had been suspected by Washington of plotting acts against the patriot army. On June 21, 1776, this suspicion was confirmed. The committee of the Provincial Congress, already described, which was to watch for and deal with Tories, reported to Washington that Matthews was charged "with dangerous designs and treasonable conspiracies against the rights and liberties of the United Colonies of America." [41]

The accusation was based on evidence obtained by two of the committee members, John Jay and Gouverneur Morris. A man named Isaac Ketcham, who had been jailed for counterfeiting, had testified that he believed two fellow prisoners, Sergeant Thomas Hickey and Private Michael Lynch of Washington's personal guard, were receiving money from the British, for he had overheard them talking of cutting down King's Bridge and going over to the enemy when the British fleet arrived. This information also involved William Leary of New Jersey, who told the committee that a former employee of his, James Mason, had been in British pay; upon being questioned, Mason involved Hickey and others: Gilbert Forbes, "a short, thick gunsmith with a white coat," William Greene, a drummer in Washington's guard, and William Forbes. Both Leary and Mason implicated the mayor, David Matthews, with Mason testifying that this Tory official had contributed 100 pounds for the expense of the plotters.[42]

Matthews was arrested at his residence in Flatbush and surrendered without resistance, but no real evidence was found in his house. Gilbert Forbes was rather well known, for his gunsmith's shop was on Broadway just opposite Hull's Tavern. Hauled before the committee, Forbes refused to say anything. But the next morning a young minister named Robert Livingston called on him, told him he was sorry to see him so involved, and pleaded with him to tell the truth, adding perhaps designedly that since Forbes probably had only a few days to live, he should prepare himself. Whether this admonition was purposeful or not, it had the desired effect. Forbes decided to tell all he knew.[43]

The men of Washington's guard were thereupon soon surprised by soldiers of the provost marshal with fixed bayonets, and were taken into custody. William Forbes was also locked up. In explaining his acts, Mayor Matthews told Jay and Morris that he had gone aboard the British ship *Duchess of Gordon,* on which was Governor Tryon, and that as

Matthews was leaving, Tryon had put a roll of money into his hands and told him to pay Gilbert Forbes for some rifles and get some elsewhere if possible. Matthews had hesitated, he said, and then had given Forbes the money. Afterward, he testified, numbers of men had come to him to enlist in the British forces or get aboard the King's ships, but Matthews assertedly told them all to go home and keep quiet.[44]

Hearing of these arrests, Tories took to the woods and swamps, but some of them were caught and arrested. Rumors flew that Hickey had been instructed to stab General Washington; that he had poisoned a dish of green peas meant for the general, who had been warned just in time, the peas being thrown to some chickens which died soon afterward. Another nebulous report accused Washington's housekeeper, Mrs. Lorenda Holmes, who was said to be in the kitchen at the time the meal was prepared. She denied the charge and soon left the household. Later, she said, she was caught and her right foot was burned with live coals by a patriot officer who suspected her of helping the Tories. Still other charges hinted at hostile risings of Indians and Negroes. "The Hickey plot" was said to be "a barbarous and infernal conspiracy of the loyalists to murder all of Washington's staff officers, kidnap him, and blow up the magazines, arm all loyalists and capture the city upon the arrival of the British." [45]

As for Washington himself, who never recorded much about this matter although he probably felt that Matthews was guilty, his chief concern, stern disciplinarian that he was, was the troops of his own army. Drummer William Greene, of the General's guard, showed himself willing to confess all he knew and to throw himself upon the mercy of the court-martial. Gilbert Forbes would also turn on his fellow-conspirators, it was found. The most stubborn of the group was Thomas Hickey. It was thought wise to make an example of this sergeant, a former resident of Wethersfield, Connecticut, but now believed to be a deserter from the royal army.[46]

Hickey was accordingly arraigned before a court-martial on June 26, at which Greene, Forbes and other witnesses adhered to their previous statements. The evidence showed that Hickey had signed the list setting forth those who would help the King when the fleet arrived; that he had received half a dollar in payment; and that he had endeavored to persuade others to join the cause of Great Britain against her colonies in America. Hickey was either not very astute or not concerned, for he produced no witnesses in his own behalf and simply stated that he had formed the plan at first to cheat the Tories and get some money from them, and that later he had agreed to let his name be sent to the ship so that he might be sure of being safe in case the British came, defeated the American army and made him a prisoner. No one believed him. Even without introducing all its witnesses, the prosecution won its case hands down. Hickey was sentenced to be hanged on the next day. Asked if he wanted a chaplain, he contemptuously refused, saying, "They are all cut throats." [47]

A gallows had been erected near the Bowery and Hickey was taken there. He maintained his sullen, rebellious attitude almost to the last, but burst into tears as the noose and blindfold were placed on him. Then he quickly wiped away the tears and faced his captors defiantly. Soon his body hung limp in the early summer breeze. A newspaper reported the event crisply: "June 28—This forenoon was executed in a field near the Bowery Lane, New York, in the presence of near 20,000 spectators, a soldier belonging to his Excellency General Washington's guards, for mutiny and conspiracy; being one of those who formed and was soon to have put in execution, that horrid plot of assassinating the staff officers, blowing up the magazines and securing the passes of the town, on the arrival of the hungry, ministerial myrmidons. It is hoped the remainder of these miscreants, now in our possessions, will meet with a punishment adequate to their crimes." [48]

Washington seemed determined to make a lesson for his men out of the Hickey episode. In his general orders he mentioned that he hoped the case would be a warning to every soldier in the army. In order to avoid such crimes and consequences, the Commander-in-Chief continued, the most certain method was to keep out of the temptation of them, and particularly to avoid lewd women, who, it was strangely reported in the last confession of Hickey, first led him into undesirable practices which ended in an untimely and ignominious death. Not only did such involvement mean the end of this prisoner, but the Hickey plot, magnified and falsified, blackened the reputation of the Tories throughout the country and retarded their cause. [49]

Although no proof was ever found against Mayor Matthews, the suspicions his actions aroused were virtually as condemning. He was finally sent, by order of the New York Provincial Congress, as a prisoner to Governor Trumbull at Hartford, Connecticut, being charged with "treasonable practices against the states of America," and was confined in various places in that state, "until he effected his escape from thence on the evening of the twenty-first of November following and with much difficulty and expense got into New York on the third day of December." In a letter to his friend John McKesson, Secretary of the Provincial Congress, Matthews wrote, "It is very odd that the Convention will not furnish me with some resolve or certificate to enable me to contradict a most hellish report that has been propagated and is verily believed throughout this colony, that I am concerned in a plot to assassinate General Washington and blow up the magazine in New York. The Convention well know it is as false as hell is false. . . . It is too much for mortal man to bear. . . . May God only spare my life to meet my enemies face to face." After the war, Matthews went to the island of Cape Breton, off Novia Scotia, where he rapidly gained prominence, becoming president of its council and, later, commander-in-chief of that colony. [50]

To Nova Scotia General William Howe and his army also had come early in the war, along with the thousand-odd Tories from Boston. In this number were 102 officials of the Crown, 18 clergymen, 105 rural residents, 213 merchants and similar tradesmen, as well as some 382 farmers and mechanics. Massachusetts had lost some of her best citizens. But they received no sympathy from Washington, whose determined stand had driven Howe from Boston. Writing to his brother, the American commander said that some of the Tories had "done what a great number ought to have done a long time ago, committed suicide . . . there never existed a more miserable set of beings than these wretched creatures . . . no electric shock, no sudden explosion of thunder, in a word, not the last trump could have struck them with greater consternation." [51]

General Howe was in an embarrassing position regarding the evacuation. He had, in previous letters to the ministry, scorned the idea that he was in any danger from Washington and had wished the rebels would attempt so rash a step as to attack him. Nor was this all. He had given the ministry strong reasons why his army should not move from Boston until reinforced. Ironically enough, as Howe was sailing out of the harbor he received the reply of the ministry who, supposing him still at his post there, approved of his resolution to remain, since they felt that an evacuation under such circumstances would be an inadvisable measure.

The immediate concern of Howe was not the Tories he had tried to rescue, however. Their worst troubles were just beginning, as were his, for that matter. He still had a war—or a peace—to win, so he sailed his army to New York, arriving there in early July of 1776, where he also took charge of the "cattle and Tories." He was soon joined by his brother, Admiral Richard Howe, with a huge fleet from England which ringed Staten Island with yellow masts and spars. The local people watched with fascination as squads, companies, battalions, regiments, brigades and divisions of redcoats were landed, until the bright green meadows of the island were transformed into towns of tents in which drums rolled every day as the soldiers drilled and drilled.

Staten Island Tories welcomed Howe. It was here that he and his brother, who had been appointed peace commissioners as well, held a conference with American delegates, but got nowhere when it was learned that the Americans would not repudiate their Declaration of Independence. The first Tory troops raised by Howe were a provincial corps and a company of horse on Staten Island. Howe offered commissions and bounties as well as the pay of regular troops, and was encouraged by the response. [52]

A leader in the large Tory element of Staten Island was Christopher Billopp, who owned an estate on the west end of the region, and as a colonel of the royal militia had charge of military posts for a distance of fifteen miles along the waterfront. Soon after the Lexington and Concord battles, Billopp wrote General Gage asking him not to send troops to New York at that time, hoping the storm of rebellion would blow over. The Staten Islander did succeed "in keeping the inhabitants of the Island quiet until the arrival of the British in 1776, and after General Howe did come, did everything in his power to assist him." Later Colonel Billopp was captured and imprisoned in Burlington, New Jersey, by the patriots, and reported that he was "ironed and chained to the floor of a common jail" and allowed no food "except bread and water, for his attachment to Government." During his imprisonment, Billopp was informed by General Washington that if he would resign his command in the British militia, "he should be permitted to go home and not be molested in his person or property [he owned 1,078 acres of land and 13,500 pounds in New York currency], during the war or after it. This he refused." [53]

All of those loyal were not so unfortunate, although many such as Andrew Elliot, Collector of the Port of New York, fled before Howe arrived and wished themselves back after he had taken New York City. Elliot had already been assured by Lord Dartmouth that the King's ships would be available as refuges for the loyal subjects who needed to leave the land and go aboard. The collector went to Monmouth in New Jersey with his family, but when he heard that Howe was in New York, he slipped over the Jersey highlands on foot and made his way back to New York, only to find his former customs house had been burned in the recent great fire. Howe made Elliot superintendent of police.[54]

Helping Howe, or trying to at least, was Governor William Tryon, who had come up from a similar position in North Carolina. A few years before, Tryon had won, at the battle of Alamance, a decisive victory with his provincial militia against a larger number of Western North Carolina insurgents called the Regulators. Although this event had strengthened the hand of the Crown in North Carolina, it had also served to solidify the opposition, who later faced the British in the Revolution. Now, in New York, Tryon had asked to be and was appointed "Major General of the Provincial Forces." By August, he had raised a body of some 2,000 Tories, later suppressing the Whigs in Suffolk County, then marching to Connecticut, where he burned Danbury, Fairfield and Norwalk. For his services in the battle of Long Island, Tryon was thanked by Howe, and until he went to England in 1780, this Tory governor who claimed New York as his civil-military domain was very helpful in keeping up the spirits of loyal persons. The historian Trevelyan called Tryon "from first to last, the evil genius of the royal cause in America." [55]

The genius of the patriots, George Washington, had given orders that no one should pass the New York ferries without a pass from the city's commandant. The story is told of a lady who did not know who the commandant was, so wrote a note to Washington asking permission to use the ferry to visit her family on Long Island. Upon receiving the note, Washington is said, by this Tory source, to have read it and tossed it back with a disdainful remark to the man who brought it, saying, "Carry the note back to your Tory relation, I have nothing to do with it."

The man then learned that Lord Stirling was actually the commandant of the city, so applied to him and received permission for the woman to go to Long Island, but "without any male attendant." Upon the man's protesting that she could not drive a coach herself to make the trip,

Stirling replied, "Then let her stay where she is and be damned!" Eventually she did manage to find friends in New York who helped her get to Long Island, much to her relief.[56]

As if to return such courtesy, a few weeks later the Tories on Staten Island paid their respects to Washington and some of his officers. They prepared effigies of Generals Washington, Lee and Putnam for burning. A great rain prevented this, although by the time of the downpour, all of the figures had been tarred and feathered except that of Washington. The British troops eventually did manage to set fire to the effigies, and all burned except that of Washington. His sturdy figure remaining intact was said to have caused much superstitious fear among the Hessian troops, who thought this might be an evil omen. Actually, it was probably because the figure had become too wet to burn. On Staten Island at the time was a young girl who was to be the mother of Cornelius Vanderbilt, richest American of his time. She was Phebe Hand, daughter of Obadiah Hand of Rahway, New Jersey, an ardent Tory. His brother, Edward Hand, however, later became a brigadier general in Washington's army. This difference of loyalties caused a schism in the Hand family and Phebe was sent to live with her Tory sister on Staten Island, where she met Cornelius Vanderbilt, a young resident of the place. Later, Phebe saw British vessels leaving the island for Nova Scotia, not knowing that among the Tories aboard was her father, Obadiah Hand.[57]

But though there was action in the environs, Manhattan was the center of the more important events. The Howe brothers were known to be friends of America, but their authority was limited. When the Tories in America were legally authorized by the King to help the British, this helped the Howes. As part of the propagandizing action, a Tory recruiting officer in September, 1776, told his listeners that the American Congress and the various committees had deluded the populace and betrayed their trust, forfeited the confidence of the public and ruined the country. When the Howes took New York, nearly 1,000 of the Tories signed their names to an address, declaring that "we bear true allegiance to our rightful sovereign, George III, as well as warm affection to his righteous person, crown and dignity." [58]

Despite pledges of loyalty on the part of the residents, the British found New York a different place from the pleasant and bustling town it had been a few years before when it was studded with parks, shady streets, Georgian mansions and sturdy buildings. Now many of the trees had been cut down and barricades erected in their place. Only about 3,-000 people remained in the city, including Dutch, German, the sick, aged, and Tories. Much of the city had been destroyed by the fire of September 21, 1776, which each side blamed the other for starting. Nathanael Greene had reasoned that "two-thirds of the property of the city of New York and the suburbs belong to the Tories. We have no great reason to run any considerable risk for its defence." Ironically, the British had refused to bombard the city because of the large amount of

Tory property there, and only the interference of Howe and his men prevented the entire city from being burned.[59]

Women and children perished in the fire, and an enraged mob searched through its charred length for the incendiaries. A carpenter with the intriguing name of Wright White, a Tory, had chosen that night to go on a roaring drunk. He was unmolested until he tried to interfere with the fire-fighting; then, eager for any likely victim, the mob seized him, placed a rope about his neck and hanged him from a tavern post. St. Paul's Church escaped the fire, while Trinity Church just down the street on Broadway was destroyed. The Tories of course lost much of their property, but they nevertheless flocked back into this British stronghold, until by February, 1777, the city had grown again to 11,000 people.[60]

In and around New York City, the Tories were active, but usually to their sorrow. Joshua Pell of Pelham Manor, near the city, was captured by the rebels and escaped. He gave the British much information about the Americans, including valuable data before the battle of White Plains. But Pell was finally forced to leave his "vast estates that afforded him every necessary and comfort of life" and flee for his life with his wife and eight children. John Hamilton, surgeon of the British ship *Centaur,* later lived in Dutchess County and was seized at his house. "The Revolters . . . barbarously wounded him . . . and imprisoned him in a dungeon for five months." Colonel William Bayard, of an old New York family, lived on the Hudson River just above New York, and was forced to fly from the rebels. His wife sent word to him that the British were in New York, so he ran "at least sixteen miles that night through the woods" and escaped. His wife followed him and was compelled "to take herself and her little children and to wade through a river to get between two hills to secure herself and them from danger." Bayard was active in trying to prevent the spread of the fire, which almost destroyed New York, and sent Lord North "some bundles of the fagots that must have been laid to set fire to the town." He raised a battalion of troops, the King's Orange Rangers, in which two of his sons were officers. Bayard claimed he lost over 133,000 pounds to the rebels. Even widows were robbed. Sarah Simpson, whose husband had been the land surveyor of New York City, claimed that the American Army in 1776 stole from her 27 fine shirts, 4 cloth coats, 2 dozen fine drill breeches, 1 dozen beaver hats, 2,000 weight of cheese, 4 barrels of pork, 60 pounds of tea, 128 gallons of brandy, 110 gallons of rum and 26 barrels of cider, among other articles. Catharine Cryderman, who sent three sons to the British Army, said her late husband was too old to go as a soldier. He was captured, and became so ill because of his suffering that he never recovered. "He lost his senses, was confined to his bed a long time and died." [61]

Alexander and James Robertson were printers at Albany who published newspapers and other such materials which might help the King. James was obliged to leave his home and hide in the woods thirteen miles from the city, where he carried on his activity as best he could. He left for New York, and the rebel committee at Albany "was so exasperated that they seized upon the body of Alexander Robertson, who for a series of years had been entirely deprived of the use of both legs," and also upon his printers, and put them in jail. When the British troops approached, all the prisoners who could walk were allowed to leave, but Alexander remained until the jail building was on fire. "He, however, made his way through the house on his hands and knees, and attained a cabbage garden, where by digging a pit with his hands and bringing cabbages to it, he saved himself by lying on his belly, and chewing them to prevent being suffocated. Three days later, he was found amongst the ruins by the returning foe, who were so little moved with compassionate feelings, though his hair and most of his clothing were burnt and his body, particularly his hands and knees were in blisters," that they ordered him to another jail, from which he was exchanged and sent to New York. The Robertsons set up papers for the British in New York, Philadelphia, and Charleston, South Carolina.[62]

One of the most important Tories in New York was Brigadier General Oliver De Lancey. Upon being summoned by the "Rebel Committee and Provincial Congress to appear before them," he fled to the British ship *Asia* in the harbor. He remained there until General Howe arrived and landed with the first troops on Staten Island, then helped them in securing guides and selecting routes of approach. This fighting De Lancey could hardly be classed as one of those referred to by John Adams when he said that "Howe is surrounded with disaffected Americans, Machiavellian exiles from Boston and elsewhere, who are instigating him to mingle art with force." General De Lancey was active in the battle of Long Island, especially at Brooklyn Heights and Flatbush, where he was of great value to the British because of his knowledge of the land and local people. He was a wealthy man, and later claimed that he had lost over 100,000 pounds in property to the patriots. Twenty-three of his houses were burned by the rebels. It is easy to see that he took delight in raising three battalions of Tories which he commanded in the service of the British.[63]

Sometimes it was hard to know which side a person was on—or at least that seemed to be the case of a farmer in Westchester County. He had helped the Tory troops when they were there and when the rebels came to his farm, they took his fat cattle "to the number of about 40," and when the royal army retired, they attempted to take him prisoner, but he escaped them by half an hour. Then they stripped him of everything worth carrying away, except his food, "because he was a damned Tory." But apparently this farmer had not clearly established his affiliation. For the next day, the King's light dragoons arrived, "provided with bags, and carried off all his beef, pork and other food, because he was a damned rebel." [64]

5. Advancing Backward

The explosive and incendiary actions of certain key persons in the South in the early period of the Revolution reverberated throughout the colonies. John Murray, Earl of Dunmore in the Scottish peerage and royal governor of Virginia, was a leader in such overt acts. He was a quick-tempered and violent man, not the type of individual to bring order easily out of the prevailing chaos. After the patriot leaders of the colony had reared their powdered heads in rebellion, Lord Dunmore swore he would declare freedom to the slaves and lay the patriots' homes in ashes.

The Governor hoped to alarm and suppress the rebellious planters by this call for an uprising of their Negroes and indentured servants, many of whom were ex-convicts. He undertook to raise a regiment of white people to be called "The Queen's Own Loyal Virginians," consisting of local Tories, and another composed of Negroes, to be named, "Lord Dunmore's Ethiopians." If he had tried to conceive of the most infuriating action he could take, he could not have succeeded better in arousing the ire of the planters. They had earlier reminded the Governor, through their representatives in the General Assembly, that "on former occasions when called upon as a free people in emergencies, we have liberally contributed to the common defense." They now redoubled their efforts to raise rebel regiments.[1]

Apparently Dunmore was exceedingly offended by the Virginia press, which he thought was "presuming to furnish the public with a faithful relation of occurrences, and now and then making a few strictures upon his lordship's own conduct, as well as that of some of his associates . . ." From the patriot standpoint, Dunmore wanted to destroy "every chan-

nel of public intelligence that is inimical to his designs upon the liberties
of this country, alleging that they poison the minds of the people." [2]

John Hunter Holt, who published the *Virginia Gazette* or *Norfolk Intelligencer* right under the guns of the British fleet in the harbor where
Dunmore, as will be seen, took refuge, urged the people not to give up
their liberties without a struggle. He denounced the royal governor as a
coward and tyrant, which of course the British considered to be treasonable expressions. On one occasion, Captain Matthew Squire of the *Otter*
threatened to kidnap Holt if he kept accusing him of "Negro-catching"
and similar "falsities." Finally, on September 30, 1775, after Holt had
published a disparaging "biography" of Lord Dunmore, a landing party
of twelve British soldiers and five sailors landed and wrecked Holt's
printing shop in Norfolk. They carried off the type, part of the press and
two of the journeymen. Holt himself barely escaped.

The *Gazette* now could not be published in Norfolk. When the citizens
protested, Dunmore replied that he was doing them a favor by removing
this source of public poison. Thereafter, for a time, the paper appeared
sporadically, being printed on shipboard under the direction of the Governor's principal secretary, Hector M'Alester. Now Dunmore had not
only wreaked revenge but had obtained a news organ of his own. In Virginia, indignation over the act arose. Richard Henry Lee wrote Washington that he considered the conduct of the Norfolk people disgraceful in
allowing Dunmore's few men to take away their printing press. [3]

Holt announced on October 12 that "having been prevented from continuing business by a most unjustifiable stretch of arbitrary power," he
wanted to inform the public that he hoped to obtain some new materials
with which "once more to inform his countrymen of the danger they may
be in from the machinations and black designs of their common enemy."
In lieu of other redress, Holt collected partial damages by stealing several of Dunmore's horses. But when Norfolk was burned on New Year's
Day, 1776, Holt had no town left to furnish with a newspaper, so he
joined the patriot army. After the war, he helped publish the Richmond
Virginia Gazette and *Independent Chronicle*. [4]

Meanwhile, Lord Dunmore had issued a proclamation requiring every
person capable of bearing arms "to resort to His Majesty's standard or
be looked upon as traitors, subject to forfeiture of life, confiscation of
lands etc." He also declared that all indentured servants and slaves who
were willing and able to bear arms would be freed if they joined his
forces. To make the plan more vivid, he had emblazoned across the
breast of each Negro uniform the slogan, "Liberty to Slaves." Said
Richard Henry Lee, "If the administration had searched through the
world for a person best fitted to ruin their cause and procure union and
success for these colonies, they could not have found a more complete
agent than Lord Dunmore." George Washington, now at Cambridge,
Massachusetts, trying to organize his motley Continental troops, took
time to comment on Dunmore to the effect that "Nothing less than de-

priving him of his life or liberty will secure peace to Virginia." James Madison stated that some believed Dunmore "removed from Williamsburg and pretended danger that he might with more force and consistency misrepresent us to the ministry." [5]

Dunmore had his own ideas about securing peace, so when he had collected about 1,200 men from his recruiting campaign, the patriot leaders felt it was time to take action. Accordingly, Colonel William Woodford with a patriot regiment which included Lieutenant John Marshall, the future chief justice, marched against Dunmore. Across the route of Woodford was a place called Great Bridge, nine miles south of Norfolk. There the Americans were met by a detachment of Tories sent by Dunmore, led by a Captain Fordyce, whose troops included some Negroes. Soon the opposing forces faced each other across the bridge which joined two marshy shores. Woodford had erected fortifications and Dunmore's men did not know how many men were behind them. In order to deceive him and induce an attack, Woodford arranged for a Negro to "desert" to Dunmore and inform him that there were only 300 "shirtmen" (riflemen) in the opposing force and that they had little ammunition. Actually, Woodford had three times that number of men. Dunmore swallowed the bait and at once sent 600 of his mixed garrison against the rebels. Behind the strong breastworks, the rebels held their fire until the Tories were within fifty yards, then at the command cut loose with a sharp fire which mowed down sixty of the oncoming and surprised loyal force. Among those who went down was Captain Fordyce, who fell dead with fourteen bullets through his body. The rest of his force fled precipitately back across the bridge. Dunmore's men were compelled to withdraw to Norfolk, and then to the British ships in the harbor. The patriot soldiers entered the Tory town.[6]

But they were not yet rid of Lord Dunmore. Norfolk was too valuable to him and his followers for them to let it slip away easily. This town of 6,000 at the mouth of the James River had for many years been a prosperous trading center, and was largely owned by merchants whose warehouses were in faraway Virginia Street in Glasgow. Their clerks and agents made up a large part of the population of Norfolk, and, had they been left alone, would probably have lived peacefully enough. But when forced to show their colors, they proved to be Tories almost to a man, and so formed themselves into loyal militia. But the arrival of the rebel riflemen caused consternation among them, as the riflemen usually did in the Revolution, and the Norfolk Tories hurried with their families to the protection of the King's ships in the harbor.[7]

Being aboard Dunmore's vessels, however, was more protective than comfortable. Things there were literally in a mess. The four sizable warships and seven small tenders were swarming with crews, soldiers, Norfolk refugees and "Ethiopians." Food became scarce. Dunmore sent foraging parties ashore to obtain fresh provisions, but these detachments were either driven back or captured. As the long days went by, hunger and disease began to take their toll of the crowded vessels, until dead bodies were thrown overboard daily. Dunmore and the captain of the largest ship conferred in desperation and came to the understandable conclusion that Norfolk was "a town in actual rebellion, accessible to the King's ships" and that there was no choice but to attack it. After giving notice that he would burn the town, Dunmore ordered a bombardment which began on the afternoon of New Year's Day, 1776. For seven terrible hours, red-hot shot and shell rained from the smoking guns of the ships onto the pinewood buildings of Norfolk. These sturdy structures were covered with paint and soon were aflame; the fire, fanned by the wind, spread fast. While the aroused Americans there turned their attention to one part of the burning town, Dunmore sent ashore landing parties in boats to another section. The Tories soon set the match to the sheds where the Scotch factors kept their stores of tobacco, "which they intended eventually to be burned, but not by so wholesale and unremunerative a process." [8]

Deliberately aiming their sixty cannon at the very points where the flames were advancing, the ships' gunners made sure that the whole town was soon virtually in ashes. The rebel riflemen inside the place made even more sure that the buildings belonging to Tories did not escape the flames. For two full days, the engulfing conflagration raged, leaving only a few houses standing. Interestingly enough, Dunmore's fleet had destroyed only fifty houses, the Americans an estimated 863. Weeks later, by order of the American military leaders, the remainder of the houses were destroyed to prevent their falling again into the hands of the Tories. "The most flourishing town in Virginia was reduced to a mere name on a map." A French traveler to Norfolk, more than a year later, noted that the town which had contained more handsome houses and buildings than Philadelphia and Boston now had but ten families lodged in seven wooden shacks. Almost a century later, George Bancroft was to write, "The Royal Governor burned and laid waste the best town in the oldest and most loyal colony of England, to which Elizabeth had given a name and Raleigh devoted his fortune, and Shakespeare and Bacon and Herbert foretokened greatness; a colony where the people themselves had established the Church of England and where many were still proud of their ancestors, and in the day of the British Commonwealth, had been faithful to the line of kings." [9]

Even those Tories who helped Lord Dunmore at Norfolk received little or no reward for their services. Thomas Macknight, formerly of Belville, North Carolina, reported that he had erected a "rampart above a mile in length, which with the river, completely surrounded the place." Later he lost his large Virginia property holdings and fled to England. Andrew Sproule, one of the wealthiest men in Virginia, provided barracks for the King's soldiers when Dunmore held Norfolk. As the patriots entered the town, Sproule and his wife took refuge on board one of the British ships. Sproule was an elderly man, and on hearing that the rebels had taken his plantation and destroyed his property, he died from shock. His mourning wife then went ashore to see her son, but found that he was in jail and she could not see him. She next tried to get back on the ship and was refused by Dunmore. After being driven back and forth between patriots and Tories, this poor woman finally obtained passage to Glasgow.[10]

There seems little doubt that the destruction of Norfolk by Dunmore was a crowning piece of stupidity. It was "the one place in Virginia where the King had supporters and where the royal governor had been given a warm reception; and when he turned his guns against it, he insured the ruin of his own friends." Probably sensing this futile loss, Dunmore left Norfolk in February, 1776, after lingering in the nearby waters until the confinement and filth of his small vessels, in which the fugitives were closely crowded, the badness and scarcity of water and provisions produced fever which wrought great havoc, especially among the Negroes. He was forced to stop at Gwynn's Island and bury 500 persons. This latter catastrophe caused even Dunmore special concern. "Had it not been for this horrid disaster," he reported to London, "I am satisfied I should have had 2,000 blacks, with whom I should have had no doubt of penetrating into the heart of this colony." [11]

Dunmore had to burn several of his smaller ships; the rest, with their refugees, he sent to Florida and the West Indies, where many of the Negroes were sold again into slavery. He himself joined the British fleet off Staten Island in August and soon returned to England, where he was made Governor of the Bahamas. Thus the royal governor's scheme to stir up the slaves against their owners had backfired. Dunmore served chiefly to infuriate the Virginians and to drive them along the road to independence. He claimed that he lost 646 slaves himself, and a large number of horses, cattle, and sheep, as well as a library of 1,300 volumes. The Governor stated that he made various applications and propositions to the Government for putting an end to the rebellion, which he was certain would have been successful had they been attended to. A delegate to the Continental Congress reported that he was told, "Lord North was astonished at the union and strength of the colonies, declaring that he did not think it was possible for such things to be brought about, that he had no idea of such resistance. He feels the matter of the war itself might be easily settled with England if America would pay only a small sum annually to save appearances." [12]

The Virginia Tories were now virtually crushed. Dunmore had deserted them and patriots harassed them from every side. Some went to England, others to the West Indies; many of the merchants sought safety with the British army in the North. When the British occupied Philadelphia, 112 Scottish merchants from Virginia opened shops in that city. Dunmore's Tory regiment, The Queen's Own Loyal Virginia, was incorporated into The Queen's Rangers in New York. So instead of intimidating Virginia colonists, as well as those elsewhere, the burning of Norfolk gave impetus to the growing demand for independence, and was greatly responsible both for Virginia's increasingly fervent involvement in the Revolution and for the pressing desire of her aristocrats to supply vital leadership. George Washington told Joseph Reed, "A few more such flaming arguments . . . will not leave numbers at a loss to decide upon the propriety of a separation." [13]

There were still Tory leaders in Virginia whom the Americans tried to hang, although one of them, Attorney General John Randolph, left the country for England before they could carry out their plans. William Byrd III, Richard Corbin and Ralph Wormely were other marked Tories in Virginia. As early as 1776, men active in behalf of the Crown were declared to be subject to penalties of imprisonment or death or loss of property. The next year, those who refused to take the oath of allegiance to the American cause were denied suffrage and the right to sue for debts. They were not permitted to acquire land and were taxed doubly, later triply.

In neighboring North Carolina, a Tory leader of enduring notoriety arose from a tangled net of contradicting circumstances. He was David Fanning and his name has for too long been associated only with murder and coldly calculated cruelty. A fifty-page manuscript which he left vividly sets forth his exploits and those of other Tories in the region. In it, Fanning tries to explain his side of the terrifying activities which have lent such a bloody aspect to his career as it was known until recently. He points out that he was at first on the patriot side and was a sergeant in the South Carolina militia when fellow rebels caught Tory Colonel Thomas Brown, burned his feet, tarred and feathered him and cut off his hair. Brown escaped and later commanded the regiment of East Florida Rangers. Affected by such scenes as this, it appears that Fanning was becoming interested in joining the Tories himself. Suspected by the rebels, he was imprisoned and tried for treason, but managed to elude his captors. In March of 1778, Fanning joined a party of loyal militia and started with them for East Florida. But at the Savannah River the force turned back, and he and a companion hid from rebels in the region for six weeks in the woods, without bread or salt and eating only what wild game they were able to kill. Eventually the patriot troops captured Fanning near Ninety-six, placed him in an old, empty house, stripped him naked and chained him to the floor. He remained in this condition, his narrative states, from October 11 until December 20, "the snow beating in through the roof, with four grates open day and night." Somehow he managed to survive the weather, escaped again, obtained a horse and rode off, only to be sighted by a band of rebels who fired two bullets into his side. He turned his horse into the woods and remained there for eight days, living only on three eggs he found. His wounds became "troublesome and offensive for want of dressing," until finally he managed to stumble upon the house of a friend. Fanning was gladdened at the sight of a young girl coming out to meet him. "But when she came near enough to see me," he recalled, "she was so frightened at the sight, she ran off, while I pursued her on horseback, trying to tell her who I was. She said she knew it was me, but that I was dead; that I was then a spirit and stunk yet. It was a long time before I could get her to come to me, I looked so much like a rack of nothing but skin and bones, my wounds not having been dressed, my clothes all bloody." [14]

Fanning recovered and understandably was more determined than ever to fight for the Tories. In 1781 he was commissioned a colonel in the Loyal Militia of North Carolina and set about at once to organize an effective military force. But he found it was easier to recruit than to equip his men, a typical situation for the Tories. At Deep River, 450 men flocked to his colors, but because they had no arms, he had to send all of them home except fifty-three. He made quick use of these. The court at Petersboro was to hold a trial for several Tories who had refused to bear arms against the King. Although the court was not yet in session, Fanning and his men attacked the town itself and captured fifty-three rebels, the same number as he had troops. These captives included a militia colonel, a major, a Continental captain and three delegates to the general assembly. All were paroled except fourteen who had been extremely violent against the British, these being sent to Wilmington for confinement. En route, George H. Ramsey and others of the prisoners wrote a letter to Governor Burke stating that most of Fanning's men were Tories who had suffered great cruelties at the hands of the Whigs, having been unlawfully drafted, whipped and ill-treated without trial, their houses plundered and burned and their neighbors barbarously treated. Despite this, the letter continued, the captive rebels were treated with respect and politeness by Fanning and his followers.

Colonel Fanning, whose military talents evidently had been recognized early by the British and Tories, proceeded through the region with little opposition. In particular, he sought Philip Alston, who had been accused of putting a Tory to death. At length Fanning came upon Alston, who with twenty-five companions had taken refuge inside a large house. The pursuers surrounded the building, fired into it and killed several of those within, then set fire to the house. Mrs. Alston came bravely out of the burning structure and faced Fanning.

"We will surrender," she said, "on condition that no one of us shall be injured; otherwise, we shall make the best defense we can and sell our lives as dearly as possible."

Fanning agreed and spared the occupants.[15]

It was now the summer of 1781, and Fanning marched through the country alongside the Cape Fear River, capturing prisoners, arms and horses, helping fellow Tories whenever he heard of their being attacked. He took time to burn the plantations of two patriot brothers named Robertson. In a notable episode, Fanning marched to the aid of a Tory group of seventy men who were said to be in danger of capture on Drowning Creek. By pushing his men all night, the intrepid Fanning appeared early the next morning with 155 men opposite the threatening patriot force which outnumbered him ten to one. Nevertheless, he ordered an immediate attack on the surprised enemy, who in little more than an hour was defeated with nearly a hundred casualties. Fanning lost only five wounded, one of whom later died. He captured 250 horses laden with loot from Tory homes and farms. As to Fanning's leadership—which almost always included the elements of surprise and rapid, unorthodox movements, often taking place at night—the Reverend Eli Caruthers has said, "he certainly acquitted himself with honor. Cool and self-possessed everywhere, judicious in his arrangements, ready to expose himself when really necessary, vigilant and quick to perceive where an advantage might be gained . . . he showed he might have been a commanding officer of much distinction." [16]

This victory brought Fanning distinction, at least among his own kind. It was a sort of reprisal for the Tory defeat at Moore's Creek Bridge. Fanning had a notice printed which called for Tory volunteers and circulated it throughout the region. The response gladdened his heart, for 450 men immediately responded, then others later until he had a force of almost a thousand men. The Colonel now determined to carry through a grand scheme he had nourished for some time. It was nothing less than capturing Governor Thomas Burke of North Carolina. Acting with characteristic dispatch, Fanning marched his men all day and the next night and arrived at Hillsboro on September 12, 1781. He moved at once against the defending patriot soldiers and quickly overcame them. The results were impressive: the Tories killed 15, wounded 20 and took over 200 prisoners, including the Governor, the council, some Continental colonels, captains, subalterns and 71 soldiers. Fanning sustained the loss of but one man wounded. This was one of the most remarkable feats of the Revolution.

After releasing all Tory and British prisoners who were held by the patriots, one of whom was to have been hanged that day, Fanning left Hillsboro for Wilmington. At Lindley's Mill he was attacked by 400 Continental troops and found it difficult to defeat them, but he finally did. In this encounter, however, Fanning's men were still tired from their Hillsboro victory, and the casualties were heavy. He lost 27 killed and 90 wounded, Fanning himself receiving a bullet in his left arm which broke the bone in several places. So weak was he from loss of blood that he was forced to stay behind in the woods and turn the command of his men over to subordinate officers. Governor Burke was nonetheless escorted to Wilmington, where he was kept in jail for two weeks and then paroled on his promise to remain in the vicinity and not try to assume his official duties. But local Tories threatened his life, so he fled from the neighborhood in the following January. Even his former patriot associates condemned this breaking of his promise, and though Burke wrote a long letter to General Nathanael Greene trying to justify his actions, that generous-minded individual was not convinced by it.[17]

Fanning found it better after this to concentrate on striking at small bands of patriots on their way home from various fighting engagements. These frequently stopped at the homes of Tories and carried off their food and furniture. One such group of eleven was captured and their leader, a Captain Kennedy, revealed that a band of some sixty patriots were on their way to attack Fanning. Undaunted, although his men numbered only thirteen at that time, the Colonel attacked the rebels and dispersed them. For the helpful information, Kennedy was given back his horse, bridle and saddle as well as his eleven men. Many more such clashes took place between Fanning and his foes, a large number of whom were so afraid of him that they scattered and fled even upon hearing of his approach.

A recent account states that "Fanning's last barbaric incident" occurred in the woods of Moore County on Bear Creek. According to this version, Fanning had heard that Andrew Hunter of that neighborhood had "made some remarks about him and sought to kill him." Hunter was caught as he fled and given fifteen minutes to prepare for hanging. Instead Hunter broke away from his guards, sprang upon Fanning's favorite mare, Red Doe, and galloped away. Five shots were fired at Hunter, one of them striking him in the shoulder, but he escaped. Fanning, who loved horses, was sorely disappointed at losing the mare and planned to get even with Hunter. According to this account, Fanning went to Hunter's house, where he found Mrs. Hunter, who was "far advanced in pregnancy, and took her and their slaves to hold as hostages." Fanning then sent word to Hunter that he would exchange the wife and slaves for his horse and pistols which were strapped to Red Doe. Hunter's reply was that unfortunately the mare had gotten away. The account states that this so enraged Fanning that he abandoned the wife in the woods, but she learned from one of his men of a path which led to a house nearby where she was taken in and cared for.[18]

By the spring of 1782, Colonel David Fanning was weary of fighting. The war had been virtually over for six months anyway, since Yorktown marked the end of the line for Cornwallis. Also, Fanning had found a woman he wanted to marry. Two of his officers, Captains William Hooker and William Carr, had themselves discovered prospective brides and all three couples were to be married on the same day. But the day before the appointed time, Captain Hooker was killed. Fanning and Carr went ahead with their weddings, but because their enemies were so close, they had to hide their brides in the woods and give out news that Fanning had gone to Charleston. By May 7, a truce had been arranged and Fanning and his new wife did go to Charleston, where they remained until the city was evacuated by the British. They then took passage to East Florida and resided there until that colony was ceded to Spain. In 1784 the Fannings sought refuge at Halifax, Nova Scotia, and remained there. To the British commissioners, Fanning reported he "was engaged in six and thirty skirmishes in North Carolina and four in South Carolina, all of his own planning in which he had the honor to command." He asked for the seemingly reasonable sum of 1,635 pounds; his extraordinary service was rewarded with the sum of 60 pounds instead. Sometimes cruel and vindictive, he frankly avowed that he had returned an eye for an eye in the Old Testament manner. He had seen his Tory friends being abused, even being tried in civil courts for treason and hanged, so he had thought of his own bitter experiences at the hands of the rebels, and avenged rebel crimes with ruthless efficiency often tempered with mercy. It is interesting to speculate what would have happened if the Tories had had more daring leaders such as Fanning; it is fairly certain that if they had won the war, the name of David Fanning would be a celebrated one today.[19]

It would hardly be fair to suggest that the military and naval leaders of the British could have anticipated harsh treatment of their adhering subjects when the ships carrying the troops of Lord Cornwallis and Sir Henry Clinton arrived at the mouth of the Cape Fear River in May of 1776. They had been scheduled to reach North Carolina in February, but winter storms caused high, heavy seas which delayed them. Had they kept their schedule and as a result helped the Tories to victory in the battle of Moore's Creek Bridge, some 10,000 loyal subjects would probably have joined these two important generals on their arrival, and North Carolina quite possibly would have remained in the royal fold. Such dreams as this beguiled the British ministry until it was often misled into undue optimism. As it happened, the *patriots* turned out 10,000 men to meet and repulse Clinton. Local Tory influence was given a blow by the delay and defeat, and was virtually eliminated from public favor there and in South Carolina.

The adjoining colony of Georgia, newest of the thirteen colonies, was the last to leave the maternal cause. One cogent reason for the delay was the fact that the colony was annually receiving financial aid from the British parliament. Also, the inhabitants were in constant danger of attack from the Creek Indians and felt they needed outside protection. Sir James Wright, royal governor of Georgia, wise and prudent executive, was able through his Tory party to prevent the sending of any delegate to the first Continental Congress, and sent but one to the second. The Tories in Georgia were composed mainly of the officeholders and clergy from England, the wealthier residents of Savannah, most of the Indian traders, recent immigrants from Great Britain, and some Germans and Quakers. The Whigs generally were composed of younger and less wealthy men. So the impetus to join the Revolution finally came not so much from conditions within the colony as was the case in the Carolinas, Virginia and Massachusetts. As a recent historian, Kenneth Coleman, has said about Georgia, "Her actions often did not go as far as those in other colonies, and they always came later. There certainly would have been no revolution had it been left to Georgians to begin." [20]

But as in so many other instances, the British furnished the overt actions which led their American colonies away from the Empire. Once hostility to the royal rule seemed possible in Georgia, England sent a threatening naval squadron to Savannah, and this precipitous step ruined the effective work of Governor Wright. The Whigs seized him and other officers of the Crown, and in February of 1776 assembled a provincial congress, its delegates being instructed to concur in all measures calculated for the common good, a rather innocuous sentiment at that. There was nothing indefinite, however, in the feelings of a Savannah Tory, John Hopkins, who soon afterward showed marked disrespect for the newly organized Sons of Liberty. He was charged by the patriots with having drunk a toast and muttered the words, "Damnation to America!" Hopkins was accordingly taken from his home by the same Sons of Liberty he had been so free with, tarred and feathered, and paraded through the streets of Savannah. Arriving at the liberty tree—there seemed to be one in every city—he was told that he would be hanged unless he retracted his words and drank another toast as proof of it. He did as directed, his new toast being, "Damnation to all Tories and success to American liberty." [21]

Jeremy Wright, a Tory, escaped to Amelia Island off the coast, and from there could see the flames of several of his Georgia houses which the rebels had set afire. He claimed that he was driven from his cool house and plentiful provisions to hunger and thirst in the hot month of August, 1776, and had in "exchange, a solitary, starved wood, destitute and comfortless, frequently soaked to the skin with heavy thunder and rain, almost devoured with cow flies or venomous insects, and day and night with the lamentable groans and cries of about 180 refugees." [22]

Continuing their violence, the Sons of Liberty sent a deputation from Augusta, Georgia, to New Richmond, South Carolina, to apprehend two young men who had just come over from England, William Thompson and Thomas Brown. They allegedly had made public statements opposing American independence and had tried to persuade others of that area to join them in their attitude. Brown was reported to be the son of Lord North, sent to poison the minds of Americans. Apparently these ardent Georgians felt it their duty to put down such sentiment, even in South Carolina. Thompson was absent when the Sons arrived, and Brown quite naturally refused to go with them to Augusta. Whereupon he was seized and taken to that town, tarred and feathered and ridden about in a cart. The next day he "voluntarily" swore that he repented of his past actions and would do his utmost to protect American liberties in the future, as well as try to get others to follow his tardy example of allegiance to the cause of independence. Young Brown was evidently roughly handled, for he later stated that as a result of harsh treatment he lost the use of two toes and could not walk for six months afterward. As soon as he was released, Brown repudiated his oath. Later he was to wreak vengeance on his persecutors, when he rode at the head of the dreaded band of fighter-marauders known as the Florida Rangers.[23]

The head of the Sons of Liberty in Charleston, South Carolina, grew so to dread the hasty and frequent "meetings of the liberty tree" that he asked significantly, "Is not this a disease amongst us, far more dangerous than anything that can arise from the whole herd of contemptible, exportable Tories?" [24]

In the Carolina back country, many people tried desperately to avoid taking oaths of loyalty to either side. Some, like Alexander Chesney and Moses Kirkland, bore arms against the Crown but switched sides when the first opportunity came. So service in the revolutionary militia could not always be considered as prima facie evidence of patriotism. In the three low-country districts of Charleston, Beaufort and Georgetown, the Tories interestingly included forty-seven merchants, eighteen planters, three overseers, twenty-two laborers, seven schoolmasters, two keepers of ferries, one organ player, one midwife and a sprinkling of physicians and lawyers.

Fratricide and patricide were particularly acute in this region. Lieutenant Governor William Bull stood by the Crown, although three of his sons supported the Revolution. Thomas Heyward, a signer of the Declaration of Independence, was the son of a Tory. Gabriel Manigault on the other hand was a vigorous Whig, while his son supported the old order. During the desperate fighting in the Carolinas, members of the same family sometimes faced each other across the firing line. The historian Sabine in reference to this asked, "Did the Whigs and their opponents meet in open and fair fight, and give and take the courtesies and observe the rules of civilized warfare? Alas, no! They murdered one another." Nathanael Greene deplored the hand-to-hand strife in the South, saying that one side seemed determined to extinguish the other by evil and violent means, and felt that if it continued, the country there might actually become depopulated.[25]

Across the waters of Chesapeake Bay, the movement for independence in the new colony of Delaware was getting a slow start. This interesting section, which until 1776 was under the authority of Pennsylvania, was described by John Adams as having "from various causes, more Tories in proportion than any other." Even after the defeat of the British at Yorktown, Lord George Germain felt that the Delaware "inhabitants in general wish to return to their allegiance." This was in contrast to the fact that Delaware furnished two regiments to the Continental Army, the best known of these—and one of the best regiments in the army—being known as The Delaware Blues. This designation was derived from the number of gamecocks carried by the regiment, said to have been the brood of a blue hen that belonged to one of the officers; the soldiers of the outfit were said to be as brave fighters as these roosters. Later the people of Delaware itself became known as the "Blue Hen's Chickens." [26]

When a petition for an independent government was being circulated in Delaware in June, 1776, there was a sharp division of opinion on the proposal, with a majority of the people being opposed. "The few Whigs," wrote one observer, "became desperate and dreaded the consequence of being captured and treated as rebels. They attacked the disaffected with tar and feathers, rotten eggs etc. and succeeded in silencing the disaffection." [27]

Although the Delaware Tories committed their share of the acts of violence, they were not the murderous, scheming plotters described by the Whigs, but generally men with honest differences of opinion. Here as elsewhere, many Tories had gladly supported peaceful measures against Great Britain, but they refused to consider the extremes of actual independence or war; for this stand, they were condemned by the Whigs as traitors. The patriots insisted that everyone take sides, preferably on the side of independence. For example, Joshua Hill, a wealthy Tory exiled from Sussex County, Delaware, reported that having "taken part with the British Government when troubles broke out, he refused to take part with the Americans; therefore they [the patriots] said as he was not with them, he was against them; he was ill used and abused, had the oath of allegiance offered, but refused, was carried before their Committees, but refused." Finally, having set some kind of record for refusals, Hill was driven from his home when plundering Whigs threatened his life.[28]

Even more stringent action was meted out to a resigned Tory taxcollector named Byrnes who had seized two wagons near Duck Creek Crossing and was endeavoring to drive them out of the state of Delaware. A group of Whigs seized him, took his gun and broke it, tied a grapevine around his neck, gave him a drink of "Newberry rum" (muddy water) out of a duck hole, then forced him to "damn Bute, North and their brethren for a parcel of Ministerial Sons of Bitches." Finally he was "varnished and feathered" and then expelled from the colony. Daniel Varnum was hauled before a Whig committee charged with saying he "had as lief be under a tyrannical king as a tyrannical Commonwealth, especially if the damned Presbyterians had the control of it." But Reverend Aeneas Ross, brother-in-law of Betsy Ross, kept his Anglican church open during the Revolution, by omitting prayers for the royal family. John Cowgill was also denounced; the neighborhood millers refused to grind his corn because he was a Tory, the schoolmaster sent his children home, and he was paraded through the streets of Dover, Delaware, with a sign on his back which stated, "On the Circulation of the Continental Currency Depends the Fate of America." [29]

Tory activity in the neighboring state of Maryland was mixed with patriotic tendencies which took different forms. At first the men of Maryland who were in the Continental Congress had supported the drastic stand for independence of the Virginia delegation, but then had switched and favored the more moderate plan of Joseph Galloway. This is understandable when it is considered that Maryland had enjoyed comparatively smooth relations with George III. Also, the state is split by the Chesapeake Bay: the maritime Eastern Shore was then Tory, while the tobacco-growing western sections were Whig. In the early part of the conflict, Maryland and Virginia merchants apparently were eager for

Anglo-American differences to be settled, especially in the interest of maintaining their profitable tobacco trade. Charles Grahame of Lower Marlboro, Maryland, wrote to James Russell, a London merchant, saying that the people of his country were "almost unanimous against that part of the Annapolis Resolves which regarded non-exportation. We choose to export at least the present crop." William Fitzhugh of Maryland told the same merchant that Charles Carroll of Carrollton and Samuel Chase were the ringleaders of "mischief in this province . . . carrying on their diabolical machinations." [30]

Quite an intriguing scheme was fostered by a Maryland Tory named Hugh Kelly. He organized about 2,000 men to oppose the Whigs, obtained shot and powder from Lord Dunmore, then returned home. He quietly summoned potential Tories from their homes by a silent nod or significant touch on the arm, following which they walked through the forest together and secretly made their plans. As the Tory leaders strolled along, they would heap imprecations on the heads of members of congress, and express the opinion that there would be no peace until those heads were off. If the companion of a Tory agreed, he was at once admitted to membership in the loyal organization and an oath of secrecy administered. Military exercises followed under the direction of Kelly, during which the Tories pulled off their hats and cheered the King. If any failed to do this he was suspected of being a spy and warned that he had better watch his step or he might be brained by a broadaxe. This whole adventurous Tory scheme fell through, however. Delay and lack of effective organization enabled the patriots to suppress it and other such measures, until a parodist was moved to write, "Thus dread of want makes Rebels of us all; and thus the native hue of Loyalty is sicklied o'er with a pale cast of *trimming.*" [31]

All Marylanders did not give up easily. The Reverend Jonathan Boucher, combative clergyman of the Anglican Church, lived on the western shore and strongly advocated the cause of the King. In fear of the numerous Whigs around him, he preached regularly for six months with two loaded pistols lying beside him on the pulpit cushion, and explained that if he were forced to use them, he believed the Lord would approve such self-defense. In keeping with his belief, Boucher made efforts to stop the mischief against the King, but in vain. He found on one Sunday that his church doors were shut against him and that a rebel had paid eight dollars for as many loads of stones to drive him and his friends from the church—which attempt did not succeed. This resolute parson felt that if the people would flaunt one law, they later would flaunt others. To another minister he wrote, "The people who now bid defiance to this great and glorious nation are, in every point of view, worthless in the extreme." Yet in 1797 when Boucher published a book of his sermons about the Revolution, he dedicated it to George Washington. Boucher was finally persuaded, against his preference, to leave the colony. Yet the strength of the Maryland Tories was indicated by the report of a patriotic committee in Worcester County which stated not long before the Declaration of Independence that "the Tories exceed our number." In Somerset County, a militia company met for drill, and half of the men drew apart and put on the red cockades of the Tories, instead of the black ones signifying the patriots.[32]

Maryland produced a man who has been described as "the most persuasive polemicist in the defense of American rights in the first great Anglo-American crisis," Daniel Dulany. An able and opulent man, he had been educated in law in England and had become a successful attorney in Annapolis. Dulany opposed the Stamp Act, brilliantly demolished the argument that Americans were "virtually" represented in Parliament if not actually, and wrote a famous pamphlet on the proper means of taxation as seen by the colonists. His sons were divided in allegiance, but Dulany remained neutral during the war, living quietly in Maryland. Charles Carroll of Carrollton accused him of not being sincere, of keeping "on the reserve until he saw which way the tide would turn; he now swims with the stream." But Dulany opposed the "upstart government as he opposed parliamentary tyranny" and would neither take up arms against his countrymen nor assist the British in quelling the revolt. "The effects of war," he said, "are so calamitous, that 'Give us peace in our time' is always part of my prayer." Neville Chamberlain, involved in another war over a century and a half later, echoed these words.[33]

From Maryland to Pennsylvania went the man who was called the most active of all the Tory leaders, Joseph Galloway. Leaving the home of his wealthy trading family, he journeyed to Philadelphia at an early age, became a successful lawyer, and while still young was Benjamin Franklin's deputy in the Pennsylvania Assembly. In this body, young Galloway represented mainly the conservative merchants of the region in and around Philadelphia, who showed a growing uneasiness about the Scotch-Irish and New England people now settling in the western counties of the state and who were opposite to the conservatives in wealth and viewpoint. Galloway, influenced by Franklin, soon became convinced of the desirability of making Pennsylvania a royal province with direct colonial representation in Parliament.[34]

Having opposed such disorders as that caused by the Paxton Boys in Pennsylvania, Galloway saw the true solution of the imperial problem, in a written English constitution for America. He had a plan of reconciliation based upon the idea of limiting the powers of Parliament, but not including separation of the American colonies from the mother country. This plan gained him intercolonial repute. He aimed "to define American rights, and explicitly and dutifully to petition for the remedy which would redress the grievances justly complained of—to form a more solid and constitutional union between the two countries, and to avoid every measure which tended to sedition or acts of violent opposition." The other faction, he declared, "consisted of persons whose design, from the beginning of their opposition to the Stamp Act, was to throw off all subordination and connection with Great Britain; who meant by every fiction, falsehood and fraud, to delude the people from their due allegiance; to throw the subsisting governments into anarchy, to incite the ignorant and vulgar to arms, and with those arms, to establish American independence. The one were men of loyal principles and possessed of the greatest fortunes in America; the others were Congregational Presbyterian republicans, or men of bankrupt fortunes, overwhelmed in debt to the British merchants. The first suspected the designs of the last, and were therefore cautious; but as they meant to do nothing but what was reasonable and just, they were open and ingenuous. The second, fearing the opposition of the first, were secret and hypocritical, and left no art, no falsehood, no fraud unessayed to conceal their intentions. The loyalists rested for the most part on the defensive, and opposed with success, every measure which tended to violent opposition." Although subjective, this statement is probably the clearest presentation of the Tory viewpoint on record. Nor did its author, Joseph Galloway, underestimate his opponents. Of Samuel Adams he said, "He eats little, drinks little, sleeps little, thinks much and is indefatigable in the pursuit of his objects." [35]

Galloway did not have the ability or inclination to stoop to the kind of politics which Adams and his colleagues sometimes employed. But he was not afraid to oppose the radical leaders. "I am as much a friend of liberty as exists," Galloway said, and John Adams noted, "No man shall go further in point of fortune or in point of blood, than the man [Galloway] who now addresses you." The Pennsylvania Tory argued for appointive councils with legislative power which would help to correct the basic defect of the colonial constitutions, a "lack of independent aristocratic authority." Such authority was part of the remarkably effective balance between king and people in Great Britain. Galloway also emphasized the value of order, conformity and harmony in society. Such ideas would appear to be of considerable interest today, but the unfortunate fact is that the complete works of Galloway, Daniel Leonard and Jonathan Boucher have not been republished since the eighteenth century, and in a late work on American political thought, the works of Galloway are not even mentioned. [36]

The setting for the consideration of Galloway's plan was not auspicious. Benjamin Franklin may have leaned toward conciliatory measures earlier, but by 1774 he was disgusted with England, where he was then living. "When I consider the extreme corruption prevalent among all orders of men in this rotten state," he wrote Galloway, "and the glorious public virtue so predominant in our rising country, I cannot but apprehend more mischief than benefit from a closer union. Such a union would be like coupling and binding together the dead and the living." Also, instead of meeting in the dignified Pennsylvania State House which was offered by Galloway, the first Continental Congress met in what they thought to be the more democratic Carpenters' Hall in Philadelphia. To add to the handicaps, Paul Revere swept into the city on another of his memorable

horseback rides, bringing alarming news for Galloway and the other conservatives. He had with him a copy of the Suffolk Resolves from Massachusetts, passed by a meeting of the patriots in Suffolk County, acclaim-
ing liberty and opposing the Coercive Acts. It was read to great applause
in the Congress and adopted. Galloway commented that the Resolves
"contained a complete declaration of war against Great Britain." [37]

To offset these Resolves and to reestablish harmony with England,
Galloway introduced his plan, which recommended a kind of federal
government for the colonies. "It was an enlightened proposal," a historian
has commented, "and if it had been adopted in Philadelphia and ratified
in London, would have prevented war." Under the proposal, the central
administration would consist of a president-general appointed by the
King and holding office at the King's pleasure, with a veto over the acts of
a grand council whose members would be chosen for a three-year term
by the assemblies of each province. The president and council would
constitute an "inferior and distinctive branch of the British legislature."
Measures dealing with America could originate in either this body or in
the British Parliament. Consent of both would be required for passage.[38]

The plan sounded reasonable, as had Franklin's Albany Plan of twenty
years before. John Jay, Edward Rutledge and James Duane spoke in
favor of the plan. But the New Englanders for the most part sat in silence
as Patrick Henry and Richard Henry Lee opposed it. For a time it appeared that the Galloway Plan would win and moderation reign. On the
vote, however, it lost by a bare six to five unit votes. "The best chance
for a negotiated settlement of the dispute with Britain had gone." Now
Samuel Adams moved that the minutes of the discussion of the plan be
expunged from the record, and the motion carried, though in this vote
the advocates of the plan were reportedly absent. The radicals tried to
make their victory appear complete and harmonious.[39]

Galloway's plan proved to be a good argument delivered at a bad time.
It was based on the idea that the colonists were members of the British
state and owed obedience to its legislative authority. But soon after publication of the plan came the battles of Lexington, Concord and Bunker
Hill. Then as at other times, bullets spoke louder than ballots. Though
Galloway opposed violence, he himself had helped to put down demonstrations against him by the Sons of Liberty in Philadelphia. Declining
election to the second Continental Congress, although urged to run by
Franklin and John Dickinson, Galloway predicted three dreadful pros-
pects for the American colonies: British conquest and prolonged military
occupation; independence and subsequent conquest by a foreign power;
and perspicaciously enough, independence and later a civil war between
North and South, with the former victorious.

Finding that a strong tide was running against him, Joseph Galloway
withdrew from Philadelphia to his country estate, Trevose, in Bucks
County, Pennsylvania, where, as he said, he remained several months in
"the utmost danger from mobs raised by Mr. Adams to hang him at his

own door." He was sent a box containing a halter and an anonymous letter advising him to hang himself in a few days or it would be done for him. Threatened with tar and feathers, he loaded some valuables into a wagon and left his home to join the British Army in New Jersey in 1776. Had Galloway's idea been carried out, the United States of America might now be greater by half a continent and millions more people. Certain it is that he deserved more than the following "tribute" in the *Freeman's Journal* of March 15, 1777:

> Galloway has fled and joined the venal Howe
> To prove his baseness, see him cringe and bow;
> A traitor to his country and its laws,
> A friend to tyrants and their cursed cause.[40]

6. A More Ominous Storm

As Joseph Galloway fled across New Jersey, he must have had mixed feelings about its people. Here there were more Tories than in any of the other twelve colonies except perhaps New York or Georgia. But here too was a potent group of Whigs, and residing on prosperous farms in the charming countryside were many satisfied farmers whose last wish was to have anything to do with a revolution. This indifference was vividly brought out when the retreating Americans were marching through the state and scarcely one of the inhabitants joined them, although quite a number did flock to the royal army. The New Jersey people "saw on the one side a numerous, well-appointed and full-clad army, dazzling their eyes with their elegance of uniforms; on the other, a few poor fellows who, from their shabby clothing, were called ragamuffins, fleeing for their safety." [1]

Before Howe's forces had spread over the state in the winter of 1776, the Whigs had plundered the property of the Tories. Then with the advent of the British, these same patriots paid with interest for their depredations by being plundered themselves. Called the "Cockpit of the Revolution," New Jersey was so divided in sentiment that it was impossible for one faction ever completely to root out the other. Living mainly in places which were exposed throughout the war to sudden raids from either army, the inhabitants grew bitter and more brutal as the tides and backwashes of the conflict swept over them again and again. [2]

Indentured servants and Negroes, trying to take advantage of the most favorable opportunities, deserted their masters for whichever side was available, although of course the tendency was for them to go to the

British and perhaps obtain freedom. One such case was advertised in a newspaper of the time, the owner offering forty shillings for the return of an English servant lad, Thomas Day, who had run away. He was described as "about twenty years of age, wears his own light-colored bushy hair, a half-worn beaver hat, a Wilton coatee, buckskin breeches much wore and broke on the knees, quite new yarn stockings lately footed and old shoes with plated buckles." [3]

There was little running away in the higher Tory circles, until flight was forced upon them. The King's party, which supported the last royal governor, William Franklin, the only—and illegitimate—son of Benjamin Franklin, was for a considerable time strong and effective. In the military phase of the war, three Jersey battalions were raised and placed in the field, under the command of Cortlandt Skinner, attorney general of the colony. In New Jersey the losses dealt by the Revolution affected the local people probably more severely than in any other colony. Here Washington fought his best battles, encountered the most difficulties and earned his most lasting military laurels.

Much of the fighting done by the Jersey Tories was not orthodox, to say the least. They became so desperate, and often depraved, in their demeanor that they plundered friends as well as foes, warred upon aged persons and defenseless youths, committed hostilities against professors and ministers, destroyed public records and private monuments, butchered the wounded while they were begging for mercy, allowed prisoners to starve, and destroyed churches as well as public buildings. After Galloway had eventually retired to England, he stated in a controversy with Sir William Howe about the crimes committed by the American Tories, that "in respect to rapes, the fact alleged does not depend on the credit of newspapers; a solemn inquiry was made and affidavits taken, by which it appears that no less than twenty-three were committed in one neighborhood in New Jersey, some of them on married women, in the presence of their husbands, and others on daughters, while the unhappy parents, with unavailing tears and cries, could only deplore the savage brutality." [4]

Nor was the opposing side in this respect idle. For example, a Quibbletown cooper who had used abusive language against the local patriot committee and the Continental Congress was stripped naked, "well coated with tar and feathers and taken round the village in a cart." A local patriot commented, "The ceremony was conducted with the regularity and decorum that ought to be observed in all public punishments." [5]

Not only were Whigs and Tories ravaged and punished by each other, but the patriots refused to sell food and other necessities to those loyal to the Crown. These measures were naturally effective in driving the latter from their farms and firesides. Some relented and recanted; most did not. Oaths were tendered to them by the patriots which they conscientiously could not take, although refusal to do so meant fines and imprisonment and eventually confiscation of their estates. The Tories were not forced to join the British Army although inducements were held out for them to do so. But these soldiers hesitated to leave their families because of the danger of raiders from the opposite side. In their refusal to join the movement for independence, they were inspired and sustained by some of New Jersey's ablest leaders, such as Frederick Smyth, chief justice of the state for twelve years; Justice David Ogden; Cortlandt Skinner; Richard W. Stockton; Judge Daniel Coxe, speaker of the state assembly; lawyers Isaac Allen and Edward Dongan; Colonel Abraham Van Buskirk, a noted surgeon who at first joined the Americans, then took his friends to the British side; and Major Robert Drummond, a prominent merchant. Nearly all the Episcopal clergy of the state were Tories, including Abraham Beach, Jonathan Odell and Isaac Brown. Most Presbyterian leaders were on the patriot side.[6]

The cause of the Jersey Tories was hurt, of course, by the brutalities already discussed which some of their number carried out. Some companies of the Tory troops plundered far worse than did the British or even the notorious Hessian troops. In regard to the last-named soldiers, a Tory historian has remarked that "It was unnatural and disgraceful for the British ministry to employ German mercenaries and savage Indians to subdue the American colonists to unconditional obedience; but was it less unnatural for the colonists themselves to seek and obtain the alliance of the King of France, whose government was a despotism, and who had for a hundred years sought to destroy the colonists, had murdered them without mercy?"

High on the list of violent excesses in the Revolution was that of fratricide. As one Connecticut Tory expressed it, "Neighbor was against neighbor, father against son and son against father, and he that would not thrust his own blade through his brother's heart was called an infamous villain." In Massachusetts, Josiah Quincy was an ardent Whig, his brother Samuel a Tory refugee. The Virginia Tory, John Randolph, was father of the young Whig leader, Edmund Randolph. In South Carolina, Lieutenant Governor William Bull was a Tory while his three nephews supported the Revolution. Thomas Heyward, signer of the Declaration of Independence, also from South Carolina, was the son of a Tory, and Gabriel Manigualt of the same state was a vigorous Whig, while his son was loyal to the King. Tory Governor John Wentworth of New Hampshire had a Whig father. John Jay of New York had a neutralist brother and Gouverneur Morris a Tory mother. As the De Lancey family in New York was divided in loyalty, so were the Livingstons, Philip, John and Robert G. Livingston being Tories, while Robert R. Livingston and his family were active Whigs.[7]

William Franklin proved to be as unrelenting a Tory as his father was a Whig, even more perhaps, considering the moderate attitude of Benjamin in the earlier colonial days. The son did his best as governor to keep New Jersey within the royal fold and out of the Revolution. In the autumn of 1775, young Franklin had instigated a petition to the state

assembly asking that it "discourage an independency on Great Britain."
That body accordingly instructed the New Jersey delegates to the Continental Congress to "utterly reject any propositions, if such should be
made, that may separate this Colony from the Mother Country." Following these instructions, the assembly drafted a petition to the King, urging
him to prevent bloodshed and restore peace and harmony. But hearing
of this action, the Congress hastily sent John Jay and John Dickinson to
warn the assembly on the danger of acting separately from the other
colonies. So eloquently did Dickinson plead that the legislative body
dropped its petition. William Franklin immediately prorogued the assembly.[8]

Why Benjamin and William Franklin were at opposite political poles
is difficult to determine. Aside from the embarrassing illegitimate relationship, there seems to have been a generally friendly feeling between
father and son from the first, but there was also some indication that at
times the elder Franklin did not regard his offspring with any particular
pride. Born in America in 1731, William was a handsome and friendly
young man when he accompanied his father to England in 1757. He was
described as "one of the prettiest young gentlemen that ever came over
from America." But Peter Oliver, who naturally was not fond of the
father anyway, pointed out that when William "was in arrears 100 pounds
sterling . . . the father refused to assist him, and a private gentleman, out
of compassion, lent him the money." [9]

William Franklin served as a captain in the French and Indian War
and made a good military record, although his father did not appear enthusiastic about such service, even when William distinguished himself
at Ticonderoga. In England the son later received a Master of Arts degree from Cambridge University, where he became acquainted with the
Earl of Bute and Lord Halifax. As a result of this valuable connection,
Franklin was made royal governor of New Jersey at the age of thirty-two.
This appointment made no good impression with the patriots because
they thought William was only an opportunist, nor did it please the
Tories who, probably because of his "natural" birth, did not regard him
as a gentleman.[10]

At least a year before the start of the Revolution, Benjamin Franklin
knew of the royalist attitude of his son, and friendly relations between
them ceased, not to be resumed for ten years, when the war was over.
The father, commenting on the estrangement, said that "nothing ever has
hurt me so much." Yet the elder Franklin was known as a moderate from
the earliest part of the Revolutionary struggle. He was author of the
Albany Plan of Union, which in 1754 advocated what seemed a reasonable compromise between Great Britain and her colonies. In spite of his
evidently strong patriotism, Benjamin Franklin at times appeared to have
a viewpoint nearer to that of his son than is generally recognized.

Whether William Franklin received a favorable impression of England
when he was there or whether he simply agreed with the imperial view-

point as he understood it, he was unquestionably a sincere Tory. Doing his best to hold the colony in line, he declared, "Not the most furious rage of the most intemperate zealots would ever induce to swerve me from the duty I owe His Majesty." [11]

As the storm clouds of conflict thickened, the more timid Tories fled to places of safety; but not William Franklin. Having been helped by his father to affluence as well as political success, he and his wife had a mansion at Perth Amboy, and that was where he stayed. But his most trusted supporters had left him, he was regarded with suspicion by both sides, and lacking a single soldier in the barracks or a single warship in the harbor to sustain his authority, he could do little but watch while the government crumbled before his eyes. Yet he stayed on. Eventually, he was arrested and hailed before the Provincial Congress of New Jersey, which regarded him as an "enemy to the liberties of his country." When the Governor refused to sign a parole obliging him to remain quietly at Princeton, Bordentown or Rancocas, he was brought before Congress for examination. And though he was the personal representative of the King to whom the Provincial Congress still professed allegiance, Franklin was abused in a speech by Dr. John Witherspoon, president of the college at Princeton, who wound up with a sarcastic allusion to the Governor's illegitimate birth. [12]

Believing that it was not advisable to allow Franklin to remain in New Jersey, Congress ordered that he be sent to Connecticut, so he was dispatched there under guard and lodged in the house of Captain Ebenezer Grant in East Windsor. In 1777, Franklin requested permission to see his wife, who was only a few miles distant from him and quite ill. The request was forwarded to George Washington, who declined to approve it, explaining that he did not have the authority to supersede the resolution of Congress which had ordered the confinement of Franklin. Washington did recommend to Congress, however, that Franklin be allowed to visit his wife. "Humanity and generosity plead powerfully in favor of his application," the American commander wrote, pointing out that Mrs. Franklin might die. Congress refused on the grounds that Franklin had not complied with the obligations of his parole. [13] Whether they acted as they did from negligence or wilfulness, Washington and Congress might have done something to bring Franklin and his dying wife together, or at least it now seems so.

Mrs. William Franklin, a native of the West Indies, had apparently been much upset over the plight of her husband and the failure of his father to alleviate his condition of imprisonment. She had come to Connecticut to be as close to him as possible; then she became ill and longed to see her husband, hence his request. She never saw William again, for she died not long after his request was refused, and was buried under the chancel in St. Paul's Church in New York City. Nine years later, her husband had a memorial tablet placed in the chancel of the church, with the inscription which may still be read there: "Compelled to part from the husband she loved, and at length despairing of the soothing hope of his speedy return, she sunk under accumulated distresses and departed this life, 28th July, 1778, in the forty-ninth year of her age." [14]

Franklin was continued in confinement for two years. He complained that he was in a loathesome room, previously used as a dungeon for common felons and overrun with vermin. He claimed he was deprived of the use of pen, ink and paper, barred from conversation except with the sheriff or jailer and "often subjected to the grossest insults from the rebel soldiery and others." However, Sabine says that Franklin was allowed to select his place of confinement, and Trevelyan states that the ex-governor "led a free and jovial existence, giving tea parties to ladies of the neighborhood and treating his male fellow-captives to more potent and much more treacherous beverages." The account adds that Franklin and his convivial associates held at least one party at which there was hallooing and shouting in the night, the group roaring out, "King George's health!" and a song with a chorus to the effect that Howe was a brave commander. The noise became so great that guards arrived, whereupon Franklin and his friends were said to have cursed the soldiers and uttered "the most terrible oaths ever heard." Upon being asked not to take God's name in vain, they told their remonstrator that this was no sin and that he could not get to heaven anyway, because he had nothing but Continental currency with which to pay his way. Blows followed words, and in the end the whole party was marched to the guardhouse. [15]

Just after the surrender at Yorktown, Franklin wrote Lord Germain that but for this event, most of the colonists were ready to take up arms to force the Congress to come to an agreement with Great Britain.

Soon after his wife died, Franklin was exchanged for an American officer and went to England. He received a pension from the British government of 800 pounds a year, which was continued throughout his long life. The appreciative government also compensated him for the loss of his estates in New Jersey and New York. (He claimed 650,000 acres of land on the Ohio River as well.) His own illegitimate son, William Temple Franklin, became secretary to his grandfather, Benjamin Franklin, and later edited his works. That sagacious and unforgetting old gentleman acted with characteristic craftiness when in his will he bequeathed his land in Nova Scotia to his son, William, whose title to them was doubtful on account of the part he had taken in the Revolution. Just why a Tory would have difficulty in obtaining Nova Scotia land is not clear. The elder Franklin was evidently serious, however, when he ended this portion of his will with the following reference to his son: "The part he acted against me in the late war, which is of public notoriety, will account for my leaving him no more of an estate he endeavored to deprive me of." But in a letter dated August 16, 1784, from Passy, France, Benjamin said he could not blame his son for differing with him. [16]

The royal governor may have gone, but the sentiment of many faithful to the King in New Jersey remained. It has been estimated that there were about 5,000 Tories in New Jersey, with Bergen County, just across the Hudson River from New York City, their chief stronghold. Only fourteen families in Bergen County reportedly sympathized with the patriots. Following the adoption of its constitution on July 2, 1776, New Jersey quickly enacted strict measures to insure the safety of the state against the action of the Tories. Laws were passed to punish treason and counterfeiting, to appraise the personal estates of those who had left New Jersey to join the British, to repeal the loyalty oath to the King and supplant it with a new oath of allegiance to the government of the people, and to punish by fine and imprisonment any person defending the authority of Great Britain or reviling the governments of New Jersey or the United States. The very severity of these laws indicates there had been much Tory activity within the colony, which it was now felt necessary to suppress.[17]

A combination of self-interest, military pressure and natural conservatism seems to account for the larger than average number of Tories in New Jersey. They had the outlook characteristic of an agrarian society of small landowners who generally felt secure and independent and clung to the status quo which they had little reason to wish changed. Many of them were near New York City, and their prosperous trade with the British within this bastion for nearly all the war increased their desire to remain with a king and government which had served them to their high satisfaction. Had their local status been the only determining element, these Jersey Tories might have been left alone by the patriots. But other factors helped to turn public opinion against them and to bring about their persecution. British and Hessian soldiers alike seemed to consider plundering as part of the legitimate rewards of war. So as the British armies moved in and out of New Jersey, they took a heavy toll of the residents, especially farmers with inviting food products. If a farm along the line of march escaped wholesale robbery by the regular troops, it was likely to be stripped by those who followed the armed forces: that is, women, officers' servants and Negro workers.

This situation was emphasized by the gentlemanly John André, who was to meet a lamentable fate toward the end of the war, but who rendered valuable service to the British while he was active, and appeared to be more sensitive of the depredations his countrymen were committing than some of his superiors. He told Sir Henry Clinton, "I have seen soldiers loaded with household goods which they have taken for the wanton pleasure of spoil and which they have thrown aside an hour afterwards." Often the owner was a "harmless peasant," a decrepit father, or a poor widow, it was pointed out. "But when the property is plundered of a man who is conducting us, fighting with us or complying with what is by the General's proclamation the price of protection, what can be said to vindicate a conduct so atrocious which involves our friends in ruin and falsifies the word of the General?" Andre asked.[18]

Another future victim of the Americans, Captain Patrick Ferguson, who later was to lead the Tories in a major engagement at King's Mountain, observed and deplored the raids made by the redcoats and their followers. He stated that he was horrified to see in New Jersey the "ravages everywhere wantonly committed, without regard to sex or age, friend or traitor, and the consequent alienation of every thinking mind from the royal cause. Most of the houses are thoroughly and indiscriminately plundered, the beds cut up and windows broke to pieces, the men robbed of their watches, shoe buckles and money, while their wives and daughters have their pockets and clothes torn from their bodies, and the father or husband who does not survey all this with a placid countenance is beat or branded with the name of traitor and rebel." [19]

Actually, New Jersey had suffered the ravages of war before the British had set foot upon its shores in the Revolution. The undisciplined Continental troops and the militia in their turn had torn down fences and used almost anything movable and combustible for fuel. The situation became so menacing that on February 3, 1777, Governor William Livingston, the patriot who had succeeded William Franklin in New Jersey, reminded the legislature that persons and their property must be protected from plunder by the American militia. He asked for stricter laws to hold them in line, explaining that George Washington himself, who did not admire militia anyway, had reported that many of the militia officers were of the lowest class of people, and instead of setting a good example for their men, were leading them into every kind of mischief, one species of which was plundering the inhabitants under pretense of their being Tories. [20]

It does seem clear that the word "Tory" had become such a symbol for evil among the opponents of the King, that many ravages were committed under this name and the blame thus placed unfairly. Under the New Jersey laws, Governor Livingston could send into the enemy's lines any of the wives and children of the Tories who had fled. This was often done, not only from humane motives but because these dependents tended to "obstruct the Commissioners from seizing and disposing of the personal estate and effects of their husbands in the execution of their commission, by secreting and concealing the same." Even for seasoned troops, women and children have always been problems in wartime. [21]

Women played an active if sometimes amusing part in the war. For instance, when an attack of the redcoats was expected near Elizabethtown, New Jersey, three young men, all brothers, were going from their home to fight against the invaders. As they were leaving, their grandmother appeared in the doorway and encouraged them thus: "My children, you are going out in a just cause to fight for the rights and liberties of your country. You have my blessings and prayers that God will protect and assist you. But if you fall, his will be done. Let me beg of you, my children, that if you fall, it may be like men; and that your wounds may not be in your back parts." [22]

There was cleverness too in the New Jersey legislature of that day. That body even contrived a way to entice some of the Tories into the patriot fold. This was achieved by the Act of Free and General Pardon of June 5, 1777, which aimed to attract the Tories to the new government and enable persons who had at first supported the King to change sides if they wished. The act provided that inhabitants who declared their allegiance to the state were to be freed of restrictions affecting persons considered to be traitors. These forgiven persons were thus "fully, freely and absolutely pardoned, released and discharged of and from all treasons and other offenses and restored to all rights, privileges and liberties of other good subjects of this state." Persons who failed to comply had their estates seized and converted into cash which was to be held for their use in the event they recanted within the time prescribed, otherwise the money was to accrue to the state. Later, laws were passed prohibiting Tories from passing through New Jersey without proper legal clearance. Persons disobeying were to be "pilloried, cropped and imprisoned during the war," or if they were ablebodied males were to serve on board a vessel during the war, unless they moved into an interior part of the state: a sort of legalized shanghaiing. These victims were to be disfranchised and never allowed to hold state office, and made to forfeit their real and personal estates.[23]

This situation was viewed in a whimsical manner by a gentle Quakeress of New Jersey, Mrs. Margaret Morris, who despite her peaceful nature dared to hide the Tory preacher, Reverend Jonathan Odell, in a room in her house in Burlington a few days before Washington and his army made the night-attack on Trenton. Some patriot troops approached her residence; and, though she was frightened, she was able to get her "ruffled face a little composed," she said in typical feminine concern. At length she opened the door, confronted the armed men, and asked what they wanted. They replied they were looking for "a damned Tory" who had been spying on them. Now it was difficult for the Quakeress to regard the minister in exactly this condemned light and "dignified by that name," so she rang a bell which had been placed within as a signal, and hoped that Odell would hear it in time to be "concealed like a thief in an augur hole." This "augur hole" was a secret chamber entered through a closet which had removable shelves for the purpose of entrance. Odell, also a Tory chaplain, satirist and poet, evidently hid successfully; for he survived to handle the treasonable correspondence between Benedict Arnold and John Andre and later to go to Nova Scotia.[24]

Taking a more open way of avoiding trouble, James Parker, brother-in-law of the Tory leader Cortlandt Skinner and resident of Perth Amboy, probably came as close to neutrality as any person of note in the Revolution. Parker found the region around his home to be a sort of no man's land, occupied first by one side, then the other, so he moved to Hunterdon County and settled on a 650-acre estate named "Shipley" on the road from Clinton to Pittstown. Though he apparently did nothing against the patriots, he was seized and imprisoned at Morristown. Why he should have been jailed is hard to fathom, especially in view of a speech he had made, the gist of which is in the following part: "We shall with all sincere loyalty to our most gracious Sovereign, and all due regard to the true welfare of the inhabitants of this Province, endeavor to prevent the mischiefs which our present state of affairs seems to threaten; and by our zeal for the authority of the government on the one hand, and for the constitutional rights of the people on the other, aim at restoring that health of the political body—which every good subject must earnestly desire." [25]

Even a rereading of this masterpiece of the middle course does not reveal any degree of leaning one way or the other which would call for a reprimand, much less the arrest, of the author. While he was in jail, Parker's wife wrote and asked the Council of Safety if he could be "indulged the liberty of returning from his place of confinement to his own house for one fortnight only," and the Council indulged her. Parker did go so far as to criticize the quarters furnished him by the patriots, stating that the glass windows of the jail were broken and that the large holes in the wall which let prisoners out and winter weather in still did not eliminate the plentiful vermin which kept him company. But then as if to emphasize his studied neutrality, he criticized Lord North for lack of foresight and paid his respects to General Howe who, Parker said, was "pulled all to pieces for not pushing; he might have ended the affair at Long Island, at White Plains, in New Jersey etc." [26]

If Howe procrastinated, Washington was said to be Fabian, after the Roman general who delayed so much going into action. When Washington and General Nathanael Greene joined forces at Hackensack, New Jersey, Cornwallis was at their heels. Isaac Ogden, Newark lawyer and Tory, had spied on the Americans. He was said to have given General Skinner the "exact returns of General Washington's army." In a desperate move, Washington ordered General Charles Lee to bring his troops across the Hudson from New York to help the stricken Americans in New Jersey. Lee delayed, made excuses, and finally crossed, only to be captured at Basking Ridge ignominiously by a British patrol led by eighteen-year-old William Robins, a New Jersey Tory. The irascible Lee was only half-dressed, was breakfasting in a tavern and had just finished writing a note to General Gates critical of Washington. Suddenly shots rang out, bullets whizzed through the tavern windows and doors, and up came Colonel William Harcourt with some British dragoons led by young Robins, a favorite then and later of Cornwallis. Lee was overcome and hurried away, a ludicrous captive without coat, hat or shoes. At New Brunswick, where he was taken, the redcoats celebrated the capture of this major general by getting his horse drunk and having the band play all night long.[27]

General Greene, who had mixed feelings about Lee, was well aware of the Tory situation in New Jersey. He felt that had New Jersey been New England, the British would not have marched twenty miles into the country before being stopped. "But the fright and disaffection was so great in the Jersies," he told Governor Nicholas Cooke of Rhode Island, that "in our retreat of one hundred odd miles, we were never joined by more than one hundred men. You in New England think you are greatly infested with the Tories and disaffected, but there is but the shadow of disaffection with you to what there is here." Then he added with what may have been a jocular note, certainly an understatement, "Many have the effrontery to refuse the Continental currency." Not only currency was involved, but plunder. A Pennsylvania newspaper charged that the English soldiers were so jealous of the plunder the Hessians got that they insisted on the same privilege, and that General Howe was obliged to allow it in order to pacify them. "They make no distinction," the article stated. "Whig and Tory is all one to them . . . infants, children, old men and women are left in their shirts without a blanket, furniture of every kind is destroyed, windows and doors broke, the houses left unhabitable and the people without provisions. . . . A most respectable gentleman near Woodbridge was alarmed by the cries and shrieks of a most lovely daughter; he found a British officer in the act of ravishing her and instantly put him to death; two other officers rushed in with fusees and fired two balls into the father, who is now languishing under his wounds." A Newark militia captain, James Nutman, was so exceedingly pleased with the arrival of the British that he invited his friends to celebrate with him, saying, " 'Aren't you glad they are come?' The next day they arrived in Newark and his dear friends and protectors stripped him of all his moveable property, even to his shoes and stockings; and the poor wretch of a Tory was under the necessity of begging from his neighbors something to cover his nakedness." [28]

Other such difficulties were encountered. Weart Banta of Hackensack was in New York, but was forced to leave that city because he helped to remove a Tory named Moore from a cart hauling him to be tarred and feathered. Banta fled to Albany and remained there for some time, then was imprisoned for ten months, eventually making the usual escape into the British lines. Another Tory, William Clark, had a brief but active career, being termed "a noted horse thief who stole upwards of 100 valuable horses in New Jersey, which he sold to the Royal Army." He was shot in 1782. Edward Dongan of Elizabethtown, a young Loyalist lawyer and a lieutenant colonel in the Third New Jersey Volunteers, was wounded in an engagement against the Americans on Staten Island in August, 1777, and died within three days. His wife fled from New Jersey with their baby son, an only child, through "marshes and ditches and mire frequently up to her knees, until she reached a boat by which she was conveyed to New York." The baby died as a result of these hardships, on the same day as his father, and was buried in the same grave. Thomas Long, a Rahway schoolmaster, was captured and charged with being a British spy, and was tried and hanged at Kinsey's Corner in New Jersey. He was brutally tortured before he died, and his body later dug up and made sport of. Stephen Skinner, younger brother of the attorney general and a retired merchant, had become unpopular in the province even before the coming of the patriot army, having been charged with robbery of the state's funds when he was treasurer. With the threat of prosecution and advent of the patriots, he took his wife, their ten children, his sister and a few friends, and four pipes of Lisbon wine, and boarded a British brigantine. Philip Van Cortlandt, Morris County Tory, was turned out of doors in a snowstorm "by orders of General George Washington." [29]

Such disturbances apparently did not disturb the British ministry unduly, that is, if they even heard of them. John Robinson, secretary to the ill but still alert Lord North, wrote Sir William Howe, thanking him for the reports that the American rebellion appeared to be "considerably abated." He added, "nothing whatever is more ardently the wish or could give higher satisfaction to Lord North than to see this war terminate with honor to this country and in a happy union with its parent State." [30] As if to augment such wishes, the Tories began to help the Howe brothers after they had established control over Philadelphia and the river region below it. Now the British sympathizers in that region lost no time in opening a brisk trade with the city. For months they had been feeling a scarcity of imported goods and hard money, and now with comparative ease they satisfied their needs for sugar, tea, molasses, liquors and coin by furnishing the hungry redcoats with native products.

But if the province of New Jersey had gained in Tory activity, it lost its attorney general, Cortlandt Skinner, who went aboard the British man-of-war *Asia* anchored off New York. This ship must have been a haven for such legal lights, for Attorney General John Taylor Kempe of New York was already on board. Apparently not limited to the law in his talents, Kempe wrote a greeting to his fellow barrister:

> Welcome, welcome brother Tory
> To this merry floating place;
> I came here awhile before ye
> Coming here is no disgrace.
> As you serve, like us, the King Sir
> In a hammock you must lay.
> Better far 'tis so to swing Sir,
> Than to swing another way.[31]

The pendulum of martial activity was swinging away from the coastal sections to upstate New York, where complications were developing in the plans of General John Burgoyne to move down the Hudson River and be met at Albany by another British expedition coming from Lake Ontario via Oswego and the Mohawk River. This latter force was to occupy the beautiful and strategic Mohawk Valley, which was both the gateway to the great western country and the territory of the Iroquois Indians, whose support was valuable to the cause of the Crown. The valley of the Mohawk was fertile and inviting, but was as yet sparsely settled by German, Dutch, Irish and Scotch-Irish residents. The whole country was

generally regarded as a Tory stronghold, one historian estimating that
"the loyalists in that valley were probably more numerous than in almost
any other section of the northern states." [32]   Here also was the seat of the
Iroquois or the great Six Nations of Indians: the Mohawks, Onondagas,
Cayugas, Senecas, Oneidas and Tuscaroras. The ruling family of the region was that of the Johnsons, headed by Sir William, the fabulous
British Superintendent of Indian Affairs until his death in 1774, and after
that by his son, Sir John, and his son-in-law, Colonel Guy Johnson, all
strongly Tories. The mansion of Sir William at Johnstown, since restored,
was the biggest and finest house in the countryside, an imposing symbol
of the wealth and splendor of the old British Empire. He was not only
influential among the Indians, but had lived with several of their women,
including a sister of Joseph Brant, chief of the Mohawks, an able man
educated in England but loyal to his red kinsmen and serving as their
war leader. The "natural" children of Sir William Johnson by his Indian
mistresses were so numerous that to the present day there is geometric
speculation about them.

These Tories had been electrified by the news of Bunker Hill, and soon
afterward Colonel Guy Johnson, Colonel John Butler (a friend), and his
son, Walter Butler, all colorful leaders of the King's cause, left their
homes and held a council with their Indian allies on the shore of Lake
Ontario at Oswego. From the meeting, the Tory leaders, along with some
of the Indian chiefs, made their way to Montreal and had an interview
with Sir Guy Carleton, the British commander there. Patriots such as
General Philip Schuyler at Albany, hearing of this meeting, feared that
menacing plans were on foot against them. So Schuyler ordered out the
Tryon, now Herkimer County, militia, and under General Nicholas
Herkimer they marched to Johnson Hall, met Sir William and obtained
a promise from him not to engage in hostilities against the Americans—a
promise which he promptly broke. With his tenants and other Tories
Johnson made his way to Canada within four months. There, measures
against the upstart rebels in the South were planned with the British. Sir
John Johnson became a colonel and raised a Tory regiment called the
Royal Greens, from the distinctive color of their uniforms. Colonel John
Butler also enlisted a similarly clad corps of Tory Rangers who were
eventually to bring terror to the countryside below.[33]

Focal point of this activity was to be Fort Stanwix in the picturesque
Mohawk Valley. Built in 1758 as a strong fortification with bastions believed to be artillery-proof, a covered way and a well-picketed ditch, it
had been allowed to fall into decay. Now it had been occupied by American Colonel Peter Gansevoort, a competent twenty-eight-year-old officer,
Lieutenant Colonel Marinus Willett, and a patriot garrison which had
soon restored the fort to a defensible condition. Any force going from
Oswego to Albany would have to reduce this fort. Brigadier Barry St.
Leger of the British forces was given the task. His command included
regulars, a regiment of Royal Greens, a company of the Tory Rangers

and about 350 Hanau *jagers*. His artillery consisted of two 6-pounder
guns, two 3-pounders and four small mortars. In all, his force numbered
approximately 875 men. At Oswego, Joseph Brant, also known as Chief
Thayendanegea, joined him with almost a thousand Indians. On July 25,
1777, the expedition started for Stanwix. But their information about the
fort was faulty. Someone had done St. Leger the "favor" of telling him
that Stanwix was in a ruined condition and was garrisoned by only sixty
men. He was to learn better.

When the British force arrived at the meeting with the Indians, one of
its officers, Colonel Daniel Claus, was told by Brant that his redskins
"were destitute of necessaries, ammunition and some arms such as pipe
hatchets, tomahawks, knives, kettles and vermillion," which he wanted to
equip and color the Indians for the forthcoming foray. This was not the
only problem connected with the Indians. For some reason, perhaps to
spur their eagerness to fight, St. Leger had obtained for the red men a
quart of rum apiece, "which made them all beastly drunk and riotous,"
and considerable time was required to calm them down after their celebration and the subsequent hangovers.[34]

Hearing of the advance of this formidable force, the Tories of the valley became more active and bold, and many of the lukewarm patriots
who were uncertain of their intentions either aligned themselves with
the British or professed neutrality. It became the task of the patriot leadership to counteract this situation, and Brigadier General Herkimer of
the Tryon County militia was handed this thankless assignment. He was
the son of a Palatine German immigrant, fifty years of age and a veteran
of the French and Indian War. Short, slender, of dark complexion, with
black hair and bright eyes, Herkimer, like many of his Mohawk Valley
neighbors, knew the German tongue better than he did the English. He
called on all ablebodied men between sixteen and sixty to mobilize; even
invalids and old men must be ready to defend their homes in the absence
of the younger ones; all Tories and others reluctant to fight for the patriot
cause were to be arrested and confined. This strong appeal, along with
the dread of a horrible invasion by the Indians, aroused the spirit of
Tryon County patriots to a fighting pitch. Gathering his men in a body,
General Herkimer made a speech to them in his familiar foreign accent
which further aroused their defiant determination to defend their homeland beside the lovely Mohawk. He appealed to their valor and patriotism, then inspected their arms. It was none too soon.[35]

Not far away, the mixed and menacing forces of Barry St. Leger were
forming. Single columns of Indians, widely spaced from each other, pre-
ceded the main force by a quarter of a mile. Between these and the
soldiers, other redskins, ten paces apart, maintained communications
with the central body of troops. Sixty marksmen of the Royal Greens
formed an advance guard for the main body, in two columns, a hundred
yards ahead of the British regulars who marched in two detachments
side by side. On each flank, swift and stealthy Indians moved in watch-

ful, woodland style. A guard of seasoned troops brought up the rear of
this excellent, effective formation perfectly suited to the wild terrain.
Cautiously but swiftly St. Leger moved through the forests, over streams
and through swamps, marching ten miles a day in spite of the trees which
the Americans had cut and strewn across the path of the invaders to slow
their progress.[36]

Despite this steady progress, the British commander called for still
more speed. He had heard of a convoy of provisions on its way to Fort
Stanwix and was anxious to cut it off. So he sent thirty regular troops and
200 Indians out for this purpose. They reached Fort Stanwix on August 2
—just barely too late to intercept the supply convoy and its accompanying 200 men who managed to get safely into the fort, though several of
their boatmen were caught and killed by the British troops near the river,
on the present site of Rome, New York, some 110 miles northwest of
Albany.

Friendly Oneida Indians had warned Colonel Gansevoort inside the
fort of the approach of St. Leger, and the Colonel immediately evacuated
the women, children and invalids, for he expected no quarter. Then he
prepared to defend the star-shaped fortification with his 750 men against
a force estimated at twice that number. St. Leger and his main force arrived, and in order to awe the defenders inside the fort, the British commander proceeded to parade his strength along the outer reaches of the
surrounding palisaded earthworks. The red uniforms of the British, the
blue of the Germans and the green of the Tory Rangers flashed impres-
sively in the summer sun, while the naked bodies of the vermillion-hued
Indians looked even more colorfully sinister. This boastfulness of St.
Leger backfired, however, for the ominous appearance of the British
forces struck such fear for the safety of their families in the nearby settlements into the hearts of the fort's defenders that they resolved to hold it
at any cost.

Lieutenant Colonel Marinus Willett, second in command of the fort,
who was described as a "bold, enterprising fellow," reported that "the
enemy appeared in the edge of the woods . . . sent in a flag who told us
of their great power, strength and determination, in such a manner as
gave us reason to suppose they were not possessed of great strength sufficient to take the fort. Our answer was a determination to support it."
The first action of the invaders was to station snipers in the woods
around the fort in order to pick off the defenders when they appeared to
work on the fortifications. As a result, two of the workers were killed and
seven wounded. In further defiance, the defenders made a Continental
flag, hoisted it high on a parapet, and "a cannon levelled at the enemy's
camp was fired on the occasion." A small party was sent out to rescue
any men left in the boats on the river, and found one who had been
"wounded through the brain, stabbed in the right breast and scalped."
He was still alive and was brought in, but died soon afterward.[37]

Convinced that the fort would not surrender, St. Leger had his Indians

sneak through the bushes, weeds and potato plants in a nearby garden
and set fire to a section of new barracks near the fortifications. This too
had little effect, so the British commander laid plans for a siege. Fort
Stanwix, later called Fort Schuyler, stood on a slight rise on the north
side of the Mohawk River, near a road from Wood Creek which led to a
lower landing on the Hudson. Being an important portage, the location
was also called the Great Carrying Place. Behind the fort on an even
higher elevation, St. Leger placed his regular troops. At the lower landing, he stationed his Canadians, Tories and Indians. More Tories held a
position on Wood Creek to the west of the fort, thus virtually surrounding the bastion, although some sections of the encirclement were thin
because of heavily wooded, swampy ground. On August 5 St. Leger put
his axmen and other noncombatants to work clearing a road back to Lake
Ontario, over which he would have to bring up more supplies and heavier
artillery. With this work going on and the job of removing the trees felled
in his path in progress, the commander had less than 250 troops in his
camp when he heard that reinforcements were on the way to his enemy.

This of course was the advancing force of General Herkimer. On hearing of the march of St. Leger, he had set out on August 4, though encumbered with a string of "four hundred shrieking oxcarts of baggage and
supplies." Herkimer sent three scouts ahead who managed to evade the
men surrounding the fort, slip inside and tell the officers that reinforcements for the garrison were on the way. They asked Colonel Gansevoort
to fire three cannon shots in acknowledgment of the news that relief was
approaching, and to signal his readiness to make a sortie when the
column of Herkimer was near, in order to engage the British and hold
them off as long as possible.[38]

By the morning of August 6, General Herkimer and his men were not
far away. They listened eagerly for the signal guns of Stanwix to sound.
But by eleven in the morning they still had heard no guns. William Colbraith of Gansevoort's regiment reported that three cannon were fired
that morning as agreed; if so, their sounds must have died away in the
thickness of the forests before reaching the ears of the men from the
Mohawk Valley. By now the young and eager officers of Herkimer's command were badgering him to move on, regardless of whether the guns
were heard or not. But to venture into such a risky and uncertain situation without careful reconnoitering was against the judgment of the
veteran commander. "Herkimer hesitated. The officers boldly accused him
of timidity and hinted that perhaps he was a Tory like his brother who
was with St. Leger. Herkimer yielded."

"Forward and follow me!" General Herkimer shouted.[39]

His men pressed forward. In front of them went sixty Oneida Indians
who had been engaged by the General to be the eyes and ears of the
expedition. Just what happened to them is still a mystery. As if to make
himself conspicuous and to show his men that he was not afraid, Herkimer mounted his white horse and led the way. Behind him a disorderly,

noisy column of undisciplined troops strung out in a double column for almost a mile. About 600 were in the main body; then came the screechy wagon train, followed by a cumbersome rear guard of 200 men. It was almost as reckless and spectacular an undertaking as that of Braddock and his redcoats, winding toward their disastrous destiny at Fort Duquesne twenty-two years before. So ostentatious was Herkimer's noisy march that St. Leger's scouts reported it as soon as it was under way.[40]

Meanwhile, Colonel Marinus Willett and a detachment of 200 men slipped out of Fort Stanwix to meet Herkimer. They came upon an encampment of the enemy half a mile from the fort, "which they totally routed and plundered of as much baggage as the soldiers could carry," also capturing a few prisoners. Apparently this haul changed their minds about meeting Herkimer, for Willett's men returned to the fort with more than a hundred blankets, fifty brass kettles, some muskets, powder and ball, tomahawks, a variety of clothes, Indian trinkets and hard cash, and four scalps the Indians had taken, which were entirely fresh and had been left in their camp. "Two of the scalps taken are supposed to be that of girls," observed William Colbraith, "being neatly dressed and the hair plaited." [41]

This loss, amounting to an estimated thousand pounds in value, was distressing to St. Leger, but was not so important as the approach of General Herkimer and his men, now only a few miles away. Colonel St. Leger made ready to receive them before they got to the fort. "I did not think it prudent to wait for them and thereby subject myself to be attacked by a sally from the garrison in the rear, while the reinforcement employed me in front," St. Leger wrote to General Burgoyne. "I therefore determined to attack them on the march, either openly or covertly as circumstances should offer." [42]

The circumstances did offer and were rare indeed. Six miles short of Stanwix and near the village of Oriskany, the road on which Herkimer marched led through a wide ravine about fifty feet wide and with steep sides. Through it ran a small stream bordered by marshes. Across this mucky bottom had been thrown loose logs, these forming a sort of corduroy surface, making a rough and narrow avenue for the movement of the troops over its irregular surface. It was logical that here St. Leger would try to meet and destroy the men of Nicholas Herkimer. For this task he detailed part of the Royal Greens, Butler's Rangers and all of the Indians under Brant. It was a formidable combination, especially in such a fortuitous situation for ambush.

St. Leger's plans were well laid. The white men were posted on the west of the ravine and the Indians along its margin in a curve which almost encircled it, leaving the east end of the trap open for Herkimer to enter. The plan was that after the middle of the straggling column was deep within the ravine, the Tories and Rangers were to fall upon its head and crush it, the Indians to close the circle from behind. In this dire but masterly trap, the men from the Mohawk Valley were to be completely surrounded by enemies who, under cover of rocks and trees, were literally to cut their victims to pieces.

On they came, these 800-odd militiamen from the towns and farms of Tryon County, neighbors from the quaintly-named settlements of Stone Arabia, German Flats, Palatine, Deerfield and Fairfield. They were sure that if Fort Stanwix fell, Brant's Indians would strike their farms and homes with the torch and tomahawk, and some of them also feared the vengeance of the forces of Johnson and the Butlers, whose feudal ideas they had combatted in the valley for years. Now these feuds had reached a climax which was more intensely bitter between former friends and relatives than was any broader phase of the Revolution itself.[43]

"What a column they must have been," remarked a modern writer, Howard Swiggett, who felt that the barbarousness of the Butlers was exaggerated. "Halts unorganized, men drinking water when they wanted to; bad discipline, some officers joking with their men who called them by their first names; some, good soldiers, bawling at them to close up, catch the step and cover in file, the wagons sticking in the ruts and mud." [44]

It was nearly noon and along the higher stretches of the road the day was bright and clear when Herkimer reached the ravine. Why his Oneida scouts did not detect the ominous trap awaiting him is impossible to understand, unless they themselves were treacherous. Even a few flankers on either side would certainly have stumbled upon the hundreds of redmen crouching in the dark brush. But such simple precautions were evidently not taken, the vulnerable, jostling column being confined to the narrow, rough and gloomy road, making the procession as tempting a target as the historic British Light Brigade.

Within minutes, Herkimer on his big white horse had made his way deep into the ravine, followed by the lumbering, creaking supply wagons which he was to have little opportunity to use; and behind them slogged his troops.

Suddenly the trap was sprung.

From both sides of the wooded ravine the war whoop split the summer air, as crimson-colored warriors leaped from their cover, fired at close range, then rushed in with more chilling yells, brandishing spears and hatchets with which to complete the job. The crackle of muskets and the cries of wounded were mixed with the melee as the thunderstruck forces of Herkimer tried to put up some kind of resistance.

Up at the head of his column, the General wheeled his white horse to see what had happened. As he did so, Tories and Indians on the west side of the ravine poured in a hot fire, and the horse fell dead. Trying to extricate himself from beneath the stricken animal, Herkimer found a gaping bullet hole in his knee, but he did not panic. Breaking from their ordered line, the Americans singly or in groups took cover behind what trees they could find unoccupied. Some of them found they were fired upon from the rear. A number of the attacking Indians dashed too

eagerly toward the rear guard of Herkimer, causing this contingent to
flee backward along the road. "The impetuosity of the Indians is not to
be described," St. Leger related. "On the sight of the enemy . . . they
rushed in, hatchet in hand, and thereby gave the enemy's rear an opportunity to escape." [45]

Groups of the patriots formed a little circle facing out from around
the trees. The wounded general was carried to a knob of rising ground
near the ravine. A beech tree was on this knob, and Herkimer ordered
that his saddle be brought and placed at the foot of it. Propped up with
his back against the tree, his bandaged knee resting on the saddle, he
coolly lighted his pipe and drew his sword, "animating his men" to form
one great circle and thus resist with their own fire that which came from
all sides. [46]

Dr. Moses Younglove, a physician riding with the General, dismounted
when the firing began and evidently lost his medicine case, judging from
the lack of treatment of the wounded commander. Younglove reported
that Colonel Ebenezer Cox of the American forces saw some of the men
running and ordered them to stop and fight or he would shoot the next
one who passed, "and he did shoot and kill one dead in the road." [47]

The fighting became irregular, there being much hand-to-hand combat,
the tomahawks and knives of the Indians and the dreaded bayonets of
the Tories vying against the clubbed muskets of their opponents. Here
the Indians had an advantage, for as soon as an American had fired, they
would rush in and tomahawk him before he could reload the cumbersome muzzle-loading weapon of that day. Those of Herkimer's men who
could reload, "levelled their guns with the most unerring and deadly
aim. Though the enemy were so strong that they would sometimes break
in upon the encircled patriots, those who did were all put to death in
a few minutes. Not one of them escaped who made the attempt," said
an eye-witness. Dr. Younglove added that more than once he saw Herkimer's men take tomahawks from the hands of Indians and dash out
their brains with their own weapons. Herkimer all the while exhorted
his men to be valiant, telling them how famous they would become. The
General being wounded and becoming too weak to command, his two
colonels were sent for and, when found, were snugly packed away under
the roots of a fallen tree. [48]

A captain observed some men at a distance and, thinking they were
patriots, asked Younglove to bring them to the main party. They turned
out to be Hessians instead and fired at him. As he fled from them, Younglove saw a body of Indians scalping and cutting the throats of the
wounded, one of them sucking the blood from the throat of a white man.
The doctor also passed a white man and an Indian fighting, both so badly
wounded that they could not stand but lay on the ground cutting each
other with their knives. Finally Younglove was captured and taken to the
foot of a hill where Sir John Johnson of St. Leger's force was sitting
with other officers. Younglove was placed on a log where some Tories

were seated. Some of the Indians had become so enraged at the loss of their chiefs in the battle that they turned on their own side and began to "dash out the brains" of these Tories. Johnson himself was in danger and Younglove begged for the life of the officer, who then succeeded in driving the mutinous Indians off. "Then he [Younglove] wiped the blood and brains from his face, that flew from the heads of the Tories who had been tomahawked by the Indians." [49]

After an hour of this bloody, desperate conflict, providence in the form of weather took a hand. The clear skies filled with clouds, symbolically it seems, and a downpour of rain wetted the flintlocks of the muskets, bringing the firing to a sudden stop. This interim lasted about an hour, then the sun came out and the fighting resumed with hatchets and hunting knives. But meanwhile Herkimer had learned, even though he was badly wounded, the trick of the Indians who pounced upon his marksmen behind the trees before they had time to reload. Now he placed two men behind each tree, one firing at a time, and when a savage sprang forward after the first shot as before, he was shot down by the second man behind the tree.

By this time the Indians had had enough of fighting anyway, and began to cry, "Oonah, Oonah," meaning to retreat. As silently as they had come, they withdrew into the woods and disappeared. Seeing such defection, the Tories did likewise. On a crude stretcher, the patriots bore General Herkimer back to his own country, where in ten days he died from the effects of the crude amputation of his wounded leg. Fewer than half of his men had survived.

Barry St. Leger now closely besieged Fort Stanwix. As a ruse, he sent some officers to the fort with a flag of truce saying that Herkimer was defeated and that "the Indians . . . were determined to go down the Mohawk River and destroy the women and children; also, that they would kill every man in the garrison when they got in." Not believing the message, Colonel Gansevoort answered that he was determined to defend the fort to the last extremity.

Stung by this rebuff, St. Leger set about building new redoubts in order to bombard and reduce the fort. But his guns, he found, were too light for the job. Then he tried digging trenches to undermine and breach the walls. This also failed. By this time, news of the siege and battle had reached General Schuyler, who sent Benedict Arnold and a relieving force of Continental troops to drive off the British. Among some prisoners from Tryon County, Arnold had a half-wit nephew of General Herkimer called "Hon-Yost Schuyler." This simple soul was persuaded to go to the camp of St. Leger and spread the word that Arnold and 3,000 men were approaching—though actually only a third of that number were in the patriot force. The trick worked and St. Leger's Indians deserted him.

But another gesture of this kind had an opposite effect. Mrs. Sarah Cass McGinn, whose husband and son had been officers with the British forces, lived on the Mohawk River in Tryon County. Her husband had been killed and the son wounded in the knee and put out of action. In revenge, she "was tampering with the Indians in favor of the British Government." Years later, she stated that her other son "she was obliged to leave to the mercy of the rebels" who had destroyed nearly all of her property, because "he was out of his senses and bound in chains, as he had been for several years, and sometime afterward was burned alive in this situation." Mrs. McGinn met an Indian who was being sent by General Schuyler with a belt which conveyed an appeal for the co-operation of the Indians. She "got the belt and prevailed upon the Indian to carry an account of a different nature favorable to the British, and encouraged the Six Nations to continue the war against the rebels on the frontier." [50]

Realizing after more than two weeks of unsuccessful siege that he was in danger, St. Leger "in a mixture of rage and despair, broke up his camp with such haste that he left his tents, cannon and stores to the besieged. The flight of his army through a deep forest was not a little embarrassed and distressing." [51] While on their retreat, St. Leger and Sir John Johnson got into an argument, each blaming the other for the failure of their expedition. Two Indian chiefs who were left observed this altercation and decided to have some fun. Near a bog of clay mud, they directed a young warrior to loiter in the rear and suddenly cry out, "They are coming, they are coming!"

On hearing this, "the two commanders took to their heels, rushed into the bog, often falling and sticking in the mud, and their men threw away their packs and hurried off." [52]

This battle at Oriskany crippled the forces of St. Leger and seriously hurt the chances of the British from this direction, for after this, General Burgoyne could expect no help from the royal right wing thrust, which might have contributed materially to his success. This was a battle between relatives and friends, and to political differences were added spite and thirst for revenge. A doctor's bill for attending the wounded Americans showed women and children to have been stabbed and scalped.

"In this fratricidal butchery, most of the males of the Mohawk Valley perished, and if Tryon County smiled again during the war, it smiled through tears." [53]

7. The Role of Religion

Although the American Revolution held few aspects of a holy war and some of its elements might in fact be classed as unholy, there was a significant influence of religion on the Tory side. The word "Tory" itself was first used in Ireland to apply to the outlawed Papists in the reign of Charles II, and came to have the connotation of a conservative oppositionist.[1]

The distance from a charitable attitude toward the Tories which some ministers attained may be exemplified in the attacks made by Reverend Nathaniel Whitaker, an able preacher of Massachusetts. He may have been serving God, but he did not hesitate to use words more becoming to the devil in his denunciation. "A Revolutionary politician little less than ferocious," he evidently made himself believe that the American Tories closely resembled certain evil children in the Old Testament, on whom had fallen the wrath of God and the curses of the prophets.[2] In the Tabernacle Church at Salem in 1777, Whitaker preached a sermon which he entitled "An Antidote Against Toryism; or the Curse of Meroz." This tirade of vehement hatred, along with another in the same vein, became his most famous utterances and were published. With virulent scorn for the Tories, he exhorted his congregation as follows: "When such characters as these present themselves to our view, if we are possessed with the spirit of love required in the law and gospel, we must feel a holy abhorrence of them." He went on to say that while God says to turn the other cheek to an enemy in some instances, he also wants us to "punish certain vile enemies." Waxing more vitriolic, Whitaker thundered that while "Liberty is the cause of God, laxity in taking up arms against an enemy is sin!" He explained that the cause of the colonies against Great Britain was like a crusade, and he cried savagely, "Cursed be he that holdeth back his hand from blood!"

This irate minister continued his torrent of condemnation by comparing the Tories to Jabin, king of Canaan, who ruled Israel severely for twenty years. Then God commanded his people to wage war on the tyrant and overthrow him—and they did. So must the Americans overthrow English rule, Whitaker declared. He vilified those who refused to draw a sword in the conflict as violating that law of nature which requires all to exert themselves to promote happiness among mankind. Those who refused to do so, he added, sin against posterity.

"Every soldier should enter the field with benevolent, tender, compassionate sentiments, which is the temper of Jesus Christ," Whitaker explained; then asked, "What curse is too heavy for the wretch that can tamely see our country enslaved!" [3]

On the opposite side of the religious picture, many loyal ministers were forbidden to preach, some being put in prison while others were confined within the limits of their parishes and threatened with death if they were seen outside those limits. A notable exception to this situation was the Reverend Mather Byles of Boston, descendant of the Cottons and the Mathers, and a friend of Benjamin Franklin, who if he lived in the present day would doubtless be one of our leading comedians. A graduate of Harvard in 1725, he had read Pope, Lansdowne and Watts and was so impressed by their ideas that, of the prominent Congregational clergy, Byles alone stood against the Revolution. Once when watching thousands of mourners from the slums of Boston marching in the funeral procession of the mulatto, Crispus Attucks, who had been killed in the "Boston Massacre," Byles remarked to a friend, "They call me a brainless Tory, but which is better—to be ruled by one tyrant 3,000 miles away or by 3,000 tyrants not a mile away?" [4] He left no doubt that he was an ardent Tory, but he publicly disclaimed interest in politics, explaining to his congregation: "I have thrown up four breastworks, behind which I have entrenched myself. In the first place, I do not understand politics; in the second place, you all do, every man and mother's son of you; in the third place, you have politics all week, pray let one day in seven be devoted to religion; in the fourth place, I am engaged in a work of infinitely greater importance; give me any subject to preach on of more consequence than the truth I bring you, and I will preach on it the next Sabbath." [5]

In 1777, "the celebrated Dr. Byles," though he wrote many well-regarded articles and poems and became the poet laureate and official literary greeter of the province, was denounced in a town meeting in Boston, pronounced guilty of being a Tory at a later trial, and sentenced to confinement until he could be sent to England with his family. Byles steadfastly refused exile; the banishment was never enforced and he was permitted to remain in Boston. For a while he was held a prisoner in his own house. On one occasion, while under guard, he persuaded the sentinel to go on an errand for him, promising to perform the sentinel's duty himself. To the great amusement of all concerned, the Reverend Mr. Byles marched gravely before his own door with a musket on his shoulder, keeping close watch on the house until his keeper returned. He called the sentry an observe-a-Tory, and—referring to the careless changing of his guard—he remarked that he had "been guarded, re-guarded and disregarded." [6]

With such delightful antics and comments, Byles created many a laugh, some of them at the expense of patriots who did not exactly appreciate such cleverness. "The memory of his wit," Clifford K. Shipton has aptly observed, "has obscured the fact that he was in some ways the best and most popular preacher of his generation." Byles was a tall and commanding person, his voice strong and harmonious and his delivery graceful. He knew very well young and stout Henry Knox, who owned a bookstore in Boston before he himself married a Tory, the marriage separating her from her parents, whom she never saw again after they fled to England. Knox joined the army of George Washington and went on the memorable trek to Ticonderoga to bring back the captured British artillery with which Washington frightened the British from Boston. As the victorious patriot forces entered Boston after the departure of General Howe and his army and the Tories, Mather Byles was standing on a street corner watching the procession with much interest. Spying the bulky Knox riding with Washington, the parson punned, "I never saw an (Kn)ox fatter in my life!" [7]

Some visitors called at Byles's house one morning while Mrs. Byles was ironing clothes. She did not want the ladies who called to see her at the ironing board, so her husband put her inside a closet and closed the door. After a few remarks, the ladies asked to see the "doctor's curiosities," which he proceeded to exhibit one by one. After entertaining them greatly, he informed them that he had kept the greatest curiosity to the last. So he went to the closet, opened the door and showed them Mrs. Byles.

At one time the minister had a rather stupid and literal-minded servant girl, and one day in order to frighten her he assumed a look of great terror and said to her in a solemn tone, "Go and say to your mistress that Dr. Byles has put an end to himself!"

The maid ran upstairs and told the wife, who with her daughter dashed down in great alarm. They found the good doctor calmly waltzing about the room with a cow's tail, which he had picked up in the street, tied behind his coat.

It seems that in his younger days, the Reverend Mr. Byles had courted a lady who refused him. Afterward, she married a Mr. Quincy. Seeing her in later life, Byles remarked, "So, madam, it appears you prefer a Quincy to Byles."

"Yes," she reportedly replied, "for if there had been anything worse than biles, God would have afflicted Job with them."

A sufferer from toothache asked Byles for the address of someone capable of drawing a tooth, and was sent to John Singleton Copley, the celebrated artist. Some selectmen of Boston, when their carriage stuck fast in a mudhole in front of his house, were met by his greeting, "Ah, gentlemen, I have often complained to you of this nuisance, and I am very glad to see you stirring in the matter now."

Once the Reverend Thomas Prince was supposed to preach at the Hollis Street Church in Boston and did not appear at the appointed time. Byles arose and conducted the service, using the text, "Put not your trust in princes."

Byles painted his study brown so that he could say he was "in a brown study." Late in his life, he suffered a stroke and was confined to his chair. Said he to a visitor who approached, "You must excuse my not getting up to receive you, for I am not one of the rising generation."

Had all those involved taken the Revolution with as little seriousness as the Reverend Mather Byles, the whole affair would have had a happier and perhaps better aspect. He continued to live in Boston after the war was over, dying in 1788 at the age of 82, admired and esteemed, as well as being the subject of warmly amusing memories, some even expressed in quatrains:

> With strutting gait and wig so great
> He walks along the streets,
> He throws out wit, or what's like it,
> To every one he meets.[8]

More outspoken on the political side of the crisis, but given only one opportunity to express such ideas from his pulpit, was the Reverend John Bullman, already mentioned, of St. Michael's Church in Charleston, South Carolina. According to a contemporary, "the best minister in the province," Bullman preached a sermon on August 14, 1774, on "The Christian Duty of Peaceableness." In it, after taking a slap at Whigs who could not run their own homes but were now trying to run a nation, he asserted that "every silly clown and illiterate mechanic will take upon himself to censure the conduct of his Prince or Governor." Telling his parishioners that instead of rebelling against the King they should mind their own business, this Tory minister stated, "There is no greater Instrument or Ornament of Peace, no more effectual method for securing the advantage of civil society, than for every man to keep in his own rank and do his duty in his own station, without pretending to judge affairs beyond the reach of his understanding and erudition." Soon after this sermon was delivered, the parishioners called a meeting, expressed by a majority their disapproval, and voted to ask Mr. Bullman to resign. He did.[9]

Jonathan Boucher of Maryland did not acquiesce so easily. This dynamic and high-minded Tory preacher was born in England but came to Virginia when twenty-one, and soon thereafter he was ordained by the Bishop of London, having to return there for the ceremony, since no

Anglican bishop was as yet in America. He became a minister somewhat
by accident, at the request of a neighboring parish which had lost its
rector, but once having donned the cloth, he pursued his career with
vigorous precision. He had been a teacher before, and after his entry into
the ministry he led a versatile life, owning a large plantation with many
slaves, conducting a boarding school for boys, indulging in colonial politics, drawing up and introducing bills in the assembly at Annapolis where
he had come as a young preacher, writing speeches for the governor and
plays and songs as well. He also engaged in newspaper controversies
over affairs of church and state.

Nor was the prowess of Boucher confined to affairs of the mind. A
burly blacksmith who owned a cornfield next to Boucher's pasture, becoming angry at seeing the minister's horse eating his corn, shot at the
animal and lamed it. Not satisfied with this, he abused Boucher in the
presence of the latter's wife, approached the minister himself and cursed
him, shaking his big fist in Boucher's face. "No alternative seemed now
to be left, and so as we were to come to blows, I was determined to
have the first," Boucher recalled. "I struck him but once, when prostrate
he fell and measured o'er a length of ground." After this successful
encounter, Boucher was accorded more honor, he added, than if he had
had the brains of a Newton. His wit, as strong as his fists, was shown
on another occasion when a Dr. Brookes gave a toast with the words,
"May the Americans all hang together in accord and discord!"

To which Boucher quickly replied, "In any cord, Doctor, so it be but
a strong cord." [10]

Even after he had almost been mobbed, Boucher continued to preach
from his pulpit, arming himself, as has been noted, with two pistols. He
advised the forming of church schools in which the instructors would
take an oath to support church and state, and regretted that his orderly
and fruitful life must be interrupted by the Revolution, which "put an
end to everything that was pleasant and proper." To Boucher, the very
idea of armed revolt was foreign to his old-fashioned belief in the divine
right of king and government.

Jonathan Boucher knew George Washington and frankly gave his opinion of him. He told of meeting the Virginian as he was going to Massachusetts to take charge of the new Continental army. "There had been
a great meeting of people, and great doings, in Alexandria on the occasion," Boucher recalled, "and everybody seemed to be on fire, either with
rum or patriotism or both." The two talked briefly and Boucher warned
Washington that "there would certainly be a civil war and that the
Americans would soon declare for independency. With more earnestness
than was usual with his great reserve, he scouted my apprehensions,"
Boucher added, "saying (and I believe with perfect sincerity) that if
I ever heard of his joining in any such measures, I had his leave to set
him down for everything wicked." [11]

In the Tory opinion of Boucher, Washington "acquitted himself decently but never greatly. I did know Mr. Washington well and cannot conceive how he could have been spoken of as a great man. He is shy, silent, stern, slow and cautious," the minister added, "but has no quickness of parts, extraordinary penetration nor an elevated style of thinking . . . he seems to have nothing generous in his nature. At Mount Vernon, the most distinguished part of his character was that he was an admirable farmer." [12]

Boucher blamed not only the leaders of the Revolution, but some American institutions as well. He felt that "the chief abbetors of violence are young men of good parts but spoiled by a strange, imperfect, desultory kind of Education which has crept into fashion all over America. Some of these Northern academies, which in my wrath I can scarcely forbear calling Seminars of Sedition, led the way, and like other Plagues, it soon spread. . . . It is plainly and truly a war against the Constitution, a Catalinian Combination of individual Scoundrels." [13]

Doubtless the fiery Boucher had in mind in his denunciation the patriot ministers as well as other leaders of the colonial cause. These from their own pulpits defended their position, quoting especially John Locke's principle that "it was the people's right to choose their rulers and fix the bounds of their authority." The mother country was pictured as a monster.[14]

Not only with words did the ministers fight. Some of them joined members of their congregations in going into battle. Others aided the combatants in various ways, such as in the picturesque community of Springfield, New Jersey. When the American artillery ammunition ran low in the significant battle there, the local pastor, Reverend James Caldwell, was said to have grabbed up some hymn books by Isaac Watts, offered them to the gunners for wadding and cried, "Now, boys, give 'em Watts!" [15]

So the fight for freedom was joined in the pulpit and on the field by most of the colonial churches. The Congregationalists, Presbyterians, Baptists, Lutherans, the Reformed Church and the Roman Catholics all mainly supported the move for independence. The Quakers, Mennonites, Moravians and Amish refused to fight because they believed that war was wrong, and as a consequence these pacifist groups were distrusted and harassed by both sides. A rather recent estimate of the number of religious congregations in the colonies at the close of the colonial period gives the total as 3,105, with about 1,000 each for New England, the Middle Colonies and the South. Of this total, the Congregationalists had 658, most of which were in New England. Next were the Presbyterians with 543, mainly in the Middle Colonies; then the Baptists with 498, the Anglicans with 480, Quakers, 295, German and Dutch Reformed, 251, Lutherans, 151, Catholics, 50, and the Methodists with 37 circuits largely in Maryland and Virginia, although John Wesley, Methodist leader and Tory, fled from Maryland to Delaware. The comparatively small number of Jews in America were nearly all patriots, some aiding greatly with finances. One Jewish Tory, however, was Lieutenant Colonel David S. Frank, aide to Benedict Arnold until the time of Arnold's treachery, after which Frank was exonerated from any complicity. Nine of the colonies had established churches. In Massachusetts, Connecticut and New Hampshire, this was the Congregational Church, established by law and supported by taxation, although the Reverend Daniel Collins of New Hampshire was a Tory. In six of the colonies, the established church was the Anglican; these included all the colonies south of Pennsylvania and New York, although in the latter, the Anglican church was established only in New York City and in the three adjoining counties.[16]

As an indication of the loyalty of the New York City churches, a resident wrote to a friend in London in May, 1774, excoriating the clergy of New England for "their most wicked, malicious and inflammatory harangues . . . spiriting their godly hearers to the most violent opposition to Government; persuading them that the intention of the Government was to rule them with a rod of iron and to make them all slaves." [17] In contrast to this sweeping indictment, Governor Hutchinson had thought that while the Congregationalists had been most extreme in their wish for independence, the Baptists, Quakers, Presbyterians and Methodists were neutral.[18]

Fiery Peter Oliver apparently entertained no doubts as to the hostility of the ministers in New England. One of them he quoted as saying in a public prayer, "O Lord, bind up all the Tories on this and the other side of the water, into one bundle and cast them into the bottomless pit, and let the smoke of their torment ascend forever and ever." As to their pulpits, Oliver said, "many of them were converted into Gutters of Sedition, the Torrent bore down all before them, like after a city shower, dead cats and turnip tops come tumbling with the flood. The clergy had quite unlearned the Gospel and substituted Politics in its stead." The acid-tongued Tory added that he knew one of the preachers "with the reputation of learning, preaching upon the Sixth Commandment to his large parish, declared to them that *it was no sin to kill Tories.*" [19]

Aiding in such an objective, the dissident clergymen often gave addresses when the militia mustered or when recruiting was to be done. Before the battle of Lexington, a number of ministers called upon the patriots of the congregations to be of stout heart and good courage and to be ready to wield the sword of the Lord. On numerous occasions the fiery preachers won more recruits and filled more empty regiments than the military officers themselves. This was especially true in Connecticut and Massachusetts. For instance, after Falmouth, Massachusetts, was burned in August of 1775, a recruiting officer who was trying to raise troops nearby asked the Reverend Samuel Eaton of Harpswell, in what is now Maine, to speak on the next Sunday morning to the people, who seemed reluctant to join the Continental colors. The minister declined to do this at the communion service, but after sundown, out of doors before the steps of the meeting house, he altered the sanguine aspects of the ritual and preached on the text, "Cursed be he who keepeth back his sword from blood." Before the night was over, forty men had volunteered.[20] Recruiting officers worked for four days in Boothbay, Maine, and, having little success, asked Pastor John Murray to try his hand. He agreed, spoke in the Presbyterian church, and so fired the audience with patriotic enthusiasm that within two hours an entire company had enlisted.[21]

The virulence of these ministers in aiding the cause of independence was matched by their violence in abusive language against the British. The venom-tongued old preacher John Cleaveland, of Ipswitch, held forth in unbridled billingsgate against General Thomas Gage, the British military governor at Boston. On June 17, 1775, Cleaveland saluted Gage as follows: "Thou profane, wicked monster of falsehood and perfidy . . . your late infamous proclamation is as full of notorious lies as a toad or rattlesnake of deadly poison—you are an abandoned wretch . . . without speedy repentance, you will have an aggravated damnation in hell . . . you are not only a robber, a murderer and usurper, but a wicked rebel: a rebel against the authority of truth, law, equity, the English constitution of government, these colony states, and humanity itself." [22]

In perhaps a poetic vein, Reverend Jonathan Odell, Tory minister of New Jersey, replied:

> From the back woods, half savages came down
> And awkward troops paraded every town.
> Committees and conventions met by scores:
> Justice was banished, Law turned out of doors;
> Disorder seemed to overset the land;
> Those who appeared to rule, the tumult fanned.[23]

Odell, who has been compared with Philip Freneau, the outstanding Whig satirist, was a graduate of the College of New Jersey and a grandson of its first president. He was a friend of Governor William Franklin and had to leave that state when the Americans took over, whereupon he came to New York and tried to support himself, his wife and three children on the six shillings a day he received as a Tory chaplain. He was helpful to Major John André during that ill-fated young officer's earlier and more successful days as aide to Sir Henry Clinton.[24]

Regardless of the religious ups and downs of the Revolution, leaders in the evangelical churches feared that Parliament would appoint bishops in America and thereby hurt their own organizations. John Adams thought this situation was as contributory as any other to arousing the patriots to question the authority of Parliament over the colonies. This situation brought the Congregational and Episcopal churches into open opposition to each other in New England. The Presbyterians had received harsh treatment from the Anglicans in Ireland, and the Baptists had also been persecuted by the Anglicans. Such experiences caused resentment toward establishing the Church of England officially in Amer-

ica.[25] A fervent leader in this opposition movement was Jonathan Mayhew, pastor of the West Church in Boston, who was called by Robert
Treat Paine "the father of civil and religious liberty in Massachusetts and
America." His was the first church in that region to avow itself as Uni-
tarian. The distinctive trait of Mayhew's work was intellectuality, and he
thought the Church of England with its sedate hierarchy was foreign to
the new American nation and would, if established here, eventually ruin
it, by "a flood of Episcopacy." [26]

Such dissension divided the Anglican Church in America, those favoring an American bishop generally being Tories, those opposed, patriots.
Not only did such division damage the church of the mother country,
whose titular head was George III, but the Anglican ministers were embarrassed because, after the Declaration of Independence, it was disloyal
to the new republic to use that part of the liturgy which required that
prayers be said to the King. Yet if they did not use this part, they were
not properly doing their priestly duties. There followed a newspaper and
pamphlet war on each side of the Atlantic, and the American evangelical
churches banded together to prevent "the establishment of an Episcopacy in America." [27]

Such a decline of the Anglican Church in this country was a far cry
from the situation before the Declaration of Independence when, in
North Carolina, for example, no marriages were considered legal unless
they were performed by Episcopal clergymen. Another North Carolina
law forbade any man to teach school unless he was an Episcopalian,
although the colony direly needed education. Some intrusive Philadelphia ministers wrote to those in North Carolina saying popery had been
established in Quebec, why not in North Carolina? Boston Harbor had
been closed, why not Charleston? [28]

The Anglican Church was also rocked in Virginia by the doctrine laid
down in the Declaration of Rights in 1776, with George Mason and
James Madison urging complete religious freedom. Not only did this
movement come about because of the political struggle for freedom, but
the Tory cause was hurt by the personal conduct of the Anglican ministers themselves. Perhaps such stories were exaggerated, but one such
Tory parson was said to have had dinner every Sunday with the chief
planter of his neighborhood, and afterward was in such an inebriated
condition that he had to be tied in his carriage to prevent his falling out,
and was sent home with a servant. Another preacher had a fist fight with
his vestrymen, then compounded his unorthodox conduct by preaching to
them next day on the text, "And I contended with them and cursed them
and smote certain of them and plucked off their hair." [29]

In Delaware, the clergy was less violent, but nonetheless devoted. Four
of the five Anglican ministers there had been born in the colonies, one of
them, Aeneas Ross, being a brother of a signer of the Declaration of Independence and the brother-in-law of another. But their being born in
the colonies was countered by important factors: England was the most

dependable source of their income; prayers for the royal family were part of the Anglican services; and at ordination, the ministers had taken an oath of loyalty to the King. The Reverend Samuel Tingley found that prayers for the royal family would not be tolerated by his neighbors. Yet if he did not officiate, his flock "would be unavoidably scattered." So in order to satisfy everyone, instead of praying, "O Lord, save the King," he said, "O Lord, save those who Thou hast made it our special duty to pray for." To him this meant the King; others could think what they would.[30]

Less concern was shown for many churches. During the Revolution, numerous places of worship were destroyed, damaged or desecrated. In Boston, the Old South Church was used as a riding school by the British cavalry, as was a Dutch Reformed Church in New York City, while another there was used as a hospital. It was reported that if the redcoats found a large Bible and a metrical version of the Psalms in any church or house, they considered this prima facie evidence that it was a rebel habitation. The Presbyterian Church at Newtown, Long Island, was used as a prison and a guardhouse until its steeple was sawed off, the building torn down and its lumber used to construct huts for British soldiers. Churches at Cumpond and Mount Holly in New Jersey were burned to save them from occupation by the British, while the church at Princeton was seized by the Hessians, and its pews and galleries torn up for fuel. A fireplace was built inside with the chimney extending through the roof, causing Henry Knox, chief of the American Army artillery, to consider it a fair military target and shell it. In all, an estimated fifty churches were destroyed during the Revolution, both patriot and Tory taking part in the needless destruction.[31]

Even if they were not closed or destroyed, many Anglican churches suspended public services. In Connecticut, after a meeting of church officials at Hartford on July 23, 1776, all Anglican churches were closed except those at Newtown and Redding. These two were presided over by the Reverend John Beach, who was almost eighty years of age. Disregarding the instructions to close, he declared he would pray for the King "till the rebels cut out my tongue." [32] When a band of patriot soldiers visited his church at Newtown, he calmly continued the sermon he was preaching, saying in the presence of the troops, "I am firm in my resolution . . . to conform to the unmutilated liturgy of the church and pray for the King and all in authority under him."

This was too much for the soldiers. They seized the aged preacher and as they dragged him out of the church, threatened to cut out his tongue.

"Now, you old devil," they said, "say your last prayer!"

Without flinching, the venerable clergyman entreated, "God bless King George, and forgive all his and mine enemies."

So impressed were the soldiers with such courage that they let the old man go. Never again was he molested in his church services.[33]

Other Connecticut ministers were not so fortunate. The Reverend

Matthew Graves of New London, who refused to omit the prayer for the King, was driven from his church. The Reverend James Nichols of Bristol was shot at several times, tarred and feathered and dragged in a brook, and finally sent to jail in Litchfield. He was tried for treason but acquitted. The Reverend Roger Viets of Simsbury was convicted of assisting Tories to escape from prison and himself received a prison term of one year. Four months later, he was placed in the dreadful Simsbury mines prison and cautioned "not to do or say anything against the United States of America or detrimental to their interests." The Reverend Benajah Phelps of Manchester had to choose between leaving town or taking up arms against the King. He fled, leaving his family and possessions.[34]

One who early felt the bitter wrath of his countrymen was the Reverend Samuel Peters, wealthy landowner and Church of England missionary at Hebron, Connecticut. A law graduate of Yale, he had gone to England to complete his education, had donned the Episcopal cloth and returned to America. He maintained his church without pay at the Biblically-named town of Hebron. At one time he owned some 60,000 acres of wilderness land in the territory of what is now New Hampshire, Massachusetts, Connecticut and New York, which he inherited from his ancestors. His home estate at Hebron consisted of a thousand acres fenced in by a stone wall and having within its picturesque confines seven houses, four barns, 4,000 apple trees, "six Negroes, a library, chaises, horses, neat cattle, hogs, sheep, shays, carts, wagons, cider mills, blacksmith shop and four thousand pounds sterling." [35]

Apparently the wealth and position of the Reverend Mr. Peters aroused the envy of dissenters in the region. His manner also was offensive, since he "aped the style of an English nobleman, built his house in a forest, kept his coach and looked with some degree of scorn upon republicans," as well as evincing from time to time an "ill-balanced character." A climax came in the summer of 1774 when some enterprising Whig in London advised the people of America in a letter to take good care of the Episcopal clergy, as they were believed to be enemies to America, to religion and liberty, and spies for Lord North and the Bishops. Confirmation of this could be found by seizing the papers of the clergy, the letter continued. Copies of this communication were read in every Meeting House on Sunday, August 14. Whereupon, the papers of Peters were taken from his house by a mob and examined, but they found no cause for complaint and so returned part of them. Governor Trumbull of Connecticut was evidently not satisfied. On September 6, he sent what Peters estimated to be "about 4,000 armed men" (this figure was probably exaggerated) to subdue the affluent and loyal minister, explaining that by punishing Peters, all such dissident forces in the colony would be subdued and liberty preserved. "The mob obeyed his instructions by breaking my house," Peters related, "my furniture, by wounding with swords my daughter, eleven years of age, my mother, my two brothers, one of whom died of wounds soon after, and the nurse of my son; by tearing off my gown and clothes, by carrying me naked two miles to their Liberty Pole; by ordering me to sign their Covenant, by condemning me as a traitor to the rights and liberties of America, first because I had advised the people of Hebron not to arm and fight General Gage; secondly because I had peremptorily refused to take their Covenant." [36]

Some of the victims were said to have had "their bowels crushed out of their bodies. Others were covered with filth and marked with the sign of the cross, in token of loyalty to bishops and kings. . . . Even the women were tarred and feathered . . . their tears produced nothing but peals of laughter." [37]

Later Mr. Peters thus analyzed the treatment:

Take the herb of Hypocrisy and roots of Pride three handfuls . . . two ounces of Ambition and Vainglory. . . . Pound them in the mortar of Faction and Discord . . . leave over the fire of Sedition until you see the scum of Deceit at the top . . . strain it through the cloak of Rebellion . . . then make it into pills of Conspiracy . . . take nine. . . . The next day you will be disposed to censure the church, burn all the Bishops, murder the King, plunder the nation and cut the throats of all honest men.[38]

The mob sentenced Peters to be tarred and feathered, but their leader objected, saying he thought that by this time Peters was "insane in consequence of some blows on the head," and allowed him to be carried back to his home. The next day, however, the resilient minister went straight to see Governor Trumbull to complain. According to the account later given by Peters—whose veracity has been questioned—the only consolation he got from the Governor was the admonition to submit "to the Lord's anointed (the good people of America)." The Reverend Mr. Peters then fled to New Haven and demanded protection from the twelve magistrates of that town, "which was not granted by reason of three 'mobs' headed by [Benedict] Arnold, Mansfield and Wooster." Obtaining a sword and aided by two friends with muskets, the irate preacher then returned to Hebron, having to fight off some attackers along the way. On the evening of September 19, Peters decided understandably that he was no longer safe at home, so he fled on foot for four miles, then procured a horse and set out for Boston, 110 miles away. En route he was stopped by three troops of rebel horsemen, he said, but apparently was prepared for them, since he informed them he was a messenger from Governor Trumbull going to see John Hancock to find out what measures were being taken to destroy General Gage and his army. Evidently this falsehood (which apparently did not bother the conscience of the minister) had the desired effect, for the patriot soldiers took him into their confidence and told him *their* plans for disposing of General Gage. As soon as he arrived in Boston, Peters communicated the information to Gage, who evidently interpreted it as meaning an imminent attack on him, for he "forthwith made three cuts and formed three batteries on Boston Neck which saved his own life and the lives of his army and the Loyalists then in Boston." [39]

Gage advised Peters to go on to Portsmouth and take a ship for England. Peters agreed, but on his way he was pursued by a party of rebels, finally managing by night to make his way "to the seashore where he existed between the rocks by the help of friends fourteen days, when Admiral Samuel Graves sent a tender and took him off." The tender put him aboard the ship *Fox* bound for London, and despite a mob which had heard of his presence and which "fired several cannon to prevent its sailing," the vessel made off and Peters arrived in London eight weeks later.

After his disappearance from Connecticut, a reward for the Reverend Samuel Peters was offered by Governor Jonathan Trumbull. Peters explained that he "left his daughter and infant son, his aged mother and his friends and property to save his life, to strengthen the minds of the loyal Episcopalians in Loyalty and to convince the Republicans that he acted from principles above all temptations which had been offered by Mr. Trumbull and the judges of the Supreme Court to induce him to abjure his King, his ordination vows and internal integrity."

In 1776, Admiral Graves sent the daughter of Mr. Peters to England aboard the man-of-war *Somerset*, after she had been secretly conveyed from Hebron to Boston. The General Assembly of Connecticut had decreed in 1774 that all people were forbidden to correspond with Samuel Peters, so for the next two years he heard nothing from home. Finally he heard from his brother Jonathan that the latter had been "overtaken by a mob of about 300 men . . . who took all our papers from us, swore they would tar and feather us, beat and kicked us without mercy. . . . As I was undressing to go to bed," the brother related, "a large mob rushed me, dragged me downstairs, took me into the street and mounted me on a rail, two of them having hold of my arms and two hanging on to my legs. In this position, they carried me about the streets for half an hour, treating me at the same time with abusive language, crying 'A Tory, a Tory, a cursed, damned churchman!'" [40]

In England the Reverend Mr. Peters was introduced to Lord North by the Archbishop of Canterbury. The Prime Minister received the American clergyman with great politeness and bestowed upon him an allowance of 1,000 pounds a year. This was helpful, but not anywhere near the usual income of the refugee. "I am deprived of my living as a Clergyman," he wrote, "my Negroes and estate, lying waste if not destroyed. My incomes are nothing, from aplenty I am reduced to poverty, and for what reason I cannot conceive unless for my loyalty to my King and attachment to Government." Peters added, however, that he was willing to sacrifice all his property in America "for such a blessing" as having his children with him. "In my present state," he said, "I have some happiness in knowing myself a Rebel to the Congress and a loyal subject of the King of England." [41]

Other ministers and friends of Peters wrote him while he was in England, among them, the Reverend John Troutbeck, who was himself exiled in Nova Scotia. Troutbeck had helped Peters get from Boston to Portsmouth en route to England, and he now chided Peters for complaining, saying they both should be thankful that they had not remained in Boston until Howe's army was forced to leave, for they might have thereby lost their lives. A "Reverend Doctor Byler," also in Halifax, wrote Peters condemning "those unprincipled and infamous wretches who first wantonly kindled the rebellion" in the colonies, but criticizing even more the British who had "been sent for the express purpose of suppressing that Rebellion and with a force sufficiently abundant for that purpose, and yet have done all in their power to encourage it and to crush and ruin many thousands of the most faithful friends of Government. . . . Such guilty Heads ought not to go down to the grave in peace." After expressing this interesting opinion, which perhaps exemplified that of others and set forth an important reason why the American Tories were not more successful, Byler concluded with a spirited offer to Peters: "I will give you my head for a football if there is any further difficulty." [42]

A request to Peters for help by Tory Thomas Brown, exiled in Halifax, was based on intriguing reasons. Brown claimed he was due money from the British government, which he had advanced to General Gage in Boston, "for paying jurors, coffin-makers, grave diggers etc. and which General Gage promised me should be refunded. But when I applied to him to pay me what I had expended in consequence of his express directions, he begged to be excused from doing it out of his own pocket, and told me in the presence of General Burgoyne that I should be rewarded in Heaven."[43]

Such was the account of his hardships which Samuel Peters left for posterity. How accurate it is of course depends on the veracity and memory of the minister himself. On this subject, Moses Coit Tyler charmingly wrote, after spending some years investigating the reliability of Peters' accounts: "Somewhere in the debatable land between history, fiction and burlesque, there wanders a notorious book, first published anonymously in London in 1781, and entitled 'A General History of Connecticut etc. by a Gentleman of the Province.'" Though the authorship of the book was never acknowledged, Tyler was sure that it was the work of Samuel . Peters. Tyler found the work "grotesque fabrications in disparagement of a community of Puritan dissenters which seem to have proved a convenient quarry for ready-made calumnies upon that sort of people there and elsewhere." In the generous thought that perhaps the whole book was a kind of jesting satire, Tyler tried to interpret it in that light. Alas, he ended up by describing it as "a narrative obviously intended to be taken by its readers as a truthful and faithful record of facts, which yet is saturated by exaggerations and perversions of those facts." Peters appeared to "have been one of those exceedingly creative minds, which are unable to give an account of the simplest facts, without adding to them great and perhaps unconscious embellishments of fancy." [44] With this appraisal in mind, one can still be reasonably sure of the main facts of his life as set forth in the letters of Peters, which are used for this account.

The Church of England evidently had great and abiding faith in the

Reverend Samuel Peters, for he was elected Bishop of the State of Vermont by a state convention of Episcopalians, and doubtless would have been consecrated by the Archbishop of Canterbury had not the latter been limited in this respect by Parliament because of the unsettled state of the relation of the church to America at the time. So Peters could not accept the honor, although he did prepare a conciliatory sermon in anticipation of delivering it. In describing Vermont, he paid it a dubious compliment, probably more in line with his whimsical fancy than the facts: the people of Vermont, he said, wished "to be a neutral and sovereign power like a Swiss canton in order to be a barrier between the United States of America and the two Canadas." Though not as a bishop, the Reverend Samuel Peters did return to America to try to help settle the estate of a friend, his own property having been confiscated. He died in New York at the age of 90, ironically on April 19, 1826, the anniversary date of the battles of Lexington and Concord, and like John Adams and Thomas Jefferson, just half a century after the Declaration of Independence.[45]

It was of course more than a difference in belief that made the dissenting ministers oppose the Church of England and its clerical representatives in America, such as the Reverend Mr. Peters. The dissenters were afraid that the heads of the Anglican church would close the independent churches which, in their quest for religious freedom, the settlers had established in America.[46] Yet viewing their own English background with pride, the Anglicans logically believed that the Church of England, by the same token of religious liberty, deserved at least equal prestige with the other denominations in English colonies. These Episcopalians also believed that since their church was the only one among English-speaking Protestant organizations that was founded on the principle of Apostolic Succession, it was the only church which could claim to be historically valid. They did not acknowledge the Congregational ministers, for example, as true clergymen, holding that their lack of episcopal ordination made them merely "dissenting teachers."[47]

In many instances the Anglican ministers tried to show that they were the true orthodox persons as far as leading religious flocks was concerned, as well as by adherence to their oaths and firmness under the assaults of their enemies. As a Maryland rector who had been removed from his pulpit expressed it, if he could not prevent the rebellious disturbances, "he shewed at least by his example what his parishioners owed to their Sovereign and Mother Country."[48] Great effort was exerted by the Anglican ministers to preach submission to the English state, and to use the church as a bond of union and a vitalizing force for upholding prestige and power. Often the Anglican clergy used as a text: "My son, fear thou the Lord and the King; and meddle not with them that are given to change."[49]

Not only sons but also daughters were active in the struggle between

Whigs and Tories. At Kinderhook, New York, a young Tory went to a quilting party where there were a number of young women; in fact, he was the only man present. Although even under the loquacious circumstances he should have known better, he sounded off against the Continental Congress vociferously and at great length. Finally the girls, growing increasingly impatient and patriotic, became tired of his outbursts, pounced upon him and stripped him naked to the waist. Not deigning to employ the common, masculine practice of tarring and feathering, they took a more feminine approach and covered him with sticky molasses, to which they applied the downy tops of irises that grew in the meadows, and when he was well coated they turned him loose. One of these girls was the daughter of a Parson Buel of Southold, Long Island, who was a friend of Governor Tryon and the British general, Sir William Erskine. The General reportedly told the minister one Saturday, "I have ordered the people of your parish to appear with their teams at Southampton, tomorrow."

Whereupon, the witty Buel replied, "I know, but as commander-in-chief on the Sabbath, I have annulled the order."

Sir William did not insist. In fact, he allowed the parson to get by with even more impertinence. When Buel met Lord Percy, an aide to Erskine, he asked what troops Percy commanded.

"A legion of devils from hell," Percy jauntily replied.

"Then," said the Reverend Mr. Buel with a low bow, "I suppose I have the honor of addressing Beelzebub, the prince of devils!"

Aroused, Percy placed his hand on his sword. But Erskine restrained him and soon the joke was on Percy instead of on Buel.[50]

But it was no joke when John Vardill, minister, educator and man of strikingly diverse aptitudes, became in 1773, at the age of twenty-one, Professor of Natural Law and Moral Philosophy at King's College (now Columbia University). For the patriots detested this man with the ironic titles because he had opposed their ideas of freedom from the Crown, and particularly because he had dared to write a scholarly answer to the utterances of Dr. John Witherspoon, president of the College of New Jersey (now Princeton University), a strong Whig.

A pupil of Vardill was John Parke Custis, stepson of George Washington, and the teacher at one time wrote to Washington about the lad, praising his character and affability.[51] Vardill was also elected Assistant Rector of Trinity Church in New York, and had every prospect of succeeding to the rectorship of that most important Episcopal stronghold in America, when the war broke out. A native of New York, he was regarded as one of the finest scholars ever sent to England from America when he went there for his ordination in 1774, a trip then necessary for this ceremony, a requirement which those desiring a bishopric for this country were trying to eliminate. According to one appraisal of Vardill, he had "a devout, religious turn of mind which solely induced him to enter into holy orders." [52] But there was another side to this clergyman, and it was at least hinted at in "M'Fingal":

> In Vardill that poetic zealot
> I view a lawn bedizened prelate.

Professor Vardill himself, under the refreshing pseudonym of "Poplicola," wrote several Tory pamphlets and composed a funny song for the loyal circles of New York. But still being in England when "the unexpected fray at Lexington in April, 1775," as he called it, occurred, he decided to remain until it should be safe to return. Here he received a pension of 200 pounds a year and the government's thanks for his loyalty. Defending the American policies of the British cabinet, he wrote extensively to both Tory and patriot leaders in this country, including John Jay, Robert Livingston, Gouverneur Morris and John Parke Custis. Vardill claimed that as a result of his work along this line, he had won over two members of the Continental Congress to the cause of the Crown, by promising them judgeships in America. He did not include in this statement, however, the names of those converted. [53]

So active did the Reverend John Vardill become in behalf of the King that he was given an office at 17 Downing Street close to that of the Prime Minister. The subsequent activities of the clergyman resemble more those of an espionage agent than a minister, with most of his work being centered on those in England who sympathized with America. The British officials apparently felt they had here an American Tory who was superbly equipped in both background and sympathies to deal with any doubtful persons who might afford some help to the cause of the Crown. When the Abbé Raynal arrived in London bringing letters from Benjamin Franklin in Paris, Vardill succeeded by some secret means in examining this correspondence, unknown to the bearer. He did likewise when Jonathan Austin arrived as Franklin's confidential agent for the purpose of conferring with Lord Shelburne. This ingenious and versatile parson also placed an American medical student professing patriotic sympathies in the same boardinghouse with a suspect to watch his activities.

At another time Vardill met quite by accident a "gentleman of birth and fortune and considerable confidence with Dr. Franklin," who conceded after much persuasion that he had come from Paris at the instigation of the American Congress, with letters from Franklin, and he was about to return to the French capital. By some astute means, Vardill persuaded this man, Jacobus Van Zandt, who had assumed the name of George Lupton, to disclose the contents of his important correspondence for "a certain reward." Van Zandt also agreed to continue his residence in Paris and obtain all the information on the American war activities he could and pass it along to the British ambassador in Paris, Lord Stormont. This was an important connection, since Van Zandt often dined with Franklin and knew well the other American leaders then in France, and by this means obtained the assumed names and addresses under which the American spies in London received their mail.[54]

These exploits, although of value, were minor in importance to the crowning feat of Vardill's activities. In order to attain his objectives, he did not hesitate to descend from the sublime to the promiscuous and to personally deal with members of the oldest profession. He became acquainted with Mrs. Elizabeth Jamp, who kept a "boardinghouse" in London, the "menu" of which included not only edibles but obliging female companions for the pleasure of masculine patrons. One of the latter, a sea captain from the eastern shore of Maryland, was Joseph Hynson, uncouth, illiterate and conceited, but apparently gifted with certain qualities suitable for espionage. Hynson was the stepbrother of Lambert Wickes, who had brought Franklin to France and who had the reputation of being an honest man. At least, so thought Silas Deane, American commissioner in Paris, who wanted a sailor to carry dispatches to America. Deane wrote to Congress about Hynson, "I can vouch for his fidelity." [55]

If the gullible Deane could vouch for the fidelity of Hynson, Mrs. Jamp could vouch for his wantonness. From Dover, where Deane had sent him to buy a vessel, Hynson found his way to her house, "where he passed his time most agreeably in a feminine society congenial to his sailor tastes." There he took up with one of the girls, Isabelle Cleghorn, who apparently became quite attached to him. He in turn not only reciprocated the affection, but sounded off freely to her about the confidential errand he was on in behalf of the American commissioners in Paris. Mrs. Jamp overheard these conversations and reported what Hynson had said to the eager ears of the Reverend Mr. Vardill.[56]

This talented Tory clergyman called at once at the Jamp house and made the acquaintance of the sailor, who was soon persuaded to "unbosom himself." To enhance his channels of information, Vardill also cultivated the acquaintance of Miss Cleghorn, who waxed warmly grateful for the interest of a minister of the gospel in her irregular relationship with Hynson. This new friendship of Vardill progressed so well that the next time he visited Mrs. Jamp, he wrote to Hynson, who had gone back to Dover, that he was sitting on the parlor sofa beside the landlady "and your fair Isabelle" and that the sailor was a mighty lucky fellow to be so highly respected by the fair sex. The ebullient parson went on to say that it was his wish to "crack a bottle" with Hynson and that he looked forward to the coming summer when the two might do "a little junketing together." [57]

Whatever Vardill meant by this expressed wish, there was no doubt as to what Isabelle meant when she wrote to Hynson upbraiding him for leaving her. He replied with an apology, and since the house of Mrs. Jamp and its occupants had now become so involved with the King's business, the letters between Hynson and his mistress were intercepted and sent to Lord North, and even George III was informed of the activities of the sea captain, the Tory clergyman and their interesting female friends.[58] Encouraged by his progress in these clandestine carryings-on, Vardill even suggested to William Eden, Undersecretary of State who was in charge of the British Secret Service, that Hynson might steal the entire correspondence of the American commissioners in Paris.

Hynson was directed to retain the confidence of Silas Deane, obtain a ship, get the secret dispatches from the American commissioners to Congress, and as soon as possible steer the vessel to some designated point, where British cruisers would lie in wait, and there dump the package of correspondence overboard from his ship, to be picked up by the cruisers. Lord North agreed to ask Lord Sandwich to prepare two 16-gun warships for this purpose, and a retired army colonel was to accompany Hynson to France. From there, this extraordinary sea captain, upon whom fortune had so smiled, passed back information about vessels bound for America, which was said by Vardill to have resulted in the capture of many of them.[59]

Fortune in the form of Isabelle Cleghorn smiled again on Joseph Hynson. She went to Paris and joined him. There he labored diligently to live up to his undercover assignments, keeping in frequent touch with Deane and his British counterparts as well. Deane cautioned him that soon he was to be furnished the dispatches which would tell Congress fully about the delicate and important negotiations at Versailles regarding French help for the American cause, and which would also describe the vessels which were to be sent to aid America from French ports. But Hynson managed so that whenever a ship was fitted out for him, he would find something wrong with it and inform Deane accordingly. Deane would then write Hynson an apology, promising him a better ship—and these letters were sent at once by the captain to the British cabinet. This went on for nine months, and still the project was unfulfilled. Finally in this fantastic and complicated situation, even Deane began to suspect Hynson, who by now was considering squirming out of his duty to his English employers.

At length, when the dispatches were sent to a Captain Folger, a relative of Franklin, Hynson discovered them on board the former's ship and managed while Folger was absent for a short time to open the package, take out the papers, and substitute blank pages of equal length and width, tying the package back as it was before. The next morning, Folger sailed for America and Hynson for England, the latter carrying the entire confidential correspondence which passed between the American commissioners and the French court from March 12 to October 7, 1777, as well as many public and private letters sent by Arthur Lee, the third American commissioner in Paris, all enclosed in a cover addressed to the Chairman of Foreign Correspondence of the Continental Congress in Philadelphia. These important papers were handed on October 20 to William Eden.[60]

For his services along the primrose path and on the water front in behalf of the intelligence department of the crown, the Reverend Mr. Vardill received a reward which fulfilled his fondest dream. Bestowed within three months of the purloining of Benjamin Franklin's and the other commissioners' papers, this recognition was in the form of a royal warrant, signed by the King himself, and countersigned by Lord George Germain:

> Whereas we have received a good report of the ability, loyalty, prudent conduct and sober conversation of our Trusty and Well beloved John Vardill . . . we have therefore appointed him to be our Professor of Divinity in the said College.[61]

The "said College" was King's, now Columbia University, in America, and even if the position never materialized for Vardill, it signified nevertheless the gratitude of the monarch and his government for services ardently if not divinely performed.

The theft of the papers was later discovered in America, to the chagrin of Silas Deane and the amazement of the Congress. Vardill continued in the employ of the British cabinet until the end of the war. After that, the government did little for him, even though it had promised him a salary of 200 pounds a year as Professor of Divinity. When he died in 1811 at the age of fifty-nine, this remarkable Tory preacher-professor and espionage agent extraordinary was described by the *Gentleman's Magazine* in an obituary notice as "a rare example of splendid talents devoted to the purest philanthropy." [62]

King's College was represented in a more orthodox if not less colorful way by its president, the Reverend Myles Cooper, a Tory of the first rank. He had made trips southward in a strenuous effort to enlist the support of the clergy for an American bishopric, getting mixed support. Cooper had not helped his personal comfort any by gratuitously referring to the Sons of Liberty as the "sons of licentiousness, faction and confusion." Then it appears that the officers of the British man-of-war *Asia*, in order to test the range of her guns and having little choice, since the ship was in New York Harbor, carelessly fired a few shots into the city, producing the wildest commotion. The Sons of Liberty assembled and in their rage punished some of the ministerial adherents who tried to justify this outrage. Prominent among the Crown's defenders was Dr. Cooper.

"To the college!" shouted the Sons.

Cooper was warned that the mob was on its way, "that they were bent on shaving his head, cutting off his ears, slitting his nose, stripping him naked and setting him adrift. They had paused en route for a proper dose of Madeira, with which to strengthen themselves for their noble task." One of the students, young Alexander Hamilton, although a patriot, did not believe that "every man who differed from him was either a knave or a fool," so he and a fellow-student, Robert Troup, mounted the front steps of the college and appealed to the mob to let the old president alone. During this speech, President Cooper was said to have been on an upper floor, and raising a window and looking down on the crowd, not being able to hear what Hamilton was saying, called out to crowd, "Don't believe anything Hamilton says; he's a little fool!"

Evidently Cooper took the matter seriously enough, however, to grab some clothes, slip out the back door, climb the fence and make his way swiftly to a house on the Hudson River, where he hid until the next night. Then he joined the publisher, Rivington, aboard the *Kingfisher* and soon sailed for England. "No greater love hath an undergraduate for a college professor," John C. Miller has aptly commented, "than Hamilton demonstrated on this occasion." [63]

Cooper left no doubt as to his stand regarding Toryism in America, when in a sermon at the University of Oxford almost two years later he significantly said, "If it be right in a sovereign state to attempt the forcible suppression of a wicked and unprovoked rebellion, after all persuasive methods have failed, then this war is just and necessary. If it be right in a Prince to afford protection to his loyal and best subjects, against the tyranny and oppression of his worst and most disloyal, then the war is just and necessary, and laudable; for even in these revolted provinces there are still thousands and ten thousands of his Majesty's subjects, of inflexible loyalty, who could be induced by no menaces or persecutions to bow the knee to the *Baal of Independency*, or to swerve at all from the duties of allegiance." [64]

Assisting Cooper in his Tory activities was the Reverend Charles Inglis, rector of Trinity Church in New York, from which came so much loyal leadership. Inglis made an agreement with Cooper, Samuel Seabury and the Reverend T. B. Chandler, all Anglicans, "to watch all publications that were disrespectful to Government or the parent State, or that tended a breach between Great Britain and her Colonies and to give them an immediate answer and refutation." In 1774, Inglis wrote a series of newspaper essays which were published in the *New York Gazette* and signed them "A New York Farmer," certainly not a very accurate title for a minister holding forth in the midst of the metropolis. In these articles, he described the happy state of America, enumerated the advantages derived from their connection with the mother country, and refuted the Whig arguments that England intended to enslave America and establish popery here. Inglis visited extensively in Dutchess and Ulster counties "to warn his friends in the country as well as in the city of the evils that were approaching . . . and he could name many whom he confirmed in Loyalty when wavering or whom he prevented from joining in the rebellion." [65]

The greatest challenge came to Charles Inglis in 1776 when the famous and influential pamphlet, *Common Sense*, by Thomas Paine, appeared. Inglis felt impelled to answer it, particularly after Paine had challenged the Tory writers to show a single advantage from reconciliation. The title of the pamphlet which Inglis issued in answer to this challenge was "The

Deceiver Unmasked, or Loyalty and Interest United, in answer to a pamphlet falsely called 'Common Sense.'" Its author regarded the pamphlet
of Paine as "one of the most artful, insidious and pernicious pamphlets"
he had ever met with. In it he found "no common sense but much uncommon Phrensy. It is an outrageous insult on the common sense of
Americans. . . . The principles of government laid down in it are not only
false, but too absurd to have ever entered the head of a crazy politician
before." [66]

In his own pamphlet, Inglis made a powerful appeal to the moderates
and conservatives throughout the colonies: the calamitous war would be
stopped; peace would be restored; agriculture, commerce and industry
would assume their wonted vigor; trade would have the protection of the
greatest naval power in the world; protection would cost just a fiftieth of
what it would if the colonies were independent; England would pay a
bounty on exports, and the colonists would be able to get the best manu-
factured goods in the world at lower prices than if independent; everything would return to its pristine state of prosperity, and immigration
and population would increase with increased prosperity. [67]

This was one of the best-organized and most forcible Tory arguments set forth in America up to that time. Governor Tryon, then on
board a British warship in New York Harbor, urged that it be printed,
and at his request Mayor David Matthews took it to a printer. But as
soon as word of this leaked out, a mob of rebels gathered and demanded
to see a copy of it. As soon as they read it, the Inglis pamphlet was condemned and the whole edition burned. It was later published in Philadelphia. [68]

Another minister of Trinity Church, who probably felt the loss which
the Anglicans suffered in America most keenly, was the Reverend Samuel
Auchmuty, brother of a New England colonial judge, Robert Auchmuty,
who had served as one of the justices investigating the *Gaspee* burning
and who went to England early in the conflict. The judge remarked bitterly that he liked the mother country so much he would not ever change
it for "the rude and unsettled states of America . . . a community which
will ever be shunned by every true lover of liberty." His brother Samuel
had attended Harvard but was expelled for unexcused absences. However, that institution saw fit to grant him not only a bachelor's but a
master's degree in 1745 after the information appeared that he was to become a minister. After his ordination in England, the Reverend Mr.
Auchmuty, apparently softening in his attitude toward America, returned
to America and became a catechist in a Negro school in New York, in
which he was able to interest masters in Christianizing their slaves and
teaching them to read and write. He heartily disliked the Dutch and the
Presbyterians, feeling that the only persons in this country loyal to the
King were the members of the Church of England. He preached sermons
at Trinity Church which contained vigorous urgings for men to join the

British armed forces, and he felt that if an Episcopal bishop had been appointed twenty years before in America, the rebellion would never have taken place.

He condemned the patriots publicly, in one sermon referring to them as "a rascally Whig mob," but strangely enough they virtually ignored him. One day, however, Lord Stirling, whose chaplain Auchmuty had once been, sent the minister word that if he read the prayer for the King the following Sunday, he would be pulled out of his pulpit by a band of soldiers. A son of Auchmuty carried the message and, instead of delivering it, collected some of his Columbia classmates who went to church with concealed weapons, determined to protect the parson. When he commenced reading his prayers, Lord Stirling marched into the church with a body of soldiers and a band playing "Yankee Doodle." Doctor Auchmuty went right on with his prayers without faltering. The soldiers marched up one aisle and down the other and left without offering any violence.[69]

After this experience, Dr. Auchmuty felt "much indisposed," but was accused of expressing a desire "to throw off the gown and take up a musket in King George III's defense." He and his wife and younger children removed to New Jersey, where they stayed at New Brunswick, his two sons having joined the British Army. After the great fire in New York, he asked permission of the patriots to return there, but was refused. He then slipped out through the woods and swamps and made his way to the city, after suffering from hardship and exposure en route. There he found his beloved Trinity Church and his home both burned to the ground. Weeping bitter tears, he dug through the ruins, but found only two silver plates remaining. Within a few weeks, the sorrowing minister took to his bed with a cold and fever, doubtless resulting from his exposure, and soon died—some said from a broken heart.[70]

How the Anglican Church was losing its battle for adherence to the Crown is strongly indicated by the estimate that two-thirds of the signers of the Declaration of Independence were members of this church.[71] The Reverend William White of Christ Church in Philadelphia had an idea which he felt would solve the problem. White had succeeded the changeable Jacob Duché, who earlier had praised the patriot cause, given the first prayer in Congress and become its first chaplain, only to revert to the British when they occupied Philadelphia. White suggested that all American members of the Church of England get together and form a new church which would have its own bishops and its own organization and be truly American. Since time would be required to obtain bishops, White recommended that a "president" be elected to lead the church until it could get a bishop. This idea, while favored by some, was strongly disliked by the Anglicans in New England. They proceeded to try to arrange for their own bishop, and sent Samuel Seabury to England, asking that he be made "Bishop of Connecticut." The English laws prohibited this, so Seabury went to Scotland, where bishops "laid their hands on him" and granted him the requested title. Eventually this was to result in a united Anglican Church in this country, known as "The Protestant Episcopal Church in America." [72]

Perhaps the most learned and one of the most able clergyman in the entire thirteen colonies was Samuel Seabury, a vivid and forceful pamphleteer. A graduate of Yale, he was descended from some of the earliest settlers of New England, including John Alden. He was a man of powerful physique, bubbling with health and tremendous energy, and besides being a clergyman was also a physician, teacher, scholar, orator and brilliant writer. When first seized by "patriots," he was teaching at a little schoolhouse near his home above New York City, and as already has been described, Seabury was hurried away to Connecticut and imprisoned. The principal charge was that he had written the pamphlets of the "Westchester Farmer," which many on both sides of the conflict would have taken as a compliment. The pamphlets were not signed, however, so there was no evidence that Seabury did write them. After being jailed for a month, he was allowed to return to his home. But he found no peace there, being harassed by rebels and mere curiosity-seekers, who went out of their way to go to his house, where they reviled him, "the king, the Parliament, Lord North, the church, the bishops, the clergy and the society, and above all, that vilest of all miscreants, a 'Westchester Farmer.' One would give one hundred dollars to know who he was, that he might plunge his bayonet into his heart; another would crawl fifty miles to see him roasted." Even the strong Seabury could not stand such as this for long, so he went behind the British lines in New York and remained there, active for his cause, until the end of the war. [73]

What was this pamphlet which so infuriated people? In short, it was a masterpiece. Within three weeks from the announcement of the first Continental Congress that it had a scheme of nonimportation and nonconsumption of English goods and nonexport of American farm products, the pamphlet, ostensibly written by a farmer and addressed to farmers, appeared. Castigating the Congress for its recent actions, the contents included old prejudices, rusty jokes, and colorfully striking language designed to appeal to the average, down-to-earth American—and to others also. It presented a simple view of the situation; therefore it made a huge impact on the public, its advocates praising it with paeans of joy, its opponents cursing the writer for a diabolical demagogue. Appealing parables were used to show that the Congress was crazy in its ideas, that "from the day the exports from this province are stopped, the farmers may date the commencement of their ruin. Can you live without money?" the Farmer asked.

In regard to the invasion of his private domain, the writer stated, "My house is my castle: as such I will consider it, as such I will defend it, while I have breath. No King's officer shall enter it without being supported by a warrant from a magistrate. Nor shall my house be entered, and my mode of living be inquired into by a domineering committeeman. Before I submit, I shall die." Such statements, widely spread, were electrifying. Other pamphlets followed the first, containing "a mastery of eloquent statement, of philosophy, history, politics and constitutional law, not commonly to be met with in men of his class—or any class." Seabury, who later admitted authorship of the pamphlet, predicted that if the colonies won, civil war would eventually follow, "to determine what kind of a government we should have," a stirringly perspicacious comment. As is well known, his writings were ably answered by young Alexander Hamilton, whose cause carried the day, but this does not detract from the excellent and often devastating quality of the memorable "Westchester Farmer" pamphlets, nor make those who now live in this county less generally proud of their residence.[74]

Even with such grandeur of simplicity, the viewpoint presented by Seabury was more generous than that of a Sharon, Connecticut, minister, obviously on the other side, who told his congregation that "The York Tories are rich, the Lord permitted his people to despoil the Egyptians and that it was lawful and right, because they were all Tories and to do it was no robbery." Another allusion was made to the men of the Middle East by John Zubly, Swiss-born Georgia pamphleteer and preacher, in a sermon on "The Law of Liberty," when he protested that the English government in trying to bind its colonies completely was like the "emperor of Morocco binding his slaves." Though Zubly was not a Tory at first but rather a moderate, he became what one might class as an adherent of the Crown after he served as a delegate to the second Continental Congress. He saw the break with England coming and wanted no part of it. But Zubly, although banished for a while from Georgia, agreed with some of the patriotic principles. In his sermon on liberty, he referred to the idea of taxation without representation, and told how King James I had once asked Bishops Nelson and Andrews whether he had a right to raise money on his own authority. Nelson said yes. Andrews replied that he thought then that King James had a right to Nelson's money.[75]

While the Anglican Church was influential in its Tory role, no demonination so supported the Revolution as did the Congregationalists. From the beginning of the conflict, the ministers of this militant group were most influential in public affairs, and often their sermons were printed at the expense of the state and distributed among the towns, especially in New England. In these sermons can be found, long before the war began, the whole patriot philosophy of the Revolution. These fiery preachers not only spoke for independence from the King, but also supported the war with their pens and often their swords.

Of equal activity in some respects were the Presbyterians. Mostly Scotch-Irish, they were generally the most recent immigrants and were still burning with resentment for what they considered the wrongful causes of their migration. On the other hand, in 1775, David Varnum was brought before the Committee of Public Safety of Delaware for saying he would as soon be under a tyrannical king as under a tyrannical Presbyterian commonwealth.[76] The greatest Presbyterian leader of the period was John Witherspoon, who came from Scotland in 1768 to accept the presidency of the College of New Jersey, now Princeton University. As soon as the colonial friction began, he busied himself in the patriot cause, "applying the Presbyterian theories of republicanism to the constitution of the new civil governments." Witherspoon was one of the five New Jersey delegates to the Continental Congress and was the only minister to sign the Declaration of Independence. But the Tory preacher and satirist Jonathan Odell paid his respects to him thus:

> I've known him seek the dungeon dark as night,
> Imprisoned Tories to convert or fright;
> Whilst to myself I've hummed, in dismal tune,
> I'd rather be a dog than Witherspoon.[77]

Families were just as aligned against each other religiously as politically. For instance, the Presbyterian Livingstons opposed the Episcopalian De Lanceys in New York. The Dutch Reformed churches almost unanimously supported the Revolution, though their main congregations were located in New York City and the Hudson valley where the British were most active. As a result, many Dutch congregations were broken up and their property destroyed.

The Lutheran patriarch, Henry M. Muhlenberg, decided not to endorse openly the Revolutionary cause, since this would violate his oath of allegiance to George III. But his sons were active. One of them, Biblically named John Peter Gabriel Muhlenberg, became a general in the Continental army. At the war's outbreak, he was minister of a Lutheran church at Woodstock, Virginia, and had already accepted a commission as colonel of a regiment. Ending his sermon about patriotism, he said, "In the language of the Holy Writ, there is a time for all things. A time to preach and a time to fight." Whereupon he removed his pulpit robe and stood resplendent in a colonel's uniform. Then he stood at the front door and, with a roll of drums, enlisted his brethren to fight too.

The Baptists were said to have joined the Revolution because they had suffered most from the Episcopalians; accordingly they kept up a continual fight for religious liberty. But the Methodists, who still were not strictly separated from the Anglican Church, were on the whole regarded as Tories principally because their founder, John Wesley, was himself a strong one, writing pamphlets in behalf of the King. All the preachers sent over by Wesley from England returned to that country as ordered, except Francis Asbury, who appeared to be a patriot. He later became first Bishop of the Methodist Church in America.[78]

Though there were not many Catholics in this country at that time, they strongly supported the Revolution, especially those in Maryland and Pennsylvania. Charles Carroll of Carrollton, a Catholic, signed the Declaration of Independence. The numerous French Catholic soldiers here brought Catholicism for the first time to many American communities and helped to show Americans that Catholics could be good citizens and neighbors. The Anglican Reverend Thomas Barton of Lancaster, Pennsylvania, said of the Tory churchmen that "Some of them have been dragged from their horses, assaulted with stones and dirt, ducked in water, obliged to fly for their lives, driven from their habitations and families, laid under arrests and imprisonments." [79]

The gentle Quakers were opposed to war as well as revolution, as their founder, George Fox, had admonished them. Some sympathized with the patriots, some the Tories, so the Friends suffered from both sides. Quaker teachers were fined and imprisoned for not taking allegiance tests. John Pemberton, Clerk of the Friends Society in Philadelphia, wrote on January 1, 1776, "The inhabitants of these provinces were long signally blessed with peace and plenty. Has true thankfulness been generally manifest?" [80] Apparently he thought it had not. Quaker Samuel Shoemaker, a Philadelphia merchant, fled to London to avoid taking the oath. His diary kept from 1783 to 1785 does not once mention the words "Rebel" or "Tory." But he did write his wife, who remained in America, about the pleasant shopping he did in London. On the other hand Nathanael Greene was read out of the Friends Meeting in Rhode Island, joined the army and became a renowned major general under Washington.

Because of their pacific sentiments and lack of enthusiasm and support for the patriot cause, twenty Quakers were arrested and ordered to leave Pennsylvania and go to Winchester, Virginia, on September 11, 1777. When they asked for sustenance, the Pennsylvania patriot government ordered them to pay their own expenses. In this group were some of Philadelphia's most prominent citizens: John, James and Israel Pemberton, Thomas Wharton, Edward Bennington, Thomas Fisher and Thomas Gilpin. The last-named made a somewhat revealing comment on the leanings of the people, saying, "If George Washington hangs all that carries provisions to Howe and Howe hangs all that carries provisions to Washington, the Cause of Liberty will turn out a bad bargain to the People." In describing the spectators who gathered along the streets to watch the sad procession pass by, Gilpin noted that "lots were overheated with drink, and a rabble of boys who behaved very rude and naughty, threw dirt and they were not restrained by our guard." The leader of the guard, a Captain Wolfe, was said by Gilpin to be a man with "some very familiar sentiments about thumbing people's eyes, biting, kicking, pinching the privates. If he knows a man to be a Tory, he would take delight in hanging him or shooting him, many of his men have as delicate notions as our captain." Poor Gilpin, who wrote the foregoing comments in his diary which he kept from September 2, 1777, to January 24, 1778, died in the prison camp in Winchester a few days after his last entry, and only a few weeks before public pressure had humanely influenced the patriot government to return these harmless Quakers to their homes in Pennsylvania. [81]

The Mennonites of Pennsylvania, with beliefs somewhat like the Quakers, were split on whether or not to pay the war tax or handle the

Continental currency which might help the war effort. One of them, Christian Funk, said, "Were Christ here, he would say, give to Congress that which belongs to Congress and to God that which belongs to God." On the whole, the Mennonites were treated leniently. The Moravians suffered the most of the nonresistant groups during the Revolution, although they helped by furnishing hospitals and supplies. Both sides turned on the misunderstood Moravian Indians. Because they did not believe in serving in the armed forces, Moravians in North Carolina were granted exemption, but had to pay heavy fines instead. At the time there was apparently a lack of interest in spiritual things in that southern state anyway, for one minister commented, "Religion is so little in vogue here that it offers no temptation to undertake its cause." [82]

With hardly a pious attitude, the Reverend Nathaniel Whitaker, who had so condemned the Tories at the start of the war, cried in a sermon of May, 1783, when the conflict was over: "The Rubicon is now crossed! The oppressor is confounded, the haughty are humbled, AMERICA IS FREE!" [83]

8. *Violent Legacy*

A legacy of dubious value was left by the Tories as a result of the British occupation of New York City. It was in keeping with a custom which has attached to armies abroad from time immemorial, that of taking along women to lighten the lot of the soldiers. The American Revolution was no exception, particularly in regard to the British forces. Most celebrated have been the mistresses of Generals William Howe and John Burgoyne, and the ill-fated female friends of Major Patrick Ferguson. The enlisted men, too, were not without their distaff companions.

Having been apprised of the demand for camp followers for the British Army in America, a Captain Jackson, an English colonial trader, made a contract with the British War Office to transport 3,500 women, "whom England felt it could very well dispense with, to become the intimate property of the army quartered in New York City, thus relieving the tension now felt that at any moment these same soldiers might take to themselves such of the residents as pleased their fancy" and thus be likely to adopt American ways and viewpoints. Jackson procured these women from large cities such as London, Liverpool and Southampton and took them to a territory which held more promise of lucrative returns for theirs, the oldest profession. Specifically, such trade appeared to be centered in New York City in the Lispenard Meadows, now known as Greenwich Village. The fleet of femininity made smooth progress until rough weather was encountered and one of the ships foundered and sank, with the loss of some fifty of the women aboard. Undaunted and still determined to fill his quota, Captain Jackson forthwith repaired to the West Indies, where he soon obtained a similar number of colored women, whom he quietly interspersed among the other "ladies of the evening." Although apparently welcomed on arrival, these replacements were of course noticed as being different in appearance and became jocularly known as the "Jackson Whites." [1]

Tory newspapers of the period referred facetiously to the visits of the soldiers to "the Jackson Whites and Jackson Blacks." These women were confined in a stockade which, if not used for military purposes, served as a rallying point for soldierly diversions. When the British troops left New York City, the gates of the stockade were opened and the camp followers released. Some 150 of them went to Hoosick Falls, New York, the rest to the Ramapo Mountains of New York and New Jersey on the west shore of the broad Hudson River. Here they found ready "sympathizers" among Tories, Hessians, Dutch and Indians who had gathered there, most of them to avoid the rigors of the Revolution. In later accounts, Irish and Italian names have been ascribed to a few of the Jackson Whites.[2]

The redmen who inhabited these picturesque mountains and plateaus appear to have been the Tuscarora Indians who settled there about 1774 after having fought and been defeated by the white settlers of North Carolina and driven from that province. The Tories, led by the notorious Claudius Smith and his outlaws, holed up in the caves and glens nearby for protection. Many Hessians recruited from the German principalities of Hesse-Cassel and Brunswick had deserted the British cause—with which they had never had much sympathy—and had fled upstate in considerable numbers, and mated with the Jackson Whites when they arrived. The Dutch, a few of whose Negro slaves may have mixed with this already bizarre conglomeration, had lived in the Ramapo region for generations, some of them "taking up" with the itinerant women, as the names of their descendants show.

That the female followers released from the Lispenard stockade desired and deserved sympathy may probably be judged from their route of removal. After leaving their "quarters" in Manhattan, many of the women had tried to get passage with British ships but failed. They then went into New Jersey, crossed the Hackensack meadows and went up the Saddle River Valley, some of them carrying infants in their arms, their older children clinging to the tattered skirts of their mothers, the fathers, whoever they were, having long since left them. Driven by hunger, the desperate women raided orchards, grain fields and gardens and thus provoked the local farmers, who drove on these wanderers with hard words and harder blows, many of which were returned. No one wanted these unfortunate people. Whenever they stopped to rest, the neighborhood dogs were set on them. At last the weary caravan entered Ramapo Pass and soon found themselves in a country wild in character but hospitable. Here they settled, finding shelter in the woods and among the rocks, and solace in the arms of peaceful men.

As time went on, these sequestered persons tended more and more to keep to themselves, more by choice than necessity. Inbreeding took its toll until this motley mixture of several races became a hybrid product. One of them, Nellie Mann, descended from the Hessians, appeared with the Barnum and Bailey circus in the early 1900's, billed as "a wild girl captured in the Australian bush." Another, Aunt Albie de Frees, lived in the woods, smoked a clay pipe, talked about an imminent Armageddon and brewed sweet tea from native herbs. Her superstitious neighbors looked upon her as a witch, while they themselves lived simply and illiterately in the appropriately named sections called Horse Stable, Breadneck Mountains, Shipsail Hollow and the Valley of Dry Bones. Maxwell Anderson referred to them in his play *High Tor* as the poor folks of the region, a tri-raced people including many albinos.

The Jackson Whites have lived since in the same region, mainly in the counties of Rockland and Orange in New York, and Passaic, Morris and Sussex in New Jersey. Their community life, what there is of it, has centered around Ringwood, New Jersey, once the site of mines and iron works operated by Robert Erskine, friend of and surveyor for George Washington, who turned out cannon for the American army during the Revolution. Later, as the mines were developed for civilian use, the Jackson Whites worked in them.

Less than an hour's drive from Broadway in New York City, which once parodied the southern United States in a play called *Tobacco Road*, the settlement of the Jackson Whites has become a colorful and overly-ridiculed anachronism. The mines have closed, but somehow these descendants of Tories and others live on. A number of them have full lips, broad faces and kinky hair; others have thin lips and high cheek bones. They are classed by the United States Census Bureau as "non whites," and, at this writing, a fourth of them are on government relief. Carl Carmer, in his book on the Hudson River, refers to them as being near Nyack, New York, and compares them with the people known as Eagle's Nesters near Kingston or the Pondshiners and Bushwhackers north of Albany.[8]

About 6,000 of the Jackson Whites still live in the Ramapo mountain region, and for some reason are reluctant to leave it, although poverty-ridden. Mostly they are mulattoes. A coal-black brother may have a sister with skin and hair a fish-belly white. Some of their faces are Mongolian in type, some Negroid, others resemble Indians. A quarter of a century ago, a Hackensack physician gave a paper before the New Jersey Medical Society, in which he stated that because of inbreeding, the Jackson Whites had developed into a twelve-toed race (polydactylism), and some of them had two or more fingers or toes grown together (syndactylism). In one family it was found that seven out of nine children had one or the other of these defects, and this trait could be traced back through four generations. The condition was attributed also to dietary deficiency, poverty and isolation. Those Jackson Whites who had webbed fingers were able to grasp with their hands only to a limited extent, and the ones with extra toes could not wear shoes until the superfluous digits were removed by surgery. These odd people are mainly Episcopalian in religion and usually vote as conservative Republicans, perhaps an ironical throwback to their Tory ancestry.[4]

Such peaceful if deteriorating assimilation of different groups into local society was the exception in earlier times, however. As the war went on, violence, individual and collective, more and more replaced acceptance. For instance, a patriot carpenter named Anderson who lived in New York City had an altercation with a Tory, who was reported to have insulted the carpenter as he carried his tools along the street.

"Times are changing with you!" cried the Tory. "So, you are obliged to carry your axe. Where is your gun now, that you used to carry?"

This brought a retort from Anderson, blows were struck, and later the Tory lodged a complaint with the British general in charge of the city. Anderson, without receiving a trial, was ordered to receive 500 lashes, "and notwithstanding the intercessions of his wife and children and a number of friends, this inhuman sentence was carried into execution with the greatest vigor . . . he fainted away twice during the execution; after which, he was sent into confinement on board a man of war." [5]

These British ships in the harbor may have been effective prisons in which the Americans could slowly rot, but, sitting there, they lent comparatively little weight to the prosecution of the war by the King and his ministers. On land, operations of a sort proceeded, although the master plan of the British military leaders—if it could be called such—was surrounded by a haze of confusion. Writing in the *Gentleman's Magazine*, "An Old Soldier" commented that "any other general in the world than General Howe would have beaten General Washington; and any other general in the world than General Washington would have beaten General Howe." The failure of the St. Leger expedition was followed by a similar denouement. A sizable portion of the army of General Burgoyne was marching down the classic invasion route from Canada via Lake Champlain, Ticonderoga and thence to Albany, where a junction with Howe or Clinton was hoped for. In fairness to Burgoyne and what followed, it should be said that from the first stage of his invasion of upper New York, he lacked pack horses and provisions. His German General von Riedesel particularly grew tired of having his heavily equipped dragoons slogging along as foot soldiers, when they were supposed to be mounted. Burgoyne thereupon sent a raiding force into nearby Vermont to procure the needed supplies. Unfortunately for the British commander, he selected to head the expedition the only officer of substantial rank in his command who could not speak a word of English, Lieutenant Colonel Friederich Baum. His mission was to penetrate enemy country and try to enlist the service of English-speaking people. This appears all the more strange in view of the opinion of Burgoyne himself, expressed in later years before the House of Commons: "I knew that Bennington was the great deposit of corn, flour and store cattle, that it was only guarded by militia, and every day's account tended to confirm the persuasion of the loyalty of one description of the inhabitants and the panic of the other." [6]

If he knew this, why he did not dispatch an officer who would be able to communicate with the Tories in their own language is not easy to fathom. But then "Gentleman Johnny" Burgoyne was often unfathomable, a quality he obviously enjoyed at times. As he glibly put it, Baum's objective was "to try the affections of the people, to disconcert the councils of the enemy, to mount Riedesel's dragoons, to complete Peters' corps of Tories and to obtain large supplies of cattle, horses and carriages." [7]

How Baum did not accomplish this rather ambitious mission, how he was defeated by General John Stark and a large body of New Hampshire militia is well known. But it was not only because Burgoyne did not reinforce Baum that the latter was badly defeated in the dense setting of the thick New England woods. Although the invading force consisted of Germans, British, Tories and Indians, the Hessian hirelings were the backbone of the force. These were mainly regulars and fought well for Baum. But they were not at home in the Hampshire woodland and did not even recognize Stark's troops for what they really were. Two encircling detachments of Americans slipped around through the woods and reached the rear of Baum's men. This should have been an arousing if not alarming occurrence as far as Baum was concerned, but it was not. Colonel Philip Skene, an ex-British officer, who had established a 25,000-acre estate at the head of Lake Champlain, had advised Burgoyne to march near it, so that he would build roads which incidentally would help the estate, "Skenesborough." He had told Baum that the people of this countryside were Tories five to one. So when Baum saw some irregular groups of shirt-sleeved farmers, muskets or fowling pieces on their shoulders, approaching his rear, he thought they were friendly Tories wishing to join his ranks. Not only did he make no effort to keep them off; he actually ordered his pickets to give way and let them come closer! Little did he know how soon these farmers, Stark's men, would give him a sample of how friendly they were—with their frontier marksmanship. It may have been one of their bullets which a little later fatally wounded Colonel Baum. The Tories who were in his ranks fired once and fled when the shooting started, the shirt-sleeved militia having attacked with such suddenness that their loyal opponents did not have time to reload.

Commanding these Tories was Colonel John Peters, nephew of the Reverend Samuel Peters of Connecticut, who with his brother had gone to England to escape hanging. John, a graduate of Yale and later a judge, owned extensive lands and mills and was elected to attend the First Continental Congress as representative of Gloucester and Cumberland counties. But on his way to Philadelphia with his uncles, Samuel and Bemslee Peters, he was mobbed by Governor Trumbull's Liberty Boys, because they thought he was a Tory. Freed after being severely abused, Peters made his way to the Congress, but when he was convinced that nothing short of independence of the colonies would satisfy most of the delegates, he withdrew. On his way home, Peters was attacked by other mobs who seized him and threatened to execute him as an enemy of Congress. His house was searched for correspondence with the British, but none, he said, was found. Confined to Moor Town, Connecticut, Peters was threatened with death if he left. It is no wonder he did not favor the patriot cause. During this confinement, he later testified, "Mobs again and again visited me, and eat and drank and finally plundered me of most of my moveable effects." There was a division of loyalty in the family, for he added, "My father, Colonel Peters of Hebron, wrote against me and urged on the mob."

Finally, having had all he felt he could endure of such treatment, John Peters fled to Canada. At Montreal, he was informed that his wife, a small and delicate woman, had been turned out of their home in the midst of winter and had been sent in a sleigh with one bed for 140 miles to Ticonderoga, "through the woods, snow, storm and bad roads, with her young children in her arms. They were almost dead on arrival there." Such were the memories Colonel Peters carried with him into the fight at Bennington. He had conferred with Benjamin Franklin and Benedict Arnold at Montreal, but again was convinced that America was determined to have independence. So he raised a regiment of Tories which he named The Queen's Loyal Rangers, who fought with him at Bennington on August 16, 1777, where he lost half of the 291 men of the outfit.

Had they all fought like John Peters, the battle might have been more favorable to the Tories and British. "I observed a man fire at me, which I returned," he related. "He loaded up again as he came up and discharged at me, crying out, 'Peters, you damned Tory, I have got you!' He rushed on me with his bayonet which entered below my left breast but was turned by the bone. By this time I was loaded, and I saw he was a rebel captain, an old school fellow and playmate, and a cousin of my wife's. Though his bayonet was in my body, I felt regret at being obliged to destroy him. I received Burgoyne's approbation of my conduct in this action."

One of Peters' sons also fought with him at Bennington, and a false report was later given his wife that both were killed. Mrs. Peters received the news with dry-eyed stolidity. "My calamities are very great," she said, "but thank God they died doing their duty for king and country. I have six sons left and as soon as they are able to bear arms, I will send them against the rebels, while I and my daughter will mourn for the dead and pray for the living. I cannot say I look back with regret at the part I took, from motives of loyalty and from a foresight of the horrors and miseries of independency." [8]

Burgoyne, also a dramatist, could have asked for no more poignant action had he written a play about his campaign. The fratricidal nature of the conflict was heightened by the fate of another woman, Jane, also called Jenny, McCrea, daughter of a New Jersey Presbyterian minister.

Upon the death of her mother and the marriage of her father to a second wife, Jane went to live with her brother who had settled in the Hudson Valley near Saratoga. At the time when Burgoyne was advancing down the invasion route, her brother was a colonel in the patriot militia and decided to move to Albany. But Jane was engaged marry David Jones, who had fled to Canada and had become an officer in one of the Tory contingents then on the march with Burgoyne. Love in this case being above loyalty to family or country, Jane McCrea refused to go with her brother, but went instead to Fort Edward, just south of Ticonderoga, where she hoped to meet her lover and, as the contemporary writers expressed it, "have a tryst with him." The fort was by this time abandoned, but in a nearby cabin lived an old woman, a Mrs. McNeil, who was a Tory and cousin of British General Simon Fraser. She took the girl in as a guest.

On July 27, 1777, two days before the advancing army of General Burgoyne took over the abandoned Fort Edward, his Indian forerunners arrived at the fort. They seized Mrs. McNeill and Jane McCrea and started back toward the British army. They had not gone very far when two of the Indians, evidently attracted to the beautiful Miss McCrea, got into a dispute over who should be her guard. In anger, one of the Indians shot and scalped her and stripped the clothing from her body. They took Mrs. McNeill and the scalp of Miss McCrea to the British camp, where, reportedly, General Fraser received his cousin, and David Jones recognized the long black hair of his fiancée. She has been described as "a girl of graceful form and attractive by her intelligent countenance and endearing disposition. Her lover was a fine, dashing fellow who had brought a company of Loyalist sharpshooters to the assistance of Burgoyne." But that such an atrocity was not in keeping with the ideas of the British general is borne out in his directions for the "rules" of the campaign, set forth only three days before: "Aged men, women and children and prisoners must be held sacred from the knife or hatchet, even in the time of actual conflict. You shall receive compensation for the prisoners you take, but you shall be called to account for scalps." [9]

In accordance with this order, Burgoyne immediately ordered the arrest of the murderer of Jane McCrea and prepared to execute him. But the matter proved to be not that simple. The guilty warrior turned out to be an important Indian personage, a chief of huge physical proportions known as the Wyandot Panther, who was feared and respected by all his tribesmen. Burgoyne was advised by one of his officers, St. Luke de La Corne, that if he punished this chief, all the Indians would then desert the army, would probably return to their villages and burn the unprotected country on both sides of the Canadian border. So the Wyandot Panther was pardoned.

The feminine attributes of Jane McCrea have been variously described by historians, but regardless of her beauty and charm, she became a sort of symbol of saintly martyrdom. News of her murder spread up and down the New York and New England frontier, and her beauty grew with the increase of the tales of the horrible crime. She became a Revolutionary Joan of Arc. To many Americans who wavered in their homes, Jane McCrea became the watchword to go out and crush the cruel Tory and British enemy. Canny General Horatio Gates made capital of the situation. He wrote Burgoyne "that the savages of America should in their warfare mangle and scalp the unhappy prisoners who fall into their hands is neither new nor extraordinary; but that the famous Lieutenant General Burgoyne, in whom the fine gentleman is united with the soldier and scholar, should hire the savages of America to scalp Europeans and the descendants of Europeans . . . is more than will be believed in England. . . . Miss McCrea, a young lady lovely to the sight, of virtuous character and amiable disposition, engaged to be married to an officer of your army . . . was scalped and mangled in the most shocking manner." That the affair caused no joy in the British camp is evidenced by the statement of an officer that "the melancholy catastrophe of the unfortunate Miss McCrea affected the General and the whole army with the sincerest regret and concern for her untimely fate." [10]

Even more misfortune for Burgoyne and his men was to come at Saratoga, the battle which changed the course of the war and was most influential in bringing France into the conflict on our side. On September 20, Burgoyne wrote Clinton, "Nothing now between us but Gates." General Gates, regarded by Burgoyne as "an old midwife," turned out to be more of an adjutant general than a field commander, and let Daniel Morgan and Benedict Arnold carry the brunt of the battle. Historical appraisal developed by late research gives Morgan and his reliable and effective frontier riflemen, whose devastating marksmanship in picking off the officers shocked the British, increasing credit for the crucial victory. Morgan was the commander whom Burgoyne admittedly feared the most.

The British at Saratoga were defeated not only from outside their ranks but also from within. Bennington had deprived Burgoyne of more than 800 men, half of whom were regulars. The Indian allies of the British general, disgruntled by restrictions which he had placed on their independent operations after the McCrea affair, held a council and decided to go home. This left him, besides his insufficient regular forces, mainly the Tory troops, and these he found largely unreliable. He wrote to Lord Germain about these Tories, "I have about 400 (but not half of them armed), who may be depended upon. The rest are trimmers merely actuated by interest." Furthermore, 3,000 miles away, this very Lord Germain was supposed to sign the orders for General Howe to meet Burgoyne at Albany; but this esteemed minister, on his way to a leisurely weekend in Kent, looked in at the War Office in London, found the draft of the orders incomplete and failed to sign them—in fact never did. "So Lord George went down into the country and lost America."

Burgoyne had been told that the territory through which he had come, especially Vermont and Tryon County, New York, held numerous Tories who would rise to his standard and help him sweep the rebels before him. But circumstances, which included the lack of heart and proper organization of the Tories themselves, combined to deny him much of this help. Had he found the loyal support he fondly expected, Saratoga might have been a different story, despite Howe, and the whole course of the war changed; as it was, the civilian help went instead to Gates and his victorious Americans. Burgoyne told Howe that "a scandalous defection of the Indians, a desertion or timidity worse than desertion of provincials [Tories] and Canadians, a very few individuals excepted" were among the reasons for the defeat. "Had all my troops been British," wrote "Gentleman Johnny" wistfully, "I, in my conscience, believe I should have made my way through Mr. Gates' army." [11]

News of the British defeat at Saratoga gave great shock and setback to the cause of the Tories in America. Various explanations were set forth regarding the cause of the disaster to the redcoats. A few years after the war's end, Tory historian Thomas Jones declared that the principal cause of Burgoyne's defeat was the same as that which ruined Braddock in 1755, and which lost the Tories so many battles, "the overbearing pride of regulars and their contempt for volunteers." Another factor, stated Jones, was the acceptance by Burgoyne of the selfish advice of Colonel Skene, to proceed to Ford Edward from "Skenesborough," instead of by Ticonderoga and Lake George, although this point has been disputed. The advice of Colonel John Peters to Burgoyne, pointing out the dangers existing at Bennington and Saratoga, would have been immeasurably more valuable. But to Peters, Burgoyne was said to have replied, "When I want your advice, I shall ask for it." On the other hand, Charles Inglis wrote Joseph Galloway that Burgoyne was welcomed and greatly helped by the inhabitants of upper New York when he approached Saratoga; "provisions in abundance were brought to his army, the inhabitants cheerfully gave their beds to them and sympathized with them." A cause given for the fear of some Tories of helping the invading British was the previous trial of several Tory leaders at Claremont, New Hampshire, in December of 1775. These were charged with offering ardent support to the British side and consequently were warned by the Committee of Safety to stay within the limits of their town and to desist from helping the redcoats for the rest of the war. Apparently this warning was carried over to the Saratoga region and prevented many Tories who otherwise would have done so from aiding Burgoyne.[12]

The momentous news of the American victory at Saratoga was sent to Europe as speedily as sailing ships could carry it. John Paul Jones in the *Ranger* took dispatches containing the news to Nantes, arriving there on December 2, 1777, only to learn that he had been beaten by twelve hours by Jonathan Loring Austin of Boston, who had sailed with the information aboard a French vessel. Astute Benamin Franklin and his French friends saw to it that the story of Saratoga was spread throughout the continent. The American Tories abroad were thunderstruck. Charles William Dumas, Swiss propagandist for the patriots in America, wrote them, "This news has made the greatest possible sensation; a deep consternation among those who have all their interest in England, a marked joy among those who hate your enemies." [13]

Meanwhile, back in Pennsylvania, a pathetic episode all too typical of the Tory efforts to thwart the rising tide of patriotism was taking place. It involved James Molesworth, an Englishman who had come to Philadelphia before the Revolution and was employed as a clerk in the mayor's office. With that beleaguered city changing hands, Molesworth in the spring of 1777 found himself out of work and wandered through New Jersey until he reached New York City. There the British commanders were planning their campaigns, aided by Joseph Galloway, who met Molesworth and felt he would be valuable in the Pennsylvania activities of the British against the Americans. Galloway took him to Admiral Lord Howe, who was then outlining an expedition to Delaware. Howe offered Molesworth a commission as a lieutenant if he would go secretly to Philadelphia to obtain the services of several local pilots acquainted with the navigation and defenses of the Delaware River, these individuals to return with Molesworth to New York for instructions.[14]

Molesworth at once set out on the dangerous errand, taking a circuitous route by way of Basking Ridge and Brunswick and eventually reaching Philadelphia safely. This was not long after the battle of Princeton, when the British army was maneuvering in the upper part of New Jersey, and the patriots of Philadelphia and the surrounding country were encouraged by Washington's recent victories and were especially on the alert. In the city, Molesworth took "retired lodgings" and soon communicated with two men named Shepard and Thomas and two women, Abigail McKay and Sarah O'Brien, to whom he naïvely told his whole plot without being sure of their reliability. Three pilots were to be engaged to pilot the ship, the *Eagle*, to Philadelphia from New York, the British fleet under Howe to follow immediately. Arrangements were to be made among the Philadelphia Tories to have the guns in the forts near there spiked and the bridges demolished. If this went off successfully, Molesworth was to receive handsome rewards.

Alas for the naïveté of poor Molesworth. His "trusted pilots" at once revealed the plot to Philadelphia patriot officials, Molesworth was arrested, his male confederates escaped, the women were jailed and he was executed. Commented Joseph Reed, a patriot leader, "Had Molesworth been spared, the execution of André would have been unpardonable butchery." [15]

This example marked a tendency of many Tories in Pennsylvania. These disaffected persons went to little trouble to conceal their pro-British sentiments, even after the Declaration of Independence. They exposed themselves to the dangers of arrest and were incarcerated daily. Some of the leading men of the Moravian congregation at Bethlehem were Tories, one of them, the Reverend George Kribel, being compelled to serve a term in the Easton jail bcause he would not "adjure the King according to the specific requirements of the militia bill." John Francis Oberlin was required to resign the custody of the church store, after serving as its keeper for many years, because he hotly remarked that he "had sufficient rope in his store to hang all Congress." Tories were with General Howe when he and his army landed at the head of the Elk River in August of 1777, including Joseph Galloway, who was now an adviser to the British commander. Galloway felt that Howe had deliberately allowed Washington to escape into New Jersey, then Pennsylvania, and had told Governor Hutchinson that there was never a week when Howe could not have destroyed the Continental Army had he wanted to. Furthermore, if Philadelphia was the object of Howe's advance, why, Galloway asked, was his army sent 600 miles by sea to get 60 miles by land? Part of this question was answered by Ambrose Serle, secretary to General Howe, who was a friend of Galloway and sympathetic to the Tories. As to their helping Howe in Pennsylvania, Serle commented, "Alas, they will prate and profess much; but when you call upon them, they will *do* nothing." Galloway had to agree to some extent, but explained such inaction by saying the Tories had been disarmed and had never been supported by the British when they had attempted to resist the Congress, a body which he felt was composed of the most violent men in the colonies and which had an army to support its measures. For his part, Serle recalled New York, where he had seen in May an attempt by "a very sanguine gentleman to raise a corps of 300 men for the defense and security of New York City"; yet scarcely a Tory had enlisted. Even so, Galloway said before the war was over, "I am convinced that . . . if the new states were disbanded, the British troops withdrawn and the people left to themselves and their free and unbridled suffrage, that nine persons out of ten in the whole revolted colonies would vote for a constitutional union with and dependence on the British state." [16]

George Washington evidently felt somewhat the same way, for he had written to Congress not long before Howe's arrival in Pennsylvania that the activity of such men as Governor Franklin of New Jersey had so stirred up the Tories of that and adjoining states that he would not be surprised "if a large number of the inhabitants in some of the counties should openly appear in arms, as soon as the enemy begin their operations." The head of that enemy, William Howe, doubtless felt proud of the new honor his king had bestowed upon him just before he set out for Pennsylvania. It was the coveted Order of the Bath. But Thomas Jones, the Tory historian, took a dim view of the bestowal. The investiture, said Jones, was "a reward for evacuating Boston, for lying indolent upon Staten Island for nearly two months, for suffering the whole rebel army to escape him on Long Island and again at White Plains; for not putting an end to rebellion in 1776, when so often in his power; for making such injudicious cantonments of his troops in Jersey as he did, and for suffering 10,000 veterans under experienced generals to be cooped up in

Brunswick and Amboy for nearly six months, by about 6,000 militia, under the command of an inexperienced general." [17]

Regardless of what his military efforts deserved, Howe received from the Tories who lived in the Head of Elk region where he landed helpful intelligence on the current situation there. With Howe were two Tory units, the Queen's Rangers and a detachment of Royal Guides and Pioneers, both of which received many recruits from the local inhabitants. Howe encouraged such activity by issuing a proclamation offering protection to all Tories who would appear and swear allegiance to the crown within sixty days. Advancing to Philadelphia, Howe was ready to cross the Schuylkill River on September 21, when he learned from Tory intelligence that the Pennsylvania patriot officer, Anthony Wayne, was approaching his rear with 1,500 men and four pieces of artillery. Howe simply cut Wayne's men off and held them powerless while he crossed over the river without interruption. The British general approved the officers of additional Tory organizations, the first battalion of Pennsylvania Loyalists, the Roman Catholic Volunteers and the first battalion of Maryland Loyalists, these three units eventually totaling about 500 men. An estimated thousand men were recruited from three times that number of qualified Tories in the Philadelphia area, including some deserters from the Continental forces. One factor which apparently was detrimental to the recruiting was the bad impression made by those seeking the enlistments upon their fellow Tories.

Howe's campaign had been undertaken on the theory that a large majority of Tories from New Jersey, Pennsylvania and Maryland would rise to his standard as soon as he came and especially after Washington was defeated. Then the rich and populous central colonies, administered by an efficient and stable government of prominent Tories, would be a stronghold of loyalism just as New England was a citadel of rebellion. But this did not come about. In eight months, Howe had recruited less than a thousand Tories, whereas ten times that number of New England farmers and frontiersmen had taken up their weapons and marched forth to oppose Burgoyne. In Pennsylvania there was not a Franklin, an Adams or a Washington to lead the Tories, and the military authorities showed themselves incapable of governing properly. The patriot leaders, on the whole, were trusted and supported by the people, took good care of their finances and defense, and acted on a friendly, equal footing with the generals of their army. On the British side, military arrogance, class-consciousness and domination abounded, as well as dishonesty; and civilians, Whigs as well as Tories, were subject to rigid military discipline instead of the more applicable peacetime methods of justice.[18]

Probably the busiest and most effective of the loyal individuals in the city was Joseph Galloway himself. He numbered the loyal persons in the area, secured horses for the army, obtained intelligence of the movements of American troops through the help of about eighty spies, rendered the capture of Mud Island in the river more speedy by erecting batteries, compiled a chart of all the roads in the vicinity and administered oaths of allegiance to the King under Howe's proclamation. Galloway was appointed superintendent of police, imports and exports of Philadelphia and thus became virtually the civil governor of the city. Local Tories were urged to raise vegetables for the British troops and to aid the farmers of the Pennsylvania countryside in bringing in their produce for sale—which they did to such an extent that lack of supplies was a greater problem for Washington and his needy troops at nearby Valley Forge than the storied weather of that winter, which has been exaggerated. Tory troops raided the surrounding country, and others escorted provisions into the city. Some of these loyal soldiers proved adept at capturing supplies badly needed by the patriots, such as the cloth anxiously awaited by the chilled Americans in their crude and cold encampment. In the winter of 1777–78, a vote in all the colonies might have shown a majority in favor of the Tories. One reason for this was a fear among many of the patriots of being informed on by Tory inhabitants for any help given to the young nationals. For example, Charles Stedman of Philadelphia was informed on by a Tory named John Fox, then in London, and as a result Stedman was jailed for high treason, "locked day and night in a damp room, debarred the use of pen, ink and paper and was obliged sometimes to drink the water he washed his face and hands in." In the *Virginia Gazette*, an advertisement expressed that journalistic medium's opinion:

WANTED: for his Majesty's service, as an assistant to his excellency General Howe, a gentleman who can lie with ingenuity. Inquire of Peter Numbskull, compiler and collector of lies. A good hand will receive the honor of knighthood.[19]

In like spirit appeared a notice from London in the *Freeman's Journal* in Portsmouth, New Hampshire, on March 22, 1777:

His Majesty intends to open this year's campaign with 90,000 Hessians, Tories, Negroes, Japanese, Moors, Eskimoes, Persian archers, Laplanders, Fiji Islanders and light horse. . . . He is resolved to terminate this unnatural war next summer . . . for heaven's sake ye poor deluded, misguided, bewildered, cajoled and bamboozled Whigs! ye dumb-founded, infatuated, back-bestridden, nose-led-about, priest-ridden, demagogue-beshackled and Congress-becrafted independents, fly, fly oh fly for protection to the royal standard, or ye will be swept from the face of the earth with the besom of destruction, and cannonaded into nullities and nonentities, and no mortal can tell into what other kind of quiddities and quoddities.

Following the entry of the British into Philadelphia, they commanded the bay and river along the whole coast of Delaware and ended all patriot water traffic. A Wilmington mob broke into the home of Jonathan Rumford, a wealthy merchant accused of Tory trading along the coast, and scattered firebrands through the residence, and the leader of the mob, a blacksmith, crushed Rumford's skull with a hammer. Caesar Rodney, militia commander of Delaware, led the struggle against the Tories with such success that the loyal people in that state had little chance to express themselves either in words or deeds. Joshua North was probably the wealthiest Tory in Delaware. He lost real and personal property which sold for 38,439 pounds.[20]

In "the City of Brotherly Love" itself, there was an unusual amount of gaiety during the winter of 1777–78. The British soldiers had plenty of time on their hands and indulged freely in amusements. Their officers organized "Loyal Association Clubs," held cricket matches and patronized a cockpit where sturdy roosters squared off to the tune of as much as 100-guinea bets on the outcome. From January to the end of April, weekly balls were held in which the young Tory ladies met and entertained the military men in town. Gay evening gowns mingled with colorful dress uniforms as the royal armed forces dallied away the season. It was like a happy play with a sad ending for Sir William Howe, for it meant the end of his command in America. He was honored at the climax by a dramatic extravanganza directed by none other than the artistic and talented John André, aided by the Tory ladies of the city. The spectacular outdoor exhibition, known as the "Mischianza," meaning in Italian a brilliant medley, was given at the Joseph Wharton residence half a mile below Philadelphia. It was, Andre said, "in honor of Sir William Howe, two pavilions being erected on either side of a square prepared for a tournament. Seated in the front were seven young ladies wearing dazzling Turkish costumes, and attached to their turbans were the favors they intended to reward the knights who were to contest in their honor." These were the Knights of the Burning Mountain and the Knights of the Blended Rose. Present as a symbol was Neptune with his trident, two sisters guarding it with drawn swords. Andre was one of the Knights of the Blended Rose, resplendent on a gray charger, answering the challenge of the knights on the other side to a dashing jousting match on the green lawn. At the wharves was a British fleet of 300 sails, each vessel decorated in bright colors. By 10 P.M., the challenge having been successfully met, the windows of the hall were thrown open and a magnificent display of fireworks arranged by Captain John Montresor, chief engineer, was shown. Twenty succeeding exhibitions featured bands playing "God Save the King" and an uninterrupted flight of rockets and bursting balloons, while military trophies on each side shone in a variety of transparent colors. At midnight, supper was announced, and large folding doors, heretofore artfully concealed, were suddenly thrown open to reveal a magnificent salon 210 feet long, 40 feet wide and 22 feet high, with three alcoves on each side. Dancing continued until 4 A.M. Howe literally left in a blaze of glory.[21]

But not all those who viewed the brilliant spectacle were happy about it. Mrs. Henry Drinker, whose husband had been punished for being a Tory, commented, "This day may be remembered by many for the scenes of folly and vanity. . . . How insensible do these people appear, while our land is so greatly desolated, and death and sore destruction have overtaken and impends over so many." One of the young Tory ladies taking part in the spectacle was the beautiful Miss Margaret Shippen, future wife of the traitor, Benedict Arnold. Even Ambrose Serle was struck by the folly and extravagance of the ball. The secretary reported that General Howe told a Philadelphia magistrate before leaving the city that the official might as well "make his peace with the States, who, he supposed, would not treat him harshly; for it was possible, on account of the French war, the troops would be withdrawn." Such sentiments were especially dispiriting to Joseph Galloway, who stood to lose, besides his home, an estate of 70,000 pounds.[22]

Galloway was not the only Tory to leave his Pennsylvania estate at this time. An estimated thousand loyal families left the city with the British army, filling the waiting fleet and causing Sir Henry Clinton, who took over the command, to have to march his soldiers overland. After Howe's army had landed in New York, the various Tory regiments accompanying it were distributed among the various British posts of the vicinity, the Queen's Rangers at Kingsbridge, the Pennsylvania Loyalists on Long Island and the Roman Catholic Volunteers and Maryland Loyalists at Flushing. How efficient these units were is a doubtful matter. Such Tory forces never seemed to make an effective showing in the large and overall operations of the British Army in America, though in random raids their sting was felt violently and often.

An officer under General Howe who was with the British forces from their first landing at Boston until the end of January, 1781, made a keen appraisal of this situation. By August of 1777, he stated, the King's army was joined by 6,000 American volunteers besides 3,000 militia embodied within the lines. Had common prudence directed the measures of the British high command, this number might have been raised to 30,000, this officer believed. But unfortunately, instead of the raising of these levies being used to suppress the rebellion, it was mainly turned to the purpose of making possible higher commissions for favorite young officers of the royal army by supplying them with sufficient troops to warrant such promotions. That the receiving of the initial commissions was not always exactly a matter of long deliberation is borne out by a communication to Charles Jenkison, Secretary at War under Lord North. It was explained that "Lord Amherst always insists on every person being seen by some officer before he gives him a commission." [23]

Tory privates, Howe's critical officer further explained, instead of being allowed to serve with the officers under whom they had enlisted and under whose leadership they had expected to continue in the field, were assigned to officers strange to them in manner and custom. Most of these young enlisted men were farmers or the like, in comfortable circumstances and with considerable education. They had been accustomed to associating with their neighbors without any great distinction of rank, and most knew their recruiting officers personally, esteemed them highly and would have followed them into battle without the strict discipline of the British Army; whereas the common soldiers were largely collected from the lowest ranks of society, were without property, and were "accustomed to keep the awful distance dictated by British officers." These freeholders, instead of being allowed to continue under their chosen officers, were compelled to submit to the capricious severities of young and inexperienced English officers, who were made their captains, majors and colonels. Not understanding the gentlemanly attitude of the American Tories, these officers used the most vigorous discipline to break down their spirits. And while the enlisted men from England expected such treatment, the Tories were astonished and dismayed at it. Such a feeling of bitter disappointment was also felt by the Tory officers, many of them gentlemen who had left their estates and highly respectable positions for the specific purpose of serving the royal cause. They raised their companies or regiments among their friends and neighbors, but soon found themselves completely deprived of them and seeming to have deceived those whom they had enlisted. The officers themselves were "thrown aside and totally neglected. . . . This absurd management and breach of faith toward both officers and men [by the British] discouraged others from coming over from the rebels, and they who were enlisted sought only how to relieve themselves, choosing rather to return home and bear the abuse and contempt of the rebels, than endure the insolent caprice of strangers." [24]

When the British evacuated Philadelphia on June 18, 1778, dashing Captain Allen McLane and his Maryland troopers followed the redcoats and captured Tory Captain Thomas Sandford of the Bucks County Light Dragoons and Frederick Varnum, keeper of the prison under Galloway. This was partly in retaliation for kidnapings of Americans by Tories in the vicinity. One of the latter, William Hamet, learning that two American officers were in nearby Jersey, had organized a party and in the dead of night crossed the Delaware, slipped up to the house where the men were asleep and seized them in their beds. Hamet then took them to Philadelphia as prisoners. In Delaware, Caesar Rodney complained so loudly about patriots being kidnaped by Tories that Congress decreed the death penalty for such occurrences if they happened within seventy miles of the headquarters of an American army. Joseph Galloway stated that during Howe's occupation of Philadelphia, 2,300 deserters came over from the American army and were absorbed into the British forces.

Philadelphia was not to be without military occupation for long. The day after the British left, Major General Benedict Arnold dramatically entered the city with his American forces. Tory influence on him was to figure importantly in the war. By December the mercurial Arnold, with no complaint now about not being promoted, was being thought a Tory himself. Soon afterward, he was said to be behaving leniently toward the loyal people of the community, especially the charming Margaret Shippen, whom he married. He acquired a handsome country estate, paid for, according to an army purchasing agent, from official funds, and lived like a mogul. Thus he began his deplorable descent from duty which led eventually to his betrayal of his cause to the British at West Point. Why Washington was not aware of the deterioration of Arnold sooner is difficult to understand, but it is certain he was reluctant to believe anything adverse about his old friend and esteemed officer. Also, Washington was trying to recover from the ordeal of Valley Forge, where not only had the weather and lack of supplies plagued him, but his men had deserted in groups numbering from ten to fifty each until his force was reduced to about 4,000 effective men.

In northeastern Pennsylvania, among the early settlers along the upper Delaware and Susquehanna rivers, Tory sentiment was strong. It derived partly from the strife between Whigs and Tories across the border in Tryon County, New York, centered at Johnstown in the lower Mohawk Valley, from which, as we have seen, the Johnsons fled to Canada in 1775. Tories from the upper Susquehanna region had followed the Johnsons and some of them enlisted in the corps of rangers under Colonel John Butler at Niagara, serving under this controversial leader for the remainder of the war. Perhaps it was the reports of these itinerant Tories to Butler and Sir Guy Johnson about the rich resources of their former Pennsylvania homes that led the Tories to move against that region, aided by Indians. In this regard, it should be pointed out that the redmen were active in every part of the new America and most of them were hostile to any invader who settled on their hunting grounds. Nor were the ringing words of Edmund Burke in Parliament, that the English were the first to use Indians in war, correct. The Americans had done this even before the battle of Lexington, when they enlisted Stockbridge Indians as minutemen; and Congress in May of 1775 had instructed its Indian commissioners to try to keep the redmen neutral or, if this were not possible, to enlist them on the American side.[25]

Stretching for about twenty-five miles along the north branch of the Susquehanna River in Luzerne County was a pleasant and fertile region some three miles wide called the Wyoming Valley. Here was to be enacted a vivid and unforgettable episode of the war. Flanking the beauteous valley were two low ranges of hills, each about a thousand feet in height. "In all its aspects, it was a land formed by nature as a garden spot of peaceful fruitfulness as well as a delight to the eye." Yet from its founding in 1742, the valley settlement became a scene of sharp conflict between rival claimants, Pennsylvania holding that the valley was a part of William Penn's grant from the King, and Connecticut claiming the valley as falling between lines extending westward from its own northern and southern boundaries. When this dispute was at its height, Congress interposed and stated that until the general dispute with Britain was decided, this local controversy could go unresolved.[26]

Here for years the inhabitants lived happily, navigating the picturesque river with their flat-bottomed boats and raising on their rich meadow lands great quantities of grain, fruit, hemp, flax and livestock. With the coming of the Revolution, the settlement had supplied the Continental Army with thousands of bushels of grain and other provisions, as well as up to a thousand volunteer soldiers. For protection from the Indians, the settlers had built a number of small forts, which were actually entrenched blockhouses along the river, the most important ones being called Fort Durkee, Fort Wyoming, Ogden's Fort, the Pittsdown Redoubts, Wintermoot's Fort and Fort Jenkins. All were designed as places of refuge for the inhabitants in case of Indian attack. Thus Wyoming may have seemed a peaceful valley, but it was to be the scene of what was fancifully called "the surpassing horror of the Revolution." When the patriot settlers learned that in their midst were a number of Tory families, they took steps to banish these loyal souls to the dreaded Simsbury Mines in Connecticut. "The sinister terror and suspicion which so cruelly attends civil wars enveloped the valley. Sounds on the road at night, heard through barred doors and windows, the hooded light in the field, were not made by friends or neighbors, but those who lived in lonely houses in bitter loyalty. . . . There was something fearful in every footfall. The lone valley, pictured by so many as an Arcadia, was in reality a cauldron in the hills, boiling with greed and violence and fear." [27]

The resentment of the Tories at being forced to leave soon began to show itself. They relayed word back against their patriot enemies to the Indians who plied the forests from the Mohawk to the Wyoming valley. Eventually the people of the latter region began to suspect that the redmen were planning action against them, despite the fact that Indian delegations sent to them went to some pains to assure the residents that they had no hostile designs. But one of the visiting braves got drunk and let slip the remark that he and other red messengers were sent only to delude the people of the Wyoming community, and that some of the Six Nations intended, as soon as their plans were crystallized, to attack them. Alarmed by this inadvertent report, the local families for thirty miles up the river were collected and brought in to the more thickly settled area. By May it was noticed that strolling parties of Indians and Tories were making forays into the settlement. One of these foraging parties, bent on plunder, mistakenly killed a Tory woman and her five children who had remained in the valley.

In this spring of 1778, the headquarters of the Tory troops of Sir Guy Johnson and Colonel John Butler was at Fort Niagara on Lake Ontario. These leaders made plans to launch an expedition against Wyoming Valley, but this plan, as some legends indicate, was not born in random bloodthirstiness. One object of Butler was to bring out the families of the refugees who had left the valley for his fort. Hundreds of women, old people and children had been left behind to the "untender mercies of the rebels, and their rescue was ardently desired by the men at Niagara." Aiding the expedition was John Burch, a Tory and native of England, who had a large estate on the Delaware River. Asked to sign an oath of loyalty to the American cause, he refused. Instead, upon hearing that Colonel Butler was planning to attack nearby Wyoming, Burch wrote him and offered to bring him a supply of cattle for provisions. This offer was welcomed and the Tory and his friends furnished Butler 136 cattle. The patriots learned of this act, surrounded Burch's house and plundered his effects, he reported. Three times he was attacked in this manner until finally he was forced to leave the country, being fired at as he left for the Indian country and made his way to Niagara Falls where he settled.[28]

Carrying out Butler's plan, in late June a thousand men came down the winding Susquehanna. About half of them were white, including Butler's Rangers, a detachment of Johnson's Royal Greens, and some unattached Tories from New York, New Jersey, and Pennsylvania. Contrasting with the lush, green fields of the valley were the red skins of some 500 Indians, chiefly Senecas, the most ferocious tribe of the Six Nations, whose king, Sucingerachton, foremost man of the Iroquois, was devoted to the British and hated the French. The royal forces were still smarting under their defeats at Oriskany and Fort Stanwix, so the Wyoming expedition was variously motivated. A long string of canoes, bateaux and rafts carried the contingent downriver. Twenty miles above Wyoming, they disembarked, then quietly entered the valley through a notch in the western mountains and hid themselves in the deep woods. Near Fort Jenkins, one of the upper blockhouses, the invaders came upon seven men and a boy working in the fields. They killed three of them and captured four, and the boy escaped. The fort, its small garrison weakened by the loss of the seven, then surrendered without resistance. Nearby was another fort called Exeter, but it happened to be filled with Tories, so it gladly surrendered.

In command of the armed patriots of the valley was Colonel Zebulon Butler, said to have been a cousin of the Tory commander. He had about sixty "regulars" and had also gathered 300 militiamen, these being concentrated at a place called Forty Fort. Learning of the approach of the Tories and Indians, Zebulon Butler counseled with his men and could see no hope of deliverance except through a victory over the foe, who was twice his number and more skillful in the woods. Nevertheless it was decided to go out and fight, in the hope of taking the enemy by surprise. As they approached Wintermoot's Fort, the patriots found how hard it was to take Indians in the woods by surprise. A redman spotted them, and quickly gave the alarm to Colonel John Butler inside the fort, which he had just captured. Setting fire to the fort in order to make the attackers think he had fled, Butler and his men spread out into the woods. "We immediately treed ourselves," Richard McGinnis, a Tory carpenter, reported, "and secured every spot that was in any way advantageous to our design. When the enemy came within sight of us, they fell ablackguarding us, calling out aloud, 'Come out, ye villainous Tories! Come out if ye dare and show your heads if ye durst, to the brave Continental Sons of Liberty!' "

In reply, McGinnis called them "Sons of Sedition, Schism and Rebellion." [29]

Among the trees and in the underbrush, John Butler coolly deployed his men in line of battle. On his left, he placed the trusted Rangers, their flank on the fort; in the center were the Royal Greens; and on the right were the eager Indians. Opposing his right and left was the militia of Zebulon Butler, his regulars in the center.

The patriot line came on. No sight of the enemy appeared to its commander. Then at the foot of the opposite mountain, a flag suddenly appeared. The advancing Butler believed that this meant a request for a truce or at least a parley. He moved toward it, but as he did, the flag slowly moved back. "We lay flat on the ground awaiting their approach," said John Butler later. "When they were within 200 yards of us, they began firing. We still continued upon the ground, without returning their fire, until they had fired three volleys. By this time they had advanced within 100 yards of us, and they being quite near enough, Sucingerachton ordered his Indians who were upon the right, to begin the attack on our part, which was immediately well seconded by the Rangers on the left." As the heavy firing sounded on all sides of the Americans, they realized too late that they had been decoyed into an ambush.[30]

Even so, for half an hour a heavy fire was exchanged. During this time a body of Seneca braves succeeded in working their way unperceived to an advantageous position on the left flank of the Americans, so that they could look right down their throats. The redskins now opened up a surprising and murderous fire which threw the patriot left flank into a melee of confusion, as the white men were cut down by rifle and hatchets, and scalping followed hard on the heels of death.

To meet this unexpected thrust, American Colonel Nathan Denison ordered a company to wheel and face the flank attack. Either from fear or from misunderstanding, some of his men mistook the order for one to retreat, and as in a similar happening at the Cowpens two years later, the whole wing began to give way in disorder. This was just what the Indians wanted. Throwing down their muskets and letting out savage yells, the Senecas swarmed into the milling mass, ripping it with tomahawks and knives. The Americans fought back valiantly for a short time. Then there was a sudden break, the heart-chilling pause before flight, and the whole command gave way. Soon it was fleeing in wild array, while on its rear, the blood-crazed redmen took a heavy toll, regaining their muskets and shooting and tomahawking every man they could catch. Crèvecoeur later wrote that some of the Americans plunged into the river in hopes of reaching the other side, but that the enemy, "flushed with the intoxication of success and victory, pursued them with the most astonishing celerity, and being naked, had very great advantage over a people encumbered with clothes. This, united with their superiority in the art of swimming, enabled them to overtake most of the unfortunate fugitives, who perished in the river, pierced with the lances of the Indians. Thirty-three were so fortunate as to reach the opposite shore, and for a long time afterward the carcasses of their companions, become offensive, floated and infested the banks of the Susquehanna as low as Shamokin." [31]

The toll of the losers was heavy. John Butler reported that 227 scalps were taken in the fight and only five prisoners, the Indians being so exasperated with their loss the previous year at Fort Stanwix that it was difficult to save the lives of the few who survived. McGinnis, the Tory carpenter, said that he was told by prisoners that of 450 Americans engaged in the battle, only 45 returned to the fort. The loss to the British side was one Indian and two Tories killed, eight Indians wounded. Colonels Denison and Butler got away with what few of their men they could find, Butler feeling that he had insufficient men left for defense against the British and that those who did remain had no heart for further fighting. Consequently he put his wife on his horse behind him and left the valley for Wilkes-Barre. Colonel Denison had already surrendered before Butler made his way out of the settlement.

The subsequent and gory events which followed are termed a "massacre" by most historians, but the Tory historian, Ryerson, said that Wyoming was a "pitched battle," and cites what he terms expert opinion to show that no massacre followed except what the unrestrained Indians committed. It does appear that John Butler made efforts to prevent brutality. When his expedition set out for Wyoming, he held frequent counsels with the Indian chiefs "to deter them if possible from murdering the women and innocent, in consequence of which, they agreed not to do it on any pretence whatever. And I must say," continued Richard McGinnis, who was with John Butler, "for my part they did not commit anything of the kind to my certain knowledge." In pursuance of this purpose, when Butler entered the captured fort after the surrender, he ordered all liquor containers broken up to prevent the Indians' getting them. After he had reported that he had destroyed eight forts and a thousand dwelling houses and had driven off a thousand head of cattle, sheep and swine, he added that "not a single person has been hurt of the inhabitants but such as were in arms. To those indeed, the Indians gave no quarter." [32]

Yet Henry Melchoir Muhlenberg, the Lutheran clergyman and leader, recorded in his journal that he had heard of "the frightful and extraordinary massacres and atrocities committed by 1,300 Tories and 300 Indians upon the thickly populated region of Wyoming on the Susquehanna. The settlers were, for the most part, hacked and slashed to pieces, taken prisoner and slowly tortured to death. Pregnant women, children and gray-heads were driven into houses and barns and burned alive with the buildings. Those who could escape fled destitute into the wilderness, where there was nothing to eat." [33]

This is essentially the version accepted by George Bancroft, David Ramsay and Richard Hildreth, although the last-named historian does admit that Butler desired to fulfill the terms of surrender and marched away with his Tories, although he could not induce the Indians to follow immediately. Even Benson Lossing, certainly not inclined to favor the Tories, remarked that the survivors of the battle exaggerated their reports of what had happened and said that the "massacre" grew in bloodiness with each telling. Ryerson said that the hard fighting occurred because the Wyoming Tories had previously been "insulted, imprisoned and banished and their property confiscated." It is generally agreed that the Indians left little to the imagination when it came to barbarity in warfare, and the ruthless Senecas left behind at Wyoming doubtless ravaged, killed and burned. Seventy soldiers taken prisoner were said to have been "inhumanly butchered, with every circumstance of horrid cruelty," while a recent and respected historian states that "shrieking in anguish, men were burned at the stake and others roasted over live coals and kept pinned down by pitchforks while their horrified families looked helplessly on. Still others were arranged in a circle while a ghastly half-breed squaw, Queen Esther, chanting a wild hymn of triumph, chopped off their heads." [34]

The pleasing aspects of the beautiful valley were virtually destroyed. One account mentions that cattle which could not be taken away had their tongues cut out and were left to starve in misery. For some time, it was said, the roads through the settled country were filled with unhappy people fleeing the valley, many of them "young, bare-headed, bare-footed, shedding tears at every step, oppressed with fatigues too great for their tender age to bear, afflicted with every species of misery, with hunger, with bleeding feet and every now and then surrounding their mothers as exhausted as themselves, asking where are we going, where is father, why don't we go home?" [35]

Captain James Bedlock of the American forces was allegedly stripped, tied to a tree and stuck full of sharp pine splinters; then a heap of pine knots was piled around him and he was set on fire. Tory Thomas Hill was said with his own hands to have killed his mother, father-in-law, his sisters and their families. Another Tory, Partial Terry, was stated to have previously sent his patriot father word several times that he would wash his hands in his heart's blood. He succeeded in forcing his way into his father's house, murdered and scalped him, and also his mother, brothers and sisters, and finally hacked off his father's head and carried it away with him. So went the stories. Against them must be set the statement of Walter Butler, son of Colonel John Butler, to General James Clinton, that "We deny any cruelties to have been committed at Wyoming, either by whites or Indians; so far to the contrary that not a man, woman or child was hurt after the capitulation, or a woman or child before it or after being taken into captivity." The historian, Hildreth, commented that "These barbarities, greatly exaggerated by reports embodied in poetry and history, excited everywhere a lively indignation," which can well be understood. His contemporary, William L. Stone, who visited Wyoming in 1838 and interviewed its oldest inhabitants, remarked, "Rarely indeed does it happen that history is more at fault in regard to the facts than in the case of Wyoming." [36]

To the verdant valley of the Mohawk spread the border warfare which so intermingled the actions of Indians and Tories that it is difficult to give discredit where it is due. German Flats, where now stands the town of Herkimer on the Mohawk River, was ravaged by the Indian leader Joseph Brant, who led a band of Tories and Indians there in September. Although no lives were lost, the village was burned. In revenge, the Americans burned Unadilla, an Indian village fifty miles to the southwest.

In continuance of such retaliation, Cherry Valley was the next target of the British allies. Located in Tryon County about fifty miles west of Albany, it was an exceptional frontier settlement of highly intelligent and moral people. In 1778 Lafayette had visited this valley in preparation for a projected foray into Canada. Though the expedition never materialized, the Frenchman did direct the building of a fort in Cherry Valley for defense against the Tories and Indians. Colonel Peter Gansevoort, who had defended Fort Stanwix, wanted command of this fort, but his request for it was denied. Instead, Colonel Ichabod Alden with the Seventh Massachusetts Regiment took over, neither the 250 men nor their commander having any experience in Indian warfare. The defenders had not long to wait. From Chemung, Captain Walter Butler and 200 of his father's Rangers set out in late October on a 150-mile march up the Susquehanna River toward Cherry Valley. On the way he met Joseph Brant and 500 Indians and persuaded them to join him. Butler had heard that this would be a good time to attack Cherry Valley, because the enlistments of the patriot militia there were soon to expire—a recurring curse of the American forces. Impelling the Tories and Indians was a common interest, that of self-preservation through mutual help; and the recovery of the Mohawk Valley was a vital objective for those who had lost it.

Colonel Alden had been warned that his post might be attacked. Even so, he would not even allow the local residents to move inside the fort. He furthermore permitted his officers to live outside the fort, and in posting his scouts overlooked an old but strategic Indian trail leading to his headquarters. On the morning of November 11, Walter Butler and his men, under cover of a heavy fog, approached the fort along the overlooked trail. Silently scattering his men, Butler had them first attack the outlying houses, one of them being that of Robert Wells which was also occupied by Colonel Alden. Both were shot and scalped, as well as the family of Wells. Other houses were similarly attacked and their occupants killed. Historian Willard Wallace states that "though Brant tried to restrain the prisoner killing, particularly of women and children, Butler was less squeamish." But Howard Swiggett remarks that "while Lossing,

Simms and Timothy Dwight describe Butler as the instigator of it all, not one of them ever gives the name of a family at whose murder he was present." [37]

Butler had no artillery and could do little to reduce the fort. He did send a heavy musket fire into it for several hours, probably for psychological effect. Then the Indians took over. Dwellings and barns were burned and livestock carried away. Some thirty prisoners were taken and marched off. A newspaper reported that the invaders "committed the most inhuman barbarities on most of the dead. Robert Henderson's head was cut off, his skull bone was cut out with the scalp. Mr. Willis's sister was ripped up, a child of Mr. Willis's, two months old, scalped and arm cut off, and many there as cruelly treated. Many of the inhabitants and soldiers shut out from the fort, lay all night in the rain with the children, who suffered very much. The cattle that were not easy to drive, they shot." But Butler told General Schuyler in a letter next day from Cherry Valley: "I have done everything in my power to restrain the fury of the Indians from hurting women and children or killing prisoners who fall into our hands, and would have more effectually prevented them, but that they were so much incensed by the late destruction of their village by your people." Butler reiterated this to other officials.[38]

Falling into the same historical rut as others, Lorenzo Sabine charged that on this occasion there were committed "deeds of rapine and murder of such hellish hue that sufficient evidence remains undoubted to stamp Butler's conduct with the deepest, darkest and most damning guilt." [39] But that there were more survivors than was initially reported is a matter of record; that the Americans lost no opportunity to make rich propaganda of such occurrences on their borders, where facts often became submerged in the ornamentation of fiction, is apparent. Probably remembering his own mother and other members of the family, Butler soon released all women and children except a few whose men had been especially active against the Tories, and these he agreed to exchange with General James Clinton.[40]

Such action, however, was far from a settlement of the military situation on the borders. As the year 1778 drew to a close, Tory and Indian attacks in the valleys of upper New York and Pennsylvania spread terror through the region which echoed in the councils of the Continental high command. To avenge the ravages of the oposing forces, the next spring Washington sent General John Sullivan into the Indian country to strike a counterblow the Indians and their Tory allies would never forget.

9. Law and Disorder

If there was one consistently Tory territory during the American Revolution, it was Florida. Particularly East Florida remained steadfast in its attachment to the Crown and menaced Georgia and the Carolinas throughout the war, becoming a general refuge for Tories from the southern provinces and a constant worry to patriot leaders.

For more than two years after Sir Peter Parker literally lost his breeches in the barrage of American fire at Charleston, South Carolina, in 1776, the great flatlands from Virginia to Florida had seen little of formal warfare. Tory rangers had swept up from the loyal Florida frontier to strike often at Georgia, where the rebels flourished in parts of the province. These rangers were usually young men. Their fathers were equally flourishing as Tories, but they battled at home to retain the status quo. A relentless and bitter internecine warfare between Whigs and Tories who hated each other with a wild vengeance had kept the Carolinas and Georgia in a state of tense embroilment, now hard to understand. The aims of both sides were so diverse that they may be put down as more selfish than loyal.

In the treaty of 1763 at the end of the French and Indian Wars, Spain had ceded Florida to England. During the Revolution many of the prominent Tories who were persecuted severely fled to Florida, as did Negroes or others who ran from one kind of authority or another. One man governed Florida for more than a decade. He was Lieutenant Colonel Patrick Tonyn of the 104th British Regiment. From 1774 to 1784 he served as colonial governor, and when he left, he turned over his office to a governor from Spain, which had again come upon the lovely southern scene.

Florida formed a refuge for the Tories not only in their plots and hostilities during the war, but also in the subsequent evacuation of the province, which lasted almost two and a half years, the major part of which was conducted under Spanish auspices.[1]

The royal government, garrison and scant population of Florida had felt the first tremors of the Revolution by 1775, especially in the difficulty of obtaining ammunition and arms from Great Britain. The British brigantine *Betsy*, from London, destined with a large quantity of gunpowder for the garrison and merchants of St. Augustine, was boarded off the bar by a rebel party from the South Carolina sloop *Commerce*, and the powder was carried away. Many of the Tories who fled to Florida during the Revolution expected to make their homes there. Some of them acquired plantations along the St. Johns River or started businesses in St. Augustine. Officials of Florida were authorized by royal mandate to receive refugees and provide for them, these provisions being set forth in a letter from the Earl of Dartmouth which expressed the hope of the King that the province might become a secure asylum for those among the rebellious colonials who were too weak to resist the violence of the times and too loyal to concur in the measures of revolt. The letter directed that free grants of land be made in Florida to such persons. These orders were then embodied in a proclamation of Governor Tonyn and had a marked effect in bringing adherents of the Crown to Florida.

Measures for the defense of Florida were taken by the royal governor in 1776 and included the organization of militia consisting of a troop of horse soldiers and a company of volunteers. Opposing forces were already rising. Frequent raids on plantations along the St. Marys River impelled Governor Tonyn to commission Thomas Brown and Daniel McGirth to raise bands of rangers among the refugees and other inhabitants. These rangers did much scouting and stole cattle in Georgia, to which province the Florida Rangers continued to be a thorn in the flesh throughout the war.[2]

From 1776 to 1778, three campaigns were made from Georgia against Florida. The first of these was made by Major General Charles Lee, then Commander of the Southern Department of the Continental Army, who was dispatched by Washington because he thought the southern states might be lost by the patriot cause unless drastic steps were taken. The campaign was actually headed by Colonel William Moultrie, who got no farther than Sunbury, Georgia, because of the unhealthy season and illness among the troops. Lieutenant Colonel Lewis V. Fuser led a thousand men, part of whom were Creek Indians, in a retaliatory expedition against that of Moultrie in 1777 and took off 2,000 cattle. During the same year Thomas Brown, now a lieutenant colonel but smarting from the memory of having been tarred and feathered by the patriots, led 300 men against them with considerable success; and in April of 1778 British Brigadier General Augustine Prevost at the head of a Tory force marched against their enemies because of the strict laws passed against those still loyal to the King by North and South Carolina. Meanwhile, about 400 Tory civilians, many of them originally from South Carolina, hurried from Augusta, Georgia, to Florida because of such laws. In his report to General Howe about the situation, Prevost said in regard to Florida, "This province can in the space of a few days be invaded [by rebels] either by land or water by an army well supplied with artillery." But he added that the Rangers and Indians were not very dependable. "The Indians, entirely intent on plunder, thought of nothing but securing all the horses they could find," he said, "and the King's troops, many of them barefoot, greatly fatigued and overcome with excessive heat, could not attempt to come up with the people who fled with all possible swiftness and were on horseback." [3]

The Tory units formed in Florida, though not always effective, took part in most of the British expeditions to the South during the latter phases of the Revolution. As has been noted, in their agility and knowledge of the wild country, they at times excelled the patriot soldiers sent against them. But the chief contribution of these southern Tories was not so much in a regular military capacity as in auxiliary movements. At times they were unpredictable. Benjamin Springer, a South Carolina refugee who was sent by General Prevost to collect livestock and provisions for the Tory troops, used his agents to plunder the plantations of Tories and patriots alike in Georgia, carry their booty into East Florida and sell it. Later, Florida Tories were with Prevost when he marched into South Carolina and unsuccessfully tried to lure General Benjamin Lincoln and his patriot forces out to fight. Some of these Florida Rangers were with Sir Henry Clinton when he captured Charleston in May, 1780, which in some ways was the most decisive British victory of the war. As one pamphleteer put it, "Beyond the Southern border was the province of Florida, from which royal troops and predatory bands could be sent by the loyal governor, Patrick Tonyn." [4]

As the war wore on and the Americans gained possession of more and more posts and territory in South Carolina and Georgia, the Tory troops withdrew farther south, and not being certain even of the safety of Florida, those people loyal to the King cast their eyes toward his islands. "East Florida and the Bahamas became the next objects of my care," wrote Clinton, "and I was consequently not inattentive to them." Like Florida, the Bahamas were sparsely settled. Since the acquisition of Florida by Britain in 1763, there had been some contact between the islands and the mainland, but this was usually limited to a ship or two each year passing from St. Augustine to Nassau or the reverse. Many Floridians became planters in the Bahamas, since all these Tories were eligible for land grants there. Three Armbrister brothers, James, John and Henry, once of Charleston, South Carolina, went to the Bahamas from East Florida during this period, and ever since, the Armbristers have been prominent in the Bahamas. Robert Chrystie Armbrister, the son of James, along with Alexander Arbuthnot, a Bahamian merchant, were the two men executed by Andrew Jackson in Florida in 1818 as an example to other Tories and Indian traders who were believed to be keeping Florida in a turmoil. Robert Armbrister, described as an intelligent, fine-looking boy of about twenty and unarmed, was deeply mourned by his father, who called the execution a "flagitious mockery of justice." Jackson was severely criticized for the act, even in the United States.[5]

An expedition of about 200 Tories, called the Royal Foresters, was organized in St. Augustine in 1783 to drive the Spanish from the Bahamas, which had been recaptured from the British. The force was led by Colonel Andrew Deveaux, a native of South Carolina, who had fought for the British until hostilities had ceased in the South, then had gone to Florida with many of his soldiers. At St. Augustine, Deveaux and his volunteers outfitted several small ships, which included two privateers. One of the ships had twenty-six guns, while another mounted sixteen. This small but sturdy fleet sailed to the Bahamas and dropped anchor on March 30, 1783, at Hole-in-the-Wall, Abaco, intending to move later on Nassau. But before the invaders could attack the fort there, the Spanish abandoned it and withdrew to a nearby field. There a skirmish took place and two Spaniards were captured by the Tories. Using stolen cannon from Spanish ships in the harbor, Deveaux occupied Fort Montagu near the main stronghold, Fort Nassau. Then this resourceful officer had his men rig up some straw figures of Tory soldiers, and thus deceived the Spanish into thinking they were outnumbered. He began to fortify a ridge near the main fort, and climaxed his novel approach by lobbing a shell into a house occupied by the Spanish governor. The Spanish surrendered.[6]

Although the foregoing action took place after the peace between Great Britain and the United States had been declared, neither the Tories nor the Spanish in the Bahamas knew of it. Some accounts have therefore called this the last action of the American Revolution. At least it brought gratification to the British leaders, who rewarded Deveaux and his men with a grant of 6,000 acres of land on the islands of Eleuthera, and this land is still held by descendants of these Tories. An offspring of one of them, William Curry, moved to Key West, Florida, in 1837 and was a leading citizen there for almost fifty years. He was a merchant, a ship-builder, a wrecker, and a public official and was known as "Rich Bill" or "Florida's first millionaire."[7]

Soon after the Deveaux expedition, other Florida Tories heard with anxiety that their province was to be handed over to Spain, so they too turned their attention to the Bahamas as a future home. But they did not wish to leave their pleasant state. Governor Tonyn wrote the British colonial secretary, Thomas Townshend, that the colony was prospering and that 12,000 new inhabitants had been added to Florida during the war years. To have to abandon their happy homes in this balmy coastal region would be a sad blow to them, and furthermore most of them could not afford it, he added. "The Bahama Islands are mere rocks," said

Tonyn, "fit only for fishermen, and the inhabitants live chiefly by wreck-ing. Nova Scotia is too cold a climate for those who have lived in the southern colonies, and entirely unfit for an outlet and comfortable habita-tion for owners of slaves." Lord North wrote Tonyn and admitted that the home government was embarrassed and perplexed over the Florida refugees. But that unfortunate official, at this late stage of the conflict, could promise little except to advise them to go to the very Bahamas which Tonyn had criticized, where, the Prime Minister said, a supply of "provisions has already been provided and dispatched." In Georgia, Governor James Wright had been warned by his council about the dan-ger of allowing Tory troops to go to Florida, but little could be done to stop them. In West Florida, a British province from 1764 to 1781, Wil-liam Bartram, the botanist, found on a visit to the Alabama region near it, that the Indians and Tories in the whole section traded extensively with the northern colonies. West Florida, being somewhat isolated from the action, in general had no desire to take part in the Revolution. The local Tories were not even able to hold Pensacola from Bernard de Gal-vez, the governor of New Spain, who bombarded and captured the town.[8]

The concern of the British in the latter phases of the Revolution was greater in the Carolinas, Virginia and Georgia, however, than in Florida. Military operations not being successful in the North, they were trans-ferred to the South in hopes of better success, partly because it was felt that a larger number of helpful Tories would be found there. If the South could be returned to the royal fold, the other colonies could be more eas-ily controlled by cutting off their supplies and blockading their ports. The plan of campaign was to start in Georgia and gradually push north-ward. To facilitate this, Savannah or Charleston was needed for a base as well as a supply port for the West Indies. So Sir Henry Clinton in No-vember, 1778, sent 3,500 British, Hessians and Tories from New York and New Jersey, who landed two miles below Savannah. Help was also ex-pected from General Prevost in Florida. Some of the Tories Clinton sent, he doubtless was glad to get rid of, many being young and single New Yorkers who had shown that they preferred boating and carting of wood to soldiering. Some had formed themselves into small companies and gone on desultory expeditions, annoying and plundering the rebel inhabi-tants on the Jersey and Connecticut coasts, and not only making more bitter enemies of these already troublesome people but introducing a mode of cruel warfare which Clinton never approved of himself.[9]

Clinton was an enigmatic personality who vacillated between con-fidence in the Tories and little respect for them as fighters. He had ob-served in 1778 that "the number and zeal of those colonists who still remained attached to the sovereignty of Great Britain undoubtedly formed the firmest ground we could rest our hopes on for extinguishing the rebellion." Yet within months, he stated that certain officials had gone back to London "influenced perhaps by the too sanguine reports of overzealous loyalists," who evidently exaggerated the extent of co-operation which Clinton was receiving from this direction. In the failure of Clinton both as a subordinate and as commander-in-chief in America is generally the same inconsistency as in that of the American Tories. Perhaps the two failures are related. As Professor William B. Willcox has discerningly pointed out, Clinton played a leading role in the war longer than any officer on either side except Washington—and Henry Knox, who succeeded Washington as commander, might also be mentioned in this regard. Clinton did not get along with his superior, William Howe, or his subordinate, Lord Cornwallis. Sir Henry was excellent as a planner but could not seem to get his plans executed. From the spring of 1776 until the end of the Revolution, he maintained that effective support would be forthcoming from the Tories only where they were persuaded that the King's forces had come to stay; and that such support could never be elicited, as London fondly imagined, by the mere appearance of the royal standard. Clinton was a timid man and at times his own worst enemy. But he carried out the reduction of Charleston, which has been called the greatest British victory of the war, with supreme confidence, using the conventional European methods. He lacked what a British officer seemingly needed to win fame in that war, "the gift for spectacular failure," such as that shown by Howe, Burgoyne and Cornwallis, all of whom are now much better known than Clinton. He did at Charleston what might have been done at Manhattan—enveloped, besieged and captured the opposing army. Like his Tory friends in America, Sir Henry Clinton was a psychological puzzle and generally ineffective.[10]

The British forces which took Savannah in 1778 included four battalions of Tories, and the city became a base for the victors' operations. By the summer of 1778, most of Georgia was back in British hands, and in a move unparalleled in any other colony during the war, Sir James Wright was restored as royal governor. The last to leave the loyal fold, Georgia was the first to return. Now more Tories than ever flocked to the colors of the King in that province. Lieutenant Colonel John Hamilton, a prominent Scottish Highlander, was sent into the back country of Georgia where other Tories arose to join him. Learning of this gathering, Colonel Andrew Pickens of South Carolina assembled a force of patriot militia and went to meet Hamilton's men, who already were raiding the countryside more than necessary for supplies. On the morning of February 14, 1779, Pickens and his 400 men came upon the Tories, about 800 in number, a few miles west of Washington, Georgia. The Tories had halted for breakfast on the north side of Kettle Creek. Part of those in the camp were at the time engaged in slaughtering a herd of stolen cattle; their camp was in disorder, their horses turned out to graze—in short, they were caught by surprise. Nonetheless, a fierce fight ensued for about forty-five minutes, after which the bested Tories scattered in all directions.[11]

Wilkes County in northwestern Georgia, where the battle of Kettle Creek was fought, became known as "Hornet's Nest" because of the sharp

conflicts there between Whigs and Tories. Deserving some claim as
queen of the hornets was Nancy Hart, cross-eyed wife of a Whig soldier
of the county, who, despite her unorthodox vision, was a crack shot with
a rifle. Many legends have grown up around the name of Nancy Hart,
one to the effect that she was stirring a large pot of soap in her fireplace
and was telling her children how, although other people were leaving
the state for South Carolina from fear of the Tories, "no drat Tory could
skeer her." Just then, her child, Sukey, tugged at her skirt and whispered,
"Ma, look at that Tory peeping at you through the crack in the chimney!"

Nancy is said to have continued to stir her soap nonchalantly, hum-
ming a lively tune and at the same time taking up a large spoon and
sticking it into the hot soap. Catching sight of the peeping Tory out of
one of her cross eyes, she suddenly pulled up the spoon, swung it toward the chimney crack, and caught the Tory square in the eyes with
the boiling lye. He let out a great yell. Then Nancy snatched her rifle
from its rack, dashed outside, captured the intruder, and bound him
with rope while taunting him for allowing himself to be captured by a
woman. Then she marched him in front of her until they reached the
Broad River, crossed it with her captive and turned him over to Colonel
Elijah Clark, Whig hero of many local clashes with the Tories, who
hanged the unfortunate man on the nearest tree.

This warlike woman figured in an even more significant episode. It
concerned American Colonel John Dooly of the same neighborhood, who
was allegedly murdered by Tories even after he had offered to surrender.
Five of the men responsible for his death were said to have called at the
cabin of Nancy Hart soon afterward and demanded food. Again she was
alone—her husband seems to have been absent during her most exciting
moments—but she received the Tories coolly, that is until they insisted
she cook for them. She replied demurely that she had no food left, that
the Tories had taken it all. Spying her last old turkey gobbler in the
yard, the leader of the Tories promptly shot its head off and ordered her
to cook the bird. She had to comply, but meanwhile urged her unwel-
come visitors to help themselves to a jug of liquor which she accommodat-
ingly produced. They complied, in fact too well, for they did not notice
that Nancy kept sending her little daughter Sukey to the spring for more
and more water. At the spring, the daughter signaled on a conch shell
hidden there for her father, Captain Benjamin Hart of the Whig militia.
As the cooking and drinking progressed and the cabin waxed warmer,
Nancy would manage to edge close to the stacked muskets of the Tories
and slip the weapons out, one at a time, through cracks between the
cabin logs. Finally one of the men spied her doing this and sprang up.
Nancy grabbed a musket. "I'll shoot the first man who moves!" she cried.

One did. She fired and he fell dead on the floor. Nancy grabbed a
second musket. The remaining men looked at her intently. They knew
she was a good shot, and could not tell at which one of them her cross
eyes were looking, so they understandingly hesitated. Just then, Sukey

arrived and said her father and his men were on their way to help. The trapped Tories realized that if they were to escape, they must do it now. Another rushed at her. He joined his dead companion on the floor. Nancy called out to the remaining three to surrender their "damned Tory carcasses to a Whig woman," which they did, and when the men came, they were taken out and hanged without further ado.[12]

Drastic actions like these may have influenced the previously tarred-and-feathered Tory Colonel Thomas Brown, who had become commander of the loyal troops in Georgia as well as Indian superintendent and a terror to all back-country Whigs. At one time, Brown and his Indian allies were hard pressed by the Americans under Elijah Clark and took refuge in an Indian trading post named "the White House," just outside Augusta. Brown was wounded and, although confined to his bed, still maintained his alertness. Twelve wounded Whigs had been left by Clark in his hasty retreat, and despite the fact that he could not get up, Brown is alleged to have ordered that they be hanged from the staircase of the house where he was staying, so that he could watch their dying agonies from his bed. That this report may have been Whig propaganda is strongly suggested by the concurrent information from Governor Wright that thirteen rebels had been hanged at this time because they had broken their paroles and fought with the Whigs against the Tories.[13]

A figure of equal controversy was the Tory leader, William, or, as called by his enemies, "Bloody Bill" Cunningham, a native of Abbeyville, South Carolina. There are two distinct versions of his career, the Whig and the Tory. Even so, there is no doubt but that his career during the Revolution was marked by violence and bloodshed, regardless of motives and manner. As a young, jovial and good-natured man of nineteen, he was an active Whig, and having been induced by Captain John Caldwell to serve as an officer in a company formed to keep the peace and hold down the Tories, Cunningham was told that he could resign from the company at any time he wished to do so. So on arriving near Charleston, he asked to be relieved, but instead was arrested and put in irons. He was tried, and although acquitted, Cunningham never forgot this duplicity, which "ended in turning into gall and bitterness all the natural good humor of his heart, and speedily changed a kind and affectionate man into a vengeful and unsparing partisan" on the British side. He became so feared by the Whigs that he was hunted like a wild beast; his only secure place of rest was in the deepest recess of some all but impenetrable forest. He dared not visit any of his family, except by stealth and under the cloud of night, lest he bring down upon them the vengeance of his persecutors.

Especially active in searching for Cunningham was Whig Captain William Ritchie, who sought him dead or alive. The former heard of the search and sent Ritchie word that he had better desist. The reply of Ritchie was that not only would he not desist, but he would shoot Cunningham down on sight, and would follow him, "if necessary, to the very gates of hell." On hearing of this, according to a Tory account, Cunning-

ham at first had a desire to take Ritchie to task immediately but was
persuaded by his brother Andrew, whose farm was next to that of Ritchie,
to leave the neighborhood for a while and allow the many Whigs there
to cool off. Accordingly, Bill Cunningham left for Savannah, while Ritchie, not knowing this, continued his search. Finally, exasperated from
lack of success, Ritchie determined to wreak his vengeance on some
other member of the Cunningham family. A fit object appeared to be
John Cunningham, although he was lame from birth and an epileptic.
Using the excuse of drafting John into the militia, Ritchie and two companions went to the home of the lame brother to get him. Upset by their
demands, John berated them for entertaining such a ridiculous idea. In
answer, they threatened to whip him into silence, grabbed him, and taking turns at striking the poor cripple, beat him to death. When William
Cunningham heard of this outrage, he swore he would never rest until
he had avenged it, and though he could not obtain a horse, he set out on
foot and walked all the way from Savannah to Ninety-six. Just prior to
this, Ritchie, not being satisfied to kill one Cunningham, had entered
the home of William's father, who was sick in bed. Despite his protests
that he knew nothing of the activities of his son, the old man was dragged
from his sick bed by his hair and severely beaten by Ritchie.

Upon arriving at the scene and hearing of this additional assault, William Cunningham went straight to Ritchie's home and found him in the
yard with seven of his followers. On seeing Cunningham, Ritchie clasped
his hands together and said to one of his men, "Lord have mercy on
me, for yonder is Cunningham, and I am a dead man."

Ritchie tried desperately to escape over a fence. But the eyes of William Cunningham, filled with a terrrible vengeance, had already fixed
him in the sights of his rifle. He fired and Ritchie fell mortally wounded,
confirming his own forecast. As the victim lay dying, Cunningham bent
over him and muttered, "I walked all the way from Savannah to kill
you!" [14]

This and other violent deeds gained Cunningham the additional char-
acterization among the Whigs of "Murdering Bill Cunningham." He and
his men left "the country through which they passed in tears." Their
marches were characterized "by celerity and destruction. Burning houses,
bloodstained homesteads indicated the course he had come, but gave no
advertisement of where he was going. In an unsuspecting hour of sleep
and domestic security, they entered the houses of solitary farmers and
sacrificed to their revenge, the obnoxious head of the family," it was
charged. In the Cloud Creek section of South Carolina, a Captain James
Butler, Jr., and some twenty of his men took refuge in a house which was
surrounded by the Tories of Cunningham, who were willing to spare the
lives of all of them except Butler. But when they all marched out under
what they thought was an honorable surrender, Butler had his hands cut
off while still alive and all the rest were killed in cold blood except two
who escaped, according to the Whig version. At Hayes' Station, Cunning-

ham and his men surrounded another body of Whigs in a house, promising to spare them if they surrendered, but adding that all would be killed if they did not. The Whigs expected relief and resisted, but were forced to surrender when the house was set on fire. As they came out, Cunningham apparently thought they were still fighting, for he told his men to pick out any one of them they chose and do away with him, which they did to the number of twenty-seven, three of them falling before Cunningham's own sword.[15]

This Revolutionary Robin Hood had a horse almost as fabulous as himself. It was named Ringtail, from a white ring around that extremity, and the Tory account describes him as "a celebrity hardly less distinguished than his owner." For example, Captain Samuel Moore, who was with Ritchie when John Cunningham was murdered, went with twenty men in search of William—a pastime evidently popular with the Whigs. Moore and his men entered the house of Andrew Cunningham, who was absent, used abusive language toward his wife, destroyed a great part of the furniture, and finished by eating as much food as they could hold, which was plenty, throwing the rest to the dogs. Moore had hardly left the house when William and Andrew Cunningham arrived. What they saw boded no good for the raiders. Setting out at once, William tracked them all day and through the night, coming upon them the next morning at the foot of a long hill filled with gullies. Upon sight of Cunningham, Moore jumped into his saddle and spurred his horse, a customary occurrence when a hunted one caught sight of "Bill." But though Moore had a fast horse, it was no match for Ringtail. After a mile and a half of furious chase over the gullies and hillsides, Moore was overtaken by Cunningham, who, after a few words of taunting contempt, cut Moore down with his sword.

Many of his escapes were due to his trusted horse, which Cunningham taught to give a jerk of his head whenever he saw anyone approaching, especially when his master was forced to sleep in his saddle as he rode along. Even after Charleston was retaken by the British Army, and many Whigs hastened to join the Tories or swear belated allegiance to the King, bands of men were still out after William Cunningham. Seven different parties, it was said, tried to capture him, but each time Ringtail helped him to escape. The goal of Cunningham was the refuge of Charleston itself. He finally made it—on Ringtail—but at a great price. Twenty-three days after they had safely reached the city, Ringtail died of the violent exertions it had been necessary for him to make in order to save his master. "Bloody Bill" . . . wept like a child and had 'Ringtail' buried with all the honors of war." [16]

Yet this same man, whom Whig-minded historians have termed a monster and cold-blooded demon, is said to have come one day upon the isolated home of a Whig soldier, John Wood, who happened to be there recovering from illness. Seeing the Tories surround his house, Wood thought it wise to surrender, so he limped out to meet them, followed by

his wife and small son. His offer to surrender was reportedly met with the
words, "Shoot him, damn him, shoot him!"

According to this version, "the intercessions and prayers of his wife to
spare him were unheeded, as were the entreaties of his little son, who
was cursed as a little rebel and ordered back into the house. The command was given by Cunningham to shoot him down. A volley was fired
into him and he fell a lifeless corpse into the arms of his wife, who
caught him as he fell. His death was instantaneous and she gently laid
his body upon the ground." [17]

Even with all these deeds attributed to him, Tory William Cunningham was never taken by the Whigs. He eventually escaped to Florida
and afterward went to England, where he received for life half pay as
a major, finally dying there after a brief illness. He is an example of an
almost legendary character of the times, glorified by his friends and condemned by his adversaries. There were many others of his ilk on both
sides, of whom space does not permit description. Cunningham, more
or less bloody, may serve as a graphic example.

Although the foregoing typical episodes of men taking the law into
their own hands cannot be justified, one strong provocation for such illegal actions was the mass of laws passed by the various colonies against
the Tories. As far as the new nation was concerned, those who remained
Tories had to be outlaws. As early as 1777 the Continental Congress had
passed a resolution recommending to the several states that as soon as
possible they confiscate and sell all the real and personal property of
Tories and invest the money from such sales in Continental loan office
certificates. The Tories felt that this was adding insult to injury. But
Congress tried to soften the blow, also resolving that "no man in these
colonies, charged with being a Tory . . . be injured in his person or his
property, or in any manner whatever disturbed, unless the proceedings
against him be founded on an order of this Congress," or of the colony
within which he resided. The main exception was any person found to
be committing some act "destructive of American liberty," which was
subject to innumerable interpretations.[18]

As with other such resolutions, these were typical of the weakness of
the new government and were not binding on the states. What did the
average Whig in the recesses of the Carolina back country know or care
about such "national laws" when it came to dealing with his hated Tory
enemies? His ready remedies were usually tar and feathers or a musket
or hanging rope. For their part, in trying to fight back, the Tories were
handicapped from the beginning by lack of arms. The patriot committees, as one of their first acts, saw to it that the Tories were disarmed
as much as possible. This lack of arms, as already seen, hindered the
effectiveness of the Tory troops with Burgoyne. This situation seems
remindful of what Senator Robert Toombs of Georgia said after the Civil
War, that his people could not fight the Yankees with cornstalks. Neither
could the Revolutionary Tories in trying to fight Yankee Doodle.

Kind words were even used in an attempt to settle the Whig–Tory dispute. The Virginia Tory, John Randolph, wrote from London to his cousin, Thomas Jefferson, a polite if audacious request: "Would it not be prudent to rescind your Declaration of Independence, to be happily re-united with your ancient and natural friend, and enjoy a peace which I most religiously think would pass all understanding?" [19] The author of the Declaration must have been grimly amused at this request.

In order to force a declaration of principles from those who were indifferent or who were secret enemies of the Revolution, and thus separate the "sheep from the goats," the state legislatures enacted Test Laws. (One Whig, perhaps not facetiously, suggested that all Tory houses be painted black.) The test laws, although varying somewhat among the states, generally required the person taking the oath to swear before the Ever-living God and the world that the war of the colonies against Great Britain was just and necessary; that he would not aid and abet the forces of Great Britain; that he renounced all allegiance to the Crown and pledged faith and true allegiance to the state in which he resided. Refusal to take the oath resulted in being disarmed, imprisoned, and made subject to special taxation and confiscation of property. Many Tories did not take the rigid and encompassing oath, while some took it with tongue in cheek, an easy way to get off the horns of a dilemma, and "sooner than lose a groat, swore the state allegiance." In most of the states, justices of the peace administered the oath, a careful record being kept of all who signed and certificates given to each signer. No traveler was safe from arrest or annoyance without presentation of such a certificate. Often the justices of the peace were paid so much for each oath they administered, with the natural result that many justices searched diligently for Tories, coaxing and threatening as they herded them to the oath-taking. Of course this treatment the Tories resented as bigoted and illegal; but the patriots countered that they had created a new state with sovereign rights, one of which was to take any necessary measures to preserve its existence. [20]

It might have been possible for the two sides to compromise these and other issues, but as in the later American Civil War, it is difficult to see just how it could have been done successfully once the lines of conflict were so severely drawn. British and Tory leaders seemed unable to understand the need for compromise until it was too late. They did not realize that the colonial legislatures had grown to maturity and now required different treatment from that received in the past. As Leonard Labaree has observed, "So long as such an unenlightened attitude persisted, peaceful compromise was impossible." Nor was it, the Tories charged, only the unfairness of the laws that they resented, but also those who passed and enforced them. A Savannah merchant declared that the Georgia constitution of 1777 had "thrown power into such hands as must ruin the country, if not timely prevented by some alteration in it." Another complained that the government was the antithesis of democracy,

that it was conducted in daily meetings at taverns and by nocturnal soci-
eties which "bellow liberty, but take every method in their power to deprive the best part of the community of even the shadow of it." This was
exemplified by the Tories' being deprived early of the right to vote or hold
office. Yet Washington Irving observed that "many of the loyalists, it
must be acknowledged, were honorable men, conscientiously engaged
in the service of their sovereign and anxious to put down what they sincerely regarded as unjustifiable rebellion." The Tories reasoned that this
was *their* country, no less than that of their opponents; they wished to
keep it what it was; and they conceived that they had at least as great
a right to take up arms to maintain the government, as their antagonists
had to take arms against it. But the patriots felt that since the Tories
had not taken the required oath of allegiance to the United States, they
were not bona fide citizens of it. An alert watch was kept on the polls
to be sure that Tories did not vote, and judging from the results, the
precautions appear to have been effective. Any Tory who violated the
election laws was subject to fine and imprisonment.[21]

In addition to the hardship of being prevented from voting, a person
loyal to the King could not bring legal action in the courts of the colonies
after they rebelled, and he could be vilified or assaulted and still get no
help from the courts. Nor was the right of habeas corpus usually available
to him. For example, John Dunn of New York told how he was at home
recovering from illness when he was seized by armed men who had entered his home without permission. Taken to a coffeehouse along with
another Tory, Dunn procured a patriot attorney but was not allowed to
leave the café. Asked by what authority he was detained, Dunn's captors
replied that it was the desire of some gentlemen to the southward to
question him about his political sentiments. Dunn was then led away
by armed men and kept in jail nine months without a trial.

As to the states themselves, they varied in their attitudes much as their
people differ on political issues today. Georgia patriots were slow to act
against the Tories, but in 1778 they banished and declared forfeit the
property of dozens of Tories said to have been guilty of treason against
the state, among them Governor James Wright, who was later to return
to his office. Some Georgia Tories were simply fined eight or twelve per
cent of the value of their estates. A few of them who had fled from
the state were even authorized to return. But many Georgians were so
inflamed against the government of Great Britain and its adherents in
America that some of the Tories who sought to go back to their homes
there after the war were assaulted and mobbed. On the other hand, a
large number of the most respected people in Georgia were Tories, having
a real affection toward George III for whose father the state was named.

In South Carolina the Tories were divided into four classes, as was
shown by what happened after the fall of Charleston to the British. At
that time 210 persons who styled themselves "Addressers" stated they
were the principal inhabitants of that city and asked Sir Henry Clinton to

be allowed readmission as British subjects. Of these, sixty-three were later banished and lost their property by forfeiture because they had asked to be armed on the royal side. Others were sent away for having held positions under the Crown. After Cornwallis smashed the army of Gates at Camden, thirteen South Carolina Tories congratulated him, only to find themselves punished, when the patriots regained the upper hand, for being so obnoxious. Thus the "Addressers," "Petitioners," "Congratulators" and "Obnoxious" among the Tories eventually received short shrift in South Carolina. At the war's beginning, South Carolina had tried to prevent the departure of those remaining loyal to the King, but after the Declaration of Independence their presence proved embarrassing and the laws were changed so as to force them to leave. Four who dared to return to Charleston in 1783 were slain. Another Tory who had been tried for atrocities and legally acquitted was lynched when he came back. One reason for such bitterness at Charleston was the opposition of the tradesmen and workers to the return of the wealthy planters, who had strong reasons for remaining loyal to the Crown because of favorable bounties on indigo and rice and the general prosperity of the colony when war broke out. A South Carolina Tory was tried for having called his stray dog Tory, thus presumably intimating that the Tory led a dog's life. But he pleaded that he was intoxicated at the time he named the dog, and was let off with a reprimand from the bench.[22]

A South Carolinian whose Toryism was tested was George Walker. At Charleston he was asked by a mob to "drink damnation to King George III and all the rascals about him." He refused to comply and was seized and given a sham trial. His sentence: to be put in a cart, stripped, tarred and feathered, carried through the streets and pelted for five hours with whatever could be found in the streets, pumped water on for another hour, and then thrown off the wharf. He was given a chance, after the sentence was pronounced, to drink the toast to the rebel cause; instead, he drank damnation to them, then hurled the bowl among the mob. The sentence was carried out to the letter. He reported that his left eye was damaged by the tar, that two ribs were broken when he was thrown off the wharf, and that if a boat had not happened to be near, he would have drowned.

North Carolina, in keeping with her tradition of farsighted moderation, sought at first to persuade the Tories rather than coerce them. But few took advantage of this consideration, so in 1777 the state directed that persons who refused to take the oath of allegiance should be banished, and those who gave active support to the British should be imprisoned for the duration of the conflict and lose half of their property. Two years later, as anti-Tory sentiment deepened, sixty-eight individuals and four mercantile firms had their property confiscated. In 1783, an act of pardon extended relief to many of the less prominent and violent Tories, but even these were often unable to effect the return of their possessions, and sales of such property went on until 1790. The conspicuous, the wealthy, the inveterate loyalists, together with those who had committed atrocities, were not forgiven. Quakers, Moravians, Mennonites and Dunkards were not obligated to defend the patriot government if they had conscientiously taken the oath. By the summer of 1780, North Carolina jails were overflowing with prisoners accused of treason. Most of these were then disposed of in a reasonable manner, but the seizure of Tory property became so profitable that the state assembly had to regulate this further by law.[23]

Neighboring Virginia, as Professor Emory G. Evans has pointed out, at the outbreak of the Revolution owed two of the five million pounds of American indebtedness to Great Britain. It is significantly possible that this could have influenced her merchants in rebelling against the land to which they owed so much in so many ways. At first there were few Tories in Virginia, but these were prominent, such as Attorney General John Randolph, William Byrd III, Richard Corbin and Ralph Wormely, to name those best known and earliest prosecuted. Virginia seemed to sense that her Tories must be dealt with at once or they would prevail. So as early as 1776, Tories were declared to be subject to imprisonment, or death and loss of property. By the next year, any who refused to take the oath of allegiance to the state were denied suffrage and the right to sue for debts. Thus, by 1777, "loyalist legislation became closely identified with state finance." For example, British sympathizers were not permitted to acquire land and were taxed doubly, later triply. The state confiscated and sold Tory property promiscuously, enriching smart patriot purchasers who forced depreciated Continental currency on the Tory owners for land and buildings. Early in 1779, the Collector of the Port of Glasgow wrote the Board of Customs in England that "It is generally believed a stop would be brought to the war in North America this ensuing season. The inhabitants of Virginia and the other provinces are sick of it. General Washington has a very poor army." As this appraisal was changed, so was the feeling against the Tories in Virginia softened by the war's end. Prominent in this attitude of leniency was none other than the once fiery Patrick Henry who grew more conservative with age and affluence. Tories were allowed to return to Virginia, except those who had borne arms for the British. Thomas Jefferson in his *Notes on the State of Virginia* mentioned that not a single Tory had been executed for treason in Virginia, a fact which he attributed to "the lenity of our government and the unanimity of its inhabitants."

Nicholas Cresswell left his father's sheep-raising farm in northern England and came to Virginia, landing unintentionally in the midst of the Revolution. He soon became bored with it all and noted in his journal intriguingly, "Abundance of political puffs and lies told to amuse the public. It is a matter of dispute with me whether the Tories or the Whigs are the greatest propagators of falsehood." Discouraged with the trend of events, Cresswell took to drinking too much, but not too much to observe sarcastically in 1777 that "Washington's name is extolled to the clouds.

Alexander, Pompey and Hannibal were but pygmy generals in comparison with the magnanimous Washington. Poor General Howe is ridiculed in all companies and all my countrymen abused. I am obliged to hear this daily and dare not speak a word in their favor." [24]

In Maryland there was strong opposition to the seizure of Tory property because it was widely believed that England would compel its return in the peace treaty.

"Good God!" exclaimed a Maryland patriot in 1780. "What is this state come to . . . we cannot take the property of our enemies to pay our taxes, when if it was in their power, they would take our lives."

Sam Finley, a Tory of Washington County, Maryland, was fined ten pounds for not enrolling to fight with the patriots. He was also charged with altering a public newspaper by making an American army in an attack appear to lose 5,000 men instead of 500.

Though slow to act against the Tories, Maryland made up for lost time once it began. In a meeting of the assembly in 1777, fear was expressed by the more radical members that an uprising of the Tories might occur on the lower eastern shore. Troops were accordingly dispatched to that region and the furore and expense resulting from this activity caused a wave of resentment against prominent Tories. Persons who affirmed the authority of Great Britain were to be fined and imprisoned; no one would be allowed to travel without a pass. Finally a test law was passed, but the Quakers, Dunkards and Methodists refused to take the oath because of conscientious objections, so that about one-third of the state was not committed. Professional persons were forbidden, if they were Tories, to practice their occupations. A Maryland surgeon who was only a mild Tory reported that his business gradually declined until he had none. He said that people were afraid to employ him. Tories became social lepers and only by great sacrifices kept up their commercial activity. Half of the heavy fines for continuing any profession went to the prosecutor of the Tories—a situation of built-in corruption. Every successful man was certain to have jealous rivals who would seize upon any opportunity to accuse him and thus accomplish his downfall and diminish his fortune. Many a sin, here as elsewhere, was committed in the name of anti-Toryism.[25]

Delaware was believed by some patriot leaders to have had more Tories in proportion to its small population than any other state, though this has been questioned by recent historians. Many there certainly were loyal to the King, and there was also a significant number who did not seem to care which side triumphed, and sat on the fence as long as they could, waiting to jump into the ranks of whoever won. In time, public pressure forced the legislature to pass measures against the Tories. Persons convicted of waging war against the state were to suffer death without benefit of clergy and their lands were to be forfeited. Tory ministers of Delaware, as has been seen, were effectively silenced by the local laws. When Caesar Rodney became president of the state, as its head was then called, new loyalty laws were passed and vigorously enforced. Every white male was required to take an oath of allegiance to the state, goods of Tories caught trading with the British were confiscated, and a third law offered "free pardon and oblivion" to all Tories—except forty-six very active ones—who by August 1, 1778, should appear before a designated legal official and take the oath of allegiance. If not, their property would be sold. At least they had a plain offer.

These Tories received great encouragement after the defeat of Washington at Brandywine in the summer of 1777. At Lewes, Delaware, Tories came in by the hundreds to drink the health of the King and damn the rebels. A Whig who tried to speak for his side was assaulted with "fists, clubs and feet." But later as the Whigs gradually gained control of the legislature, Tories who did not take the oath of allegiance were excluded from voting, lost what control they had of the local government, and were broken in morale.[26]

A Tory historian in an address half a century ago made a remark applicable to the Tory in general: "It certainly was his misfortune that he was a conservative in a time of accelerated progress, and an aristocrat, as he usually was, in a democratic land." This was all too true of a Tory named Cheney Clow. He was first on the list of those not to be pardoned. He had instigated a revolt in the April, 1778, meeting of the Delaware legislature and had gathered a hundred other Tories into a sort of fort. When it was overcome by patriot troops, there was fear that in retaliation, Clow and his men would regroup and march against the capital at Dover. But instead about half of his force was captured, though Clow himself, who was called "a back-sliding Methodist," was not apprehended until 1782.[27]

The capture of Cheney Clow and his subsequent fate became a *cause célèbre* which is argued by historians to this day, his story having reached the proportions of a romantic legend in Delaware. Following the uprising, a warrant had been issued for the arrest of Clow, and Sheriff John Clayton of Kent County and a large posse found him to be in his home. But taking him was no easy task. The house was dark, its doors closed and barred. Clayton shouted that he had come for Clow and demanded that he come out and surrender. The response was a prompt and rapid succession of shots from inside the house. The sheriff and his men then spread out and surrounded the building, some of them attempting to break in, others firing volley after volley through the windows. Finally the front door was battered down, and in the ensuing melee, one of the posse, Joseph Moore, was shot and killed.

Finally succeeding in getting inside the house, the posse found only Clow and his wife. She had been seriously wounded in the breast but had been able to load several guns and hand them to her husband, so that the posse had thought there were a number of defenders. Now Clow saw that further resistance was senseless and surrendered. He asked only that he be allowed to dress for the ride to Dover, and this request being granted, he put on his uniform of a captain in the British army. Then he was placed on a horse and the party started on their ride. Halfway to Dover, they were met by a company of militia headed by one Isaac Griffin, who furiously demanded the surrender of Clow so that they could hang him without further ado. Clayton refused, and he and his men prepared to defend their prisoner. They managed to avert a fight and took their man on to jail. Soon he was indicted by a grand jury for treason, but pleaded not guilty, claiming that he was a British officer, had never sworn allegiance to any other government, was not subject to trial by a civil court and therefore should be considered a prisoner of war. The jury accepted this reasonable argument and acquitted Clow of the charge of treason. But they held him in bail of 10,000 pounds, which he could not furnish, this evidently being a device to keep him in jail.

Five months later, on May 5, 1783, Cheney Clow was put on trial for the murder of Joseph Moore. Part of the jury had been in American military service and could hardly be expected to have been impartial. In his defense, Clow contended that the state had failed to prove that he had shot Moore when the latter tried to break into his house, and that had he shot him, it would have been in self-defense, which anyone in his own home had a right to. Even Sheriff Clayton testified that in his opinion, Clow did not shoot Moore, that the nature of his fatal injuries indicated he had been accidentally shot from behind by one of his own party. Other members of the sheriff's posse testified to the same effect. Little or no direct evidence was produced to show that Clow killed Moore. But the meager testimony offered by the state was sufficient for a jury which was obviously anxious to convict anyway, so a verdict of guilty was promptly rendered. The prisoner arose and heard the sentence intoned, that he be taken to the place of execution and there be hanged by the neck until he was dead.

But the matter was not that simple. It devolved upon President Nicholas Van Dyke of Delaware to fix the time and place of execution and to issue a warrant for it. The executive was slow to act, for Van Dyke is said to have felt that the prisoner was not guilty and wanted to pardon him. However, the executive did nothing but leave poor Clow in jail. In October of 1786, the President was succeeded by Thomas Collins, who also granted Clow successive stays of execution. A few fair-minded men petitioned for clemency in this case, since the war was over, the new country independent, and much of the ill feeling between Whig and Tory had subsided. But ill feeling had not sufficiently subsided in the case of Cheney Clow, who must have had a special penchant for incurring hatred. Petitions poured in on Collins demanding that a warrant for the execution of the prisoner be issued. Meanwhile, Clow's spirit had broken. He had been confined to jail for six long and weary years and was constantly menaced by his inexorable foes. His son had died; his wife, who had faithfully pled for mercy for her husband, finally gave up her fruitless efforts; and the haunted and dejected prisoner, his heart filled with despair, himself gave up and wished to live no longer in such misery.

Clow wrote a letter to President Collins in which he requested a pardon be granted at once; if this were not forthcoming, then he asked that a warrant be issued without further delay for his execution. The pardon was not granted; the warrant was issued. Cheney Clow went bravely to his death, singing a hymn as he walked erectly to the scaffold. Caesar Rodney, to his credit, declared that day that he had never wished to be head of the state of Delaware until then, and he only wished for it then so that he might pardon Clow. According to the records of the court, "A strange but strong feeling of revulsion seized upon the crowd assembled to witness the last sad act of the tragedy which they had labored so long and so hard to get up. And a late but unavailing remorse sank deep into the hearts of many. Soon everybody agreed that Cheney Clow had fallen victim to the ill-judged violence of party feeling. But the scene had closed, and the repentance and mercy came too late to prevent an act which must ever be deplored." [28]

Sad though such cases might be, the laws against the Tories remained strict. In Pennsylvania, sixty-two persons designated by name were required by the executive council to surrender themselves to a judge or justice of peace within a specified time and await trial for treason, failure to do so to render them attainted. Later, thirty-six persons, also named, who had previously been attainted of treason, had their estates confiscated. Pennsylvania also had probably the harshest laws forbidding professional men to engage in their occupations if they were Tories. Subsequently, clerks, notaries and sergeants-at-arms were added to the proscribed list. The victims commented bitterly that the new patriot officials would "rather rule in Hell than serve in Heaven." The answer to this incisive blast was the total prohibition of any work for the Tories.

When the British were in Philadelphia, some of the trustees of the College of Philadelphia had already had their powers suspended. The key to their former activity, and that of their loyal associates in all the important walks of life, was the power of the British to support and protect them; with this power gone, the Tories were left to their own resources and to the merciless vengeance of the patriots. Rectors, professors, masters and tutors of any college might be prosecuted for performing their duties if they had Tory sympathies, the inducement for the prosecutor being half the 500 pounds which might be levied against the defendant. It was said of Pennsylvania druggists, if they were suspected of loyalty to the Crown, that they usually poisoned people. Such talk, of course, cut deeply into their trade. Fourteen Quakers were forced into the militia, compelled to serve as sentinels and to march with muskets tied to their bodies. At a meeting of militia in Philadelphia on October 4, 1779, it was planned to seize and ship Tory women and children to New York, along with candidates for election who might oppose radical patriot leaders. James Wilson was hated because he had defended a number of Tories. When he was threatened by a mob, Wilson and a group of his friends, including Thomas Mifflin, Robert Morris, George Clymer and other well-known citizens, gathered at his house and waited. The mob came, shots were fired, a member of the attackers was killed and others wounded. Mifflin opened a second story window of the house and attempted to speak to the crowd. He was fired at and almost hit, whereupon he returned the fire. At this critical moment, President Joseph Reed of Pennsylvania and the City Light Horse Troop arrived on the scene and dispersed the mob.[29]

New Jersey was the scene of reciprocal raiding of farms and homes by Tories and Whigs. They seemed to vie with each other in burning, pillaging, stealing food, driving off horses and cattle, and sometimes kidnaping the owners. Trading with the enemy was carried on by both Whigs and Tories, despite prescribed punishments by the patriot authorities, which ranged from pillorying and cropping to imprisonment. Whereas the British paid gold for provisions, the American paper money was worthless; that was the difference between patriotism and its opposite. When the British wintered in Philadelphia, they easily obtained supplies in the surrounding country from farmers who put their pocketbooks before anything else.

Major Philip Van Cortland of the New Jersey Volunteers was obliged to take refuge in the mountains, while his property was "wasted and destroyed by the rebel officers and soldiers who were continually quartered in his house," he reported. "His family was treated in a manner that would disgrace the most savage barbarians, reduced in the space of three months from affluence to want the common necessaries of life, and then by Mr. Washington's order, inhumanly turned out of doors in a snow storm to make room for the sick of the army." Daniel Coxe, Tory Trenton attorney, said he might have become wealthy and distinguished if he had sacrificed his principles, but instead, he clung to his allegiance to the King—and what did he get as a reward? Not Americans but British troops "ransacked and pillaged his house and left it in most wanton desolation." Patriot Justice Joseph Hedden was taken by the Tories in Newark and brought to New York City for punishment. A loyal newspaper stated that Mrs. Hedden was wounded and "it was what she merited by her assaulting and opposing all in her power the carrying away of her husband." The account added that the justice deserved rough treatment because of the "acts of barbarity he had frequently committed on many of his Majesty's loyal subjects. . . . Among many of his persecutions were imprisonment, keeping some several days without meat, drink or any fire in the severity of winter, reducing others to bread and water only, stripping many women and children of their clothing, beds and household furniture, and then banishing them without the necessaries of life and selling their estates, to his no small emolument." Justice Hedden had also allegedly banished a helpless woman because her husband was a Tory and sent a guard after her, who found her six miles from Newark, "very weak and unable to travel, having been delivered of twins about fourteen days before, which excited so much compassion in the guard that he returned and remonstrated to Hedden that executing his order would be the death of the woman.

" 'Let her die!' Hedden replied. 'There will be one damned Tory less.' "

So the guard was sent a second time and took her and her twins in a wagon to Newark, although she fainted from weakness. When she arrived in Newark, "her deplorable case drew tears even from the eyes of the rebels; and the kind offices of some friends of her sex enabled her the next day to go through the last stage of her journey to Bergen, where soon afterward, her death and the death of her two innocent babes closed the dismal tragedy." [30]

A tragedy of a more massive nature took place at Old Tappan, just south of the New Jersey–New York state line. There on the evening of September 28, 1778, American Colonel George Baylor and some 150 light horse troops were ensconced—safely, they thought—for the night. The Dutch barn, tan house and other buildings on the farm of Cornelius Haring made snug sleeping quarters for the tired patriots, although Baylor, when he arrived, had been warned by the farmer that British and Tory troops were nearby. Ignoring the warning, Baylor and his men were soon sound asleep.

Hardly had the patriots hit their bedding when a Tory friend of Haring's set out to warn the redcoats. Down the road just a few miles, he met the men of General Charles Grey, the British officer already nicknamed "No Flint" because of his stealthy and successful bayonet massacre of Anthony Wayne's sleeping troops at Paoli, Pennsylvania, just a year before. Now Grey was to do it again. Upon learning of the presence of the Americans at Old Tappan, the general moved decisively. He spread six companies of light infantry quietly around Haring's houses and barns, while the rest of his troops moved straight up the Paramus road toward Baylor's twelve pickets.

At 2 A.M., the redcoats struck. Bursting from the darkness with cries of "No quarter to rebels!" Grey's infantrymen poured into the sleeping quarters of the patriots. Surprised and half asleep, they were bayoneted and clubbed as they tried to rise. The orders were to kill them all and take no prisoners, though not all of the British carried out the cruel instructions. Colonel Baylor and his major tried to hide in a huge Dutch fireplace, but were found and bayoneted, the latter dying of his wounds. Americans who endeavored to hide in the hay were run through until the blood dripped freely to the floor below. Out of the 150 victims, a third were killed, many of the others wounded. Major John André jubilantly made a map of the local area where the massacre took place. In just two years, he was to be hanged a few miles from the spot.

The royal reply to the charges that Tories were ravaging the land was summed up neatly by editor James Rivington. With accustomed vitriol he wrote, "The Rebels, in their accounts of these excursions, speak of the Refugees as thieves, robbers and murderers, while they represent their people when concerned in the same kind of transactions as brave warriors, heroes and demigods." [31]

Adding to the eccentricities of Rivington was his foppishness. He dressed in the extreme fashion of the day, with curled and powdered hair, claret-colored coat, scarlet waistcoat trimmed with gold lace, buckskin breeches and top boots—to mention a few of his sartorial splendors. He was as fastidious in his wines as in his clothes. Rivington was extremely afraid of the tumultuous Ethan Allen, who had threatened him more than once. An unexpected encounter was related by Rivington himself. "I was sitting, after a good dinner, alone," he said, referring to an evening in his house at Pearl and Wall Streets in New York City, "with a bottle of Madeira before me, when I heard an unusual noise in the street. I was in the second story, and stepping to the window, saw a tall figure in tarnished regimentals, with a large cocked hat and an enormous long sword, followed by a crowd of boys, who occasionally cheered him with huzzas, of which he seemed insensible. He came to my door and stopped. I could see no more. My heart told me it was Ethan Allen. I shut down my window and retired behind my table and bottle. I was certain the hour of reckoning had come. There was no retreat. Mr. Staples, my clerk, came in, paler than ever, and clasping his hands said, 'Master, he is come.'

" 'I know it.'

" 'He entered the store and asked if James Rivington lived there. I answered, "Yes, Sir." '

" ' "Is he at home?" '

" ' "I will go and see, Sir," I said; and now, Master, what is to be done? There he is in the store and the boys peeping at him from the street.'

"I made up my mind. I looked at the bottle of Madeira—possibly took a glass.

" 'Show him up,' said I, 'and if such Madeira cannot mollify him, he must be harder than adamant.'

"There was a fearful moment of suspense. I heard him on the stairs, his long sword clanking at every step. In he walked.

" 'Is your name James Rivington?'

" 'It is, Sir, and no man could be more happy than I to see Colonel Ethan Allen.'

" 'Sir, I have come—'

" 'Not another word, my dear colonel, until you have taken a seat and a glass of old Madeira.'

" 'But, Sir, I don't think it proper—'

" 'Not another word, Colonel. Taste this wine; I have had it in glass for ten years. Old wine, you know, unless it is originally sound, never improves with age.'

"He took a glass, swallowed the wine, smacked his lips and shook his head approvingly.

" 'Sir, I come—'

" 'Not another word until you have taken another glass, and then, my dear Colonel, we will talk of old affairs, and I have some droll events to detail.'

"In short, we finished two bottles of Madeira and parted as good friends as if we never had cause to be otherwise." [32]

The general situation regarding laws against Tories in New York—which furnished more soldiers for George III than it did for George Washington—was far from humorous, however. County committees were authorized to apprehend and decide upon the guilt of any inhabitants who were supposed to conduct correspondence with the enemy or commit any similar offense, and the committee would punish those they judged to be guilty with imprisonment for three months or banishment. Americans searching for Tories were often called "Tory hunting parties," and when the unfortunate loyal people were found, they were frequently subjected to "kangaroo courts" in which full advantage was taken of them by malicious or envious neighbors. A foreman of a grand jury testified that proceedings concerning Tories were actually revealed to the patriot leaders, a violation of English common law which was held to be almost sacred in the judicial system. Hugh and Alexander Wallace, loyal brothers of New York, supplied Sir Henry Clinton "with gold and silver to a large amount for the service of the Southern expedition at a time of the greatest emergency." Mrs. John Rapelje of Brooklyn persisted in drinking tea after it was prohibited by the Americans, and as a result had a cannon ball fired into her house, almost hitting her—while she was drinking tea! She retaliated by giving intelligence of the patriot movements to the British army. Tory lawyers in New York were required by October, 1779, to produce a certificate of attachments to "the liberties and independence of America" by patriot courts, penalty being suspension of licenses. A parent whose sons joined the British was fined nine pence on the pound of his estate for each such son. Peter Van Schaak of Kinderhook, New York, prominent lawyer and friend of John Jay, Gouverneur Morris and George Clinton had an excruciating experience. In 1778, Mrs. Van Schaack became ill and her doctors felt that it was important that she go from Kinderhook to New York City where she was born and where the air and nearness to the sea were thought to do her good. Her husband accordingly applied to his "friend," George Clinton, then governor of New York, for permission for her to enter the British lines. The request was refused. She became worse, and when she had reached a dying condition, Van Schaack asked again. Again the request was refused. In desperation he asked that a renowned British surgeon who was with the army of Burgoyne be allowed to visit her. He was refused. Mrs. Van Schaack died, forgiving those who had refused her. Her husband was later banished, the order being signed by a former law student of his, Leonard Gansevoort. Van Schaak wrote to him, "Leonard, you decided from principle, so did I." [33]

The monetary emergency brought legal as well as economic difficulties to Tories in New York. Tenants depended on landlords for financial help, while Whig mortgage-holders caused feelings of insecurity among the landowners themselves. In regard to this situation, Egbert Benson, a future American Federalist, remarked in 1779 that "for two years, the Whigs have done my state more damage than the Tories." In some Tory families, the head of the house had fled and left his wife and children on the unworked farm, living among patriot officials who were torn between feelings of duty and compassion as to whether or not to evict them. "They are like the wandering Israelites and equally cursed by their maker," commented Thomas Clark at White Plains in 1778. There was also Tory discontent in Dutchess County, concentrated in three areas, "the militia, the cost of living and the land." But when the British returned to New York later in the war, a Tory rhapsodized:

> In spite of Congressional tyrants, you see
> We are once more assembled, all happy and free.
> In social good humor, to drink, chat and sing
> And toast what we love in our hearts—Church and King! [34]

Much of the life of the Long Island Tories was not "happy and free," however. It was a common sight in the afternoon to see a farmer driving a flock of turkeys, geese, ducks or "dunghill fowls" and locking them up in his cellar for the night, to secure them from the robbers of both sides of the war, who frequently plundered the farms on the island. "It was no uncommon thing for a farmer, his wife and children, to sleep in one room, while his sheep were bleating in the room adjoining, his hogs grunting in the kitchen, and the cocks crowing, hens cackling, ducks quacking and geese hissing in the cellar." [35]

In Connecticut, Toryism was less secular than sectarian in character, chiefly because of jealousies and fears engendered by strong religious prejudices. Loyal persons were in all classes; aristocratic families, farmers of moderate means, artisans, Anglican ministers, merchants, lawyers and physicians. As the patriots gained the upper hand, laws were passed providing that any person who libeled or defamed Congress or the Connecticut General Assembly should be tried. If convicted, he might be fined, disarmed, imprisoned or disfranchised. There was also a law providing for the seizure and confiscation of the estates of those who sought royal protection and absented themselves from their homes or the country. But the offenses of furnishing supplies to the royal army or navy or giving them information, of enlisting or procuring others to enlist in them, and of piloting or assisting naval vessels, were punished more mildly and resulted only in the loss of estate and personal liberty for a term not exceeding three years. As a consequence of this moderate attitude, hundreds of potential Tories retracted and became patriot citizens.

Not all loyal individuals fared well, however. Samuel Ketchum of Norwalk testified that his father was harassed by patriot mobs from 1774 until 1779, when he joined the British and escaped the persecution. The son did not himself bear arms, and for this reason, when Benedict Arnold appeared in the state at the head of patriot troops, he ordered Ketchum and "a few more Tories shut up in a house and burnt," a fate which they were able to elude. Moses Dunbar of Wallingford, Connecticut, was not so fortunate. He was a courageous and outspoken young Tory and so was attacked by a mob of forty men. Escaping to Long Island, he accepted a commission as a captain in the regiment of Colonel Fanning. Dunbar then returned to Connecticut to recruit men for the British, an activity in which he was somewhat successful, enrolling one named, ironically, John Adams. Angry patriots caught Dunbar, tried him at Hartford and sentenced him to death. He again escaped, only to be recaptured. He was executed on March 19, 1777. The young officer was described as being a "man of high character, inflexible courage and sincere devotion to his religious and political convictions." Just six months before, another young Connecticut captain, Nathan Hale, was captured by the British and hanged as a spy, saying he had only one life to give for his country. And though hardly known, as compared to that martyr, Moses Dunbar was also a hero, even though he was a Tory. He too made a parting statement: "I depart in a state of peace with God and my own conscience." [36]

Although the Continental currency was worth no more in Connecticut than elsewhere, one patriot parson owned some to his regret. He was captured by the British at Kingsbridge with some of the "dirty money" in one of his shoes, brought into New York, forced to eat the money and to swear that he would not pray again for the Congress "or their doer of dirty work, Mr. Washington." His punishment was slight compared to that of a number of Tories who were consigned to the infamous Newgate Prison at East Granby, Connecticut. It was the old abandoned Simsbury Mines where once copper was obtained. Later described as a "den of horrors which surpassed that of the Black Hole of Calcutta," the mine was some sixty feet underground, the only entrance being by means of a ladder down a narrow shaft to caverns where the darkness was intense, the caves reeked with filth, vermin abounded, water trickled from the roof and oozed from the sides from which masses of earth were frequently falling. Here twenty-eight Tories were confined on the eighteenth of May, 1781, and determined to escape even if it meant death in the attempt. At 10 P.M. when all the guards except two had gone to bed, as prearranged, the wife of one of the prisoners appeared at the entrance to the mine and asked to see her husband. The guard removed the hatch which covered the entrance and as he did, the prisoners below who had gathered for this long-awaited opportunity quickly scrambled up the ladder, seized the guards and disarmed them. The captain of the guard, now awakened, rushed out and tried to restore order, but was shot down by the prisoners using the captured guns. The Tories then herded the guards down into the prison, fastened down the hatch and made their escape from the place which they had understandably nicknamed "Hell."

The foregoing Tory account of the Newgate Prison doubtless is based upon the truth, but it should be pointed out that the infernal place was not especially designed for their punishment. The mines had been used for several years before the Revolution for the confinement of ordinary criminals, and its use was continued after the war began. "The barbarity of imprisonment in this underground dungeon," commented Epaphroditus Peck, "was a part of the crude and merciless penal practice of the time, and not evidence of any great malice against the Tories." [37]

In Rhode Island, death and confiscation were prescribed by law for any person who communicated with the British ministry or their agents or who supplied their armed forces or piloted their ships. Despite the gentle liberality imbued by the founder of the colony, this smallest of them was in one way the toughest. It passed a resolve that if any of its citizens preached or prayed for the King, or in any way acknowledged him to be their sovereign, they would be guilty of a high misdemeanor and would be fined 100,000 pounds of "lawful money," pay all costs of prosecution and be jailed until "the same be satisfied." The assembly, however, in a moment of generosity, did pass a law for the relief of "persons of tender consciences" or for those who were sincere objectors to warfare. With this escape clause in mind, there soon developed so many men with "tender consciences" that the law was made stricter within two months.

Along with New York, Rhode Island supplied a major part of the "Tories' own navy." Need for such a service arose because the British army toward the latter part of the war was in sore need of fuel and provisions. Prominent Tories accordingly fitted out vessels at their own expense, plied these along the eastern coast and did such an effective job of obtaining supplies, including medicines for their hospitals, that the prices of provisions fell considerably. The Tory sailors often carried off not only the materials but also the patriot guards protecting them, it was reported. These vessels operated under the authority of Sir Henry Clinton and undertook a sea service which obtained needed supplies for the British and gave employment and subsistence to hundreds of Tories. While not employed in this service, the ships were used to protect the harbors of Rhode Island when the British occupied this region, to furnish convoys to transports which brought in royal troops and supplies, and to cover the landings of these men when necessary. Tories from these vessels disembarked and served as guides for the troops as well as helpful flanking parties. Later the Tory ships went to Martha's Vineyard and cut many of the patriot sea communications between the northern and southern parts of the colonies. They took and destroyed a number of American vessels, some of them laden with cannon and other military equipment. Using Nantucket as a base, they also cut off much of the trade between Boston and the French West Indies. The towns of Chilmark and Edgartown on Martha's Vineyard were said to have agreed by a unanimous vote to help supply the royal garrisons of Rhode Island with fuel and fresh provisions. This service was stopped only when the British evacuated that colony.[38]

One of the prominent Tories engaged in this maritime activity was George Leonard of Rhode Island, who put all of his wealth plus all the credit he could obtain into fitting out the ships. He went to Boston where he had prepared and manned a small fleet consisting of seven armed vessels, three transports and several armed boats for the purpose of "annoying the sea coast." He reported that the people under his guidance "were at all times a faithful band of guides and pilots to the King's army and navy, also convoying transports and supply ships of the British fleet." In a letter dated September 20, 1779, to Admiral Marriot Arbuthnot, the British naval commander in America at the time, Leonard explained another important reason why the Tories formed their own navy. "The people under my direction are loyalists of this country who fled for protection to the British standard," Leonard wrote, "unwilling to be idle spectators of a contest where their happiness depends on the success of the British arms; we were also unwilling to enter as common seamen on board his Majesty's ships or as soldiers in the army, as most of us were by birth and education, gentlemen." [39]

Higher up the New England coast, barges manned by Tories often raided the homes of the settlers living near the water, sometimes at their peril. One Tory named Pomeroy guided a barge into Bay Point, Maine, and with other Tories landed and seized a rebel named Robert Jameson, a giant of a man. Several of them carried him aboard the barge while others of the group took his provisions. But when they had finished their plundering, they tried to get Jameson off the barge and he refused to budge. His wife came and tried to persuade him but he would not stir, indicating that he was planning to get even with his captors. As the barge was leaving the inlet, Jameson let out a bellowing shout for a patriot schooner just coming in, asking for help. A fog prevented such assistance and Jameson escaped. After the war, he came across Pomeroy, wrested his musket away from him, beat him unconscious, and then for good measure gave him a vengeful thrust with his own bayonet as he lay on the ground. Jameson proved to be a kind of post-war, one-man army in his personal revenge. He found John Long, another Tory, in a tavern, after peace was signed, and quietly asked the tavern keeper to build a big fire in the fireplace. When the logs were blazing brightly, the huge Jameson grabbed Long up in his arms and threw him onto the burning logs like a stick of wood. Long was blistered and singed.

"There, burn the harbor village again, will you!" his tormentor roared.[40]

New Hampshire passed acts of condemnation and confiscation and prohibited seventy-six of her former citizens from returning. The estates of twenty-eight of them were forfeited. General John Sullivan wrote Washington early in the war regarding the defenses of Portsmouth Harbor, about "that infernal crew of Tories who have laughed at the Congress and despised the friends of liberty." In Claremont was a hiding place for Tories, one of a chain extending from New York to Canada. The occupants apparently specialized in deliberately passing off the worthless Continental currency in an effort to ruin the rebellion by inflation. An especially active link in the chain of Tory hideouts extended from Londonderry, New Hampshire, to Hollis, thence to Shrewsbury, Massachusetts, to Groton, Connecticut, and on to New York, The Claremont hiding place was known as "Tory Hole" and was protected on three sides by a swamp covered with a thick growth of alder bushes, and on the fourth side by a steep bank about thirty feet high. Here meetings of the Tories were held and travelers were sheltered and fed on their "underground railroad" passage before they continued their journeys. This particular rendezvous was not discovered until 1780. Sullivan himself was publicly criticized later when he was attorney general for allegedly not pressing the sale of confiscated Tory estates. He replied that in substance he was trying to temper justice with mercy. A petition was presented to the state government asking for "some mode of procedure against those abandoned wretches known as 'Tories' who have too long infested this state."

Tory Captain Simon Baxter was condemned to death by the New Hampshire Whigs, but on the day set for his execution, he escaped with a rope around his neck and succeeded in reaching Burgoyne's army. Later he went to New Brunswick, Canada, where he was granted 5,000 acres.[41]

One of the most remarkable figures of the Revolution was Benjamin Thompson of New Hampshire, better known as Count Rumford. A handsome young man, Thompson soon married a wealthy widow and settled down on a farm near Concord, New Hampshire. He employed two deserters from the American army on his farm and was accused of being a Tory, which Thompson denied; but because of the continued suspicion under which he lived, he became disgusted, offered his services to the American army, and—when they were refused—fled to Boston and became a British spy. Later he sailed for England, leaving his wife and daughter, apparently without much regret, never to see them again.

In London, Thompson conveyed to Lord George Germain the first report of the evacuation of Boston by General Howe. He added that American soldiers were sick of their service and could hardly be prevailed upon to fight. Germain liked the young Tory and they soon became fast friends, Thompson attaining the position of Under Secretary of State for the Northern Department, in charge of the colonies, while he was still in his twenties. But as the American war went against the British, Thompson lapsed into the background and eventually resigned his position, came to New York and took charge of a regiment of dragoons. He was glad to be back in America and especially to associate with the prominent Tories of New York society. Thompson commanded the Queen's Rangers, who terrified Long Island, and in one raid forced the inhabitants to pull down a church. The Rangers used the church timbers to build a blockhouse in the middle of the cemetery and then used the tombstones in their fireplaces. The grisly result was that loaves of bread coming out of the fireplace ovens bore the reversed inscriptions of the tombstones on their lower crusts.

Later in Europe, Thompson became adjutant general to the Duke of Bavaria, with permission of the English king, attaining the rank of major general. He was also made a Count of the Holy Roman Empire, taking the name of Rumford, which Concord, New Hampshire, had originally been called. Count Rumford became a widely known philosopher. He married several more times, his last wife being Madame Lavoisier, widow of the famous chemist, from whom he was eventually separated. He died near Paris in 1814, a remarkable man whose personality and luck had amazingly propelled him into world affairs.[42]

Massachusetts provided that a person suspected of enmity to the Whig cause should be arrested and banished unless he swore fealty to the cause of liberty. A Tory could not even speak out in town meetings without risking punishment. After being criticized, Tory Daniel Bayley of Newburyport said he was resolved not to converse on politics again, "which seem so generally to disgust." [39] In this state, 308 persons, including seventeen from Maine, had fled from their homes, the law stating that any who returned should be imprisoned; if they returned a second time, death was the penalty. Responsibility for prosecuting the Tories was laid upon a remarkably wide range of officials—the selectmen, committees of correspondence, sheriff, constable, grand jurymen and tithingmen. A Tory had no legal redress against a debtor, until the Tory took the oath favoring American independence. No loyal relative or friend could be guardian of an orphan child or executor of an estate, nor could a Tory buy land or transfer it to another or speak or write unpatriotic opinions. Mrs. Freelove Scott, widow of a Tory, petitioned the General Court for sustenance for herself and five children, because her husband's estate had been confiscated and she was left without even funds for food. The mansion house of Joshua Loring, husband of the mistress of General Howe, brought the Commonwealth of Massachusetts 36,792 pounds, the Loring family evidently having prospered under the personal aegis of the general.

General Henry Knox petitioned the court for whatever portion of the estate of his wife's father, Thomas Flucker, royal secretary of the province, it thought proper. The petition explained that Mr. Flucker had left Massachusetts without having the opportunity to provide for his daughter as he would have under ordinary circumstances. This request was granted, in part at least, for Mrs. Knox and her husband came into possession of a large part of what is now the state of Maine. Colonel Richard Saltonstall, a collateral ancestor of United States Senator Leverett Salstonstall, was a prominent man, revered in general by his Haverhill neighbors, but he was a Tory in principles. Once when a mob assembled to attack him, he appeared at his door and told them in a dignified, calm way that he was under the oath of allegiance to the King and intended to remain so. He then ordered some refreshments for the "visitors" to his elegant estate; they accepted and went away cheering him. Later he wrote from England, "I have no remorse of conscience for my past conduct. I have had more satisfaction in a private life here than I should have had in being next in command to General Washington." [43]

10. King's Mountain

In the South, where the American Revolution was finally won, the fortunes of war had reached a low ebb for the patriots by the spring of 1780. Charleston, South Carolina, had fallen to Sir Henry Clinton. He had surprised virtually everyone including himself, for by applying Continental methods of seige warfare, he had neatly taken the city in a squeeze from land and sea. Had the British been as successful in all phases of the Revolution as they were in capturing the American cities of Boston, New York, Philadelphia and now Charleston (though they did not retain them) the war might have had a different outcome. But they also had a new and vast frontier to subdue, and they could or would not understand it.

While the patriots were dismayed at losing Charleston, the Tories of the Carolinas were jubilant. The opportunity for which they had waited four long and fruitless years seemed at last to have come. In the rebel troops captured by Clinton were over a thousand North Carolina militia and almost as many Continentals. Local resistance to the King was fading. Cornwallis quickly occupied the three strongholds which dominated the entrance to North Carolina, Ninety-six, Camden and Cheraw, and now felt that conquest of the rest of the state would be easy, and it was high time. For years, the state had seen almost no British troops within its borders and its Continentals had felt free to help the other embattled colonies. British emissaries were accordingly sent among the Tories to arouse them to action, especially into the Scottish settlements along the Cape Fear and upper Pee Dee rivers.[1]

Many North Carolinians were influenced to join the Tories by the actions of leading citizens of South Carolina. Among these was Charles Pinckney, who had recently been president of the South Carolina Senate and who tried to excuse his previous actions to the British by stating that he had been misled by the hurry and confusion of the times, but now voiced his devotion to the King. Rawlins Lowndes, just prior to this time "President and Commander in Chief in and over the State of South Carolina," took a similar turn, and Henry Middleton, who had been president of the First Continental Congress, declared his belated dedication to the British crown.

In the campaign to utilize the local Tories, Cornwallis characteristically urged caution. But these local subjects, many of them not appreciating his discreetness and being restless under the pressure of the Whigs, began to organize independently and tried to forge sometimes random connections with the British lines. Some sent messages to Cornwallis which glowed with eagerness for him to come and conquer. The severe heat of the summer of 1780 and the scarcity of provisions, however, inclined him to remain in camp until later in the year when the weather would be cooler and the wheat crop harvested and ready for use by his soldiers. Such dilatory ideas were too gradual for the Tory leaders, especially Colonel John Moore of Ramsour's Mill, now the site of Lincolnton, North Carolina, about midway between the cities of Charlotte and Hickory. He had served under Cornwallis and returned home early in June wearing his lustrous uniform and filled with determination to wreak vengeance upon his rebellious neighbors. Ironically, Ramsour's Mill was one of the spots where the people had assembled after the battle of Alamance and had been compelled to take the oath of allegiance to the King. They were now for the most part living up to that obligation, while the men who had forced the battle upon them were in revolution against the sovereign. Colonel Moore somehow had access to a "considerable number of guineas by which he sought to allure some of the people, while others were intimidated by the account of the British success in the South and of what they regarded as the inability of the Whigs to make further resistance." [2]

A meeting was called by Colonel Moore at Ramsour's Mill for June 10 and forty Tories showed up. To these, Moore described the plans of Cornwallis to invade the region, reward the loyal, and punish the rebellious. But even while they were meeting, word came that only eight miles away was a company of the detested patriot militia under Major Joseph McDowell. Plans were immediately made to attack McDowell, who heard of the plans, however, and escaped with his men. Moore told his followers to meet with him again in three days and they complied. By June 20, 1,300 Tories had gathered at the mill, although a fourth of them were without arms. They gathered on a ridge near the mill, which was fronted by a gentle slope dotted by trees here and there and bordered by lush glades between the Tuckasegee Ford and Sherrill's Ford Road. These Tories were more ardent than military.

Meanwhile, North Carolina patriots heard of the Tory gathering at Ramsour's Mill and determined to resist them. General Griffith Rutherford called for a turnout of militia and 800 met with him on a plantation near Charlotte. Under him, commanding dragoons, light infantry and cavalry were Colonel William L. Davidson and Major William R. Davie. They decided to surprise and attack Colonel Moore and his Tories. So did Colonel Francis Locke of nearby Mountain Creek, who gathered about 400 armed civilians and started for the enemy at once. As Locke approached the Tories, he discovered that they were badly disorganized. For example, a picket guard of twelve men was stationed fully 600 yards in front of them, and when Locke's horsemen came in sight, the guards fired and fled back to their main body in such confusion that the Tory camp was thrown into an uproar. Locke's men approached within thirty paces of the Tories and opened fire, causing some of the unarmed men to scurry off. But others soon rallied and returned the patriot fire. The surprised attackers themselves fled precipitately, riding through and almost over their own infantry.

As Locke's foot soldiers pushed up the hill, joined now by their recently frightened horsemen, the Tories fired on them, then fell back over the top of the hill. Again the attackers came forward and the loyal troops fell farther back. As the opposing forces, dressed in civilian garb, came closer to each other, it was difficult for them to distinguish friend from foe, the only tokens of identity being green pine twigs in the hats of the Tories and pieces of white paper similarly worn by the Whigs. At times, these badges fell out and as a result, patriot muskets fell unknowingly on patriot heads and Tories struck down their own kind. A big Tory of German descent saw a Whig acquaintance and said, "How do you do, Pilly! I have knowed you since you was a little poy and I never knew no harm of you, except you was a rebel."

This friendly remark apparently had no effect on Billy, for he clubbed his gun and made a pass at the German's head. The latter dodged the blow and remarked, "Stay, stay! I am not going to stand still and be killed like a damn fool, needer!"

He immediately struck a blow at Billy, who dodged. Seeing the encounter, a friend of Billy's nearby, whose musket was loaded, held it to the side of the German and shot him dead.

Many of the Tories tried to escape across a narrow bridge over Ramsour's Mill dam and were, in the rush, pushed off by each other and drowned. Others tried to escape through the pond, got mired in the mud and were either shot or drowned. As the Whig leaders vigorously led their men wherever they could, the Tories were flanked and it became clear that they were getting the worst of the haphazard conflict. They broke ranks and fled down the far side of the hill to the opposite bank of a creek, where they halted. From his post on the captured hill, Colonel Locke took a look at the Tories formed along the creek bank and thought they were rallying for another fight. Quickly he tried to form his men.

But only 110 of the original group could be found, the patriots having scattered also, so he sent word to Rutherford to hurry with his force. But this was needless; Moore's men were through. Like so many of the Tories in their other engagements during the war, they had failed because of lack of organization, arms, inspiration and plain luck. Colonel Moore sent a flag to Locke, asking for a truce in order to collect his wounded and bury the dead. But even as this request was being considered, the Tories ran away, singly and in small groups. Moore himself escaped with thirty men and when he reached the headquarters of the redcoats at Camden, he was threatened with court-martial for assembling the Tories before the time appointed by the British commander.[3]

Neighbor had fought against neighbor in the battle of Ramsour's Mill, some loyal groups holding their positions stubbornly until forced to give way by the general retreat of the Tories. Trees behind which both sides took shelter were found to be scarred with bullets. One tree on Tory ground, at the foot of which two brothers lay dead, was grazed by three balls on one side and two on the other. The results of the battle were surprisingly even: each side lost about 150 killed and wounded. Had Colonel Moore heeded the advice of Cornwallis and waited until the proper time for attack, Major Ferguson could have reinforced him, the fight might have been won, and perhaps 2,000 more Tories would have been available to help Ferguson in the forthcoming crucial engagement at King's Mountain. As it was, the defeat of Moore resulted in crushing the Tory element in much of Central North Carolina, and when Cornwallis later came this way and encamped at Ramsour's Mill, instead of getting the loyal help he had hoped for, he lost more men by desertion than he gained in recruits.[4]

Among those who were not yet impressed with patriot victories and who wished to be on the winning side were 207 residents of Charleston. They presented to Sir Henry Clinton a petition beginning with the words, "The humble address of divers inhabitants of Charleston," in which they begged for re-entry into the British fold and apologized abjectly for what the rebels had done to the King's men. Encouraged by such subservience and by his defeat of Gates at Camden, Cornwallis at the behest of Clinton determined to subdue North Carolina both in order to carry out his main strategy of conquering the South and to protect his southern posts. After North Carolina, he planned to take Virginia, then Pennsylvania, and so on. Three parallel forces moved northward: Lord Cornwallis heading the main body, Banastre Tarleton at the head of the British Legion and light infantry, and Major (brevet Lieutenant Colonel) Patrick Ferguson and his Tories. Ferguson seemed determined to teach the Americans a lesson which he thought they needed. He marched through the district along the Tiger River in South Carolina, past Spartanburg and through the Quaker Meadows in Burke County, North Carolina, plundering the local citizens of cattle, horses, beds, wearing apparel, "even wrestling rings from the fingers of ladies. . . . The desperate, the idle, the vindictive who sought plunder and revenge, all found a warm reception in the British camp, and their progress through the country was marked by blood and lighted with conflagration," comments historian J. B. O. Landrum in a hardly impartial description.[5]

By late September, Ferguson was at Gilberttown, three miles north of what is now Rutherfordton, North Carolina. His purpose was to collect and train the Tories of the region in order to utilize them effectively in behalf of the British. He wanted to train young men and fit them into his ranks so that they could fight like regulars. Had he succeeded, the British might have won the South. But he failed to sense the strength of his opposition; in fact, he strengthened it by an untimely proclamation.

On October 1, 1780, Ferguson heard that the men over the western mountains were rising to resist him. He was then at Denard's Ford on the Broad River and had just had word also of a recent atrocity against a Tory. Referring to this occurrence and its consequences, he sent the following message to the over-mountain men: "Unless you wish to be lost in an inundation of barbarians who have begun by murdering an unarmed son before the aged father, and afterward lopped off his arms, and who by their shocking cruelties and irregularities, give the best proof of their cowardice and want of discipline; I say if you wish to be pinioned, robbed, murdered and see your wives and daughters . . . abused by the dregs of mankind . . . if you choose to be degraded forever by a set of mongrels, say so at once and let your women turn their backs on you, and look out for real men to protect them." Ferguson added that if the rebels did not stop resisting British rule, he would march his army over the mountains, hang their leaders and lay their country waste with fire and sword. He could not have created from imagination a taunt more likely to bring these men down upon him.[6]

Born of titled Scottish parents, Patrick Ferguson was a cornet of horse in the British army at the age of fifteen. He was one of the best of the professional redcoats, a veteran of wars on the continent of Europe when he came to America as a captain. Slight of build with a long, oval, gentle-appearing face, his disposition was friendly, and his persistent determination won him among his fellow officers the nickname "Bull Dog." He was serious in critical moments, had high ability, sound judgment and great energy. From the plains of Flanders to the Caribbean, Ferguson had displayed his military prowess and bravery. At the battle of Minden in June, 1760, a pistol had dropped from his holster as he rode across a deep ditch. Missing it, he galloped back and in the faces of enemy hussars retrieved the weapon. That he was a born soldier was indicated by his mother's brother, Major General James Murray, in a letter to her two years later from Quebec: "You must no longer look upon him as your son," the uncle said about young Ferguson. "He is the son of Mars and will be unworthy of his father if he does not give proofs of contempt of pain and danger."

After a period of illness during which Ferguson made an intensive study of military science and tactics, he came to America in 1777 with the reputation of being the best marksman in the British army. This skill was accentuated by the fact that he had taken advantage of his enforced inactivity to invent a breech-loading rifle which fired a pointed instead of spherical bullet and which could be fired six times a minute; it was twenty-five times as fast as the ordinary muzzle-loading rifle then in use. In 1776 at Woolwich, in the presence of King George III, Lord Townshend, master of ordnance, and Generals Amherst and Hawley, during a high wind and heavy rain, Ferguson was said to have fired accurately six shots a minute at a target 200 yards away. He then climaxed the brilliant performance by hitting the bull's eye while lying on his back on the ground.

Had it been used widely in the American Revolution, this improved rifle might have meant the difference between British defeat and victory. Ferguson asked and had been given permission to test the new weapon by arming a special corps of men with it at the battle of Brandywine, but General Howe took a dim view of the rifle because he had not been consulted regarding its use. During this same battle, Ferguson felt the effect of another rifle—one fired from the ranks of the Americans, who were also skilled marksmen. One of their deadly bullets struck the bone of his right elbow and left it stiff and useless for the rest of his short life. With Ferguson disabled, Howe had most of the new rifles stored, the rest being distributed among ineffective soldiers in various units. Upon recovering from his wound, Ferguson practiced using his left arm until, despite the disability, he was adept with sword and pistol.[7]

An incident which occurred at Brandywine before Ferguson was wounded could have had a vital and lasting effect upon the war and the future leadership of the new country. The British officer was stationed with his riflemen in a wood. "We had not lain long," Ferguson recounted, "when a rebel officer, marked by a hussar dress, passed towards our army, within a hundred yards of my right flank, not perceiving us. He was followed by another, dressed in dark green and blue, mounted on a bay horse, with a remarkably high cocked hat. I ordered three good shots to steal near to and fire at them; but the idea disgusting me, I recalled the order. The hussar, in returning, made a circuit, but the other passed within a hundred yards of us, upon which I advanced from the woods toward him. Upon my calling, he stopped; but after looking at me, he proceeded. . . . I could have lodged half a dozen balls in or about him . . . but it was not pleasant to fire at the back of an unoffending individual, who was acquitting himself very coolly of his duty—so I let him alone. The day after, rebel officers who were wounded told us that General Washington was all the morning with the light troops, and only attended by a French officer in hussar dress, he himself dressed and mounted in every point as above described. I am not sorry that I did not know at the time who it was." [8]

When Philadelphia was evacuated by the British in June of 1778, Ferguson accompanied them to New York and took part en route in the hot battle of Monmouth. In September he was sent, in command of 400 men, to Egg Harbor, New Jersey, to destroy a "nest of rebel pirates," which he ruthlessly accomplished. Later he led several predatory expeditions along the coast and up the Hudson River, rising steadily by his achievements in the eyes of his superiors. In October, Ferguson was promoted to the rank of major in the Seventy-first Regiment of Highland Light Infantry. When Sir Henry Clinton sent his expedition against Charleston, Ferguson went along as commander of 300 American Tory Volunteers whom he had personally selected. For this service, he was given the brevet rank of lieutenant colonel. He and Banastre Tarleton, the best cavalry leader on either side, were ordered to secure certain bridges in the Carolinas in advance of the redcoats, which entailed a toilsome march through swamps and difficult passes. They succeeded. In the fighting involved, Ferguson was mistaken by British troops for a rebel and wounded in his left arm, thus temporarily incapacitating both his arms. Ferguson was a fit associate for Tarleton in hardy, scrambling, partisan enterprise, equally intrepid and determined, but cooler and more open to impulses of humanity.[9]

The Carolina Tories flocked to Ferguson's standard in large numbers. He took pains to explain to them his misson and would sit for hours talking to the country people about the war situation, pointing out to them what he regarded as erroneous on the rebel side. He gently reminded them that the orders of Cornwallis were to hang any man who had fought on the side of the King and then switched to the patriots. This explanation added to the number of Ferguson's recruits, though many of them fought only for a short time.

By the time Ferguson arrived at Gilberttown, the people of the Carolina countryside had gained an especially favorable impression of the progress of British and Tories. Gates had been defeated disastrously by Cornwallis, Sumter dispersed by Tarleton, and other Whig detachments so scattered that it looked for a time as if the patriot cause were hopeless. Large numbers of the residents hastened to take the oath of allegiance to the King in order to save their hides.

The immediate mission of Ferguson was to intercept Colonel Elijah Clark of Georgia, who did not seem to feel the rebel cause lost and had recently made a demonstration against Augusta, then in the hands of the British. But Clark eluded him. On the march, one of Ferguson's officers developed smallpox, and since there was little or no treatment for the disease in that day, the poor man was left with his horse in a deserted house. Both died. This could have been an omen, but Ferguson evidently did not so regard it. He showed less caution as he drew farther away from Cornwallis than he usually did in strange country. As for Cornwallis, he was later blamed by Clinton for indifference to the fate of Ferguson on this "incursion into North Carolina." Perhaps Ferguson misled his commander, for he wrote him as he swung back in the direction of head-quarters that the Americans were active but had underestimated the strength of the British. "I am on my march toward you, by a road lead-ing from Cherokee Ford, north of King's Mountain," Ferguson said. "Three or four hundred soldiers, part dragoons, would finish the business. *Something must be done soon.*" [10]

Something was done. But not what Ferguson expected.

His incendiary message to the men across the highlands had the reverse effect of what he had intended. In the picturesque reaches of these western mountains, comprising what is now East Tennessee, lived hardy frontiersmen whose daily life was a continual struggle with the rugged land and the Indians. They had no intention of adding to their difficulties by surrender to the pesky British. So they considered the challenge of Ferguson something to be dealt with quickly and effectively. Most of these people were Scotch-Irish who had come to Pennsylvania—or their forebears had—from the homeland, then down the Great Valley of Vir-ginia into this storied, hilly region which was much like their native countries of Scotland or Northern Ireland. They were expert hunters and Indian fighters, crack shots with their heavy, long-barreled rifles which could pick squirrels out of high trees at over a hundred yards. When the leaders received Ferguson's message, they decided to go and strike the "Bull Dog" on his own ground rather than wait for him to come and ravish their beautiful countryside. So a force was raised without any authority from the government; the men supplied their own muskets, rifles and shotguns and such other weapons as they could obtain. In traveling, they knew how to sustain their lean bodies off the land as they went along. Most of them had horses, so the word was given to go.[11]

The leaders of this bold expedition were as varied as they were color-ful. One of them, Colonel William Campbell, was a former officer in the forces of Lord Dunmore and had married the sister of Patrick Henry. Campbell had helped to suppress the Tories in Montgomery County, Virginia. For the march against Ferguson, he brought 400 men from Washington County. Colonel Isaac Shelby, of Welsh descent, came with some 250 men from Sullivan County, North Carolina. Colonel John "Noli-chucky Jack" Sevier, later governor of the short-lived state of Franklin, then first governor of Tennessee, brought 250 men from Watauga County, North Carolina, now Tennessee. Sevier was a daring fighter who had fought and won thirty-five battles with the Indians. He later became a bitter rival of Andrew Jackson. Though the way was rough, these men did not have a great number of miles to come, for their collective territory was all in and around where the states of North Carolina, Virginia and Tennessee adjoin today.

The men assembled at Sycamore Flats on the Watauga River near the present Elizabethton, Tennessee. Colonel Benjamin Cleveland of Wilkes County, North Carolina, who had also been active against the Tories, came with 350 men he had collected and met the others near Morganton.

Colonel Charles McDowell, retiring before the advance of Ferguson, joined the gathering with 160 men. "The whole country," wrote historian Lyman Draper, "was animated with the same glowing spirit, to do something to put down Ferguson and his Tory gang, who threatened their leaders with the halter and their homes with the torch." For their part, the British paid their respects to the nature of the mountaineers—or at least one of the officers of Cornwallis, Major George Hanger, did. "This race of men are more savage than Indians," he commented, "and possess every one of their vices and not one of their virtues. I have known one of them to travel 220 miles through the woods, never keeping any road or path, guided by the sun by day and the stars by night, to kill a particular person belonging to the opposite party." [12]

This description was exaggerated, but it held all too much truth for the good of the Tories. Even with such prowess, however, the impromptu army of the patriots needed funds. Colonel Sevier tried to borrow money on his own responsibility but found discouraging scarcity. The only person who appeared to have any substantial cash was John Adair, the Entry Taker of Sullivan County, which is now in Tennessee. He had about $12,-000 which he had collected from the sale of North Carolina lands. Sevier asked him if this could be made available for the expedition. The reply was significant: "Colonel Sevier, I have no authority by law to make that disposition of this money; it belongs to the impoverished treasury of North Carolina, and I dare not appropriate a cent of it to any purpose; but if the country is overrun by the British, our liberty is gone. Let the money go too. Take it. If the enemy by its use is driven from the country, I can trust that country to justify and vindicate my conduct—so take it!" [13]

Sevier did. He and Shelby pledged themselves to guarantee the loan, which was later legalized by the state legislature. What would have happened in this matter had the British won the war is an academic question. The necessary ammunition and equipment for the march against Ferguson were obtained. Although the men were mounted and carried their own hunting rifles, they had no baggage or the usual quartermaster supplies, for which their officers were glad, because heavy equipment would have impeded their progress on the mountain trails. Each man had a blanket, a cup for drinking water, and a pouch for food, which was usually only parched corn meal that they mixed with maple sugar for a nourishing if meager repast. Now and then a skillet appeared in the ranks, to be used for a hot meal when possible. These frontiersmen wore fringed hunting shirts made by their wives and daughters, fur skin caps, and leggings and moccasins like those of Indians. Each wore a hunting knife, with here and there a sword such as the big claymore of Colonel Campbell, a relic of his Scottish ancestors.

On the morning of September 26, before they set out on their perilous journey, the over-mountain men gathered for a solemn ceremony. Ferguson had called on Cornwallis for reinforcements; these men called on heaven, the Reverend Samuel Doak being their mouthpiece. This pioneer

Presbyterian clergyman, who often preached sermons of half a day's duration, gave a prayer—doubtless a long one—which he ended with the stirring shibboleth, "The sword of the Lord and Gideon!"

Thus these men of the mountains, mostly Presbyterians themselves, and now exceedingly inspired, mounted their horses and began their long trek through the woodland recesses to find their enemy. Leaving beautiful and green Crab Orchard Valley, they made their way slowly at first through a gap between Yellow and Roan Mountains. Even at this early time of the season they found the sides and tops of the mountains covered with snow "shoe-mouth deep." On the summit of one mountain were about a hundred acres "of beautiful table land, in which a spring issued, ran through it, and over into the Watauga. The bright rushing waters, tumbling over their rocky beds, and the lofty, blue mountains in the distance presented a weird, dreamy and bewildering appearance." On the fourth night, the men "rested at a rich Tory's, where they obtained an abundance of every necessary refreshment." [14]

Two of Sevier's men, probably Tories, James Crawford and Samuel Chambers, deserted his ranks and rushed ahead to tell Ferguson about the coming of the patriots. Ferguson at once started south toward the fort of Ninety-six, then turned east toward King's Mountain, near the North Carolina-South Carolina line. Meantime, the over-mountain men had reached a place sixteen miles from Gilberttown where they had understood Ferguson was. It was October 1, a rainy Monday, and the men remained in camp, some of them so eagerly restless that they presented problems of discipline. The officers met and decided that an overall commander was needed. So Colonel McDowell, who was older than the rest, was delegated to go to General Gates at Hillsboro and ask that a general officer be sent to command the expedition. Daniel Morgan was the man whom the men preferred above all others. This heroic officer, a Virginian and a renowned Indian fighter, had already won high laurels at Quebec and Saratoga. An expert rifleman himself, he would have been a natural leader of the frontier fighters who were to give such a great account as marksmen in the forthcoming battle. As it was, no officer arrived from Gates before the engagement took place, but Morgan was to have his memorable opportunity at the place where the over-mountain men were to encamp soon, the Cowpens. In a dramatic poem published three years before, Hugh Henry Brackenridge gave the following as Morgan's impression of the Tories:

> The cursed earth can scarcely furnish out
> So much black poison from the beasts and herbs,
> As swells the dark hearts of these Royalists.
> The toad's foul mouth, the snake's envenomed bite,
> Black spider, asp, or froth of rabid dog
> Is not so deadly as these murderers.[15]

Colonel William Campbell agreed to act as co-ordinating officer to furnish a chain of responsibility in the patriot command. The men kept on the move meanwhile and on October 6 arrived at the Cowpens in north-west South Carolina, where they were joined by Colonel John Williams of South Carolina and 400 officers and men, including Major William Chronicle. The force now totaled about 1,400, but it was decided to select 900 stalwart, mounted fighters from among these and make a rapid push against the British leader, the rest of the patriots to follow. Colonel Edward Lacey of South Carolina had ridden all night to join the mountain men and as he approached the camp at Cowpens early in the morning, he was spotted and accused of being a Tory spy. At length he was able to prove that he was not by giving valuable information about Ferguson's strength and position, so he was added to the plentiful list of colonels commanding the force.

Although the decision was to move at once against Ferguson, food was needed before starting out. Finding such was proving a problem until it was discovered that nearby lived a wealthy Tory named Hiram Saunders who kept numerous cows in the pens which gave the place its name. He had heard of the presence of the mountaineers and when some of them called on him, he feigned sickness and was in bed. But he was unceremoniously yanked out, roughed up and ordered to tell what he knew about the movements and purposes of Ferguson. Saunders declared that he did not know anything of this kind and eventually convinced the officers that he was telling the truth. Notwithstanding, they shot several of his fat cattle and cooked them for the famished force. Fifty acres of his robust corn were harvested and fed to the equally hungry horses. Now the outfit was in a more warlike condition. To emphasize this, a message was delivered to the men from their leaders, the spokesman being the colorful and rotund Colonel Cleveland, who weighed 300 pounds and was fittingly named "Old Roundabout." Taking off his huge hat with a sweeping effect, Cleveland said to the assembled men,

"My brave fellows, the enemy is at hand, and we must be up and at them. Now is the time for every man of you to do his country a priceless service—such as shall lead your children to exult in the fact that their fathers were the conquerors of Ferguson. When the pinch comes, I shall be with you. But if any of you shrink from sharing in the battle and the glory, you can have the opportunity of backing out and leaving."

This eloquent exhortation had its desired effect. But there was at least one exception, at heart anyway, as he himself revealed regarding what followed. "Each leader made a short speech in his own way," wrote James P. Collins of Major Chronicle's regiment, "desiring every coward to be off immediately. Here I confess I would willingly have been excused, for my feelings were not the most pleasant. This may be attributed to my youth, not being quite 17 years of age—but I could not well swallow the appellation of coward."

Three minutes went by. No one backed out, and a cheer went up.

"When we encounter the enemy," the voice of Colonel Shelby rang out, "don't wait for the word of command. Let each one of you be your own officer and do the very best you can, taking every care you can of yourselves and availing yourselves of every advantage. If in the woods, shelter yourselves and give them Indian play; advance from tree to tree, pressing the enemy and killing and disabling all you can." [16]

Thus was the plan of battle outlined and it was followed closely, almost too much so. The men were dismissed with orders to be ready to march within three hours, even though it was already the end of the day. By 8 P.M. they were on the move. It was a very dark night and to add to this difficulty, rain fell in a heavy downpour. In the darkness, some of Campbell's men lost their way and had to be rounded up by flankers, which required until daylight, when the heavy rain had changed to a light but impeding mist. In the gray, damp dawn, the Broad River loomed up in front of the weary and hungry men, where they paused only long enough to eat a scanty breakfast from their food pouches. Sensing the value of time, the men pushed their horses on through the rainy, dismal terrain. As the dampness continued, they were forced to slow down because of the exhausting struggle. Believing that such wearing conditions called for a halt and rest, Colonels Campbell, Sevier and Cleveland rode up to the front unit and proposed to Shelby who was in charge that it might be best to pause for awhile. To this collective suggestion, Shelby replied, "I will not stop until night, if I have to follow Ferguson into the lines of Cornwallis!"

Put on their mettle by this determined statement, the other colonels returned to their respective commands and the march continued. It was now a problem for the men to keep their weapons dry. They were able to do this only by wrapping such things as their saddle bags, blankets or hunting shirts around their precious rifles. Their discomfort was great, but it was lessened at noon when they learned that they were only eight miles from the place at which Ferguson had chosen to make a stand against those whom he regarded as contemptible rebels.

The rain had stopped. The troops had reached the farm of a man named Solomon Beason, who was said to be half Whig and half Tory "as the occasion required." From him they confirmed the information that Ferguson was near. As the soldiers left the house of the "Tory," his daughter, who evidently sympathized with the patriots, came out and informed them that Ferguson was "on that mountain," as she pointed to a nearby eminence. Within two miles of it, they captured a boy named John Ponder, fourteen, who was said to have relatives in Ferguson's camp. They searched him and found a dispatch from Ferguson to Cornwallis describing the former's situation and asking for help. Upon being questioned, young Ponder described the dress Ferguson wore, a kind of disguise over his British uniform. This information helped the mountain men later to identify Ferguson when they finally spotted him.[17]

The elevation they saw in front of them on this misty fall day was impressive but not awesome to those men who had come from other mountains to assault this one. It is difficult to understand why the wily Ferguson did not realize that on such terrain, the mountaineers would be right

at home while he would not. The name "King" was bestowed upon the
mountain not because the troops of the King occupied it, but because a
man named King lived at its foot. In the hazy visibility it loomed only as
a high ridge to the men who were accustomed to peaks several times its
height. Even so, King's Mountain afforded a defensive position of unusual strength. Shaped like a gigantic Brazil nut but flat on top, its steep
sides, wooded with chestnut and poplar trees, rose some sixty feet above
the plain below. The summit was about 500 yards long and 75 yards
wide, spreading out to 120 yards in width at the northeast end where
Ferguson had established his camp. Near him was a spring for an adequate supply of water. Patrick Ferguson characteristically declared that
he was "on King's Mountain, that he was king of that mountain, and
neither God Almighty or all the Rebels in Hell could drive him from it."
     Ferguson's forces numbered about 1,100 and were made up of 100 reg-
ulars and 1,000 Tories from New York, New Jersey and the Carolinas.
Most of them wore scarlet coats and were well-trained and disciplined,
being armed with muskets and bayonets, the use of which they well
understood. The Tories from the region around Ninety-six had guns without bayonets, but had been provided with long knives. Ferguson, with his
usual ingenuity and deftness with firearms, had these men file the butt
ends of their knife handles to a size that would fit snugly inside the muz-
zles of their muskets, thus making quite effective improvised bayonets.
In command of the Tory New Jersey Rangers was Captain Abraham de
Peyster of New York, and his adjutant was Lieutenant Anthony Allaire,
also of the Empire State, who left a good description of the ensuing
battle. Ferguson himself was the only British officer in the engagement,
which was fought otherwise by Americans on either side.[18]
     It was past noon when the frontiersmen neared the mountain and their
scouts established the fact that Ferguson and his redcoats stood squarely
atop it. A halt was called, and the leaders quickly met to plan their attack. Orders were given that there should be no talking for the rest of the
march and that the men should approach the mountain as stealthily as
possible. This was made easy by the dampness of the leaves which had
been wet by the rains of the forenoon. Hardly able to restrain their eagerness, the patriots tied all their loose baggage to their saddles, fastened
their horses to trees and left them in charge of a few of the older men
while they prepared for the assault. The position of Ferguson on top of
the mountain would have been more secure had the sides not been covered by woods, which sheltered the attackers as they approached and enabled them to fight in their favorite manner. For some strange reason, the
usually alert Ferguson did not have pickets posted at any considerable
distance from his position, and apparently did not hear the coming of his
enemies until they were only a quarter of a mile away.
     At 3 P.M. the final patriot order was given: "Fresh prime your guns.
Every man go into battle firmly resolved to fight until he dies!" [19]
     Quietly the long line of riflemen, the natural shading of their pictur-

esque frontier clothing blending inconspicuously into the autumn woodland, filed through Hambright's Gap less than a mile west of their objective. Swiftly and certainly they moved to their assigned positions around
the mountain. Colonel Shelby's regiment formed a column on the center
left, Campbell's on the right, while Sevier's men made up the right flank
column and those of Colonel Cleveland the left flank. Thus they approached and surrounded King's Mountain in a smooth, sweeping en-
velopment.

The main position of Ferguson was near the northeastern end of the
mountain. Finally the oncoming patriots were so close that his pickets
sounded the alarm. Then through the wooded stretches of the slopes
sounded a weird, shrill call. It was the silver whistle of Patrick Ferguson
calling his own men to battle.

Now that they were spotted, his men were told by Campbell, "Here
they are, boys! Shout like hell and fight like devils!"

They replied with a hair-raising, Indian-like war whoop. It reached
and reverberated high up on the mountain, where Captain De Peyster,
second in command, stopped and turned his ear toward the sound. He
had heard this murderous cry before and knew what it meant. To Ferguson, he made the portentous comment, "This is ominous. These are the
damn yelling boys!" [20]

The divided forces which began the attack were to swarm up the sides
and catch Ferguson in between them at the mountain's broad end. So
Campbell's men scrambled and worked themselves up the rough and
craggy right side. But this was not as forbidding as what they confronted
at the top. Suddenly they faced a row of glistening steel bayonets aimed
at them by rushing men in flaming red coats. The startled patriots fired
their rifles, but their aim was hampered by the rush of the oncoming
redcoats. Armed with nothing but empty guns which required at least a
minute to reload and small arms ineffective at any appreciable distance,
the attackers took one look at the cold steel bearing down on them and
turned and fled down the mountain. A few waited too long and were run
through by bayonets. The rest of them kept going until they reached the
bottom, then scurried up to the top of the next ridge. The assault was
tougher than they had anticipated.

Shelby was on the opposite, southeast, side; his group pushed up the
tree-filled slope and this gave Campbell a chance to rally his retreating
men on the other side. But on reaching the top, Shelby's men got a hot
burst of point-blank musket fire from the Tories as well as a deadly
bayonet charge which drove them back also. During this initial attack,
the rest of the rebels had worked their way around the opposite, broad
end of the mountain and were climbing, taking cover as they went, and
approaching the top. Sighting them, Ferguson sent his bayonets at them
and drove them back as he had done Campbell and Shelby. Had the
"Bull Dog" at bay been able to continue this effective procedure, King's
Mountain might have remained in the hands of the King.

But the men besieging the stronghold were utterly determined. Each time they were repulsed, they waited until the Tories had moved back into position, then they climbed back up to the work that had been cut out for them. From behind sturdy trees and sheltering rocks, they reloaded and poured a steady and accurate fire at the enemy, whose bright uniforms made them plain targets. Historian John Haywood wrote, "The mountain was covered with flame and smoke and seemed to thunder." [21]

As the battle raged more intensely and the frontiersmen neared the top of the mountain in increasing numbers, Ferguson found to his dismay that his high position held danger as well as advantage. The summit was bare of woods, making his men easily-seen targets, while down along the sides, trees sheltered the attacking riflemen and at the same time prevented the Tory musketry and bayonet charges from being effective for very long. Now Sevier had reached the summit and Ferguson had to turn on him and his coonskin-capped snipers. To add to the mounting assault, Williams, Chronicle and McDowell were also approaching the top. Ferguson suffered another disadvantage. His men, with their smooth-bore muskets and possibly a few of his new rifles, had to fire downhill and this forced them to aim at the rebels' heads as they appeared. The slope thus affected the accuracy of fire so that they often shot above their targets; but the approaching mountain men "fired upward at the plainer target of the Tories' stomachs." [22]

Finding himself being surrounded, Ferguson dashed all over the place to maneuver and encourage his men. Above the crackling roar of some 2,000 rifles and muskets, his silver whistle screeched furiously, urging his soldiers to hold on and prevail. The British commander had thrown a plaid hunting shirt over his bright uniform coat, but with his whistle clenched in his teeth and his sword swinging vigorously from his left hand, he was plainly, even to the frontiersmen, Colonel Patrick Ferguson, the "Bull Dog," and a target much to be sought. Though he was as brave as he was active, his efforts were not enough. His bayonet charges checked the attackers temporarily, but they soon rallied and pushed up again in growing numbers and fury. As Henry Lee appraised it, "King's Mountain was more assailable with the rifle than defensible with the bayonet."

On and up smashed the rebel contingents until they fought hand to hand with the defenders. Lieutenant Anthony Allaire of Ferguson's force slashed and killed a big mountaineer with one stroke of his sword. A South Carolina "patriot" who had vowed he would stand his ground, "live or die," took to his heels in a mad dash down the mountain, and, when later chided by his friends, explained that he had tried to stop, "but my confounded legs would carry me off." [23] The shouts of the mountaineers, the crackle of rifle and musket, the loud commands and entreaties of the officers on both sides, the shrill whistle of Ferguson high above the confusing din of battle, the groans of wounded and dying throughout the lines, all combined to add pandemonium to this wrathful scene above the plain. Lieutenant Reece Bowen of Virginia was seen to expose himself unnecessarily and was urged to take to a tree.

"Take to a tree!" he replied indignantly. "No. Never shall it be said that I sought safety by hiding my person from a Briton or Tory!"

Hardly had he completed the remark when a rifle ball struck him in the breast and he fell dead. Major Chronicle had just commanded his men to "face to the hill" when a bullet struck him and he too fell. Patriot William Twitty was behind a tree and receiving heavy fire from a marksman sheltered by another tree with a fork in its limbs. Twitty held his fire until he saw a head appear in the fork, then his hunting rifle spoke and the Tory fell dead behind the forked tree. Later the victim was found with his brains blown out. He had been a neighbor of Twitty. Charles Gordon, young patriot officer, encountered a Tory officer, seized him by his long hair and started dragging him down the mountain, when the Tory managed to draw his pistol and shoot Gordon, breaking his left arm. Whereupon Gordon drew his sword and killed the enemy.

"In the thickest of the fight, I saw Colonel Williams fall," wrote 16-year-old Private Thomas Young, who had lost his shoes and was barefoot. "I ran to his assistance, for I loved him as a father, he had ever been so kind to me. . . . They carried him into a tent and sprinkled water on his face. As he revived, his first words were, 'For God's sake, boys, don't give up the hill.' . . . I left him in the arms of his son, Daniel, and returned to the field to avenge his fall." Williams soon died. Alexander Chesney said that Ferguson killed him with his left hand.[24]

Samuel Abney of South Carolina was said to have been forced to fight in Ferguson's corps, and at the beginning of the battle had stationed himself behind a rock, thinking he would just stay put and do no fighting for either side. But he found that instead of being safe, he was in the midst of a shower of bullets. A ball entered the fleshy part of one arm. This made him "a little mad," he said, but he still refrained from fighting. Then another bullet struck him and made him "mighty mad," so he fell to and fought furiously for Ferguson. Before the action was over, Abney was riddled with seven bullets and left in an unconscious condition on the mountain. But when night came, the frost revived him. He managed to crawl to a branch for a drink of water, and was later found and cared for by a resident of the region, so that he completely recovered.

The furious encounter had raged for almost an hour, when Campbell and Shelby finally gained the southwestern summit of the mountain and were holding it firmly. From all sides the patriots closed in on Ferguson, not in the solid fronts which his bayonets had routed, but scattered and behind trees from which they blasted murderous fire from the fringes of the open plateau. Now completely surrounded, Ferguson's force, although fighting bravely, could not withstand the savage assault. Ripped by a torrential fusillade of bullets directed by patriot huntsmen, the Tories became disorganized and drew toward their campsite on the southeast. The British commander was urged by officers to surrender.

But not Patrick Ferguson. Even in this desperate situation, with attacks and counterattacks on all sides, the cry of his silver whistle could still be heard amidst the din and roaring whoops of mountaineers. He swore he would "never yield to such damned banditti." [25]

Ferguson, from his dashing horse, ordered de Peyster to take a full company and reinforce the position on the extreme eastern end. The officer complied, his men trying to make their way through the thick cross-fire from the enemy. When he reached his objective, de Peyster turned to look back at his men and was horrified to find that he no longer had a company but only a few who had managed to make their way through. Then he ordered his remaining cavalrymen to mount, but this was futile. As quickly as they reached their saddles, they were picked off by the devilish riflemen behind the surrounding trees.

At last Ferguson himself realized that his cause was hopeless. But he was still determined not to surrender himself to those he despised as "back-water men." Hurriedly choosing a few personal friends from among the Tories, Ferguson had them mount their horses and try to escape with him. Spurring his gray horse, he led the way toward what he thought was a gap in Cleveland's lines near the northeast crest, cutting down as he galloped a white flag one of his men had raised. But the mountain marksmen had been told to look out for Ferguson in a plaid hunting shirt with his sword in his left hand. They did. Eight rifles roared almost at once and the rider in the hunting shirt went down, pierced by eight bullets. One of them was from the Deckhard gun of Private Robert Young of Sevier's regiment, which he had named "Sweet Lips." As Ferguson fell, his sword broken from so much cutting and slashing, his left foot caught in the stirrup, and he was dragged along on the ground. When his men saw him, their spirits were crushed. They caught and untangled him, propping him forlornly against a tree, as his riderless horse dashed away and down the mountain. Ferguson died within a few minutes.[26]

This was the signal for the end. After a brief flurry of further resistance, Captain de Peyster, now in command, raised a white flag and called for quarter. His men were huddled behind their wagons in terror like cattle in a corral. The reply de Peyster received from his foes was: "Buford! Buford! Tarleton's quarter!" referring to the previous slaughter of prisoners by Tarleton at Buford.

Thus some of the mountain men kept shooting, flag or no flag. A few of them doubtless did not realize what a flag of surrender meant; others were indifferent; still others were bent on avenging the deaths of friends and relatives who had been killed by the Tories in the neighbor-against-neighbor war of a bitterness not known in the conflict between the regulars of both sides. As the frontiersmen kept firing and the helpless Tories fell, Colonel Campbell cried out to the men, "For God's sake, quit! It's murder to shoot any more."

But young Joseph Sevier, who had heard that his father, Colonel John

Sevier, had been killed, kept firing into the huddled Tories, cursing them as tears rolled down his cheeks. Then his father rode up and the son was calmed. It was an uncle, Captain Robert Sevier, who was killed.

Shelby shouted to the panicky victims to throw down their arms, to which they had instinctively held on. They obeyed, and this virtually stopped the firing at them, except that a few mountaineers came late over the crest and, not knowing of the surrender, fired into the crowd of Tories before learning what had happened. It was a hard fight to stop. Campbell, to whom de Peyster had protested about the continued killing, ordered the Tory officers to separate from the others, to take off their hats and sit down. This seemed at last to satisfy their avenging opponents.

The battle had lasted an hour. Yet it was as bloody and decisive as many a longer engagement. Campbell proposed three cheers for liberty. King's Mountain rang with the loud hurrahs of the happy victors. One of them, Robert Henry, had a desire to see Ferguson's body. He found the brave Briton had been shot in the face and breast, his right arm shattered, his thigh and skull pierced. Samuel Talbot, who was with Henry, turned the body over and took Ferguson's pistol. From his pocket dropped a bright silver whistle.[27]

After the riddled corpse had been viewed by the morbidly curious, pawed over by the avaricious and cursed by the vengeful, four of Ferguson's own men managed to take the mangled body to a spring at the foot of a slope not far from where he fell. There they wrapped him in the only covering they could find, a raw beef's hide, and buried him in a small ravine, covering the crude grave with a small mound of rocks in tribute to his solid bravery. There is a tradition that Ferguson had with him two mistresses, a not uncommon thing for British officers. Both were listed as cooks. They were handsome women, and one, who was known as Virginia Sal, was said to have been killed early in the battle and later buried in the same grave with Ferguson. In 1845, Dr. J. W. Tracy, a physician of the town of King's Mountain, North Carolina, opened the grave and found in it two skeletons, one that of a woman. The other mistress was Virginia Paul, who survived the battle, and after it was over "was seen to ride around the camp as unconcerned as though nothing of unusual moment had occurred." She was taken with the Tory prisoners to Morganton and later sent to the army of Cornwallis.[28]

Few if any of Ferguson's men escaped death, wounding or capture. Of the approximately 1,100 under him, 157 were killed, 163 were so badly wounded that they were left on the field, and 698 were taken prisoner, according to respectable records which do not account for any additional members of his command presumably missing. The patriots lost 28 killed and 62 wounded. About 1,500 muskets and rifles and a quantity of supplies and ammunition fell into their hands.[29]

When the battle ended, it was too late in the day to start homeward, so the frontiersmen remained on the mountain until morning. Both victor and vanquished passed the night in the scarred woodland amid the dead and the groans of the wounded and dying. "The next day, which was Sunday," James Collins wrote, "the scene became really distressing. The wives and children of the poor Tories came in great numbers. Their husbands, fathers and brothers lay dead in heaps, while others lay wounded or dying—a melancholy sight indeed. . . . We proceeded to bury the dead but it was badly done. They were thrown into convenient piles and covered with old logs, the bark of old trees, and rocks, yet not so as to secure them from becoming a prey to the beasts of the forests or the vultures of the air; and the wolves became so plentiful that it was dangerous for anyone to be out at night for several miles around. Also, the hogs in the neighborhood gathered in to the place to devour the flesh of men. . . . Half the dogs in the country were said to be mad and were put to death. I saw, myself, in passing the place a few weeks after, all parts of the human frame lying scattered in every direction. . . . It seemed like a calm after a heavy storm."

On the next morning, the patriots started for home under a bright sun, the first they had seen in many a day. Their march was hastened by fear that Banastre Tarleton might have been dispatched to overtake the mountain men, which indeed he had been, though he turned back when he heard of the fate of Ferguson. What to do with the many prisoners was a huge problem to the frontiersmen, who wanted to return home as fast as possible. The patriots also had their own wounded to care for. One of them, Pat Murphy, had been shot across his windpipe, cutting it considerably. A keg of rum had been captured from the Tories, and companions of Murphy bathed his wound in it. The Irishman could not resist grabbing the cup and swallowing some of the rum, remarking that "a little *in* is as good as *out!*" [30]

Colonel Campbell and a detachment stayed behind for a day to complete the burying of the dead in two shallow trenches, one for the Tories, a smaller one for the patriots. That evening these men rejoined their companions at a plantation on the Broad River, a lucky stop, for here was a sweet potato patch ample enough to supply the whole outfit, which had not tasted real food since their stop at the Cowpens prior to the battle. A couple of stray cows added to the welcome repast. As the mountain men returned, some of them evidently could not restrain their resentment against their Tory prisoners, for on October 11, Colonel Campbell issued orders to stop "the disorderly manner of slaughtering and disturbing the prisoners," adding that if this were not done, he would punish those who did not comply.

The tense situation came to a climax next day when the forces arrived at Bickerstaff's plantation where Forest City, North Carolina, now is. Officers of the Carolinians complained to Campbell that they had noticed among the prisoners a number who were said to be robbers, arsonists and murderers, and it was felt that if they were allowed to escape, they would commit "enormities worse than their former ones." These Tories, it was urged, should be tried immediately and punished. Colonel Campbell agreed. In order to make the trials "legal," a copy of the law of North Carolina was obtained, which authorized "two magistrates to summon a jury and forthwith try, and if found guilty, to execute persons who had violated its precepts." It happened that most of the North Carolina officers present were also magistrates, so it was reasoned—or rationalized—that the procedure was proper in both civil and military law. The resulting trial lasted all day; thirty-six of the accused Tories were found guilty of breaking open houses, killing the men, turning the women and children out of doors and burning the houses. To complete this sharp cycle of whirlwind "justice," a suitable oak tree nearby was selected, and those found guilty were to swing from its limbs without delay. Nine of them did. One of the others, Isaac Baldwin, was more fortunate. Just before he was to hang, his brother, a mere lad, came up to say his farewell. He threw his arms around his condemned brother and "set up the most piteous screaming and lamentation, as if he were going into convulsions or his heart would break with sorrow. While all were witnessing this touching scene, the youth managed to cut the cords which bound his brother, he darted away, breaking through a line of soldiers and easily escaped under cover of darkness into the surrounding forest."

One of those executed was Colonel Ambrose Mills, an elderly man. Later Cornwallis wrote American General William Smallwood, "I must now observe that the cruelty exercised on the prisoners taken under Major Ferguson is shocking to humanity; and the hanging of poor old Colonel Mills, who was always a fair and open enemy to your cause, was an act of the most savage barbarity." [31]

The summary execution of the nine Tories was frontier justice of a questionable type, too quick to be reasonably justified, too vengeful to be understood even in a day of Nuremberg trials. Yet those in charge undoubtedly believed such procedure to be proper, especially in view of like hangings of Americans by the British at Camden, Augusta and Ninety-six. One bloodthirsty rebel, Captain Paddy Carr, when he saw the Tories swinging dead from the tree, remarked, "Would to God every tree in the wilderness bore such fruit as this!"

He said he would have made a good soldier had God given him a less merciful heart. This is scarcely borne out in the account that on his way back to Georgia from King's Mountain, Carr killed eighteen Tories with his own hands, bringing his total to a round one hundred destroyed during the war.

These were the extreme cases. To the bulk of the over-mountain men, the battle was over and taking care of prisoners was a bore and a hindrance to the return home. About five-sixths of the Tory prisoners escaped, lending the impression that not too much care was exercised in keeping them in custody. Some were paroled and bound over for a later appearance in court. Only 130 of them remained to be delivered to General Gates at Hillsboro, and he did not know what to do with them.

Gates asked Governor Thomas Jefferson of Virginia for advice as to their disposal, but the answer was to turn them over to the civil governments of the Carolinas. Such governments hardly existed and the result was the escape of half of those still in custody. Jefferson later commented regarding King's Mountain: "This memorable victory was the joyful annunciation of that turn of the tide of success which terminated the Revolutionary War with the seal of independence." [32]

A historian of two generations later stated that "Never was a success more opportune. The most gallant charges of the royal forces were eventually crushed by the ever-increasing fatality of an aggravated fire of single shots." Lieutenant Allaire of Ferguson's command said, "There is not a regiment in all his Majesty's service that ever went through the fatigues or suffered so much as our detachment." William Gilmore Simms wrote:

> Hark, 'tis the voice of the mountain
> And it speaks to our heart in its pride,
> As it tells of the bearing of heroes
> Who conquered its summit and died.

Historian Benson Lossing believed that the battle crushed the spirit of the Tories and weakened beyond recovery the royal power in the Carolinas. There is no doubt that it altered the attitude of the British military leaders toward the local support they had fondly believed was forthcoming in the South. Lord Rawdon wrote to Sir Henry Clinton soon after the battle that though he felt they had a powerful body of friends in North Carolina, not enough evidence had yet been given, either of their numbers or activity, to justify the stake of the province for the uncertain advantages that might attend immediate junction with them. As has been noted, Clinton blamed Cornwallis for letting Ferguson advance so far into hostile country without regular support. [33]

As for Cornwallis, King's Mountain changed his plans. Ferguson's appeal had reached him on the very day of the battle, too late to do anything about it except to send Tarleton, who had returned with the shocking news of the defeat. It was now feared that the rebels would sweep into South Carolina and capture Camden and Ninety-six. Cornwallis therefore abandoned his plans for the subjugation of North Carolina, and by October 14 his troops were in hurried withdrawal. He went from Charlotte to Winnsboro in upper South Carolina just a week after the debacle at King's Mountain. The rainy season had set in, and Cornwallis' situation was worsened by a Tory guide, William McCafferty, who led him two miles off the main course and then deserted him in the dark of night. For five days, his soldiers had to live off the corn gathered from fields through which they passed and were compelled to sleep on the wet ground. American militia hung on the flanks of the redcoats, and in addition there was much sickness; Cornwallis himself came down with a fever which kept him in his wagon for days. After two weeks of such wretched conditions the British commander arrived at Winnsboro, his winter campaign drastically disrupted.[34]

The British never forgot the gallant stand of Ferguson. Colonel Robert Gray of the South Carolina Provincial Militia, who later went to Nova Scotia, said about the Tories at King's Mountain, "Our militia behaved with a degree of steadiness and spirit that would not have disgraced any regular troops." In his appraisal of the general situation, Colonel Gray revealed that the regular British officers as a rule regarded the Tory militia with contempt, but that Ferguson did not. "Had he lived," remarked Gray, "the militia would have been completely formed. He possessed all the talents and ambition necessary to accomplish this purpose." In his comment which followed, Gray probably hit upon the principal reasons why the Tories in the South and elsewhere did not perform as effectively as their opponents. He stated that when the rebel militia were made prisoners, they were immediately delivered to regular British officers who, being ignorant of the dispositions and names of the people concerned, treated them with the utmost lenity and sent them back to their homes on parole. Consequently, no sooner did the rebel prisoners get out of their captors' hands than they broke their parole, took up arms and "made it a point to murder every Tory militiaman who had any part in making them prisoners." On the other hand, Gray continued, whenever a Tory militiaman was made a prisoner, he was delivered, not to the Continentals, but to the rebel militia, who looked upon him as a state prisoner, as a man who deserved the halter, and therefore treated him with the greatest cruelty. If he was not killed after being made a prisoner, he was hurried to Virginia or North Carolina, where he was kept a prisoner without friends, money, credit or hopes of exchange. "So," the account went, "it was no longer safe to be a loyalist on the frontiers. Overwhelmed with dismay, they became dejected and timid, while the others, increasing in boldness and enterprise, made constant inroads in small parties and murdered every loyalist they found, whether in arms or at home. Their eruptions answered the descriptions we have of the Goths and Vandals. The unfortunate loyalist found the fury of the whole war let loose upon him. He was no longer safe to sleep in his own house. He hid himself in the swamps. . . . Had our militia been certain of being treated as prisoners of war by the enemy, many more would have aided the royal standard. They should have been allowed to retaliate against the rebel prisoners in kind." [35]

A vivid example of cruelty to the Tories was furnished by Colonel Benjamin Cleveland, not only in the trial and execution of the prisoners already described but also in other instances. Lieutenant Allaire stated that Cleveland knocked down Dr. Uzal Johnson, the only physician present, when he attempted to dress the wounds of a Tory whom the rebels had cut with swords on their homeward march from King's Mountain. Not long afterward, Cleveland captured two Tory outlaws and hanged them unceremoniously. Then, ironically, he himself was captured by Tories who made him write out passes for them as Whigs. He managed to delay this process until his brother came up and rescued him—and he later had the pleasure of having three of his Tory captors hanged for this enterprise on their part. A Tory horse thief was left with Cleveland's two small sons during one of his absences. Impatient, they asked their mother what their father would do with the culprits. "Hang them!" she replied, and the boys did.[36]

A nephew of Colonel Cleveland, Jesse Franklin, later governor of North Carolina, was caught during the war by Tories, who were determined to hang him. They tied a rope around his neck, as his uncle had done to so many of their number, whereupon the young man remarked that if they hanged him, his uncle would pursue them like a bloodhound as long as they had a drop of blood in their veins. They desisted and let Franklin go.

Colonel Cleveland weighed close to 300 pounds during the Revolution, but grew with the years until he was said to have weighed 450 pounds in his last days, a physical match for the huge horn which he blew from the nearby mountains to call in his fighting men. Ironically, he could not establish a proper claim to the large plantation he lived on, and left North Carolina for South Carolina, where he lived the rest of his life. Today near the courthouse in Wilkesboro, North Carolina, there is a 200-year-old "Tory oak," so called because it is said that from its sturdy branches Cleveland hanged several men who chose the hazardous course of loyalty to their king.[37]

11. *Twilight*

For a time after the taking of Charleston by Sir Henry Clinton, the people of South Carolina appeared willing to return to allegiance to the British crown and live peacefully under its government. But within a few weeks, a change in sentiment took place which pointed up the stubborn attitude and dense lack of good judgment on the part of the British in handling their American friends. The causes of this drastic and significant change were the royal attempt to make the Carolinians bear arms, the avowed plundering of the citizenry by the soldiers of the King, and the severe treatment of those who disagreed with the shortsighted objectives of the English government. The much-resented plundering took place despite the strict orders of Clinton and Cornwallis. For example, Presbyterian meeting houses containing Bibles with Scottish versions of the Psalms were destroyed, the British stupidly assuming that those using them had the same political views as the Puritans of New England.

So, with all the Tory sentiment and activity in the Carolinas, the contribution of loyal help was, in summation, generally small. They performed successful raids and annoyed their enemies to a considerable extent, but, as shown in the example of King's Mountain, failed to attain large-scale success. Here as elsewhere, the Tories lacked able leadership, partly because their leaders were not sufficiently authorized to act on their own initiative and partly because the British generals did not trust the Tory officers or hold their ability in high regard. The partisan warfare carried on between Whigs and Tories was looked upon with disdain, both by the British regular officers and by such patriot leaders as General Nathanael Greene, who commented, "They persecute each other with little less than savage fury. There is nothing but murder and devastation in every quarter." [1]

In North Carolina, a Whig, John Cornelison, was attacked by a band of Tories, beaten, shot and pushed into his own fireplace, from which he was pulled dead by his wife. A relative of his named Spiney learned the name of one of these Tories and followed him into Tennessee. Finding the man living alone in a log cabin, Spiney quietly pushed the muzzle of his gun through a crack between the logs and shot him down, then returned to North Carolina. An officer of Greene's army said he had never seen such examples of desolation, bloodshed and deliberate murder as the two warring factions showed toward each other. They were literally at each other's throats, he added, and he estimated that hardly a day passed but that some poor Tory was put to death at his own door. A British officer described a Tory refugee in 1781 as having scarcely the appearance of being human; he wore the skin of a raccoon for a hat, his beard was some inches long, and he was so thin that he looked as if he had made his escape from Surgeon's Hall. He wore no shirt, his whole dress being skins of various animals. He said he had lived for three years in the woods, underground; that he had frequently been sought after by the Americans, and was certain of instant death whenever he should be taken. [2]

Even so, many Tories continued to resist until the end of the war. Those in the region around Camden, South Carolina, were under the command of Colonel Henry Rugeley, an Englishman who had also retained the respect of the Whigs. Before his military activity was over, however, he had the respect of neither side. Rugeley gathered around him a hundred Tories and converted a long barn on his plantation into a kind of fort. Loopholes were cut within it and a platform erected on the inside for an upper tier of muskets. Around the outside, earth was piled and an abatis constructed. The "fort" was considered impregnable to any opposing force not having artillery. But General Daniel Morgan had just taken command of part of Greene's forces and, hearing of this fortified position, determined to reduce it. He sent rotund Colonel William Washington and his cavalry to do the job. Washington arrived in front of the fortification and demanded the surrender of the garrison. Rugeley felt confident he could hold out, and to his credit it should be mentioned that he had been advised by his superior, Lord Rawdon, to treat rather than risk capture by a stronger force. Rugeley refused to surrender, and Washington found that neither his bullets nor cavalry swords had much effect, so he decided to change his tactics. He assumed correctly that lack of artillery made him ineffective. Fashioning a fat pine log to look at a distance like the barrel of a cannon, Washington had the "Quaker gun" placed on the stubs of three of its limbs and mounted on a pair of wagon wheels. His dismounted men pushed it menacingly toward the fort, in plain view of the defenders. Meanwhile, a corporal of dragoons was sent with a flag, summoning the Tories to surrender or be blown to pieces.

Seeing the "cannon" approaching, Rugeley surrendered, and he and his hundred officers and men marched out as prisoners. As a result of this fiasco, Rugeley became the laughingstock of both armies. Cornwallis commented significantly, "Rugeley will not be made a brigadier." [3]

This ludicrous occurrence probably was not a great surprise to Cornwallis, for a few weeks prior to the surrender of the little fort, he had written to Germain that "the leading persons of the Loyalists are so undecided in their councils that they have lost the critical time of availing themselves of our success [at Camden] and even suffered General Gates to pass to Hillsboro with a guard of six men only. They continue, however, to give the strongest assurances of support when his Majesty's troops shall have penetrated into the interior parts of the province. The patience with which they endure the most cruel torments and suffer the most violent oppressions that a country ever labored under, convince me that they are sincere, at least as far as their affection to the cause of Great Britain." [4]

Regardless of their opinions, a number of Tories were forced to serve in the American forces against the British. One of these was Alexander Chesney, Irish by birth, who was a captain with Ferguson at King's Mountain, where he was captured; he escaped soon afterward and made his way back to South Carolina. Here he hid in a cave for three weeks before joining the corps of Tarleton. Chesney had been imprisoned by the patriots in 1776 for helping other Tories to escape, and was given the choice of standing trial or joining the American army. He chose the latter and fought later that year against Clinton at Charleston, but claimed that he had always retained his loyalty to the King. In 1778 he took part in an expedition against the Florida Tories, and he bore arms in other campaigns against the British and their sympathizers until Clinton took Charleston in 1780. The British commander issued a proclamation asking loyal persons to join him, and Chesney did. After he joined Tarleton, the "turncoat" was among the force which was routed at the Cowpens by Daniel Morgan, at which time he escaped again and helped Lord Rawdon against the patriots at Ninety-six, continuing his truly checkered military career. In 1782, Chesney returned to his native Ireland, where he became an officer in the civil service at Bangor.[5]

A similar but disputed case was that of Andrew Williamson, who was called "the Benedict Arnold of South Carolina." He was probably the most influential man in the Ninety-six district, and until the fall of Charleston, he was quite active as a brigadier general of militia against the British. Yet it was rumored that he secretly favored the British, was in communication with them, and intentionally delayed forwarding to Governor Rutledge the news of the fall of Charleston to the British, so that Rutledge was almost captured by the redcoats. Williamson surrendered command of his patriot militia at Ninety-six after they had refused his offer to lead them to North Carolina. After the war, he re-

mained in South Carolina at the request of Nathanael Greene, and his
estate was not even molested.[6]

Some persons simply wished well to both sides. One such was Redmond Burke of South Carolina, a surgeon in the American army who received the pay of a colonel. But when he saw the dispute change from
redress of grievances to avowal of independence and he perceived that
serious consequences might befall America, he resigned his commission.
His brother, Thomas Burke, had been a member of Congress and governor of North Carolina. Regardless, Redmond's house, near Combakee
Ferry, which was in the line of march of British General Prevost's army
on its way to Charleston, was not respected; for it was burned and its
livestock and furniture taken away.[7]

Not so neutral was Colonel William Fortune of the Royal Militia in
South Carolina, who was taken prisoner eight times and his house plundered as often. "He was caused to abandon all society for the space of
three years before the arrival of the royal army, and secretly retire to the
lonely wilds, being several weeks together at one time without seeing one
human creature, except when in a starving condition, at the hazard of his
life, he would venture to an appointed place in some swamp or thicket to
see his distressed and aggrieved wife, who brought him a bit of victuals;
withal, to spend some of the solitary hours, chief of which was in tears
in the dark and dismal hours of the night, there being no safety in daylight to see each other." [8]

Some Whigs were searching for Tories in the swampy district of
Cheraw in South Carolina, when they came to the edge of one morass,
hesitated, then sent one of their number, Harry Sparks, in to find the
nest of Tories they sought. He did not return in a reasonable time, so
they went in after him. Their worst fears were confirmed. Sparks was
found hanging lifeless from a tree limb. A cry for vengeance went up,
and soon Captain Daniel Sparks, brother of the dead man, succeeded in
capturing one of the leaders of the Tory band. Sparks immediately told
him he would be hanged.

"Very well," replied the Tory, "as soon as you please."

The men were ordered to proceed with the execution. The prisoner, as
good as his blithe words, assisted with apparent cheerfulness in adjusting
the rope around his own neck, sprang from the ground to the back of the
horse brought for him, asked if the rope was well secured to the limb
above, and upon being told that it was, kicked the horse "and swung off
into eternity with an oath on his lips." [9]

Soon afterward patriot Colonel Abel Kolb pressed an attack against
the local Tories, then returned to his home not far away in Marion, South
Carolina. The aroused Tories heard that he was at home with his family
and determined to make an example of him. Under cover of darkness
a band of them rode to his house and awakened him. Learning that his
enemies were outside, Kolb resolved to sell his life as dearly as possible,

so he refused to come out; instead, he fired on them. The Tories in reply threatened to burn down his house along with its occupants. Moved by the pleas of the women of his family, Kolb agreed to surrender himself as a prisoner of war. The offer was accepted and he went out, accompanied by his wife and sisters. But on the very point of presenting his sword, Colonel Kolb was shot dead by a private named Mike Goings, a Tory who had a special grudge against him.[10]

In Orangeburg, South Carolina, Tory William Haywood was less assertive. He declared that "neither threats nor allurements could stop his endeavors to preserve peace and obedience," although he was driven from one county to another and was reduced from a state of prosperity to one of poverty because of his continued adherence to the British crown. Jailed for a time, Haywood escaped, a usual sequence, wandered for eight months, and at length arrived with his wife and four small children at Wilmington, North Carolina, where, he said, "had not the hand of Providence visibly appeared in his favor, he must have sunk beneath such a load of care and fatigue, but that health, hope and resolution attended him the whole time." Later the family went to New York, where they all had smallpox, "without the least assistance from any of the British officers." Sir Henry Clinton, after questioning Haywood about approaches to Charleston, "dismissed him with a frown." [11]

As for James Alexander of Charleston, his attachment to the British was such that he used every persuasive argument in his power to get his friends to adhere to the royal cause. Despite insults and some injuries from the rebels, Alexander overcame a number of them and took them to the British headquarters. But John Felder, patriot justice of the peace at Orangeburg, a known Tory-hater, proved to be a hard one to apprehend. A group under Alexander assembled at Felder's house and called on him to surrender. The reply was a shot through the door, which killed the Tory who made the demand. The firing continued and others were killed and wounded. Then, in final desperation, the Tories set fire to the house, and in attempting to flee it, Felder was shot and killed.[12]

John Macklin kept the London Coffee House, principal tavern of Charleston, and eavesdropped on the meetings of the rebels there, reporting them to the British. Eventually, Macklin thought it safer to leave, so he removed his family to St. Augustine in an open boat. Later he was captured, taken back to Charleston and reportedly "treated with the greatest severity and then exchanged." Paul Hamilton, Tory Charleston planter, lost his home and slaves and fled to Bermuda, where he was exposed to "poverty and obscurity." Robert Williams, Charleston lawyer, listed among his losses, "Pew Number 15 in the South Aisle of Saint Philips Church, to which member hath an absolute right transmissable to his house servants named 'Mulatto Billy' and the wench, Letitia."[13]

Some of the Tories who left America returned during the war; for example, Lieutenant Governor William Bull of South Carolina, who was banished to England in 1777. After the British retook Charleston, he came back to resume his former role. Two years before, he had conveyed his South Carolina estate to a "confidential purchaser," and because of the circumstances and the fact that no payment was involved, the state had charged that the transaction was fraudulent. Actually, the purchaser was Governor Bull's nephew, General Stephen Bull, who took possession and thereafter ignored his absent uncle. The nephew even opposed in the South Carolina Assembly any move to permit his uncle to return to the state and his plantations, said to be worth more than 40,000 pounds.[14]

Sir John Colleton owned a large estate near Charleston and used his utmost endeavors on all occasions to promote due obedience to the Crown and to suppress all tumultuous and rebellious assemblies for the purpose of opposing the authority of Great Britain. His estate was known as "Fairlawn." When the British army was at Monck's Corner, a mile away, it obtained corn, peas, fodder, cattle boats and Negroes from the plantation. The house at Fairlawn was elegant, made of brick and two stories high, with cypress shingles, stables, carriage houses and a large barn. It was later converted into a storehouse and hospital for the British military forces, and in order to fortify it against the Americans, the royal officers cut down some 400 stately cedar trees, which were used in the fortifications. When they reached the house, the Americans burned it along with all its fine furniture. "Nothing remained except 115 Negroes, some plate and a few wild horses." Three-fourths of the Tories of Charleston were not so affluent, being crown and church officials, doctors and lawyers. One of Cornwallis' officers referred to "numerous friends who to the hazard of their lives, sacrifice of their families and to the utter ruin of their possessions, adhered to us under every change of fortune." [15]

That such adherence continued until at least 1782 is borne out by the report of Lieutenant James Leonard, a patriot officer who said that while he was active in South Carolina, the Tories there were "500 strong and growing stronger, with spies, stolen horses and in need of suppressing." While carrying a message from Governor John Rutledge of the state to General Greene, Leonard became lost in the Carolina woods and was not sure whether or not he was in friendly territory. Night came on and in his wandering through the trees and brush he sighted the light of a cabin and approached it. After making himself known, he was welcomed by the occupant and his wife and asked to spend the night, after the custom of the time. Leonard gladly accepted but became skeptical of the political affiliation of his hosts as he talked with them. When he lay down to sleep, he placed his sword and pistols nearby. During the night, he was awakened by the noise of men outside the cabin. Listening to their voices, he was convinced of their intentions when he heard one say, "Let's kill that damned rebel!"

Leonard lay motionless with fear. Then he heard his host tell the men that if they did kill his visitor, General Greene would certainly come in search of him and in so doing doubtless find the rendezvous of these Tories. They agreed and much to the relief of the lieutenant went on their way. The next morning, he left unmolested.[16]

James Simpson, former royal attorney general of South Carolina, was sent by Germain to ascertain the extent of Tory assistance in the South. As a result of this survey, Clinton reported to Germain that Simpson, who was believed to know the nature of the southern people, had given "flattering reports of assistance from the inhabitants." But he had also found that the Tories who had opposed the rebels had been persecuted from the beginning of the war. Simpson admitted that some of the Carolina Tories were "deservedly so obnoxious" that regardless of the fate of the government, it would be impossible for them to escape the effects of the great private resentment held against them by the patriots. This proved to be all too true. But some resentment took a humorous turn. William Campbell was now a brigadier general of militia and was serving with Lafayette in Cumberland County, Virginia. One day a Tory parson named McRea visited the command and argued eloquently with the patriots, trying to discourage them from fighting against the British. He said that the army of Cornwallis would slaughter the Americans like so many beeves. Campbell called the peppery parson before him and said he would show the Tory how they intended to treat Cornwallis. Whereupon he ordered McRea to lie flat on his stomach across a road and had every one of his soldiers step over him on their march.[17]

This minister was more fortunate than the Reverend William Andrews, rector at Portsmouth, Virginia. When that town was evacuated, Cornwallis made him chaplain of the Yorktown garrison and he was present at the surrender to the Americans. Immediately after this event, Andrews returned to Portsmouth in order to remove his family to New York, but instead he was seized, imprisoned and sentenced to banishment. His wife died during the trial. In his report to the British government about the experience, Andrews related that during an earlier American celebration of the Declaration of Independence, he had been knocked down in the street for declaring that the Declaration "was both improper and impolitic."[18]

Equally opposed to such a declaration and more involved in it was the Reverend Thomas Gwatkin, professor of languages at the College of William and Mary. He was a Tory and stated that in June of 1775, he received "several applications from Richard Henry Lee and Thomas Jefferson and other gentlemen, at that time members of Congress, to draw up memorials in vindication of the proceedings of Congress, with a promise of protection and ample rewards." Gwatkin "declined and absolutely refused." For such refusal, he said, he received ill treatment, his life was threatened and he fled for protection to Lord Dunmore.

So it ironically appears that a Tory minister-professor, the Reverend Mr. Gwatkin, was asked to write a "Declaration of Independence" a year before the well-known American one was written, with some of the same patriot figures involved! [19]

The Tories also had a Declaration of Independence of their own. It appeared in Rivington's *Royal Gazette* on November 17, 1781, and belatedly, since this was just a month after the surrender at Yorktown. It began: "When in the course of human events it becomes necessary for men, in order to preserve their lives, liberties and properties, and to secure to themselves and to their posterity, that peace, liberty and safety to which by the laws of nature's God they are entitled, to throw off and renounce all allegiance to a government, which under the insidious pretences of securing these inestimable blessings to them, has wholly deprived them of any security of either life, liberty, property, peace or safety. . . ."

Just weeks before the Yorktown surrender, that brave but disabled general, Daniel Morgan, recuperating at his Winchester home, was summoned to put down a Tory uprising on Lost Creek in what is now Hardy County, West Virginia. Under the leadership of a Scotsman, John Claypool, these Tories had refused to pay state taxes or serve in the militia. Claypool was made a colonel, his sons captains, and they announced that they would soon march out and join Cornwallis. For the veteran Morgan, smashing this small insurrection was a field day. He captured the Tories almost without firing a shot, one man who resisted being killed. Then Morgan and his exuberant followers paused and refreshed themselves at the abundant farm of one of the Tories, John Brake, whose distillery product added to the festivity.

Many such farms belonging to Tories passed into the eager hands of their adversaries. Samuel Greatrex left his Virginia plantation and joined the British to fight at the Cowpens and Guilford Courthouse. Hamilton Usher St. George complained that four whale boats attacked and plundered his "very opulent mansion" on Hog Island in the James River. He had furnished supplies to Cornwallis at Yorktown. James Parker, another plantation owner, was kept a prisoner for eight months, then with eight other Tories escaped and traveled nearly 500 miles, mostly by night, ending up on a prison ship off Rhode Island. Captain Stair Agnew of the Queen's Rangers was a Virginian whose family, he said, was known to General Washington. He and his aged father were also taken as prisoners to Rhode Island by the patriots. There, according to Agnew, the French minister was informed by Washington, "not to exchange characters so dangerous [as the Agnews], on the contrary, to detain them during the war." [21]

Of all the Tories in this region, the case of Alan Cameron, a Scotsman who went to Virginia before the Revolution, seems most incredibly piteous. At the close of a long personal narrative, he exclaims, "I was reckoned in general the greatest personal sufferer in America as a Loyalist, both within and without the British lines, of any that survived with life." Cameron was a prisoner most of the time from 1775 to 1778. Having Tory sentiments from the start, he rode to Savannah in June, 1775, 300 miles in four days, thinking it was in royal hands. He fell into the hands of rebels, came down with fever, escaped and made his way to Florida. Returning to Virginia, Cameron was sent by Lord Dunmore on a trip to Detroit, there to raise a regiment of whites and Indians to come and meet Dunmore at Alexandria, Virginia. But Cameron and his companion, Lieutenant Colonel John Connolly, were captured in Maryland and taken to "a village called Hagerstown where they were examined by a committee of the lower class. From thence to Frederick Town, there re-examined and abused by a similar set of men, and afterward confined within a small apartment for six weeks under a strong, riotous guard, who in their frolics threatened us with what they called 'Indian law,' meaning to tomahawk us, and one night we actually expected they would put an end to our existence by such means." Cameron added that by order of Congress, he and Connolly were mounted on horses with their heads "joined as close as possible to each other by a rope between," and conducted in this extraordinary manner "by an unfeeling brute in frost and snow to Philadelphia," staying at night in jails at York and Lancaster and insulted by mobs who gathered along the route. In Philadelphia, they were thrown into a jail infested with vermin, "debtors, common thieves, murderers and women of bad fame" in the winter weather, without heat, water, bedding or food for twenty-four hours. Connolly was rescued by a brother who was a patriot, but the unfortunate Cameron was continued in captivity. He used the fireplace "for a certain purpose, as least noxious, and in the most distant corner" kept the water allowance which he was issued every twenty-four hours. He had to sleep in a coat on the floor, and to add to his misery, the jailer nailed down the window sashes, which deprived the prisoner of fresh air. He was not allowed to talk to fellow prisoners.

After nine months of such close confinement, Cameron was given a cell in the upper part of the jail. He rejoiced that he was now better off—that is until Captain Neil McLean "who had a bloody flux was thrown in with him," and soon a Doctor Smyth who was equally ill with the same disorder was also added to his room, to render his confinement "more irksome, and if possible, less supportable." Cameron had to be nurse as well as prisoner, but stated that he maintained "tolerable health and spirits. Pains were taken to put an end to my life by torture and piecemeal." When the other two inmates regained strength, they helped Cameron cut a hole through the ceiling with an old knife and a gimlet. Using sheets and blankets as ropes, they hoisted Cameron to the roof of the jail, from which he made his way along its surface on all fours, the rope tied to his body. Just as he was to "clear the edge of the roof," the rope gave way and he fell about fifty feet into some rubbish, stones and brickbats below, on which he broke the heel of one foot, "snapped the tendon in the other, destroyed two ligaments and in a general manner dislocated both ankles, besides receiving a violent contusion in my breast. In short," he said, "I suffered almost everything but death by the shock." Hearing his fall, the guards came running and abused Cameron "in a most barbarous manner, alarmed the town and exposed me in this melancholy condition on a bitter cold and frosty night of December to the mob." They would not even give him a drink of water, he reported, but took him back to his bleak cell and threw him unceremoniously into it. Covered with blood and dust, Cameron was visited by a doctor, who observed that the victim was so swollen that he could do little to assist and felt Cameron would not live many hours. The jailers urged the doctor to cut Cameron's throat.

"That is the way to cure the damned rascal!" they added.

This poor Tory eventually recovered, however, much to the chagrin of his captors. A friend obtained permission to take him in a wheelbarrow to be treated by outside doctors. Cameron was thus sneaked away, ferried across the Delaware River and turned over to some friendly people who were told that he was a schoolmaster who had been wounded by the British, so that they would not "blabber" about him. Then, "Mr. Cooke, a friend, came from Philadelphia and carried me on his back," Cameron stated, "balancing himself with my crutches into the cedar swamp, where he built me a wigwam. Pestered by mosquitoes, I began to yield to despair at last." But Cooke procured a wagon and took Cameron to Cape May and there a Thomas Hand promised to row them out to a British man-of-war in sight at anchor. However, Hand betrayed them and instead called a posse which, in this fantastic series of excruciating adventures, took Cameron prisoner again. Though weary, he was placed in a cart and drawn by an ox through the wilderness paths to Philadelphia, without being given an opportunity to dress his wounds. "At one house," he recalled, "two guards seemed anxious of some pretence to murder me. Could not sleep because of bed bugs." After reaching the city, he was taken to an inn where he was exposed again to the insults of a mob. A beer dray was brought to carry him to jail, but he "rejected the illiberal idea of being carried in so very ignominious a manner through the streets" and instead hobbled along on crutches for almost a mile, until he was received by an "inhumane monster of a jailer into his inhospitable and merciless clutches." Confined until the following night in the wing of the jail reserved for criminals, Cameron was then thrown into a dungeon twenty feet under the ground, in which his only company was "a swarm of starving rats that sallied in occasionally, there being only a grated door to my paved vault. These rats were so ravenous and bold as actually to tear the cockade out of my hat, and made such a continual noise as would have disturbed my rest, if everything else had favored it."

After three weeks in this infested hole, poor Cameron was at last paroled by the Americans, who evidently were afraid of Sir William Howe's preparations to move from New York on Philadelphia. In explaining his treatment, Cameron said, Congress claimed that it had kept him jailed to protect his life from "an enraged and injured public." Their true ob-

ject in punishing him so, Cameron added, was to make him an example
so as to deter others. They named him "The Infamous Cameron." That
he might recover, he was placed in a hospital at Yellow Spring, near
Philadelphia.

After the Americans were defeated at Brandywine, Cameron tried to
join the army of General Howe, but apparently was in too weak a condition, for he fell from his horse en route and was set upon by an American
officer, who stripped him of his clothes and ripped them up to see if any
secret papers were therein. Misfortune still dogged Cameron. He was
placed in jail at Reading. Finally, on April 22, 1778, he was exchanged
after what he aptly described as "unexampled cruelty and persecution for
near three years." From Philadelphia he went to New York and from
there sought haven in England.[22]

12. The Reckoning

In the latter part of the war, there came to Virginia a man whose role in the Revolution is still somewhat veiled in mystery. He was Benedict Arnold, the arch turncoat, a designation which appears more apt than terming him a patriot or Tory, neither or both. The feeling of persecution which this undeniably brave officer had long carried with him was apparently at a fever pitch, to judge from his flurry of activity against the American cause, centered at the time in the picturesque Old Dominion state.

Arnold now commanded British and Tories as a brigadier general, commissioned by the Crown, and ironically a rank lower than his former American major generalcy. As has been seen, he had married a Tory when he was stationed in Philadelphia, Margaret Shippen, daughter of a distinguished lawyer who, though mildly loyal to he Crown himself, was so respected that after the war he became chief justice of the supreme court of Pennsylvania. While in Philadelphia, Arnold was as dazzled by the gay society as he was resentful of the American government for delaying his promotion and censuring him for selling army supplies for his own private gain. So in trying to keep up with the social set of the city, he spent money faster than he made it—by whatever means. This situation led to his assignment to West Point, his subsequent treason and then his flight to the British in New York City. From there in 1780, Arnold sent out an appeal to patriot soldiers to leave their army, give up the Continental cause and come over to him, offering the enlisted men three guineas each and commissions to those whom he considered to be worthy. To the Tories, Arnold exhorted, "Reflect on what you have lost—

consider to what you are reduced, and by your courage repel the ruin
that still threatens you. . . . What is America but a land of widows, beg-
gars and orphans?" At first, Washington tried to ignore this appeal from
Arnold, because it was felt that little attention would be paid to it. But
when a second stirring notice went out from the fiery traitor, Washington
showed his annoyance by expressing contempt for such statements.[1]

Active as usual, Benedict Arnold, at the head of a thousand British and
Tory troops, went by ship from New York to Virginia. He sailed up the
James River, capturing residents and destroying military supplies. He
raided Richmond and put the legislature to flight; Governor Thomas Jefferson was nearly captured, having just time to jump on a horse and escape to the mountains. During his Virginia raids, Arnold took an American captain prisoner and asked him what the Americans would do with
Benedict Arnold if they should capture him. The captain hesitated, but
upon being repeatedly urged to reply, finally did so:

"Why, sir, if I must answer your question, you must excuse my telling
you the plain truth. If my countrymen should catch you, I believe they
would first cut off that lame leg which was wounded in the cause of
freedom and virtue, and bury it with the honors of war, and afterwards,
hang the remainder of your body in gibbets." [2]

A convenient stopping place for Arnold during the expedition was
Westover, the renowned ancestral home of the Byrd family, about twenty-
five miles below Richmond. Here lived Mrs. Mary Willing Byrd, widow
of Colonel William Byrd, who had served with the British in the French
and Indian War. Mrs. Byrd had not only this connection with the royal
cause but she was related to Mrs. Arnold, being the daughter of Charles
and Anne (Shippen) Willing of Philadelphia. Various communications
passed between Mrs. Byrd and Arnold, which at the time were thought
by the Americans to be treasonable on her part, although this was never
proved. In February of 1781, all of her papers were seized by the patriots.
Arthur Lee commented that "Arnold, with a handful of bad troops,
marched about the country, taking and destroying what he pleased,
feasting with his Tory friends and settling a regular correspondence with
them." Mrs. Byrd petitioned Sir Guy Carleton on June 5, 1783, for losses
to her estate, stating that Arnold, Cornwallis and General Phillips promised her payment.[3]

Arnold's Virginia forays were mild compared to the raid led against
New London in his native Connecticut a few months after he had been
recalled by Clinton from the South. With a corps of 1,500 Tory and British soldiers, Arnold attacked the town, overcame the garrison, and after
the Colonel in command surrendered, had him run through with his own
sword. Eighty other men were murdered by Arnold's vengeful forces.
After that, the turncoat burned the town. Hated more than ever in both
his state and his country, Arnold then retired with his men to New York
City. This was the last battle of the war in the North.[4]

Even the British did not trust Arnold, for if a man could change sides

once, he could do it again. Colonel John Simcoe, an outstanding Tory
officer and in charge of the Queen's Rangers under Arnold in Virginia,
had been asked by Clinton to keep an eye on Arnold. Simcoe performed
expertly in this campaign, as he had in previous ones. Two years before,
he had set the New Jersey countryside agog by daringly executing one
of the most skillful exploits of the Revolution. An officer young for his
rank, he had succeeded the fabulous Robert Rogers as head of the Queen's
Rangers and had distinguished himself at the battle of Brandywine. His
men were mostly Tory refugees and warmly devoted to their dashing
commander, who in well-conducted raids and brilliant actions infused
into his men his own spirit of tireless energy. Sir Henry Clinton reported
that in three years after Simcoe had taken command, the Queen's Rangers
killed or made prisoners twice their number. Simcoe won the admiration
of friend and foe alike for the speed and success of his strokes.

On October 26, 1779, Simcoe and his Rangers set out on their most
colorful mission. He had been informed that fifty flatboats capable of
holding seventy men each were at Van Veghten's Bridge on the upper
Raritan River, on carriages waiting to be drawn across the country to
Washington's patriot forces at West Point. These boats had been built on
the Delaware by Washington's orders so as to be ready to aid in an attack
on New York City which he was then planning. Simcoe's plan was to
make a bold dash up the river, destroy the boats and other military property of the enemy there, and perhaps capture Captain Stephen Moylan,
who commanded the American Light Dragoons and was said to be staying at the home of his father-in-law, Judge Philip Van Horne, in Bound
Brook. He was also to look for Governor Livingston of New Jersey, re-
puted to be stopping at the same place. This plan was approved by both
Generals Clinton and Cornwallis.

With a detail of eighty men including hussars and light dragoons,
Simcoe embarked from Staten Island. He moved rapidly through Piscat-
away Township to Quibbletown, taking pains to impress those he met
with the idea that his force was a body of Americans. He was able to do
this well because his command wore green coats, leather breeches and
cocked hats bound with white braid, much like the uniforms worn by the
legion of patriot Colonel Henry Lee (who, incidentally, admired Simcoe
very much, and the feeling was mutual). Simcoe even stopped at a Continental forage depot at midnight, waked up the commissary, drew the
customary allowance of forage, and blithely signed the name of Lee's
quartermaster, without being discovered. On the road, the Tories met
a Justice Crow, accused him of being a Tory—as a blind—and took him
along, despite his protests that he had "only been a-sparkin." At Bound
Brook, Simcoe found not the governor but a gullible country lad, and told
him the force was going to get some boats for General Washington. The
boy was eager to be of help, so he told Simcoe what he knew, which was
that the boats had already been sent to the patriots, except for eighteen
which were still at Van Veghten's Bridge. Hurrying to the bridge, the

Simcoe raiders used hand grenades they had brought for the purpose to
destroy the boats as well as their traveling carriages and ammunition
wagon, some harness and other military stores. Then they burned the
Dutch Reformed Church building because they understood it was being used to hold forage for the patriots. All this took less than an hour.

"We there received a single shot from a distant hill," the Tory leader
reported. "After this work was completed, we crossed to Somerset, released two British prisoners, and consumed the courthouse by fire." The
reason they burned the building was that Simcoe's men were so enraged
at finding a Tory prisoner who appeared "a dreadful spectacle, half-
starved and was chained to the floor." The burning courthouse ignited
adjacent buildings and by this time the residents were so aroused that
Simcoe felt it wise to hurry away toward New Brunswick. This was part
of the preconceived plan, but unfortunately for them, the Tories missed a
landmark which was supposed to indicate their route of retreat. In addition, Colonel Simcoe had been recognized and the countryside was
rising to capture him. Patriot Colonel John Neilson of the Middlesex
militia at New Brunswick sent Captain Moses Guest with thirty-five men
to hide along the route of Simcoe and ambush him. They hid in thick
woods, unknown to the Tories until it was too late. As Simcoe approached
the woods, he saw some men behind logs and bushes and tried to turn
his horse through an opening in a fence to avoid the ambush. But just
then he heard from the brush the words, "Now! Now!" and that was the
last he heard for some time, for five bullets struck his horse, which fell,
throwing Simcoe to the ground and knocking him unconscious. When he
regained his senses, he was a prisoner of the enemy.

Jonathan Ford Morris, a young medical student, saved Simcoe's life.
He seized the bayonet of an American private as he was about to run
it through the prostrate Tory, carried Simcoe to a clearing, propped him
against a tree and bled him until he had fully regained consciousness.
Captain Sandford assumed command of the stricken Simcoe's force and
hastened to try to lead it out of the closing trap of patriot militia on
their front and rear. Sandford made a feint toward the front, then he and
his men tore into the rear and cut their way through. They killed Captain
Peter Voorhees of the rebels with sabers, a loss much lamented by the
Americans, especially because he was to be married the following day.
The Tories made their way back to Staten Island, having covered sixty
miles of hostile country with the loss of but few men, having taken
thirty prisoners, destroyed much property and exchanged many bad
horses for good ones. The raid alarmed the American army. Anthony
Wayne was detached from headquarters and sent to quell the outbreak,
while Henry Lee hurried from Monmouth to the Raritan.

Colonel John Simcoe was jailed, then exchanged. Later, he tried hard
to rescue Major John André after he was captured as a spy. He was
told by Alexander Hamilton that the only way to save André was to give
up Arnold, for which Simcoe accused Washington of playing politics. The

Tory leader surrendered with Cornwallis at Yorktown and remained "a prisoner on parole in the United States" until January, 1783, when Benjamin Franklin obtained his release. He was the first governor general of Canada and held a similar post in Santo Domingo. In 1806, Simcoe was appointed commander-in-chief of India, but was taken ill en route and returned home to die. He was an Oxford graduate and student of the classics, as well as a superior military commander.[5]

Three Tories in Maryland were less favored by the fortunes of war. John Frietschie, father-in-law of the legendary Barbara Frietschie, was accused at Frederick along with Yost Blecker and Peter Sueman of being Tories and plotting to fight against the patriots. This situation was not unusual, but the sentence which was given the three men was. It was decreed that they were to be "drawn to the gallows of Frederick Town and be hanged thereon, that they be cut down to the earth alive, and that their entrails be taken out and burned while they are yet alive, that their heads be cut off and their bodies divided into four parts and that their heads and quarters be placed where his Excellency, the Governor, shall appoint." Actually, the only part of the gruesome sentence to be carried out was that of the hanging, which took place for the three on July 6, 1781.[6]

In neighboring Pennsylvania, where the Penn family was represented at the beginning of the war by Governor John Penn, the heirs of William Penn were later to claim half a million pounds for the loss of their lands to the patriots. The position of Governor Penn in the Revolution was questioned by Governor William Franklin of New Jersey, who felt that the Pennsylvanian favored Congress more than he did Great Britain. "The power of the government of Pennsylvania was greater than any other government upon the continent of America," said Franklin. "If he [Penn] had thrown the weight of his influence in favor of Britain, and thrown the weight of his family into that scale, it might have kept the Province out of the rebellion, and Maryland would have followed the example." Even so, Governor Penn was confined for ten months by order of Congress on suspicion of his being a Tory.[7]

Not only suspicion but harsh condemnation, sometimes unjustified, plagued the Tories. For instance, standard historical accounts usually state with little or no qualification that Mrs. James Caldwell of Connecticut Farms, New Jersey, was wantonly shot by British or Tory troops in June of 1780. At the command of Clinton and under General William Tryon, the royal forces had invaded the state to demonstrate their strength and try to persuade the inhabitants to resume their allegiance to the King, as well as to try to induce American soldiers to desert their cause in large numbers. While on their march, the British were attacked intermittently by the local militia, and it has been assumed that because of such harassment, a redcoat or Tory trooper fired through a window of the home of the Reverend James Caldwell and killed his wife, who was said to be sitting with her small children at the time. As soon as her body was removed, according to patriot accounts, her house and all others in the village were burned, and also the church. Reports of the killing caused widespread resentment.

Yet a British officer writing to the *Royal Gazette,* June 21, 1780, stated that on June 8, rebels were advancing to Elizabeth and had attacked the Twenty-Second British Regiment, firing out of their own houses "from which circumstance Mrs. Caldwell had the misfortune to be shot by a random ball . . . upon inquiry, it appears beyond a doubt that the shot was fired by the rebels themselves, as it entered the side of the house from their direction and lodged in the wall nearest to the British troops, then advancing. The manner in which the rebels aggravate this unfortunate affair, in their publications, is of a piece with their uniform conduct," the officer continued, "plausible but fallacious, nor is it to be wondered at, if a rebellion which originated in falsehood, is prosecuted with deceit." A prominent Tory, Ebenezer Foster, of Woodbridge, said that he was at the Caldwell house soon after Mrs. Caldwell was shot, and that the bullet appeared to have come from the direction of the rebels. A young woman at a nearby house told him, he added, that she was sitting on the same bed with Mrs. Caldwell at the time the latter was shot, and that she had been killed by Continental troops. This is the royal version of the affair, which certainly should be considered along with the other side, particularly in the absence of definite proof.[8]

On the other hand, Jonathan Clawson of Woodbridge, a Tory, stated that he fled four miles to Perth Amboy and went back for his wife and children "with utmost difficulty and in the midst of a heavy fire from the rebels." Clawson also said that his eldest son, a youth of nineteen, was taken by the rebels and "after a short imprisonment without any trial or examination was put to an ignominious death by order of their General Maxwell for no other pretended crime than that of adhering to the government under which he was born." However, a letter to a Trenton newspaper, dated June 18, 1780, soon after young Clawson was captured, asserts that "before daybreak on a mountain near Scotch Plains, a party of villains who came from Staten Island to steal horses, were discovered by Mr. Casterline, an officer of militia, who killed one, Inslee, and took three others, Lacy, Hutchinson and Closson. A court-martial is now sitting for the trial of the latter." Despite the different spelling, the last-named is believed to have been young Clawson, and apparently a court-martial was held. The New York *Gazette and Weekly Mercury* of July 3, 1780, contains an item to the effect that "John Clawson, formerly of Woodbridge, was lately executed at Washington's camp." Such instances show that there was chicanery, or allegations of same, on both sides.[9]

A celebrated case was that of Claudius Smith, romantically known as "the Tory Cowboy of the Ramapos." Over the picturesque mountains of Rockland County, New York, he roamed in search of booty for the British, and earned his designation of "cowboy" from stealing cows and horses and driving them into the British lines. This practice was carried on also by the rebels, who called themselves "skinners." Though Smith was doubtless active in such marauding, it appears that much thievery and killing committed by other Revolutionary guerrillas of varied affiliations was handily but wrongfully attributed to him. Born on Long Island, the son of a Tory, Claudius Smith had three sons who were also loyal to the King. They served with their father in southern New York and northern New Jersey and, with companions of like sympathies, formed a band which usually struck a farm at dusk, part of the gang running off with the livestock and other plunder, while the others held the farmer and his family at gunpoint. It was said that if farmers resisted, they were killed, although this has not been established. Smith and his men seemed to specialize in taking money and silverware as well as livestock, and it was such theft, held to be treasonable then if it was for the purpose of aiding the enemy, which brought an end to his colorful career. A major of patriot militia, Jesse Brush, heard that Smith and his "cowboys" were at Brookhaven, New York, and took a detail of men and captured them. Smith was taken to Goshen in Orange County, tried for robbery, and hanged on January 22, 1779. One of his sons was hanged soon afterward and another shot. Today on Horse Stable Mountain near Wesley Chapel in the Ramapo region, hikers pass what is called "Smith's Cave," in which the raider is said to have hidden and perhaps stored some of his loot. A recent observer noted that the cave contained only "a nest full of baby swallows, and fronts a shaded grassy plot with ferns, laurels and abandoned beer cans." [10]

Such small-scale activities had little success against the patriots. Sir Henry Clinton seldom ventured outside of his garrison in New York City. In 1780, for example, he had 20,000 men idle there while Washington was only fifty miles away with 7,000. But Clinton had reached the point where he did not trust the Tories to any great extent, especially in regard to co-operating with them or even aiding them in their plight. General Charles Grey wrote him early in 1781, "For God's sake, put no confidence in any of these *loyal* Americans near you. Many are spies upon you, sending home what they know will please." At almost the same time, Major Carl Baurmeister was reporting to his Hessian superiors that "The greatest secrecy has become imperative, for the number of those who are secretly rebels (who have become the most dangerous) is, according to the openly professed rebels, greater than Washington's entire army. It is astonishing indeed how these fine enemies are spared and frequently even remain in public business under protection." Such reports doubtless contributed to Clinton's practice of not incorporating Tories into his regular forces, but instead, allowing them to carry on raids such as those of De Lancey and Claudius Smith. This resulted in resentment among the Tories for being excluded from the British military units and also increased the hatred of the rebels who felt that the Tory raiders were more severe than regular British troops. [11]

Critical also of the Tory activity at first was Peter Van Schaack of New

York, a rationalist who warmly embraced the right of revolution advocated by John Locke. Van Schaack was a deliberate man, however, and refused to rush into war. While more radical patriots were clamoring for immediate liberty, he shut himself up at his farm at Kinderhook and went through Locke, Vattel, Montesquieu, Grotius, Beccaria and Puffendorf, and annotated them. Then he wrote out his own opinions of the Revolution, which were: the British are more misguided than wicked; they do not seek to enslave us. He supported Congress until he found that it aimed to dissolve the union between Britain and America. There he stopped—and became a Tory—and in his own mind, Locke was one with him also. Van Schaack was banished to England in 1778. There, soon after the peace was signed, he was walking by Westminster Abbey and noticed a man and woman pause before the monument which had been erected to Major John André. Coming closer, Van Schaack saw that they were Benedict and Mrs. Arnold. He turned away in disgust. This was not unusual treatment of Arnold in England. On another occasion, the turncoat was noticed in the gallery of the House of Commons and asked to leave by one of the members. In 1785, after corresponding with his old friends Governor George Clinton of New York and John Jay, Van Schaack was pleased with their forgiving attitude and returned to America, where he lived on his unconfiscated Kinderhook estate until he died at the age of 85.[12]

Loyal in his actions but uncertain at times in his impressions was Maurice Mergann, a British agent who came to New York and reported regularly to Lord Shelburne, British Secretary of State. As late as May 10, 1782, the agent told Shelburne that "The language here of the most intelligent men is that a very large majority in the Province wish for a reunion with Great Britain, but they are closely and jealously watched by the ruling powers, and are without arms, concert or union, and in a political view, may be considered for the present as wholly inhibited." While this statement was made well after the surrender at Yorktown, it is an intriguing appraisal of the situation from a Tory standpoint as expressed by many of them at various times during the war. A month later, Mergann informed his chief, "One may confidently be told one hour that we never have had any real friends in this country; and in the next, be informed with equal confidence, that nineteen out of twenty throughout the provinces, are well wishers at least and probably disposed to a reunion." Then he concluded with more significance than he knew, "The Refugees of different provinces do not even unite in an Address." By this he deplored the lack of coordination in their appeals to both King and the patriot leaders. Such division of opinion, interest and activity was a prime cause of the defeat of the Tories.[13]

Helping as well as hindering the cause of the King were numerous Negroes in America, both slave and free. Some had gained their freedom in both North and South before the Revolution and even owned farms or small homes; a good number of these were Tories. On the other hand, a sizable group of Negroes fought for the patriots. Slaves were an important object of plunder on both sides. For instance, when the army of General Gates approached Camden, South Carolina, many slaves of Tories were taken by the Whig militia as they gathered. But Thomas Johnston of South Carolina told the British Claims Commission he was born free but was pressed into the royal service and had acted as a guide for Cornwallis. He was declared to have been "a very zealous Loyalist and was of great service." Scipio Handley of Charleston, also a free black man who was confined by the rebels for carrying letters to the British, heard he was to be put to death. He obtained a file from a friend, cut his irons with it and leaped two stories to the ground, being "so unfortunate as to get a rupture." Now and then, stories would be circulated from either side that the Negroes were planning an insurrection; but often this was for the purpose of rousing people to arms in one direction or another. Colonel Elias Ball claimed he lost 200 Negro slaves to the rebels in South Carolina, while Solomon Whitley of Virginia laid claim for the loss of three slaves. John Twine of the same state, a free black, fought with the British at Camden and was wounded in the thigh. He ended up in England as a servant to British army officers. Dr. William H. Mills, a militia colonel under Cornwallis, had all his slaves taken by the rebels except a few which he took with him to exile in the Bahamas. Six Negroes who appeared before the British commission and presented claims for lost property on the basis of being Tories were each granted ten pounds. Some Tories organized a settlement on the Etowah River in Cherokee County, Georgia, taking their slaves with them. Aided by Indians, they raided surrounding settlements, stealing provisions, cattle, horses and Negroes and killing some of the people who opposed them. General Andrew Pickens and Colonel Elijah Clark led a force against them. The Tories fled and dispersed.[14]

Another American officer named Clark—George Rogers Clark—was engaged in more important fighting for the new nation, his theater of operations being the West. The British did not give up their struggle for the West until 1795 when the battle of Fallen Timbers decided the fate of the region against them. The Indians between the Ohio River and the Great Lakes had been asked by the British to instigate attacks on the border settlements of Pennsylvania and Virginia, including what is now Kentucky. Rumors of savages and Tories advancing from the Ohio country alarmed the frontiersmen of this part of the West, many of whom took their families and fled. The British were rather successful in pushing the settlers out—partly because, with the help of the Tories, they had given the Indians better treatment than had the patriots. In the sporadic but bloody clashes which took place, Colonel William Crawford, former associate of George Washington in land speculation, was ambushed, tortured and killed by a force of Tories and Indians on June 4, 1782. This encouraged more Indians to raid the settlements from Pennsylvania to Kentucky. Clark, a brother of William of the Lewis and Clark expedition, and a gay, determined and daring man, had been trying, since his capture of Kaskaskia and Vincennes in 1778, to organize a force to wrest Detroit from the British. Also he wanted to build Fort Nelson where Louisville now stands. This double feat proved difficult, even for Clark. Meanwhile, Tories and Indians had besieged Bryan's Station, a fort near Lexington, Kentucky. Clark collected 1,100 mounted riflemen and on November 10, 1782, routed the Indians and Tories, burning the villages of the Shawnees who were involved, near Chillicothe, Ohio. This was the last land battle of the American Revolution.

It was not the only dramatic event of this closing year of conflict, however. At almost the same time that Clark was routing the Indians and their allies in Ohio, Congress was bringing to a close a dramatic episode which had international ramifications. It concerned retribution for the tragic death of Captain Joshua Huddy, of the New Jersey militia, at the hands of Tories. He had been especially active in suppressing the extreme acts of the Tories in New Jersey, especially those in Monmouth County, so that he became a man marked for vengeance by those he overcame. In the spring of 1782, Huddy commanded the garrison of a little fort on Tom's River in Ocean County, and was attacked by Tories who outnumbered his force. They assaulted and took the fort, killing a third of Huddy's men in the action. He was taken to New York, then to Sandy Hook and confined in irons in the hold of a ship. Six days after Huddy was captured, a Tory carpenter named Philip White was taken prisoner by the patriots. He was left in the custody of three men, the father of one of whom had been killed the year before by Tories. Later White was found dead, one arm cut off, his legs broken, and one of his eyes pulled out. The guards said that the prisoner was shot while trying to escape, an age-old "explanation." News of the death of White circulated among the Tories and brought forth furious cries for revenge.

Soon afterward, Captain Richard Lippincott of the Associated Loyalists intervened. His organization was an independent group of Tories who did not join the regular forces but were willing to oppose the patriots as raiders. William Franklin was their leader, and Colonel Simcoe reported in October, 1780, that 7,000 effective men belonged to it, though they never showed much effectiveness. Mainly, they struck at isolated villages and farms, taking off whatever could be found. Their violence was said actually to have harmed rather than helped the British cause.

With sixteen of his men, Lippincott went aboard the ship on which Huddy was being held, and presented papers purporting to show that the prisoner was to be turned over to Lippincott and then taken away to be exchanged for another prisoner. Instead of being exchanged, the unfortunate rebel was taken to the Jersey shore near Sandy Hook. There a gallows was hastily erected from three fence rails and a flour barrel, and Huddy was informed that he was to be hanged by order of former Governor William Franklin, now head of the Associated Loyalists. Asked if he had not hanged a Tory on a large oak at Monmouth Courthouse, Huddy reportedly replied, "Yes, by God, and I greased the rope well!"

Huddy then calmly drew up his will on the head of a barrel, shook hands with Lippincott who assured him there was nothing personal about this retribution, and then bravely submitted to the noose. Moments later he was dead, swinging in the soft breeze which came in off Sandy Hook. On his chest the Tories had placed a sign which read: "Up Goes Huddy for Philip White."

The hanging of Huddy threw the patriots of the country into an angry uproar, and they cried out for vengeance. Washington demanded that the British surrender Lippincott to the Americans, but Clinton refused. Instead, Lippincott was tried for murder. In the court-martial, he testified that he was serving the King without pay; that many Tories had been taken by the rebels and had not even been allowed the status of prisoners of war, but had "been tried by rebels as rebels, then executed in cold blood"; that Huddy was hanged in retaliation for the murder of Philip White, and that this should prevent more of the Tory prisoners from being murdered.

George Washington insisted that if Lippincott were not delivered to him, one of the English officers held by him would die in his stead. Thirteen captured redcoat officers were therefore ordered to Lancaster, Pennsylvania, and on the 25th of May, they assembled in the Black Bear Tavern there. Their names were placed on slips of paper and drawn from a hat by a drummer boy. The unlucky one selected for execution was Captain Charles Asgill, youngest of the officers, a gracious youth from a fine old English family. He was immediately sent to the Jersey state line at Chatham, where he was to be hanged. But public opinion rose into such an outcry that even Henry Knox and Alexander Hamilton of Washington's staff protested that Asgill did not deserve such a fate. French and British dignitaries added their voices in behalf of the unfortunate captain. William Franklin denied he had ordered the execution of Huddy. Washington himself was sympathetic toward Asgill and paroled him at Morristown. Finally, Congress directed that the prisoner be freed unconditionally.[15] This was done, but it was only another episode in the denouement of the royal raiders.

Why did the Tories lose?

It is hoped that in the foregoing pages, the answer has at least been exemplified. Trevelyan said of them that seldom in all the tragic history of revolutions did a company of worthier and more blameless people find themselves in a more pitiable and hopeless strait. Those loyal to the King believed from the first that they were right and that they were infinitely superior to their upstart opponents. The viewpoint of their leaders was colored by the artificial elegance of eighteenth-century England, personified particularly by George III, Lord North, the Howes and Burgoyne and their counterparts in the American colonies. They deluded themselves until it was too late, and grim failure shook their belief and shattered its foundations.

Lord North cried out in Parliament in regard to the American Tories and their treatment by British as well as Americans, "They have exposed their lives, endured an age of hardship, lost their interests, forfeited their possessions, their connections and ruined their families in their cause. Never was the *honor,* the *principles,* the *policy* of a nation so grossly abused as in our desertion of those men, who are now exposed to every punishment that such desertion and poverty can inflict, BECAUSE THEY WERE NOT REBELS." [16]

Not only did the Tories look down on the patriots as generally being unequal politically or socially, but those on the side of the King fully expected him to win. At first they could not conceive it possible that these colonial commoners, lacking money, military leadership, experience and supplies, could hold out very long against the stupendous strength of an empire on which the sun never set, then at a peak of prestige and power. Judging from hindsight, this assumption of the Tories seems to have been quite logical. The ultimate and fortunate result makes our Revolution all the more remarkable in its success, which is still echoing through this nation and in others with similar dreams.

The victory at Yorktown was a surprise to patriots and Tories alike for the most part, as was the peace a disappointment to many. Two months before this battle, a New Jersey newspaper publisher, Isaac Collins, asked in print if it would be a good thing to stop the war on condition that the Tories be restored to their former status. He answered the question himself, in the negative, and in so doing neatly measured the comparative situation: Britain, though powerful, had been enervated by her luxury and success, had a huge national debt, a declining trade, a half-manned marine, a disordered army and a King surrounded by fawning sychophants. On the other hand, he pictured the colonies as rapidly increasing in population, vigor, financial stability, trade, military prowess and honorable aims. While this analysis is weighted toward the American side, the conclusion pointed up the hopeless condition of the Tories. Even so, they had a reasonable side to their position, and one which deserves earnest consideration.

The success of the patriots was largely due to their positive program, as contrasted to the lack of such among their opponents. Under an inspired leadership, the Americans developed a skillful if inconsistent military organization which, coupled with frontier methods and effective propaganda, wore down the British and disheartened the Tories. George Washington himself was their greatest nemesis. He kept a close watch on those who remained loyal to the King and worked with Congress to suppress them before they could coordinate their exertions and launch effective countermeasures. Faced with hostility at home and indifference in England, these once-forceful people eventually became the loyal light that failed.

Acknowledgments

Appreciation is heartily expressed for a grant-in-aid from the Penrose Fund of the American Philosophical Society, oldest learned society in America, which has helped importantly in the research and writing of this volume.

The author wishes to thank his associates at New York University for their continued heart-warming encouragement and interest in his writing and their valuable aid in research.

Gratitude is expressed to the members of the American Revolution Round Table for their kind concern with the author's books on the subject of this, our first great war.

Editors and publishers of my syndicated newspaper column have shown a warm and welcome interest in my books, as well as articles for their papers, and to all of them go my deepest thanks.

Were sufficient space available, it would be gratifying to set forth in detail the appreciation due many individuals who have been of immense help in the making of this volume. In lieu of this, the following had a direct hand in the project: Ray Erwin, Lawrence H. Gipson, Carroll V. Newsom, Carl Bode, T. P. Abernethy, John C. Pemperton III, Mark Woods, Anthony Shaw, Jean Crawford, Preston Davie, J. V. Whitfield, Howard Peckham, William Ewing, James J. Heslin, Kenneth C. Miller, William H. Holland, David Mearns, John J. dePorry, Senator Leverett Saltonstall, Wayne C. Grover, Josephine L. Harper, Leo Flaherty, Stephen Riley, Margaret Tighe, William J. Van Schreeven, John M. Jennings, James A. Fleming, Connie C. Griffith, Richard Watson, Mary Givens Bryan, John D. Kilbourne, Dorothy Thomas Cullen, Samuel Proctor, Sherman W. Perry, David L. Jacobson, William Willcox, Robert Cecil, Clifford K. Shipton, Albert B. Corey, A. K. Cunningham, William G. Tyrrell, Donald C. Anthony, Martin H. Bush, C. Eleanor Hall, Juliet Wolohan, Mrs. John J. Burnett, Helen P. Bolman, Henry Scherer, Karl Schild, James M. Ford, B. G. Hutton, John H. G. Pell, Harold Hancock, Daniel V. Raymond, M. J. Madey, Hiram C. Todd, Ruth K. Robbins, James W. Patton, William Powell, Anna Brooke Allan, James M. Babcock, Archie Motley, Miriam V. Studley, Hugh T. Lefler, Mrs. Shirley L. Spranger, Mrs. Maud Cole, R. K. T. Larson, Howard Moreau, L. Berger Copeman, and William Raney.

Bibliography

MANUSCRIPTS

Admiralty Records, National Maritime Museum, London
Asgill Correspondence, Earl Spencer, Althorp, Northampton, England
Audley End Papers, Essex Record Office, Chelmsford, England
Bancroft Collection, New York Public Library
Blagden, Sir Charles, Letters, The Royal Society, London
Bolton Papers, Hampshire Record Office, Winchester, England
Bragg, John, Diary, Public Library, Whitehaven, England
Buckinghamshire Papers, Marquess of Lothian, Melbourne Hall, Derby, England
Burton Historical Collection, Detroit Public Library
Caner, Henry, Letter-book, University of Bristol, England
Cannon Hall Muniments, Sheffield City Libraries, England
Clinton, Henry, Papers, Clements Library, University of Michigan
Colonial and Trade Papers in Loose Archives, Royal Society of Arts, London
Customs Establishment Papers, American Colonies, Customs Library, London
Diary of Colonel Robert Gray, North Carolina State Archives, Raleigh
Draper Manuscripts, Wisconsin Historical Society, Madison
Elliot Collection, New York State Library, Albany
Emmet Collection, New York Public Library
Exchequer and Audit Papers, Public Record Office, London
Fitzwilliam Muniments, Sheffield City Libraries, England
Floyd Papers, Public Record Office of Northern Ireland, Belfast
Gates, Horatio, Papers, New York Historical Society
Germain Papers, Clements Library, University of Michigan
Greene, Nathanael, Papers, Clements Library, University of Michigan
Grenville Papers, Boconnoc, Lostwithiel, England
Haldemand Collection, Canadian Archives, Ottawa
Halsey Collection, Hertfordshire County Record Office, Hertford, England
Hartley Russell Papers, Berkshire Record Office, Reading, England
Hobart Papers, Buckinghamshire Record Office, Aylesbury, England
James Hogg Papers, Southern Historical Collection, University of North Carolina, Chapel Hill
John Peters Papers, New York Historical Society
Laing Manuscripts, Edinburgh University Library, Scotland
Letter Books of Josiah Smith, Southern Historical Collection, University of North Carolina, Chapel Hill
Macartney Papers, Public Record Office of Northern Ireland, Belfast
Manchester Collection, County Record Office, Huntingdon, England

Manuscript Collection, David Library, Washington Crossing, State Park, Pennsylvania

Marquess of Abergavenny Manuscripts, Historical Manuscripts Commission, London

Martin, George, Claims Papers, St. Mary's Kells, Whitehaven, England

Massereene-Foster Papers, Public Record Office of Northern Ireland, Belfast

McDougall, Alexander, Papers, New York Historical Society

Mellen Chamberlain Collection, Boston Public Library

Miscellaneous American Revolution Manuscripts, New York State Library, Albany, New York

Miscellaneous Manuscripts, American Revolution, Library of Congress

Miscellaneous Manuscripts, Massachusetts State Archives, Boston

Munn Manuscript Collection, Fordham University, New York City

North Carolina State Records, State Archives, Raleigh

North, Lord, Manuscripts, Bodleian Library, Oxford University, England

Preston Davie Collection, Southern Historical Collection, University of North Carolina, Chapel Hill

Privy Council Papers, Public Record Office, London

Reed, Joseph, Papers, New York Historical Society

Samuel Peters Manuscripts, New York Historical Society

Shepherd Manuscripts, Manchester College Library, Oxford, England

Temple Bodley Collection, The Filson Club, Louisville, Kentucky

Transcripts of the Manuscript Books and Papers of the Commission of Enquiry Into the Losses and Services of American Loyalists, held under Acts of Parliament of 23, 25, 26, 28 and 29 of George III, preserved Amongst the Audit Offices Records in the Public Record Office of England, 1783-1790. Transcribed for the New York Public Library, 1899

Treasury Papers in Letters, British Museum, London

Vanderhorst and Duncombe Collection, Bristol Record Office, England

Verulam Papers, Gorhambury, St. Albans, England

War Department Collection, Revolutionary War Records, National Archives, Washington, D.C.

Wedderburn Papers, Clements Library, University of Michigan, Ann Arbor

COLONIAL NEWSPAPERS

Boston Gazette

Cape Fear Mercury

Connecticut Gazette and Universal Intelligencer

Constitutional Gazette

Continental Journal and Weekly Advertiser

Essex Gazette

Georgia Gazette

Independent Chronicle and Universal Advertiser

Maryland Gazette

Massachusetts Gazette and Boston Post Boy

New Jersey Gazette

New Jersey Journal

Newport Mercury
New York Gazette and Weekly
    Mercury
New York Journal
New York Mirror
New York Packet

Pennsylvania Evening Post
Pennsylvania Gazette
Pennsylvania Journal
Rivington's New York Gazetteer
Royal Gazette
Virginia Gazette

MODERN NEWSPAPERS

Elkin (North Carolina) Tribune
Laurens (South Carolina) Advertiser
New York Herald-Tribune
New York World-Telegram and Sun
New York Times

Norfolk Virginian-Pilot and Ledger-
    Star
Philadelphia Record
Rockland County (New York) Jour-
    nal

BOOKS, PERIODICALS AND HISTORICAL COLLECTIONS

Abbott, W. C., *New York in the American Revolution* (N.Y., 1929)

Adair, Douglas, and Schutz, John A. (eds.), *Peter Oliver's Origin and Progress of the American Rebellion, a Tory View* (San Marino, Calif., 1961)

Adams, John, *Diary* (Cambridge, 1961)

Adams, John, *Works*, VI, IX (Boston, 1850-1856)

Adams, Randolph, *Political Ideas of the American Revolution* (N.Y., 1958)

A Defense of the Rockingham Party in Their Late Coalition With the Right Honorable Frederick, Lord North (London, 1783)

Albee, Allison, "The Defenses of Pines Bridge," *Westchester Historian*, V. 34, 1958

Alden, John R., *The South in the Revolution, 1763-1789* (Baton Rouge, 1957)

Allan, Herbert S., *John Hancock, Patriot in Purple* (N.Y., 1953)

American Antiquarian Society Proceedings, New Series, V, XVI

American Historical Review, IV, Jan., 1889, No. 2

An Account of the Rise and Progress of the American Revolution (London, 1780)

Anburey, Thomas, *Travels Through the Interior Parts of America* (Boston, 1923), I

Andrews, Charles M., *The Colonial Background of the American Revolution* (New Haven, 1961)

Annual Register, The, etc. (London, 1788-1792)

Arnold, Isaac, *The Life of Benedict Arnold* (Chicago, 1880)

Ashe, Samuel A., *History of North Carolina* (Greensboro, 1908-1925), I

Atlantic Monthly, May, 1884

Bailey, J. D., *Commanders at King's Mountain* (Gaffney, S.C., 1926)

Bakeless, John *Turncoats, Traitors and Heroes* (N.Y., 1959)

Baldwin, Alice, *The New England Clergy and the American Revolution* (N.Y., 1958)

Bancroft, George, *History of the United States From the Discovery of the Continent* (N.Y., 1882-1884), IV

Barck, Oscar T., *New York City During the War for Independence* (N.Y., 1931)

Barnwell, Robert W., Jr., "Loyalism in South Carolina," unpublished master's thesis, Duke University, 1941

Bates, Walter, *Kingston and the Loyalists of 1783* (St. John, N.B., 1889)

Battle, Kemp P., *History of the University of North Carolina* etc. (Raleigh, 1907)

Baxter, J. P., *The British Invasion from the North* (Albany, 1887)

Beloff, Max (ed.), *The Debate on the American Revolution, 1761-1783* (London, 1960)

Bemis, Samual Flagg, *The Diplomacy of the American Revolution* (Bloomington, Ind., 1957)

Bigelow, John, (ed.), *The Complete Works of Benjamin Franklin* (N.Y., 1887-1889)

Billias, George A., *General John Glover and his Marblehead Mariners* (N.Y., 1960)

Birdsall, R. D., *Berkshire County* (New Haven, 1959)

Boucher, Jonathan, *A View of the Causes and Consequences of the American Revolution in Thirteen Discourses* (London, 1797)

Boucher, Jonathan, *Reminisces of a Maryland Loyalist* (London, 1909)

Brinton, Crane, *The Anatomy of Revolution* (N.Y., 1960)

Burgoyne, John, *A State of the Expedition from Canada* etc. (London, 1780)

Butterfield, H., *George III, Lord North and the People* (London, 1949)

Butterfield, H., "George III, Lord North and Mr. Robinson," *The Cambridge Historical Journal*, V, No. 3, 1937

Callahan, North, *Daniel Morgan: Ranger of the Revolution* (N.Y., 1961)

Callahan, North, *Henry Knox: General Washington's General* (N.Y., 1958)

Carmer, Carl, *The Hudson* (N.Y., 1939)

Carrington, H. B., *Battles of the American Revolution* (N.Y., 1876)

Caruthers, E. W., *Interesting Revolutionary Incidents and Sketches of Character, Chiefly in the Old North State* (Philadelphia, 1854)

Chalmers, George, *The Beauties of Fox, North and Burke* (London, 1784)

Chandler, Helen D., *The Battle of King's Mountain* (Gastonia, N.C., 1930)

Chitwood, Oliver P., *A History of Colonial America* (N.Y., 1961)

Christie, Ian R., "Rockingham and Lord North's Offer of a Coalition June-July, 1780," *English Historical Review* (July, 1954)

Clark, Elmer T., *An Album of Methodist History* (Nashville, 1952)

Clark, Walter (ed.), *State Records of North Carolina* (Goldsboro, N.C., 1886-1907)

Coleman, Kenneth, *American Revolution in Georgia* (Athens, 1958)

Cooper, W. G., *The History of Georgia* (N.Y., 1948)

Crawford, Constance, "The Jackson Whites," unpublished master's thesis, New York University, 1940

Crawford, Mary C., *Social Life in Old New England* (Boston, 1914)

Crèvecoeur, Hector St. John de, *Sketches of Eighteenth Century America* (New Haven, 1925)

Curwen, Samuel, *Journal and Letters* (N.Y., 1845)

d'Auberteuil, Hilliard, *Histoire de L'Administration de Lord North* (London, 1784)

Davidson College Historical Association Magazine (Davidson, N.C., 1898), I

Davidson, Philip, *Propaganda of the American Revolution, 1763-1783* (Chapel Hill, 1941)

Dawson, Henry B., *Battles of the United States* (N.Y., 1858), I

de Fonblanque, E. B., *Political and Military Episodes . . . Derived from the Life and Correspondence of the Rt. Hon. J. Burgoyne* (London, 1876)

Delaware Register (Dover, 1838-39), I, No. 3, 224

DeMond, Robert O., *The Loyalists in North Carolina During the Revolution* (Durham, 1940)

Dix, A. Morgan, *History of Trinity Church* (N.Y., 1898)

Dorson, Richard M., *America Rebels* (N.Y., 1953)

Draper, Lyman C., *King's Mountain and Its Heroes* (Cincinnati, 1881)

Dwight, Timothy, *Travels in New England and New York* (New Haven, 1821-1822)

Eckenrode, Hamilton, *The Revolution in Virginia* (Boston, 1916)

Eddis, William, *Letters from America, Historical and Descriptive, Compromising Occurrences from 1769-1776* (London, 1792)

Einstein, Lewis, *Divided Loyalists* (London, 1933)

Erskine, John, *Reflections on the Rise, Progress and Probable Consequences of the Present Contentions with the Colonies* (Edinburgh, 1776)

Fitzmaurice, Sir Edmund, *Life of the Earl of Shelburne* (London, 1912), I

Fitzpatrick, J. C., *The Spirit of the Revolution* (Boston, 1924)

Fitzpatrick, John C. (ed.), *The Writings of George Washington* (Washington, 1931-1944)

Flick, Alexander C., *Loyalism in New York During the American Revolution* (N.Y., 1901)

Florida Historical Quarterly, XIX, No. 3, Jan., 1962; Oct., 1961, No. 2

Forbes, Esther, *Paul Revere and the World He Lived In* (Boston, 1942)

Force, Peter (ed.), *American Archives*, Fourth Series, Fifth Series (Washington, D.C., 1837-1853)

Ford, W. C. (ed.), *The Writings of George Washington* (N.Y. and London, 1899)

Fortescue, Sir John (ed.), *The Correspondence of King George the Third* (London, 1927-1928), III

Fox, Charles James, *Memoirs* (London, 1808), II

Fraser, Alexander (ed.), *Second Report of the Bureau of Archives* (Toronto, 1905)

Freeman, Douglas, *George Washington* (N.Y., 1951), IV

French, Allen, *A British Fusilier in Revolutionary Boston* (Cambridge, 1926)

Frothingham, Richard, *History of the Siege of Boston* (Boston, 1903)

Galloway, Joseph, *A Candid Examination of the Mutual Claims of Great Britain and the Colonies* (London, 1780)

Galloway, Joseph, *Examination Before the House of Commons* (London, 1780)

Galloway, Joseph, *The Examination of Joseph Galloway, Esq.* etc. (Philadelphia, 1855)

Galloway, Joseph, *Historical and Political Reflections on the Rise and Progress of the American Rebellion* (London, 1780)

Garretson, Freeborn, *The Experience and Travels of Mr. Freeborn Garretson* (Philadelphia, 1791)

George, John Alonzo, "Virginia Loyalists 1775-83," *Richmond College Historical Papers*, I, No. 2 (June, 1916)

Georgia Historical Society, *Collections* (Savannah, 1873), III

Georgia Historical Quarterly, XIX, March, 1935; I, Dec., 1917, No. 1

Gilpin, Thomas, *Diary*, New York Historical Society

Gilpin, Thomas, *Exiles in Virginia During the Revolutionary War* (Philadelphia, 1848)

Gipson, Lawrence, *The Coming of the Revolution, 1763-1775* (N.Y., 1954)

Gipson, Lawrence H., "The Great Debate in the Committee of the Whole House of Commons on the Stamp Act, 1766, as Requested by Samuel Ryder," *Pennsylvania Magazine of History and Biography*, LXXXVI, No. 1, Jan., 1962

Gould, E. W., *British and Tory Marauders* (Rockland, Me., 1932)

Graham, W. A., "The Battle of Ramsour's Mill," *North Carolina Booklet* (Raleigh, 1904)

Granger, Bruce I., *Political Satire in the American Revolution* (Ithaca, N.Y., 1960)

Greene, Evarts B., *The Revolutionary Generation* (N.Y., 1943)

Green, F. B., *Boothbay, Southport and Boothbay Harbor* (Portland, 1906)

Gregg, A. G., *History of the Old Cheraws* (N.Y., 1867)

Grimes, Alan P., *American Political Thought* (N.Y., 1960)

Grumpertz, S. G., *Jewish Legion of Valor* (N.Y., 1934)

Guedalla, Philip, *Fathers of the Revolution* (N.Y., 1926)

Hall, Captain J. of Howe's Army, *The History of the Civil War in America* (London, 1780)

Hancock, Harold B., *The Delaware Loyalists* (Wilmington, 1940)

Hammond, Otis G., "The Tories of New Hampshire in the War of the Revolution," Pamphlet (Concord, 1917)

Hansard, Thomas Curson, *The Parliamentary History of England* (London, 1813)

Harlow, Ralph, *The United States: From Wilderness to World Power* (N.Y., 1958)

Harper's Magazine, October, 1860; April, 1885

Harrell, I. S., *Loyalism in Virginia* (Durham, N.C., 1926)

Hart, Freeman, H., *The Valley of Virginia* (Chapel Hill, 1942)

Hayes, J. J., *The Land of Wilkes* (Wilkesboro, N.C., 1962)

Hays, Louise F., *Hero of Hornet's Nest, a Biography of Elijah Clark* (N.Y., 1946)

Haywood, John, *History of Tennessee* (Knoxville, 1823)

Henshaw, William, *The Orderly Books etc.* (Worcester, 1948)

Higginbotham, Don, *Daniel Morgan: Revolutionary Rifleman* (Chapel Hill, 1961)

Historical Anecdotes of the American Revolution (London, 1779), written by a "Loyalist"

Historical Magazine, IX, July, 1959, March, 1869

Historical Publication (High Point, N.C., 1916)

Hoffman, Robert V., *The Revolutionary Scene in New Jersey* (N.Y., 1942)

Holbrook, Stewart H., *Ethan Allen* (N.Y., 1951)

Holliday, Carl, *The Wit and Humor of Colonial Days* (N.Y., 1960)

Hooker, Richard J., *The Anglican Church and the American Revolution*, unpublished Ph.D. thesis, University of Chicago, 1942

Honeyman, A. Van Doren, "Concerning the New Jersey Loyalists in the Revolution," *Proceedings of the N. J. Historical Society*, Vol. 51, No. 2

Hulton, Ann, *Letters of a Loyalist Lady* (Cambridge, 1927)

Hoyt, Edwin P., *The Vanderbilts and Their Fortunes* (N.Y., 1962)

Hughes, Edward (ed.), "Lord North's Correspondence," *English Historical Review*, April, 1947

Hutchinson, Thomas, *Diary and Letters* (London, 1883-1886), I

Hutchinson, W. T., and Rachal, W. M. E. (eds.), *Papers of James Madison* (Chicago, 1962)

Inglis, Charles, "The True Interest of America Impartially Stated. In Certain Strictures on a Pamphlet Entitled 'Common Sense'" (Philadelphia, 1776)

Irving, Washington, *Life of George Washington* (N.Y., 1869)

Jackson, John W., *Margaret Morris, Her Journal* (Philadelphia, 1949)

Jameson, J. Franklin, *The American Revolution Considered as a Social Movement* (Boston, 1956)

Jensen, Merrill, *Introduction to Political Ideas of the American Revolution* (N.Y., 1958)

Johns, C. D., "The Loyalists in North Carolina," unpublished master's thesis, University of Chicago, 1911

Johnson, William, *Sketches of the Life and Correspondence of Nathanael Greene* (Charleston, S.C., 1822)

Johnson, P. D., *Claudius, the Cowboy of Ramapo Valley* (Middletown, N.Y., 1894)

Jones, Thomas, *History of New York During the Revolutionary War* (N.Y., 1879)

The Journal of Nicholas Creswell, 1774-77 (N.Y., 1924)

Journal of Southern History, XXI, Nov., 1955, No. 4

Journals of the Continental Congress, ed. by Gaillard Hunt (Washington, 1904-1937), 34 volumes

Kallich, M., and MacLeish, A., *The American Revolution Through British Eyes* (Evanston, 1962)

Keesey, Ruth M., "Loyalism in Bergen County, New Jersey," *William and Mary Quarterly*, XVIII, Oct., 1961

Keesey, Ruth M., "New Jersey Legislation Concerning the Loyalists," *Proceedings of the New Jersey Historical Society*, LXXIX, No. 2, April, 1961

Keir, D. L., *The Constitutional History of Modern Britain, 1485-1937* (N.Y., 1938)

Kenyon, Cecilia M., "Republicanism, Radicalism in the American Revolution, an Old-Fashioned Interpretation," *William and Mary Quarterly*, XIX, April, 1962

Ketchum, Richard M. (ed.), *The American Heritage Book of the Revolution* (N.Y., 1958)

Kirby, William, *Annals of Niagara* (Lundy's Lane, 1896)

Kirke, Edmund, *Rear Guard of the Revolution* (N.Y., 1888)

Knollenberg, Bernhard, *Origin of the American Revolution, 1759-1766* (N.Y., 1960)

Kuntzleman, O. C., *Joseph Galloway, Loyalist* (Philadelphia, 1941)

Labaree, Leonard W., *Conservatism in Early American History* (Ithaca, 1959)

Labaree, Leonard W., *Royal Government in America* (New Haven, 1930)

Land, A. C., *The Dulanys of Maryland* (Baltimore, 1955)

Landrum, J. B. O., *Colonial and Revolutionary History of Upper South Carolina* (Greenville, 1897)

Lee, Charles, *Memoirs* (N.Y., 1792)

Lee, Henry, *Memoirs of the War of '76* (N.Y., 1870)

Lee, Richard Henry, *The Letters of Richard Henry Lee* (N.Y., 1912), I

Levenstein, Leonard, *Loyalism in Connecticut*, unpublished master's thesis, New York University, 1955

Letters on the American War (London, 1778)

Lewis, W. S. (ed.), *A Selection of the Letters of Horace Walpole* (N.Y., 1926), II

Lloyd, Charles, *Examination of the Principles and Boasted Disinterestedness of a Late Right Honorable Gentleman in a Letter from an Old Man of Business* (London, 1766)

Locket, J. B., *East Florida, 1783-85* (Berkeley, 1940)

Lossing, Benson J., *Field Book of the Revolution* (N.Y., 1850-1852)

Lucas, Reginald, *Lord North* (London, 1913), I

Luce, Melvin G., "The Southern Loyalists in the American Revolution," unpublished master's thesis, New York University, 1951

Lundin, Leonard, *Cockpit of the Revolution* (Princeton, 1940)

Lynd, Stoughton, "Anti-Federalism in Dutchess County, New York," unpublished master's thesis, Columbia University, 1960

McCall, Hugh, *The History of Georgia* (Savannah, 1811-1816)

MacKenzie, George C., *King's Mountain* (Washington, 1955)

MacLean, J. P., *Flora MacDonald in America* (Lumberton, N.C., 1905)

Magazine of American History, I

Maryland Historical Magazine, XII, Dec., 1917; 40, 1945

Massachusettensis (London, 1819). This was the pseudonym of Daniel Leonard.

Massachusetts Historical Society, *Proceedings*, 10, 71
McIlwain, Charles H., *The American Revolution: a Constitutional Interpretation* (N.Y., 1958)
Mellick, A. D., *Lesser Crossroads* (Rutgers, 1948)
Miller, John C., *Alexander Hamilton* (N.Y., 1959)
Miller, John C., *Origins of the American Revolution* (Boston, 1943)
Miner, Charles, *History of Wyoming* (Philadelphia, 1845)
Mississippi Valley Historical Association *Proceedings*, VIII (1914-1915)
Moore, Frank, *Diary of the American Revolution* (N.Y., 1860)
Moseley, Mary, *The Bahamas Handbook* (Nassau, 1926)
Mays, David J., *Edmund Pendleton, A Biography* (Cambridge, 1952)
Montross, Lynn, *Rag, Tag and Bobtail* (N.Y., 1952)
Morgan, Edmund S., "The American Revolution: Revisions in Need of Revising," *William and Mary Quarterly*, XIV, No. 1 (January, 1957)
Morgan, Edmund S., *The Birth of the Republic, 1763-1789* (Chicago, 1956)
Morison, S. E., and Commager, H. S., *The Growth of the American Republic* (N.Y., 1962)
Morris, Richard B., *The American Revolution: A Brief History* (N.Y., 1955)
Morris, Richard B., "Class Struggle and the American Revolution," *William and Mary Quarterly*, XIX, January, 1962
Morton, Frederic, *The Story of Winchester in Virginia* (Strasburg, Va., 1925)
Mowat, Charles, *East Florida as a British Province, 1763-84* (Berkeley, 1943)
Munroe, John A., *Federalist Delaware* (New Brunswick, 1954)
Myers, Marvin Kern, and Alexander, Caweltí (eds.), *Sources of the American Republic* (Chicago, 1960), I
Nathan to Lord North (London, 1780)
National Intelligencer, May, 1851
Nelson, William H., *The American Tory* (London, 1961)
Nelson, William (ed.), *Documents Relating to the Revolutionary History of New Jersey* (Trenton, 1914)
Newcomer, Lee M., *The Embattled Farmers* (N.Y., 1953)
Nevins, Allan, *The American States During and After the Revolution* (N.Y., 1927)
New England Quarterly, III, 1930
New Yorker, The, Sept. 17, 1938
Nickerson, Hoffman, *The Turning Point of the Revolution* (Boston, 1928)
Nicolson, Sir Harold, *The Age of Reason* (N.Y., 1961)
Noble, M. C. S., *The Battle of Moore's Creek Bridge*, N.C. State Archives, III
Observations on the Fifth Article of the Treaty With America etc. (London, 1783), by various persons
Onderdonk, Henry, Jr., *Long Island and New York in Olden Times, Being Newspaper Extracts and Historical Sketches* (NYHS)
Orion Magazine, October, 1843
Padelford, Philip (ed.), *Colonial Panorama, Robert Honyman's Journal* (San Marino, 1935)

Papers of Alexander Hamilton, The, Syrett, H. C., and Cooke, J. E. (eds.) (N.Y., 1961), 2 vols.

Papers of the Delaware Historical Society, LVII, Feb., 1911

Pares, Richard, *King George III and the Politicians* (London, 1953)

Parker, Charles W., "Shipley: the Country Seat of a Jersey Loyalist," *Proceedings* of the New Jersey Historical Society, XVI, No. 2, April, 1931

Parker, James, *The Parker and Kearney Families of New Jersey* (Perth Amboy, 1929)

Peck, Epaphroditus, *The Loyalists of Connecticut* (New Haven, 1934)

Pemberton, William Baring, *Lord North* (N.Y., 1938)

Pennsylvania Magazine of History and Biography, Oct., 1885; Oct., 1889

Plumb, J. H., "Our Last King," *American Heritage,* XI, No. 4 (June, 1960)

Political Magazine, 60, 1781

Proceedings, South Carolina Historical Association, 6, 1936

Pynchon, William, *Diary* (Boston, 1890)

Quarterly Review, The, Vol. 188

Quennell, Peter, and Hoge, Alan, *The Past We Share* (N.Y., 1960)

Ramsay, David, *History of the Revolution in South Carolina* (Trenton, N.J., 1785)

Ramsay, J. G. M., *The Annals of Tennessee to the End of the Eighteenth Century* (Charleston, 1853)

Rankin, Hugh F., *North Carolina in the American Revolution* (Raleigh, 1959)

Reed, W. B., *Life and Correspondence of Joseph Reed* (Philadelphia, 1847), II

Reid, W. Max, *The Story of Old Fort Johnson* (N.Y., 1906)

Report on American Manuscripts in the Institutions of Great Britain (London, 1904), I

Revolutionary Records of the State of Georgia, The (Atlanta, 1908)

Ritcheson, Charles B., *British Politics and the American Revolution* (Norman, Okla., 1954)

Roberts, J. M. (ed.), *James P. Collins: Autobiography of a Revolutionary Soldier* (Clinton, La., 1899)

Robinson, Blackwell P., *A History of Moore County, N.C.* (Southern Pines, 1956)

Robson, Eric, *The American Revolution, 1763-1783* (London, 1955)

Rossiter, Clinton, *Conservatism in America* (London, 1955)

Rossman, Kenneth R., *Thomas Mifflin and the Politics of the American Revolution* (Chapel Hill, 1952)

Ryden, George H. (ed.), *Letters to and from Caesar Rodney, 1756-84* (Philadelphia, 1933)

Ryerson, A. E., *The Loyalists of America and Their Times* (Toronto, 1880)

Sabine, Lorenzo, *A Historical Essay on the Loyalists of the American Revolution* (Springfield, Mass., 1957)

Sabine, L., *Loyalists of the American Revolution* (Boston, 1864), 2 vols.

Sargent, Winthrop, *Loyalist Poetry of the Revolution* (Philadelphia, 1857)

Saunders, William L. (ed.), *Colonial Records of North Carolina* (1886-1890)

Scheer, George F. (ed.), *Private Yankee Doodle: Joseph P. Martin* (Boston, 1962)

Schlesinger, Arthur M., *Prelude to Independence, the Newspaper War on Britain, 1764-1776* (N.Y., 1958)

Schlesinger, Arthur M., *The Colonial Merchants and the American Revolution* (N.Y., 1957)

Seabury, Samuel, *The Congress Canvassed* (N.Y., 1774)

Sedgwick, Theodore, Jr., *A Memoir of the Life of William Livingston* (N.Y., 1833)

Seeber, E. D. (ed.), *On the Threshold of Liberty* (Bloomington, Ind., 1959)

Shepard, James, "The Tories of Connecticut," *Connecticut Quarterly*, IV, 1898

Shoemaker, Samuel, *Diary*, Historical Society of Pennsylvania

Sibley, John L., *Harvard Graduates*, Clifford L. Shipton (ed.), (Boston, 1951), V, VIII

Siebert, F. S., "The Confiscated Revolutionary Press," *Journalism Quarterly*, XIII (1936)

Siebert, W. H., "The Loyalists of Pennsylvania," *Ohio State University Bulletin*, XXIV, No. 20, April 1, 1929; "Loyalists of West Florida," MVHR, II, 1916, 465; "Loyalists of New Hampshire," *Ohio State University Bulletin*, 21, 1916; *Loyalists in East Florida* (De Land, Fla., 1929), 2 vols.

Smith, G. G., *The Story of Georgia and the Georgia People* (Atlanta, 1900)

Smith, Page, "David Ramsay and the Causes of the American Revolution," *William and Mary Quarterly*, XVII, No. 1, January, 1960

South Carolina Historical Association *Proceedings*, 1937, 34

Southern and Western Literary Messenger and Review, XII, Oct., 1846

Sprague, W. B., *Annals of the American Pulpit* (N.Y., 1866-1877)

Stark, James H., *Loyalists of Massachusetts* (Boston, 1910)

State Records of North Carolina, XV, XXII

Stevens, B. F., *Facsimiles of Manuscripts in European Archives Relating to America, 1773-1783* (London, 1889-1895)

Storms, J. C., *Origin of the Jackson Whites of the Ramapo Mountains* (Park Ridge, N.J., 1936)

Stone, W. L., *Border Wars of the American Revolution* (N.Y., 1864)

Sweet, W. W., *The Story of Religion in America* (N.Y., 1950)

Swiggett, Howard, *War Out of Niagara* (N.Y., 1933)

Tappert, T. G., and Doberstein, J. W. (translators), *Journals of Henry Melchior Muhlenberg* (Philadelphia, 1958), III

Tarleton, Banastre, *A History of the Campaigns of 1780 and 1781* (Dublin, 1787)

Tatum, E. H. (ed.), *The American Journal of Ambrose Serle* (San Marino, 1940)

Taylor, Robert J. (ed.), *Massachusetts, Colony to Commonwealth* (Chapel Hill, 1961)

Thacher, James, *A Military Journal During the Revolutionary War* (Boston, 1827)

Thayer, Theodore, *Nathanael Greene* (N.Y., 1960)
Tiffany, Consider, "The American Colonies and the Revolution," Mss. in Library of Congress
Torrey, Rufus C., *History of the Town of Fitchburg, Mass.* (Fitchburg, 1865)
Tourtellot, Arthur B., *William Diamond's Drum* (N.Y., 1959)
Trevelyan, Sir George Otto, *The American Revolution* (London, 1921), 6 vols.
Trumbull, J. R., *History of Northampton, Massachusetts* (Northampton, 1902)
Tyler, Moses Coit, *The Literary History of the American Revolution* (N.Y., 1957), 2 vols.
Updike, Wilkins, *A History of the Episcopal Church in Narragansett* (Boston, 1907)
Van Doren, Carl, *Secret History of the American Revolution* (N.Y., 1951)
Van Schaack, H. C., *Life of Peter Van Schaack* (N.Y., 1842)
Van Tyne, C. H., *Causes of the War of Independence* (Boston, 1929)
Van Tyne, C. H., *The Loyalists in the American Revolution* (N.Y., 1959)
Virginia Magazine of History and Biography, VI, VII
Wallace, Willard M., *Appeal to Arms* (N.Y., 1951)
Walsh, Richard, *Charleston's Sons of Liberty: a Study of the Artisans, 1763-1789* (Columbia, S.C., 1959)
Ward, Christopher, *The War of the Revolution* (N.Y., 1952), I, II
Watson, J. Steven, *The Reign of George III, 1760-1815* (London, 1960)
Wertenbaker, Thomas J., *Father Knickerbocker Rebels* (N.Y., 1948)
The Westchester Historian, 34, No. 3, July-Sept., 1958; No. 5, Oct.-Dec., 1958
Wharton, Francis, *Revolutionary Diplomatic Correspondence* (Washington, 1889), II
Whitaker, Nathaniel, *An Antidote Against the Reward of Toryism* (Salem, 1911)
Whiteley, William G., "The Revolutionary Soldier of Delaware," *Papers of the Historical Society of Delaware*, XIV (Wilmington, 1896)
Whittemore, Charles P., *John Sullivan of New Hampshire* (N.Y., 1961)
Willcox, William B. (ed.), *Sir Henry Clinton, the American Rebellion* (New Haven, 1954)
Willett, Marinus, *Narrative of Colonel Marinus Willett* (N.Y., 1831)
Williamson, Chilton, *American Suffrage From Property to Democracy* (Princeton, 1960)
Wilson, James, *Works* (Philadelphia, 1804)
Winfield, Charles H., *History of the County of Hudson, New Jersey* (N.Y., 1874)
Wish, Harvey, *The American Historian* (N.Y., 1960)
Wolf, Richard C., *Our Protestant Heritage* (Philadelphia, 1956)
Worcester Town Records (Worcester, Mass., 1882), IV
Wright, Louis B., *The First Gentlemen of Virginia: Intellectual Qualities of the Early Colonial Ruling Class* (San Marino, 1940)
Zeichner, Oscar, *Connecticut's Years of Controversy, 1750-1776* (Williamsburg, 1949)

Notes

Whenever more than one citation appears in a note, the order of their reference is the same as that of statements on the pages to which they refer.

1

THE BRIDGE THAT WASN'T THERE

1. Alden, John R., *The South in the Revolution, 1763-1789* (Baton Rouge, 1957), 323-324; Governor Josiah Martin to Earl of Dartmouth, Sept. 12, 1775, Clark, Walter (ed.), *State Records of North Carolina, 1777-1790* (Goldsboro, 1895-1905), X, 244; Meyer, Duane, *The Highland Scots of North Carolina, 1732-1776* (Chapel Hill, 1961), 156.
2. *Gentlemen's Magazine*, June, 1776; Hubbell, S. M., "Research Material for Moore's Creek Bridge National Military Park," Oct. 6, 1961, 3.
3. MacLean, J. P., *Flora MacDonald in America* (Lumberton, N.C., 1905), 35-50.
4. DeMond, Robert O., *The Loyalists in North Carolina During the Revolution* (Durham, 1940), 92.
5. Ashe, Samuel A., *History of North Carolina* (Greensboro, 1908-1925), 501.
6. Dawson, Henry B., *Battles of the United States* (N.Y., 1858), I, 129.
7. Rankin, Hugh F., *North Carolina in the American Revolution* (Raleigh, 1959), 14.
8. Saunders, W. L. (ed.), *The Colonial Records of North Carolina* (Raleigh, 1886-1890), X, 494; Meyer, 158-159.
9. Caruthers, Rev. Eli Washington, *Interesting Revolutionary Incidents and Sketches of Character, etc.* (Philadelphia, 1854), 86.
10. Montross, Lynn, *Rag, Tag and Bobtail* (N.Y., 1952), 98.
11. Noble, M. C. S., *The Battle of Moore's Creek Bridge*, Booklet in *N.C. State Archives*, III, Raleigh.
12. *Pennsylvania Evening Post*, March 23, 1776.
13. *New York Packet*, March 28, 1776.
14. Force, Peter, *American Archives, Fourth Series* (Washington, 1837-46), V, 62; *Colonial Records of N.C.*, X, 485-486. The money amounted to about $75,000 in American specie.
15. *Ibid.*, V, 1342; Governor Josiah Martin to Lord George Germain, March 21, 1776, *Colonial Records of N.C.*, 429, 486.
16. Montross, 99; Alden, 198; MacLean, 65-66.
17. Bancroft, George, *History of the United States of America, from the Discovery of the Continent* (N.Y., 1882-1884), IV, 391.

2

BACKSTAGE

1. Gipson, Lawrence Henry, *The Coming of the Revolution, 1763-1775* (N.Y., 1954), 215.
2. Ritcheson, Charles B., *British Politics of the American Revolution* (Norman, Okla., 1954), 136.
3. Adair, Douglass, and Schutz, John A. (eds.), *Peter Oliver's Origin and Progress of the American Rebellion* (San Marino, 1961), 113-114.
4. Pares, Richard, *King George III and the Politicians* (London, 1953), 47.
5. Ritcheson, 158.
6. Gipson, 223.
7. Jensen, Merrill, *Introduction to Political Ideas of the American Revolution* (N.Y., 1958), 3.
8. Hansard, Thomas C., *The Parliamentary History of England* (London, 1813), XVII, 1288; Fitzmaurice, Sir Edmund, *Life of the Earl of Shelburne* (London, 1912), I, 224.
9. Butterfield, H., *George III, Lord North and the People* (London, 1949), 20.
10. Hughes, Edward (ed.), "Lord North's Correspondence," *English Historical Review* (April, 1947), 17. These letters were selected from the North manuscripts in the Bodleian Library of Oxford University.
11. Lewis, W. S. (ed.), *A Selection of the Letters of Horace Walpole* (N.Y., 1926), II, 301.
12. North to George III, Jan. 29, 1778, Fortescue, Sir John (ed.), *The Correspondence of King George the Third* (London, 1927-1928), III, 196.
13. Lewis, 303.
14. Quoted in Butterfield, 40.
15. North to George III, Fortescue, IV, 3412.
16. *Nathan to Lord North* (London, 1780), 2; Christie, I. R., "Rockingham and Lord North's Offer of a Coalition, June-July, 1780," *English Historical Review* (July, 1954), 380.
17. *A Defense of the Rockingham Party in Their Late Coalition With the Right Honorable Frederick Lord North* (London, 1783), 7.
18. Fortescue, IV, 3536 and Pares, 73, 79.
19. Fortescue, V, 337.
20. d'Auberteuil, Hilliard, *Histoire de L'Administration de Lord North* (London, 1784), 120; Chalmers, George, *The Beauties of Fox, North and Burke* (London, 1784), 71.
21. Fox, Charles James, *Memoirs* (London, 1808), II, 38; Lucas, Reginald, *Lord North* (London, 1913), I, viii, 329, 339.
22. Lucas, 388.
23. Guedalla, Philip, *Fathers of the Revolution* (N.Y., 1926), 80.
24. *Ibid.*, 86.

25. Robson, Eric, *The American Revolution, 1763-1783* (London, 1955), 151.
26. Pemberton, William Baring, *Lord North* (N.Y., 1938), 21.
27. *Ibid.*, quoted on page 185.
28. *Ibid.*, 260.
29. Burke, Edmund, "A Letter to a Noble Lord," quoted in Pemberton, 341.
30. Watson, J. Steven, *The Reign of George III, 1760-1815* (London, 1960), 147-172.

3

INTO THREE PARTS

1. Dorson, Richard M., *America Rebels* (N.Y., 1953), 115; Champagne, R. J., "The Sons of Liberty and the Aristocracy of New York," unpublished Ph.D. dissertation, U. of Wis., 1960.
2. Capen to James Otis and Court of Enquiry, Dec. 11, 1776, Miscellaneous Manuscripts, Massachusetts State Archives, Boston.
3. Tyler, Moses Coit, "The Party of the Loyalists in the American Revolution," *American Historical Review*, Oct., 1895, I, 24-28.
4. Becker, Carl, *The History of Political Parties in the Province of New York* (Madison, Wis., 1909), 31.
5. *American Loyalist Transcripts*, New York Public Library, V, 58, 93. These important documents will be hereafter known as *ALT*.
6. Trevelyan, George Otto, *The American Revolution* (N.Y., 1926), I, 374-375.
7. Miscellaneous American Revolution Manuscripts, Library of Congress.
8. Adams, C. F. (ed.), *Works of John Adams* (Boston, 1850-56), IX, 597.
9. Wright, Louis B., *The First Gentlemen of Virginia etc.* (San Marino, 1940), 132-133.
10. Ryerson, A. E., *The Loyalists of America and Their Times* (Toronto, 1880), I, 504.
11. Erskine, John, *Reflections on the Rise, Progress and Probable Consequences of the Present Contentions With the Colonies* (Edinburgh, 1776), 12, 13.
12. Gipson, Lawrence H., "The Great Debate in the Committee of the Whole House of Commons on the Stamp Act, 1766, as Reported by Samuel Ryder," *Pennsylvania Magazine of History and Biography*, LXXXVI, No. 1, Jan., 1962, p. 40.
13. Hall, Captain J. of Howe's Army, *The History of the Civil War in America* (London, 1780), 3.
14. Robson, 39.
15. *Ibid.*, 74.
16. Brinton, Crane, *The Anatomy of Revolution* (London, 1953), 166-168.
17. Labaree, Leonard W., *Conservatism in Early American History* (Ithaca, 1959), 130, 146-147.
18. Morgan, Edmund S., *The Birth of the Republic, 1763-1789* (Chicago, 1956), 74.

19. Rossiter, Clinton, *Conservatism in America* (London, 1955), 104-105.
20. Greene to George Washington, Aug. 6, 1775, Mass. State Archives, Boston.
21. *Boston Gazette,* Nov. 28, 1774; Schlesinger, A. M., *The Colonial Merchants and the American Revolution* (N.Y., 1957), 47.
22. *Massachusetts Gazette and Post Boy,* Dec. 26, 1774.
23. *American Archives,* 4th Ser., I, 515.
24. McIlwain, Charles H., *The American Revolution: a Constitutional Interpretation* (N.Y., 1958), 186-187.
25. Andrews, Charles M., *The Colonial Background of the American Revolution* (New Haven, 1961), 53.
26. Flick, Alexander C., *Loyalism in New York During the American Revolution* (N.Y., 1901), 12.
27. Seabury, Samuel, "A View of the Controversy Between Great Britain and Her Colonies," pamphlet, New York, 1774.
28. Nelson, William H., *The American Tory* (London, 1961), 2.
29. Trevelyan, I, 376.
30. *Letters of a Loyalist Lady* (Being the letters of Anne Hulton, sister of Henry Hulton, Commissioner of Customs at Boston, 1767-1776, dated Jan. 31, 1774, and written from Boston to Mrs. Adam Lightbody of Liverpool.) (Cambridge, 1927, 70-73.)
31. *Ibid.,* 85-86.
32. *The London Packet,* Feb. 19, 1787.
33. Billias, George A., *General John Glover and His Marblehead Mariners* (N.Y., 1960), 61; *Worcester Town Records* (Worcester, Mass., 1882), IV, 242.
34. *American Archives,* 4th Ser., I, 745.
35. Newcomer, Lee N., *The Embattled Farmers* (N.Y., 1953), 68.
36. Torrey, Rufus C., *History of the Town of Fitchburg, Mass.* (Fitchburg, 1865), 96-99.
37. *American Archives,* 4th Ser., V, 806-807.
38. *Ibid.,* III, 824.
39. *Americana,* XXII, No. 2, April, 1928.
40. Proclamation of the Massachusetts General Court, Jan. 23, 1776, quoted in *Massachusetts, Colony and Commonwealth,* Taylor, Robert J. (ed.) (Chapel Hill, 1961), 20.
41. Crawford, Mary C., *Social Life in Old New England* (Boston, 1914), 488.
42. Nicolson, Sir Harold, *The Age of Reason* (N.Y., 1961), 36.
43. *Massachusetts Spy,* March 17, 1775.
44. Hammond, Otis G., "Tories of New Hampshire in the War of the Revolution," New Hampshire Historical *Proceedings* (Concord, 1917).
45. Trumbull, J. R., *History of Northampton, Massachusetts* (Northampton, 1902), I, 373-374.
46. Tourtellot, Arthur B., *William Diamond's Drum* (N.Y., 1959), 159-60; Collections with Regard to the Care of the American Loyalists, Public Record Office of Northern Ireland.

47. Massachusettensis (London, 1819), 159, 165. This was the pseudonym of Daniel Leonard, used in a series of letters. John Adams found these letters "shining among the Tory writings like the moon among the lesser stars" (*Works*, II, 405).
48. Stark, James H., *The Loyalists of Massachusetts* (Boston, 1910), 38.
49. Hutchinson, Thomas, *The History of the Colony and Province of Massachusetts Bay*, L. S. Mayo (ed.) (Cambridge, 1936), III, 294.
50. Shipton, Clifford K. (ed.), Sibley, John L., *Harvard Graduates* (Boston, 1951), VIII, 149.
51. Adams, John, *Diary* (Cambridge, 1961), 93, entry of March 12, 1774.
52. Adams, John, *Works*, VI, 189.
53. Shipton, 204-213.
54. *Proceedings* of the Massachusetts Historical Society, May, 1895, 163.
55. Petition of Phoebe Oliver to Mass. General Court, Jan. 29, 1776, in Miscellaneous Documents, Mass. State Archives.
56. Adair and Schutz, 34.
57. *Ibid.*, xviii; *Atlantic Monthly*, May, 1884.
58. Hutchinson, Thomas, *Diary and Letters* (London, 1883-1886), I, 201; Einstein, Lewis, *Divided Loyalties* (London, 1933), 156-157.
59. Beloff, Max (ed.), *The Debate on the American Revolution* (London, 1960), 134.
60. Mass. Archives, XXIV, 535; Adams, Randolph G., *Political Ideas of the American Revolution* (N.Y., 1958), 17.
61. Davidson, Philip, *Propaganda and the American Revolution, 1763-1783* (Chapel Hill, 1941), 292-293.
62. Taylor, Robert J. (ed.), *Massachusetts, Colony to Commonwealth* (Chapel Hill, 1961), 8, 9; *Works* of John Adams, III, 12-23.
63. Wish, Harvey, *The American Historian* (N.Y., 1960), 30-33; Adams quoted in Trevelyan, I, 92n.
64. Schlesinger, A. M., *Prelude to Independence, the Newspaper War on Britain, 1764-1776* (N.Y., 1958), 40; Davidson, 304-310.
65. Forbes, Esther, *Paul Revere and the World He Lived In* (Boston, 1942), 220; Stark, 247.
66. Curwen, Samuel, *Journals and Letters* (N.Y., 1845), 4.
67. *Ibid.*, 207.
68. Shipton, V, 518; Curwen, 210.
69. Adams, *Works*, IV, 7, 8.
70. *Proceedings*, Mass. Historical Society, 2nd Ser., X, 413, 418; Stark, 455.
71. Adams, *Works*, IV, 10.
72. Stark, 326.
73. Tyler, Moses Coit, *The Literary History of the American Revolution* (N.Y., 1957), I, 356-363; "Massachusettensis," Dec. 19, 1774.

4

WHERE TORIES HELD SWAY

1. *New York Journal,* Feb. 9, 1775.
2. *Holt's Journal,* April 27, 1775.
3. *Gaine's New York Gazette,* Jan. 9, 1775.
4. Quoted in Holliday, Carl, *The Wit and Humor of Colonial Days* (N.Y., 1960), 110.
5. Jameson, J. Franklin, *The American Revolution Considered as a Social Movement*(Boston, 1956), 16; Kenney, Alice P., "The Albany Dutch: Loyalists and Patriots," *N.Y. History,* XLII, Oct., 1961.
6. Seabury, Samuel, "The Congress Canvassed" (N.Y., 1774); *American Archives,* 4th Ser., V, 1067; Flick, 52; "The Tories: 1763-1774," a paper delivered before the American Historical Association, December 28, 1960, by Professor David L. Jacobson of the University of California; Morison, S. E., and Commager, H. S., *The Growth of the American Republic* (N.Y., 1962), 199-201.
7. Einstein, 196.
8. John Pringle to William Tilghman, Aug. 7, 1775, Preston Davie Collection, *Southern Historical Collection,* University of North Carolina Library. (Hereafter known as *SHS,* UNC.)
9. Entries of Sept. 4 and Oct. 26, 1775, in Volume 766, Customs Establishment Papers, *American Colonies, 1771-1776,* Customs Library, London.
10. Van Tyne, Claude H., *The Loyalists in the American Revolution* (Reprint, N.Y., 1959), 108; *American Archives,* 4th Ser., IV, 1066; *New York Gazette,* Oct. 21, 1776.
11. Tyler, I, 500-505.
12. Ryerson, I, 493, 517.
13. *Rivington's Gazette,* March 9, 1775.
14. *Ibid.,* April 20, 1775.
15. Smith, Edward J., "Long Island's Revolutionary Counterfeiting Plot," *Journal of Long Island History,* II, Spring, 1962, No. 1.
16. ALT, Vol. 19, 135-147; Vol. 21, 53-68; Vol. 43, 139, 315-371.
17. ALT, Vol. 42, 459-540; Vol. 43, 5-10.
18. Callahan, North, *Henry Knox: General Washington's General* (N.Y., 1958), 154-155.
19. Wertenbaker, Thomas J., *Father Knickerbocker Rebels* (N.Y., 1948), 64.
20. *New York Gazette,* Aug. 18, 1774.
21. Moore, Frank, *Diary of the American Revolution* (N.Y., 1860), 174.
22. Sears to Sherman, Dyer and Deane, Nov. 28, 1775, in Manuscript Collection of the David Library of the American Revolution, at Washington Crossing State Park, Pennsylvania; Syrett, H. C., and Cooke, J. E. (eds.), *The Papers of Alexander Hamilton* (N.Y., 1961), I, 176.

23. Quoted in Granger, Bruce I., *Political Satire in the American Revolution, 1763-1783* (Ithaca, N.Y., 1960), 291.

24. Lee, Charles, *Memoirs* (N.Y., 1792), 84; Snell, Catharine C., "The Tory and the Spy: the Double Life of James Rivington," *William and Mary Quarterly*, XVI, No. 1, Jan., 1959.

25. Harlow, Ralph, *The United States: from Wilderness to World Power* (N.Y., 1958), 125-127; ALT, Vol. 19, 73-89.

26. Letter of Spalding, 1775, to unknown recipient, Colonel John Peters Papers, New York Historical Society (hereafter known as NYHS).

27. Zeichner, Oscar, *Connecticut's Years of Controversy, 1750-1776* (Williamsburg, Va., 1949), 206; Moore's *Diary*, 184.

28. Callahan, North, *Daniel Morgan: Ranger of the Revolution* (N.Y., 1961), 50; Moore's *Diary*, 123.

29. *Middlesex Journal*, Jan. 30, 1776.

30. *New York Packet*, Jan. 18, 1776; *Newport Mercury*, Sept. 2, 1771.

31. *American Archives*, 4th Ser., 582-583 and 5th Ser., 1491-1493.

32. Morris, Richard B., "Class Struggle and the American Revolution," *William and Mary Quarterly*, XIX (Jan., 1962), 4-30.

33. Jones, Thomas, *History of New York During the Revolutionary War* (N.Y., 1879), I, 101-103; Flick, 74; *American Archives*, 4th Ser., VI, 1397.

34. Elting to Richard Varick, June 13, 1776, New York Mercantile Library Association, *New York City During the American Revolution* (N.Y., 1861), 97; Henshaw, William, *Orderly Books*, Oct. 1775-Oct. 1776 (Worcester, 1948), 131.

35. Orderly book of George Washington, July 26-Aug. 6, 1776, Charles Allen Munn Collection, Manuscripts Division, Fordham University.

36. Allan, H. S., *John Hancock, Patriot in Purple* (N.Y., 1953), 212-13.

37. Manuscripts in George Washington Headquarters, Newburgh, N.Y.; Jones, II, 271.

38. ALT, Vol. 41, 575.

39. Albee, Allison, "The Defenses of Pines Bridge," *Westchester Historian*, Westchester County Historical Society, Vol. 34, 1958, Nos. 3 and 4.

40. *Ibid.*

41. *American Archives*, 4th Ser., VI, 1158.

42. Bakeless, John, *Turncoats, Traitors and Heroes* (N.Y., 1959), 102.

43. *Pennsylvania Gazette*, July 3, 1776.

44. *American Archives*, 4th Ser., VI, 1154-1155.

45. Flick, 104.

46. Freeman, Douglas S., *George Washington* (N.Y., 1951), IV, 119.

47. *Ibid.*, IV, 120.

48. *Pennsylvania Evening Post*, July 2, 1776.

49. Fitzpatrick, John C. (ed.), *The Writings of George Washington* (Washington, 1931-1944), V, 195; Van Doren, Carl, *Secret History of the American Revolution* (N.Y., 1951), 15.

50. Jones, 416-417; ALT, Vol., 41, 471, 498.

51. Quoted in Sabine, Lorenzo, *A Historical Essay on the Loyalists of the American Revolution*, Padelford, Philip (ed.) (Springfield, Mass., 1957), 13-14.
52. Frothingham, Richard, *History of the Siege of Boston* (Boston, 1903), 301; Flick, 104; *American Archives*, 5th Ser., XX, 109, 120; *Colonial Panorama, Robert Honyman's Journal* (San Marino, 1939), 50.
53. ALT, Vol. 41, 53-65.
54. Dartmouth to Elliot, Nov. 6, 1775; Elliot to Lords of Treasury, Nov. 30, 1776; Elliot to Commissioners of the Customs, Nov. 30, 1776, Andrew Elliot Collection, New York State Library, Albany.
55. Trevelyan, II, 191.
56. Jones, I, 104-105.
57. Moore, I, 278; Hoyt, E. P., *The Vanderbilts and Their Fortunes* (N.Y., 1962), 25.
58. Moore, I, 307; Van Doren, 12.
59. Wertenbaker, 98; *American Archives*, Ser. 5, II, 182.
60. *St. James Chronicle*, Nov. 9, 10, 1776, and March 22, 25, 1777.
61. ALT, Vol. 17, 951; Vol. 19, 37; Vol. 23, 485; Vol. 41, 35; Vol. 42, 177.
62. ALT, Vol. 41, 453-469.
63. Adams, John, *Autobiography*, 424; ALT, Vol. 41, 101-216.
64. *Historical Anecdotes of the American Revolution*, written by "A Loyalist" (London, 1779), 2.

5

ADVANCING BACKWARD

1. Virginia Assembly to Dunmore, June 10, 1775, Hartley Russell Manuscripts, Berkshire Record Office, Reading, England; Harrell, I. S., *Loyalism in Virginia* (Durham, 1926), 41.
2. *Virginia Gazette*, Oct. 7, 1775.
3. Mays, D. J., *Edmund Pendleton: a Biography* (Cambridge, 1952), II, 14; Siebert, F. S., "The Confiscated Revolutionary Press," *Journalism Quarterly*, XIII (1936), 179-181; American Archives, 4th Ser., II, 1137.
4. *Norfolk Virginian-Pilot* and *Ledger-Star* files; also *Virginia Gazette*, Dec. 6, 1775.
5. Lee, Richard Henry, *The Letters of Richard Henry Lee* (N.Y., 1912), I, 162; Fitzpatrick, IV, 186.
6. Dunmore to Dartmouth, Dec. 23, 1775, Public Record Office, London, Loyalist Transcripts, V, 1353.
7. State Records of N.C., X, 429-430.
8. Lossing, Benson J., *Pictorial Field Book of the American Revolution* (N.Y., 1850-1852), II, 333; Trevelyan, I, 346.
9. Bancroft, VIII, 231.
10. Harrell, 45.

11. Eckenrode, H. J., *The Revolution in Virginia* (Boston, 1916), 88; George, John A., "Virginia Loyalists, 1775-1783," Richmond College Historical Papers, I, No. 2 (June, 1916), 195; *American Archives*, 5th Ser., II, 162.
12. Joseph Hewes to Samuel Johnston, Jan. 6, 1776, *Colonial Records of N.C.*, X, 391.
13. Siebert, W. H., "The Loyalists of Pennsylvania," *Ohio State University Bulletin*, XXIV, 23; Washington to Reed, Jan. 21, 1776, Fitzpatrick, IV, 297.
14. *State Records of N.C.*, XXII, 181-189.
15. Robards, Sadie R., *Sketch of Colonel Fanning*, SHC, UNC.
16. Caruthers, Rev. Eli, *Interesting Revolutionary Incidents and Sketches etc.* (Philadelphia, 1854), 165, 166, 173.
17. *Narrative of Fanning*, in SHC, UNC Library; State Records of N.C., XVI, 184; Connor, R. W. D., "Revolutionary Leaders of North Carolina," State Normal and Industrial College *Historical Publication* (High Point, 1916), I, 493.
18. Robinson, Blackwell, *A History of Moore County, North Carolina* (Southern Pines, N.C., 1956), 85.
19. ALT, Vol. 27, 159; DeMond, 152; Fanning, *Narrative*, 12.
20. Coleman, Kenneth, *The American Revolution in Georgia, 1763-1789* (Athens, 1958), 75.
21. Wright to Lord Dartmouth, July 29, 1775, *Collections*, Georgia Historical Society (Savannah, 1873), III, 200-203.
22. ALT, Vol. 34, 349.
23. *Georgia Gazette*, Aug. 30, 1775. Tarring and feathering as a punishment was used as early as 1189 by Richard I of England, who, when he set out for the Holy Land, instituted penalties for his soldiers and sailors to keep them well-behaved. One such punishment was shaving of the heads, having boiling pitch dropped upon their crowns, cushion feathers stuck in this—then the poor victim was "set adrift." French, Allen, *A British Fusilier in Revolutionary Boston* (Cambridge, 1926), 40.
24. Walsh, Richard, *Charleston's Sons of Liberty: a Study of the Artisans, 1763-1789* (Columbia, S.C., 1959), 87.
25. Sabine, Essay, 33; Greene, E. B., *The Revolutionary Generation* (N.Y., 1943), 227.
26. Adams, *Works*, X, 277; Historical Manuscripts Commission, *Report on the Manuscripts of Mrs. Stopford-Sackville* (London, 1910), II, 218; Whiteley, W. G., "The Revolutionary Soldiers of Delaware," *Papers of the Historical Society of Delaware*, XIV (Wilmington, 1896), 69.
27. Ryden, George H. (ed.), *Letters to and from Caesar Rodney, 1756-1784* (Philadelphia, 1933), 263.
28. Hancock, Harold B., *The Delaware Loyalists*, in the Papers of the HSD,

New Series, IV, 6; Fraser, Alexander (ed.), *Second Report of the Bureau of Archives* (Toronto, 1905), I, 519-520.

29. *Pennsylvania Journal*, March 22, 1775, Nov. 29, 1775; *American Archives*, 4th Series, III, 1072; IV, 564.

30. Graham to Russell, June 6, 1774; Fitzhugh to Russell, Jan. 25, 1775, Hartley Russell Papers.

31. Van Tyne, 82-83; Nelson, 107.

32. *American Archives*, 4th Ser., III, 1571-1574; Blau, Joseph L., "Jonathan Boucher, Tory," *History 4*, 1961, 93-111; *Maryland Historical Magazine*, X, Dec. 1915.

33. Alden, 83; Land, A. C., *The Dulanys of Maryland* (Baltimore, 1955), 308-325.

34. Kuntzleman, O. C., *Joseph Galloway, Loyalist* (Philadelphia, 1941), 24.

35. Galloway, Joseph, *Historical and Political Reflections on the Rise and Progress of the American Rebellion* (London, 1780), 66-70.

36. Adams, *Works*, II, 388; Jacobson, 6; Adair and Schutz, ix; the book referred to is *American Political Thought* by Alan P. Grimes (N.Y., 1960).

37. Bigelow, John (ed.), *The Complete Works of Benjamin Franklin* (N.Y. and London, 1887-1888), V, 435-439; Burnett, E. C. (ed.), *Letters of Members of the Continental Congress* (Washington, 1921-1936), I, 55.

38. Morris, Richard B., *The American Revolution: a Brief History* (N.Y., 1955), 46.

39. Burnett, I, 53, 54, 57, 59; *Magazine of American History*, I, 442.

40. Miller, John C., *Origins of the American Revolution* (Boston, 1943), 136; Galloway, Joseph, *A Candid Examination of the Mutual Claims of Great Britain and the Colonies* (London, 1780), 59; Stevens, B. F., *Facsimiles of Manuscripts in European Archives Relating to America, 1773-1783* (London, 1889-1895), No. 2090, March 4, 1778; Galloway, Joseph, *The Examination of Joseph Galloway, Esq. by a Committee of the House of Commons* (Thomas Balch, ed.) (Philadelphia, 1855), 51n. Samuel Adams is probably the Adams to whom he referred.

6

A MORE OMINOUS STORM

1. Ryerson, I, 511.

2. Lundin, Leonard, *Cockpit of the Revolution* (Princeton, 1940), 218-219.

3. *Pennsylvania Gazette*, Jan. 3, 1774.

4. Quoted in Sabine, *Essay*, 21.

5. American Archives, 4th Ser., IV, 203.

6. Moreau, D. H., *Old Times in Hunterdon* (Flemington, N.J., 1961), 22;

Honeyman, A. Van Doren, "Concerning the New Jersey Loyalists in the Revolution," *Proceedings of the New Jersey Historical Society,* Vol. 51, No. 2, April, 1933, 119-120.

7. Ryerson, I, 495.
8. *American Archives,* 4th Ser., IV, 203.
9. Adair and Schutz, 81.
10. Trevelyan, 48.
11. Stark, 481; Curwen, 553.
12. McFadden, Elizabeth, "Last Royal Governor Left a Prisoner" in *Newark Sunday News,* March 10, 1963; *American Archives,* 4th Ser., III, 1871-1875.
13. Lundin, 71-73.
14. Stark, 481-482; Curwen, 554-555; visit by the author to St. Paul's Church.
15. Trevelyan, IV, 49.
16. Jones, E. A., "The Loyalists of New Jersey," *Collections* of New Jersey Historical Society, X (March, 1927), 75.
17. Winfield, Charles H., *History of the County of Hudson, New Jersey* (N.Y., 1874), 14, 141; Keesey, Ruth M., "Loyalism in Bergen County, New Jersey," *William and Mary Quarterly,* XVIII, Oct., 1961, No. 4.
18. "Report of Major André," Sir Henry Clinton Papers, Clements Library, University of Michigan, Ann Arbor, Mich.
19. "Patrick Ferguson re Marauding," Clinton Papers, Clements Library.
20. Sedgwick, Theodore, Jr., *A Memoir of the Life of William Livingston* (N.Y., 1833), 224; Fitzpatrick, VII, 57.
21. Keesey, Ruth M., "New Jersey Legislation Concerning the Loyalists," *Proceedings* of the NJHS, LXXIX, No. 2, April, 1961.
22. *Pennsylvania Evening Post,* Aug. 10, 1776.
23. Keesey, "New Jersey Legislation etc."
24. Jackson, John W., *Margaret Morris, Her Journal* (Philadelphia, 1949), 48, 87.
25. Parker, James, *The Parker and Kearney Families of New Jersey* (Perth Amboy, 1929), 13-15.
26. Parker, Charles W., "Shipley: The Country Seat of a Jersey Loyalist," *Proceedings* of the NJHS, XVI, No. 2, April, 1931, 117-138.
27. Thayer, Theodore, *Nathanael Greene* (N.Y., 1960), 135; *N.J. Historical Collections,* X, 1927. Robins became a captain and served with the British at the battle of Guilford Courthouse, breaking through the American lines three times. He was commended by Lord Cornwallis, the commanding general.
28. *Pennsylvania Evening Post,* Dec. 7, 1776; *American Archives,* 4th Ser., III, 1342.
29. NJHS *Proceedings,* XVI, No. 2, April, 1931, 17-18, 43, 61-62, 132, 197, 228; Lundin, 77.
30. Robinson to Howe, March 5, 1777, *Report on American Manuscripts in the Royal Institution of Great Britain* (London, 1904), I, 93.

31. Sargent, Winthrop, *Loyalist Poetry of the Revolution* (Philadelphia, 1857), 18.
32. Stone, William L., *Border Wars of the American Revolution* (N.Y., 1864), I, 37.
33. Ward, Christopher, *The War of the Revolution* (N.Y., 1952), II, 481.
34. Claus to William Knox, Oct. 11, 1777, Manuscript in N.Y. State Library.
35. Nickerson, Hoffman, *The Turning Point of the Revolution* (Boston, 1928), 197.
36. Claus to Knox, and Ward, II, 483; Commager, H. S., and Morris, Richard (eds.), *The Spirit of Seventy-Six* (Indianapolis and N.Y., 1958), I, 563.
37. *Continental Journal and Weekly Advertiser*, Sept. 4, 1777; Reid, W. Max, *The Story of Old Fort Johnson* (N.Y., 1906), 89-92.
38. *Continental Journal and Weekly Advertiser*, Sept. 4, 1777.
39. *Ibid.*
40. Scheer, George F., and Rankin, Hugh, *Rebels and Redcoats* (Cleveland and N.Y., 1957), 268.
41. Willett, Marinus, *Narrative of Colonel Marinus Willett* (N.Y., 1831), 131-133.
42. St. Leger to Burgoyne, Aug. 27, 1777, from Burgoyne, John, *A State of the Expedition from Canada* etc. (London, 1780), xliv-v.
43. Ketchum, Richard M. (ed.), *The American Heritage Book of the Revolution* (N.Y., 1958), 240.
44. Swiggett, Howard, *War Out of Niagara* (N.Y., 1933), 86.
45. Burgoyne, *A State of the Expedition* etc., xliv-v.
46. Scheer and Rankin, 268; Ward, II, 486.
47. "Narrative of Dr. Moses Younglove," in Herkimer Portfolio, being an undated newspaper clipping, N.Y. State Library.
48. *Ibid.*
49. *Ibid.*
50. ALT, Vol. 21, 399-408.
51. Dwight, Timothy, *Travels in New England and New York* (New Haven, 1821-1822), III, 196-198.
52. Thacher, James, *A Military Journal During the Revolutionary War* (Boston, 1827), 89-91.
53. Bill of Dr. William Petry after Oriskany battle, *Gotshall Collection*, VII, 100, N.Y. State Library; Flick, 111.

7

THE ROLE OF RELIGION

1. Hammond, Otis G., "The Tories of New Hampshire in the Age of the Revolution," a pamphlet (Concord, 1917), by the N.H. Historical Society.
2. Tyler, II, 308.

3. Whitaker, Nathaniel, *An Antidote Against the Reward of Toryism* (Salem, 1811), 3-12.
4. Tiffany, Consider, "The American Colonies and the Revolution," Manuscript in Library of Congress, Book IV, 11.
5. Stark, 276.
6. *Ibid.*
7. Callahan, *Knox*, 59; Shipton, Clifford K., *New England Life in the Eighteenth Century* (Cambridge, 1963), 237.
8. Stark, 277-278; Tuell, H. E., "Reverend Mather Byles, Parson and Punster," *Magazine of History*, VI, Dec., 1907, No. 6, 31-37.
9. John Pringle to William Tilghman, Sept. 15, 1774, Preston Davie Collection *SHS*, UNC.
10. Boucher, Jonathan, *A View of the Cause and Consequences of the American Revolution in Thirteen Discourses* (London, 1797), 115-116.
11. Boucher, Jonathan, *Reminisces of a Maryland Loyalist* (London, 1909), 215.
12. Correspondence of Rev. J. Boucher, in Md. Historical Society, Nov. 25, 1775.
13. *Ibid.*
14. Van Tyne, C. H., *Causes of the War of Independence* (Boston, 1929), 356.
15. Wolf, Richard C., *Our Protestant Heritage* (Philadelphia, 1956), 21-22.
16. Sweet, W. W., *The Story of Religion in America* (N.Y., 1950), 172-173; Birdsall, R. D., *Berkshire County* (New Haven, 1959), 57; Grumpertz, S. G., *Jewish Legion of Valor* (N.Y., 1934), 72-73.
17. *American Archives*, 4th Ser., I, 301-302.
18. Baldwin, Alice M., *The New England Clergy and the American Revolution* (N.Y., 1958), 123n.
19. Adair and Schutz, 104-105.
20. Sprague, W. B., *Annals of the American Pulpit* (N.Y., 1866-1877), I, 615.
21. Green, F. B., *Boothbay, Southport and Boothbay Harbor* (Portland, 1906), 233.
22. *Essex Gazette*, July 13, 1775.
23. Holliday, Carl, *The Wit and Humor of Colonial Days* (N.Y., 1960), 130-131.
24. Van Doren, 197-198.
25. Boucher, *Reminisces* etc., 104-105.
26. Chitwood, Oliver P., *A History of Colonial America* (N.Y., 1961), 593; Tyler, I, 121-140; Adams, *Works*, X, 185.
27. Hooker, Richard, *The Anglican Church and the American Revolution*, unpublished Ph.D. thesis, University of Chicago, 1942, 174.
28. *Cape Fear Mercury*, Aug. 25, 1775.
29. Jameson, 31.
30. Munroe, John A., *Federalist Delaware* (New Brunswick, 1954), 45.
31. Jameson, 92.

32. Shepard, James, "The Tories of Connecticut," *Connecticut Quarterly,* 1898, IV, 259.
33. Levenstein, Leonard, "Loyalism in Connecticut," unpublished master's thesis, New York University, 1955, 87-88.
34. *Connecticut Quarterly,* 1897, III, 435.
35. Samuel Peters manuscripts in *Archives of the Protestant Episcopal Church in the U.S.A.,* Vols. I and VIII, NYHS. This collection comprises about 200 letters which cast interesting light on the religious side of this turbulent period in America.
36. *Ibid.;* Tyler, II, 412-413.
37. Bates, Walter, *Kingston and the Loyalists of 1783* (St. John, N.B., 1889), 6.
38. *Ibid.*
39. Peters Mss. NYHS.
40. Bates, 7.
41. Peters Mss. NYHS.
42. Nicolson, Harold, *The Age of Reason* (N.Y., 1961), 36.
43. Peters Mss. NYHS.
44. Tyler, II, 412-415.
45. Peters Papers, NYHS.
46. Peck, Epaphroditus, *The Loyalists of Connecticut* (New Haven, 1934), 4.
47. Labaree, Leonard W., *Conservatism in Early American History* (N.Y. and London, 1948), 64.
48. Rev. David Love to Commissioners of the English Treasury, Dec. 4, 1780, Mss. in David Library, Washington Crossing, Pa.
49. Bates, Walter, *Kingston and the Loyalists of 1783, With Reminisces of Early Days in Connecticut* (St. John, N.B., 1889), 1; Proverbs, 24:21.
50. Moore, I, 141.
51. Vardill to Washington, Sept. 20, 1773, Ford, W. C. (ed.), *The Writings of George Washington* (N.Y. and London, 1899), 45.
52. Dix, A. Morgan, *History of Trinity Church* (N.Y., 1898), 365.
53. "The Memorial of John Vardill," Nov. 16, 1783, Public Records Office, London.
54. *Letters on the American War* (London, 1778), 34; Einstein, 55.
55. Deane to Congress, date unknown, Deane Papers, II, 256, NYHS.
56. Einstein, 56.
57. Stevens, *Facsimiles,* 12, Vardill to Hynson, Feb. 13, 1777.
58. Vardill to Lord North, Feb. 10, 1777, Stevens, 12.
59. Papers in Public Record Office, A/O, 12/20.
60. Eden to George III, Oct. 20, 1777, British Museum, 34414 f., 239 sq.
61. In Public Record Office, A/O, 13/67.
62. Einstein, 71.
63. Bartram, F. S., *History of New York City* (N.Y., 1888), 78, 79; Wertenbaker, 55; Miller, John C., *Alexander Hamilton* (N.Y., 1959), 17.
64. *Gentlemen's Magazine,* Jan., 1777; Kallich, M., and MacLeish, A., *The American Revolution Through British Eyes* (Evanston, 1962), 99.

65. ALT, Vol, 42, 163.
66. ALT, Vol, 42, 541-567.
67. Tyler, II, 287-292.
68. ALT, Vol, 42, 555-567.
69. Updike, Wilkins, *A History of the Episcopal Church in Narragansett* (Boston, 1907), I, 168.
70. Auchmuty to his sister, Caty, in America, March 13, 1779, NYHS.
71. Sweet, 176.
72. Wolf, 22.
73. Tyler, I, 350-355; ALT, Vol. 41, 559-573.
74. Tyler, I, 334-345.
75. Daniel, Marjorie, "John Joachim Zubly, Georgia Pamphleteer of the Revolution," *Georgia Historical Quarterly*, XIX, March, 1935, No. 1; Mahitable Danbury to Jesse Shepherd, Feb. 26, 1776, Burton Historical Collection, Detroit Public Library.
76. Hancock, 45.
77. Sweet, 178-179.
78. Clark, Elmer T., *An Album of Methodist History* (Nashville, 1952), 170.
79. Perry, W. S. (ed.), *Historical Collections Relating to the American Colonial Church* (Hartford, 1870-1873), II, 490.
80. Gilpin, Thomas, *Exiles in Virginia during the Revolutionary War* (Philadelphia, 1848), 288.
81. Gilpin, *Diary*.
82. Battle, Kemp P., *History of the University of North Carolina* (Raleigh, 1907), 115.
83. Whitaker, 31-42.

8

VIOLENT LEGACY

1. Storms, J. C., *Origin of the Jackson Whites of the Ramapo Mountains* (Park Ridge, N.J., 1936), 8-10; Weller, George, "The Jackson Whites," *The New Yorker*, Sept. 17, 1938, 29-39.
2. Barck, Oscar T., *New York City During the War for Independence* (N.Y., 1931), 82.
3. Carmer, Carl, *The Hudson* (N.Y., 1939), 100; *New York Herald-Tribune*, May 14, 1961; Crawford, Constance, "The Jackson Whites," unpublished master's thesis, NYU, 1940, 3-79.
4. Crawford, 96; Storms, 29; *Philadelphia Record*, June 6 and July 30, 1940; *New York World-Telegram*, April 27, 1937.
5. *The Connecticut Gazette and Universal Intelligencer*, July 11, 1777.
6. *Gentlemen's Magazine*, Aug., 1778; quoted in Carrington, H. B., *Battles of the American Revolution* (N.Y., 1876), 328.
7. Burgoyne, Lt. Gen. John, *A State of the Expedition from Canada etc.* (London, 1780), Appendix lxiii.

8. John Peters Papers, NYHS.
9. Trevelyan, IV, 126; Anburey, Thomas, *Travels Through the Interior Parts of America* (Boston, 1923), I, 171.
10. Horatio Gates Papers, NYHS, Box XIXb; Baxter, J. P., *The British Invasion from the North* (Albany, 1887), 233.
11. de Fonblanque, E. B., *Political and Military Episodes . . . Derived from the Life and Correspondence of the Rt. Hon. J. Burgoyne* (London, 1876); Guedalla, 166-167.
12. Jones, 682, 684; Upham, G. B., "Burgoyne's Great Mistake," *New England Quarterly*, III, 1930, 657-680.
13. Wharton, Francis (ed.), *Revolutionary Diplomatic Correspondence* (Washington, 1889), II, 451.
14. Reed, W. B., *Life and Correspondence of Joseph Reed* (Philadelphia, 1847), II, 30.
15. *Pennsylvania Archives* (Philadelphia, 1853), V, 270-282.
16. Siebert, W. H., "The Loyalists of Pennsylvania" etc., 29; Galloway, Joseph, *Examination etc.*, 71-72; *An Account of the Rise and Progress of the American Revolution* (London, 1780), 13, 18; Tatum, E. H., Jr. (ed.), *The American Journal of Ambrose Serle, etc.* (San Marino, 1940), 6, 123, 166.
17. Washington to Congress, April 26, 1777, Mss. in Library of Congress; Jones, I, 177.
18. *Pennsylvania Magazine of History and Biography*, Oct., 1885, Oct., 1889; Trevelyan, IV, 344-350.
19. Fitzgerald, J. C., *The Spirit of the Revolution* (Boston, 1924), 97; Scheer, G. F. (ed.), *Private Yankee Doodle* (Boston, 1962), 68; ALT, Vol. 50, 499; *Virginia Gazette*, May 16, 1777.
20. Hancock, Harold, "The Newcastle County Loyalists," *Delaware History*, IV, No. 4, Sept. 1951; Munroe, 35, 38.
21. *The Annual Register, or a View of the History, Politics and Literature for the Years, 1777-1778, 1781* (London, 1778-1782), 267-270; *Continental Journal and Weekly Advertiser*, Feb. 19 and March 26, 1778; Wharton, Anne H., *Through Colonial Doorways* (Philadelphia, 1893), 23-64.
22. Scheer and Rankin, 323; *Journal* of Ambrose Serle, 295-299.
23. A Mr. Dutton to Jenkison, Oct. 7, 1779, Liverpool Papers, British Museum, London, Vol. 118, 52.
24. A public letter, 1781, on the service of the American Loyalists, by an officer in the army of General William Howe, author unknown. Germain Papers, Clements Library.
25. Commager and Morris, II, 999-1,000.
26. Moore, II, 71; Ward, II, 629; Ryerson, II, 88.
27. Swiggett, 126.
28. Kirby, William, *Annals of Niagara* (Lundy's Lane, 1896), 55; ALT, Vol. 22, 133-142.

29. Bancroft, X, 137; *Journal* of Richard McGinnis, privately owned, quoted in Commager and Morris, II, 1006.
30. Butler to Lt. Col. Bolton, July 8, 1778, quoted in Willcox, *American Rebellion*, 387.
31. Crèvecoeur, Hector St. John de, *Sketches of Eighteenth Century America* (New Haven, 1925), 197.
32. Lossing, I, 358; Ryerson, II, 90-99; McGinnis, *Journal*, 12; Swiggett, 129.
33. *Journals of Henry Melchior Muhlenberg*, translated by T. G. Tappert and J. W. Doberstein (Philadelphia, 1958), III, 175.
34. Wallace, Willard M., *Appeal to Arms* (N.Y., 1951), 199; Ryerson, 92; *New York Journal*, July 20, 1778; Miner, Charles, *History of Wyoming* (Philadelphia, 1845), 225.
35. Crèvecoeur, 206.
36. Muhlenberg, *Journal*, III, 175; Butler to Clinton, Feb. 18, 1779, Library of Congress; Hildreth, Richard, *History of the United States* (N.Y., 1849-1852), III, 262-263; Stone, William L., *Border Wars of the American Revolution* (N.Y., 1864), I, 334-339.
37. Wallace, 199; Swiggett, 153.
38. *New Jersey Gazette*, Dec. 31, 1778; Butler to Schuyler, Nov. 12, 1778, British Museum; Butler to Mason Bolton, *Haldimand Collection*, Series B, V. 100, 82-83, Canadian Archives, Ottawa.
39. Sabine, Lorenzo, *Loyalists of the American Revolution* (Boston, 1864), I, 278.
40. Butler to Clinton, Feb. 18, 1779, Henry Clinton Papers, Clements Library.

9

LAW AND DISORDER

1. Siebert, W. H., "East Florida as a Refuge for Southern Loyalists, 1774-1785," American Antiquarian Society *Proceedings*, New Series, Oct., 1928, V, 37.
2. Hays, Louise F., *Hero of Hornet's Nest, a Biography of Elijah Clark* (N.Y., 1946), 40.
3. Barnwell, Robert W., "Migration of Loyalists from South Carolina," *Proceedings* of South Carolina Historical Association, 1937; Siebert, 235; Prevost to Howe, June 14, 1777, *Report on American Manuscripts in the Institutions of Great Britain* (London, 1904), I, 119.
4. Fortescue, Sir John W., *History of the British Army* (London, 1899-1930), III, 270-277; Coleman, 109.
5. Peters, Thelma, "The American Loyalists in the Bahama Islands: Who They Were," *Florida Historical Quarterly*, XXX, No. 3, Jan., 1962, 226-240; Wilcox, *The American Rebellion*, 357.
6. Peters, Thelma, "The Loyalist Migration" etc., *Florida Historical Quarterly*, XXX, Oct., 1961, No. 2, 123-141; Mowat, Charles, *East Florida as a British Province, 1763-84* (Berkeley, 1943), 157; Lockey, J. B., *East Florida, 1783-85*, etc. (Berkeley, 1940), 99.

7. Moseley, Mary, *The Bahamas Handbook* (Nassau, 1926), 72.

8. Lockey, 104-105, 178-180; Siebert, 240; Miss. Valley Hist. *Proceedings,* VIII (1914-1915), 102-122; Mss. in Revolutionary Collection, Duke University Library, 1781-1783.

9. Wallace, 204; Germain to Clinton, March 8, 1778, *Stopford-Sackville Mss.,* II, 94-99; "New York in the Revolution," Albany etc. NYSL, 81.

10. Willcox, William B., "Sir Henry Clinton and the Problem of Unconscious Motivation," an address delivered before the American Historical Association, New York City, Dec. 29, 1960.

11. *Virginia Gazette,* April 2, 1779.

12. Coulter, E. Merton, "Nancy Hart, Georgia Heroine of the Revolution," *Georgia Historical Quarterly,* XXXIX, 118-151; Coleman, 132; Hays, 83-85.

13. McCall, Hugh, *The History of Georgia* (Savannah, 1811-1816), II, 326-327.

14. Curwen, 638-641.

15. *Laurens (S.C.) Advertiser,* Nov. 1, 1961; biographical sketch of the career of William Cunningham in *Southern and Western Literary Messenger and Review,* XII, Oct., 1846, 577-579; Landrum, J. B. O., *Colonial and Revolutionary History of Upper South Carolina* (Greenville, 1897), 346-349; Johnson, William, *Sketches of the Life and Correspondence of Nathanael Greene* (Charleston, S.C., 1822), II, 301.

16. Curwen, 642-646.

17. Landrum, 353.

18. Ford, W. C., Hunt, Gaillard, Fitzpatrick, J. C., Hill, R. R. (eds.), *Journals of the Continental Congress,* 1774-1778 (Washington, 1904-1937), V, 464 and IX, 971.

19. Mackall, Leonard L. (ed.), "A Letter from the Virginia Loyalist, John Randolph to Thomas Jefferson, Written in London in 1779," American Antiquarian Society *Proceedings* (April, 1920), 16.

20. Luce, Melvin G., unpublished master's thesis, "The Southern Loyalists in the American Revolution," NYU, 1951, 44-48; Van Tyne, 130-134.

21. Labaree, Leonard W., *Royal Government in America* (New Haven, 1930), 268; *The Revolutionary Records of the State of Georgia* (Atlanta, 1908), I, 254-255; Williamson, Chilton, *American Suffrage from Property to Democracy* (Princeton, 1960), 105; Abbott, W. C. (N.Y., 1929), 211-212; Irving, W., *Life of George Washington,* II, 392.

22. Van Tyne, 137-138; Alden, 326-327; Sabine, 80-81; Smith, G. G., *The Story of the Georgia People* (Atlanta, 1900), 98.

23. Barnwell, Robert W. (ed.), "The Migration of Loyalists" etc., 34; De-Mond, 153-60; ALT, Vol. 52, 90.

24. Evans, E. G., "Planter Indebtedness and the Coming of the Revolution in Virginia," *William and Mary Quarterly,* XIX, No. 4, Oct. 1962, 512-533; Eckenrode, H. J., *The Revolution in Virginia* (Boston, 1916), 114-122; Harrell, 78; *The Journal of Nicholas Creswell, 1774-77* (N.Y., 1924), 104-181.

25. *Maryland Gazette*, March 3, 1780; *Maryland Historical Magazine*, XII, Dec., 1917, 388; Nevins, Allan, *The American States During and After the Revolution* (N.Y., 1927), 310; Van Tyne, 196-98.

26. Hancock, 27-34.

27. Turner, Rev. J. B., "Cheney Clow's Rebellion," address delivered to students of Delaware College, Feb. 20, 1911. Reprinted in Papers of Hist. Society of Del., LVII, Wilmington, 1912; Garretson, Freeborn, *The Experience and Travels of Mr. Freeborn Garretson* (Philadelphia, 1791), 77.

28. *Delaware Register* (Dover, 1838-1839), I, No. 3, 224; Hancock, 35; Munroe, 53.

29. Rossman, Kenneth R., *Thomas Mifflin and the Politics of the American Revolution* (Chapel Hill, 1952), 170-171; Van Tyne, 194, 207.

30. ALT, Vol. 36, 295-443; ALT, Vol. 44, 191-233; *The Royal Gazette*, Feb. 16, 1780.

31. Leiby, Adrian C., *The Revolutionary War in the Hackensack Valley* (New Brunswick, 1962), 167-173; Stryker, W. S., *The Massacre Near Old Tappan* (Trenton, 1882), 56; *Major André's Journal* (Yonkers, N.Y.), 47-48; *Rivington's Gazette*, June 5, 1779.

32. Lossing, I, 508. Lossing said he could find no verification for this story, but Allen had disagreed with Rivington's editorial policies, and had threatened to "knock the hell out of Editor Rivington." Holbrook, Stewart, *Ethan Allen* (N.Y., 1951), 124.

33. ALT, Vol. 42, 351-389; Onderdonk, Henry, Jr., "Long Island and New York in Olden Times, Being Newspaper Extracts and Historical Sketches," NYHS; Sabine, *Biographical Sketches* etc., II, 379-380.

34. *New York Journal*, March 15, 1779; Thomas Clark to James Hogg, Sept. 6, 1778; SHC, UNC; Lynd, Stoughton, "Anti-Federalism in Dutchess County, New York," unpublished master's thesis, Columbia University, 1960.

35. Jones, Thomas I, 362.

36. *Smythe's Journal*, April 1, 1777; Peck, 20-23; Gilbert, G. A., "The Connecticut Loyalists," *American Historical Review*, Jan., 1899, IV, 276.

37. *Rivington's Gazette*, June 9, 1781.

38. *Constitutional Gazette*, July 31, 1776.

39. ALT, Vol. 14, 117-118.

40. Gould, E. W., *British and Tory Marauders* (Rockland, Me., 1932), 9.

41. *The Continental Journal and Weekly Advertiser*, Oct. 27, 1777; Hammond, Otis G., "Tories of New Hampshire in the War of the Revolution" (Concord, 1917), pamphlet in NYHS; Whittemore, Charles P., *John Sullivan of New Hampshire* (N.Y., 1961), 185; material in War Department Collection, Revolutionary War Records, Record Group 93, National Archives, Washington, D.C.

42. *Essex Journal*, Aug. 3, 1774; Stopford-Sackville Mss. II, Aug. 6, 1782; Einstein, 114-50; Siebert, W. H., "The Loyalists Refugees of New Hampshire" (Columbia, 1916), 5.

43. Stark, 55, 272-275; Trevelyan, I, 187; letter from Senator Saltonstall to the author, May 25, 1962; Holten, Samuel, to the Selectmen of Salem, Mass., June 27, 1777, in Boston Public Library; Petition of Mrs. Scott to Mass. General Court, Sept. 30, 1779; Mass. State Archives; Petition of Henry Knox to Mass. General Court, March, 1778, Mass. State Archives.

10
KING'S MOUNTAIN

1. *State Records of North Carolina*, XIV, 816; DeMond, 124.
2. "Appeal from Jamaica, The *Guana* vs. Great Britain" etc. in Court Documents, South Caroliniana Library of the University of S.C., Columbia; John, C. D., "The Loyalists in North Carolina," unpublished master's thesis, University of Chicago, 1911, 35.
3. Graham, W. A., "The Battle of Ramsour's Mill, June 20, 1780," *North Carolina Booklet* (Raleigh, 1904), IV, 8-17; M. L. McCorkle to Rev. Bicknell, Jan. 20, 1849, *SHC*, UNC.
4. Barringer, G. R., "Battle of Ramsour's Mill," *Davidson College Historical Association Magazine* (Davidson, N.C., 1898), I, 54; Graham, 20; *Catawba Journal*, July 7, 1825.
5. Levett, Ella P., "Loyalism in Charleston, 1861-1784," *Proceedings*, SCHA, 1936, 6; Landrum, 175.
6. *Virginia Gazette*, Nov. 11, 1780; Ramsey, J. G. M., *The Annals of Tennessee to the End of the Eighteenth Century* (Charleston, 1853), 203; *N.C. State Records*, XV, 105.
7. Draper, Lyman C., *King's Mountain and Its Heroes* (Cincinnati, 1881), 51; Bailey, J.D., *Commanders at King's Mountain* (Gaffney, S.C., 1926), 383.
8. *Political Magazine*, March 1781, 60; Irving, IV, 51-52; *National Intelligencer*, May, 1851. James Fenimore Cooper stated in the *New York Mirror*, April 16, 1831, that, according to his father-in-law, John de Lancey, the officer in Ferguson's sights was Washington, though some felt it was Count Pulaski instead.
9. Irving, IV, 51.
10. Gen. John S. Bynum to Lyman Draper, Feb. 8, 1854, Draper Manuscripts in Wisconsin Historical Society, Madison, 4DD21; Ferguson to Cornwallis, Sept. 6, 1780, Willcox, 456.
11. *Virginia Magazine of History and Biography*, VII, 121; Draper Mss., 3DD316.
12. New York Packet, Nov. 23, 1780; *Colonel George Hanger, the Life, Adventures and Opinions of* (London, 1801), II, 403; Kirke, Edmund, *Rear Guard of the Revolution* (N.Y., 1888), 265.
13. *Harper's Magazine*, April, 1885; Draper, 174.
14. Chandler, Helen D., *The Battle of King's Mountain* (Gastonia, 1930), 21; Draper, 177-180.

15. Callahan, *Daniel Morgan*, 195-226; Landrum, 186; Tyler, II, 224.
16. Roberts, J. M. (ed.), Collins, James P., *Autobiography of a Revolutionary Soldier* (Clinton, La., 1859), 259-261.
17. Landrum, 200; Draper, 233, 542.
18. Ward, II, 741; Draper, 211.
19. Chesney, 17; Draper, 235.
20. Wilson to Draper, 247.
21. Haywood, John, *History of Tennessee* (Knoxville, 1823), 71.
22. Statement of Samuel Marion Callahan to the author. The former was a grandson of Captain John Callahan who fought under Sevier at King's Mountain, and he told his grandson, Samuel, about the battle, who passed it on down to his grandson, the author.
23. Lee, Henry, *Memoirs of the War in the Southern Department* (N.Y., 1870), 200; Draper, 255.
24. Twitty to Draper, 254; *Orion Magazine*, Oct., 1843; Chesney, *Journal*, 18.
25. *Historical Magazine*, March, 1869; Draper, 311-312.
26. *N.C. State Records*, XV, 101-103; Draper, 275; Bailey, 421.
27. Scheer and Rankin, 419; Draper, 283.
28. James J. Hampton to L. C. Draper, from Rutherford City, N.C., June 29, 1874, Draper Mss. 6DD126; Chandler, 29; Bailey, 428.
29. Draper, 292, 297.
30. Collins, 53; Draper, 303.
31. Draper, 330-332; Landrum, 218; Cornwallis to Smallwood, Nov. 10, 1780, 1822, Draper Mss., Vol. 16.
32. *Rutherford Enquirer*, May 24, 1859; Jefferson to William Campbell, Nov. 10, 1822, copy in Draper Mss., Vol. 16.
33. de Peyster, J. Walter, "King's Mountain," *The Historical Magazine*, V, 1869; *Harper's Magazine*, Oct., 1860; Rawdon to Clinton, Oct. 29, 1780, *N.C. State Records*, XV, 287.
34. Lee, Henry, 201.
35. "Diary of Colonel Robert Gray," N.C. State Archives, Raleigh, 6-12.
36. Bailey, 240-270.
37. *Elkin (N.C.) Tribune*, Nov. 16, 1961; Hayes, Johnson J., *The Land of Wilkes* (Wilkesboro, N.C., 1962), 60.

11

TWILIGHT

1. Ramsay, David, *History of the Revolution in South Carolina* (Trenton, 1785), I, 340; Syrett, Harold C., and Cooke, J. E. (eds.), *The Papers of Alexander Hamilton* (N.Y., 1961), II, 385, 529.
2. DeMond, 122; Montross, 444.
3. Barnwell, 280; William Smallwood to Nathanael Greene, Dec. 6, 1780, Preston Davie Papers, 3406, SHC, UNC; Tarleton, Banastre, *A History of the Campaigns of 1780 and 1781* (Dublin, 1787), 205.

4. Cornwallis to Germain, Sept. 19, 1780, Germain Papers, Clements Library.
5. Chesney, *Journal*, iii-x, 7-10, 130-131.
6. Alden, 242, 328n.
7. ALT, Vol. 5, 52.
8. ALT, Vol. 5, 105.
9. Gregg, Alexander G., *History of the Old Cheraws* (N.Y., 1867), 358-361.
10. *Ibid.*
11. ALT, Vol. 53, 172.
12. ALT, Vol. 5, 54.
13. ALT, Vol. 5, 92.
14. ALT, Vol. 57, 160.
15. ALT, Vol. 57, 62; Andreano, A. L., and Werner, H. D., "Charleston Loyalists: a Statistical Note," *South Carolina Historical Magazine*, IX (July, 1959), 64-68.
16. Leonard to Colonel Henry Young, March 21, 1782, N.C. State Archives, Raleigh, 6-12.
17. Brown, Alan S. (ed.), "James Simpson—Report on the Carolina Loyalists, 1779-1780," *Journal of Southern History*, Nov., 1955, XXI, No. 4, 514-519; Bailey, 72; Draper, 396.
18. ALT, Vol. 58, 372.
19. ALT, Vol. 58, 296.
20. Callahan, *Daniel Morgan*, 250-252; Morton, Frederic, *The Story of Winchester in Virginia* (Strasburg, Va., 1925), 88.
21. ALT, Vol. 58, 124, 303, 383; Vol. 59, 203.
22. ALT, 59, 18-25.

12

THE RECKONING

1. Arnold, Isaac, *The Life of Benedict Arnold* (Chicago, 1880), 330-332; Fitzpatrick, *Writings of George Washington*, XX, 189.
2. *New Jersey Journal*, Aug. 1, 1781.
3. *Virginia Magazine of History and Biography*, VI, No. 1, July, 1898, 346-348; Am. Loyalist Royal Institute Transcripts, Vol. 35, 37, NYPL.
4. Levenstein, Leonard, "Loyalism in Connecticut," unpublished master's thesis, NYU, May, 1955, 38.
5. Hoffman, Robert V., *The Revolutionary Scene in New Jersey* (N.Y., 1942), 144-150; Moore, II, 233-236; Mellick, Andrew D., Jr., *Lesser Crossroads* (New Brunswick, N.J., 1948), 292-299.
6. Quyn, Dorothy M., "The Loyalist Plot in Frederick," *Maryland Historical Magazine*, XXXX, 1945, 201-208.
7. ALT, Vol. 51, 233-235.
8. Nelson, William (ed.), *Documents Relating to the Revolutionary History of New Jersey*, IV (Trenton, 1914), 453, 564; Ward II, 621.
9. ALT, Vol. 39, 145-149.

10. Albee in *Westchester Historian*, Vol. 34, No. 3, July-Sept., 1958, 61; Johnson, P. D., *Claudius, the Cowboy of the Ramapo Valley* (Middleton, N.Y., 1894), 58; *N.Y. World Telegram and Sun*, July 16, 1962; *Rockland County Journal-News*, Sept. 8, 1962.
11. Albee, in *Westchester Historian*, Vol. 34, Oct.-Dec., 1958, 92-100; Jones, II, 179; Uhlendorf, B. A., and Vosper, Edna (eds.), *Letters from Major Baurmeister to Colonel von Jungkenn* (Philadelphia, 1937), 419.
12. Van Schaack, H. C., *Life of Peter Van Schaack* (N.Y., 1842), 260-261; Nelson, 122; Curwen, 339.
13. Mergann to Shelburne, Clements Library, copies in NYHS.
14. ALT, Vol. 5, 171; Vol. 7, 230; Vol. 8, 100; Vol. 53, 166; Vol. 56, 417; Vol. 57, 80; Vol. 58, 234; Hart, F. H., *The Valley of Virginia* (Chapel Hill, 1942), 105; Cooper, W. G., *The History of Georgia* (N.Y., 1938), II, 110-111.
15. "Trial of Capt. Richard Lippincott of the Associated Loyalists, for Hanging Joshua Huddy etc.," Mss. Div. Lib. of Congress; "Copy of Minutes of General Court Martial on Richard Lippincott, 3 May, 1782-22 June, 1782," Clinton Papers, Clements Library; Mellick, 327-332.
16. *Observations on the Fifth Article of the Treaty With America* etc. (London, 1783), by various persons, 86. Copy in Howard Tilton Library, Tulane University, New Orleans, La.

Index

A

Adams, John, 7, 38, 39, 50, 54, 56, 61, 69, 80, 92, 96, 127
Adams, Samuel, 8, 47, 49, 52, 96, 97
Alamance, Battle of, 16, 44, 77
Albany Plan of Union, 102
Allaire, Lt. Anthony, 213, 215, 221, 222
Allen, Ethan, 193-194
Allen, Isaac, 101
American Antiquarian Society, 10
American attitude of 18th Century, 7
American Loyalist Transcripts in New York Public Library, 10
Amherst, Gen. Jeffrey, 25, 46, 162, 206
André, John, 105, 192, 238
Andrews, Charles M., 7, 43
Anglican Church, beliefs, 134
Arbuthnott, Admiral Marriot, 198
Armbrister brothers, 174
Arnold, Benedict, 26, 118, 155, 163, 235-236, 242
Asbury, Francis, 145
Asia, the, 70, 110
Associated Loyalists, 244
Auchmuty, Robert, 141
Auchmuty, Rev. Samuel, 141-142

B

Bahamas, 174-176
Bancroft, George, 84, 169
Baylor, Col. George, 192
Beach, Rev. John, 129
Becker, Carl, 38, 40
Bennington, Battle of, 151-152
Betsy, the, 173
Billopp, Christopher, 76
"Bonnie Prince Charlie," 16
Boston Gazette, 52
"Boston Massacre," 53, 121
Boston News-Letter, 54
Boucher, Rev. Jonathan, 94, 96, 123-125
Brant, Joseph, 111, 112, 170
Brinton, Crane, 40
British Army, Tories in, 9
British military system, why Tories disliked to serve in it, 162-163
Broad River, 212
Brown, Col. Thomas, 86, 91, 173, 179
Brown, Wallace, 9
Bull, Gen. Stephen, 229

Bull, Lt. Gov. William, 92, 101, 228
Bullman, Rev. John, 53, 123
Burgoyne, Gen. John, 34, 64, 110, 119, 148, 151, 152
Burke, Edmund, 29, 31, 34, 164
Burke, Gov. Thomas, 87, 88
Butler, Col. John, 111, 165
Butler, Walter, 111, 169, 170, 171
Butler, Col. Zebulon, 166
Butterfield, H., 33
Byles, Rev. Mather, 121-123
Byrd, Mrs. Mary Willing, 236
Byrd, William, III, 186

C

Caldwell, Rev. James, 125, 239
Caldwell, Mrs. James, 239-240
Campbell, Farquhard, 17
Campbell, Col. William, 208-220
Cameron, Alan, 231-235
Canada, attempts to make it the 14th colony, 26
Canada, Tories in, 8
Cape Fear, 15, 16
Cape Fear River, 20, 87, 90
Capen, Hopestill, 37
Carleton, Sir Guy, 64, 111, 236
Carlisle Peace Commission, 30
Carmer, Carl, 150
Carpenters' Hall, Philadelphia, 96
Carroll, Charles, of Carrollton, 94-95, 145
Centaur, the, 79
Charleston, taken by British, 201
Cherry Valley, 170
Chesney, Alexander, 92, 216, 226
Chicago Historical Society, 10
Church, Benjamin, 47
Clark, Col. Elijah, 178, 179, 207, 243
Clark, George Rogers, 243-244
Clawson, Jonathan, 240
Claymores, Scottish swords, 17, 20, 21
Clements Library of the University of Michigan, 10
Cleveland, Col. Benjamin, 208-223
Clinton, Sir Henry, 18, 55, 90, 105, 162, 174, 176, 177, 184, 197, 201, 204, 207, 221, 224, 237, 241
Clinton, Gen. James, 169, 171
Clow, Cheney, 188-190
Caswell, Col. Richard, 18, 19, 20, 22

Washington, Col. William, 225-226
Wentworth, Gov. John, 101
Wesley, John, 145
West Indies, flight of Tories to, 10
West Point, New York, 164, 235, 237
"Whigs" in Scotland, 68
Whig, derivation of word, 68
Whitaker, Rev. Nathaniel, 120-121, 147
White, Philip, 244-245
Willcox, William B., 177
Willett, Lt. Col. Marinus, 113, 115
Williams, Col. John, 211, 216
Williams, Roger, 46
Wilson, James, 190
Wisconsin, State Historical Society of, 10
Wish, Harvey, 53

Witherspoon, John, 103, 135, 145
Wolfe, Gen. James, 25
Woodford, Col. William, 83
Wormely, Ralph, 186
Wright, Sir James, 90, 91, 176, 177, 184
Wyoming Valley, Battle of, 164-170

Y

Yale University, 130, 152
"Yankee Doodle," singing of, 65
Yorktown, Battle of, 31, 37, 89, 104, 246
Younglove, Dr. Moses, 117, 118

Z

Zenger, John Peter, trial of, 71
Zubly, John, 144